A Tree in Winter

*Sometimes our fate resembles
a tree in winter. Who would
think that those branches would
turn green again and blossom,
but we hope...*

Goethe

Also from **Kingdom Press**—

LEARNING—LIFE IN THE CASTLE

LABORING—LIFE IN THE OUTPOST

LEADING—LIFE AT THE BATTLEFRONT

A Tree in Winter

A Romance
by

Sherry Newcomb

SAN# 254-1106

TM

published by

Kingdom Press

Editor, Jean Nava
Mountain Grove, Missouri 65711

Library of Congress Control Number: 00-134041
ISBN 0-9659952-5-9

Printed in the United States of America.
by

MORRIS PUBLISHING

3212 East Highway 30 • Kearney, NE 68847 • 1-800-650-7888

Dedicated with all my love
to my husband Keith,
for all his support and encouragement,
and to my children,
Guy, Ginger, Heather, and Heath,
for believing in me.

*Short as life is, some find it long enough to outlive
their characters, their constitutions and their estates.*
—Charles Caleb Colton

Chapter 1

Sleet pelted the window like angry buckshot, and the eternal Chicago wind managed to seep through every fissure of chipped wood and cracked plaster that had developed in fifty years of neglect. I stood at the window of what had served as both living room and my bedroom and watched him leave—watched him leave for the third time in as many nights. He paused for a moment under a street lamp, whose usefulness as a light was in serious question. Hands deep in the pockets of his cashmere overcoat, his dark head hatless even in this weather, he stood perfectly still as though he were oblivious to the sleet, the neighborhood, and eyes that may have watched from windows other than mine.

For a few frantic seconds I thought he might come back into the building and make his way up those two flights of stairs and bully Missouri into making me see him. But Missouri had said that he was a gentleman, and Missouri was seldom wrong about people. Even as my fears were diminishing I watched him pull his car keys from his pocket. He went to the driver's side of his Cadillac and opened the door. Then he glanced up at the window where I stood. I took a step back, but I doubted that he could have seen me. By the time I resumed my position at the window the Cadillac was roaring into life. My unwelcome visitor was gone at last, and I breathed a heavy sigh of relief. He wouldn't be back tonight, and tomorrow I would be gone from this place for good and would never have to worry about John Ransom again.

1

I went to the dilapidated sofa and switched on the cheap floor lamp that stood next to it. It threw the room into long, dim shadows. Newspapers were scattered all over the threadbare carpet. He would have seen them, but never mind. I was sure that he was as familiar with the headlines as I was.

I heard the minutes tick by on the old clock that hung above what was once a working fireplace. The fireplace had been sealed up years ago with the advent of steam heat. That was too bad; the fireplace was the only thing about this apartment that was in the least homey. Otherwise the place was as dismal as the November weather outside. I stood in the middle of the small room and looked around. Pieces of plaster fell daily from the ceiling and the walls had so many holes it made a playground for the mice that infested the whole building. The wood floor was warped, and the cheap linoleum that covered the kitchen area was scuffed and torn. Only one burner on the stove worked, and I couldn't remember the last time we were able to use the oven. We had an old icebox, but it was seldom that I lugged the ice up two flights of stairs; it was easier for me to buy fresh food on a daily basis.

I stepped over the scattered newspapers and sat down on the couch. I sat there for more than half an hour as the clocked ticked on and on. Missouri was in David's room, humming to herself as she packed the bedding. But I also knew she was, in a rare display of tact, allowing me time to myself. I desperately needed this time, too. I looked at my bandaged hands. I wanted to cry, but couldn't. Why did everything, both blessings and curses, have to come with a price tag? Was this the price I had to pay for mine and David's freedom? Or was this the price I had to pay for my part in the tragedy?

Just this once I would let my memories, both good and bad, wash over me. For so many years I had held them at bay, not allowing them to intrude into my life. For so many years I had not allowed myself to even think about how, or why, we had come to this. Now I needed to deal with the past and put it behind me, for only then could I face the future—mine—and David's.

1955 1954 1953 1952 1951 1950 1949 1948 1947 1946 →
1945 1944 1943 1942 1941 1940 1939 1938 1937 1936 1935

"Von, two, tree, von, two, tree.. No, no! Move over. I show you how it is done. Now vatch!"

Long, lean fingers moved up and down the ivory keys, dexterously and with no apparent effort. I sat on my side of the piano bench and watched, mesmerized.

"Will I ever play as good as you, Mr. Laski?" I asked.

He looked down at me. "No von vill ever play like Laski," he, the unpredictable, predicted. "But you—if you try real hard and practice, practice, practice—you might come close."

Grandfather came into the room. "How is she doing?"

Moshe Laski shrugged. "How is she doing? This is how she is doing." And he pounded on the keys willy-nilly.

"She is only six," my grandfather said.

"I could play 'Grande Fantasie' ven I vas six," Moshe told him. "And Brittany, vat can she play? Chopsticks."

I laughed. "I can play the 'Minute Waltz', Grandfather. Honest I can."

"Hrumph!" Mr. Laski grunted. "It takes her two minutes, though."

"Well, to tell the truth, Laski, I wouldn't know the 'Minute Waltz' from Chopsticks," Grandfather told my temperamental piano teacher.

"It's a good ting," he shot back, "because the vay your granddaughter plays, it'd be hard to tell the difference."

And so went my piano lessons, week after week, month after month, year after year. My grandfather wanted me to be the greatest pianist with Polish grandparents the world had ever known.

Frederic and Sophia Morrowitz were the kindest, most loving grandparents I could have been blessed with. It was inconceivable to me, even at an early age, how they could have produced such a shallow, selfish child as my mother. They named her Camille, and lavished on her all of the love, attention, and worldly goods they could give. And they could give quite a lot. Frederic Morrowitz came to the United States from Poland shortly after the turn of the century, before the government stemmed the flow of immigrants from Eastern Europe. He married a dainty little woman from his own country, and together they built a life on hard work and honesty.

Starting from scratch in a basement shop in the factory district of Chicago, they made little items one might take for granted—unless one happened to be a soldier fighting a war. They manufactured things necessary to the relative comfort of a doughboy in the trenches, things like canteens and eating utensils, cups and plates. World War I brought them prosperity, and they bought an estate on Lake Michigan. There they raised their only child.

Wild speculation was never for my grandfather. He was content with what he had and smart enough to keep it, so when the Depression hit they were sound enough financially to weather the storm. The creation of plastic opened a new world, and my grandfather was one of the first adventurers. He made his second fortune on, of all things, plastic frames for eyeglasses.

Perhaps my grandparents didn't keep a close enough watch on their daughter, or maybe they indulged her whims so often it became a habit. Or maybe she was just willful and uncaring, having been so used to having her own way. Whatever the reason, and whoever was to blame, she ran off with a scoundrel named Patrick Thornton, an Irish immigrant most recently from parts unknown. She lavished her adoration on him; she was totally obsessed with him. Had he been more of a man that obsession would have smothered him. But he was as vain and shallow as she was. A rich and fawning wife was his due. My grandparents accepted him only because they didn't want to risk alienation from their daughter.

Patrick Thornton decided it was easier marrying money than working for it, so he turned down all offers of joining Morrowitz Plastics. He had his own fish to fry, as he would say. One of those fish fries was in St. Louis, and it was there that I was born, in 1930.

I immediately became the center of my grandparents' world. They made up for my parents' obvious lack of interest in me. But they had recognized an essential mistake they had made concerning their daughter, and they didn't want to make that mistake with me. So, no matter how much they pampered me with attention and luxuries, I was not allowed to have my own way, or talk back. When I was naughty I was disciplined.

In looks I favor my tall, slender father who had the aura of the Black Irishman about him. I have an olive complexion and dark brown hair and eyes. My nose is straight, my cheekbones high, and my fingers long and slender. In temperament, I am like my Grandmother Sophia. Shy and diffident, seldom at ease in a crowd unless I am at the piano, I hate people staring at me. I always feel self-conscious, although part of the problem could be that my mother tried to make me feel that way, so that I wouldn't steal the spotlight from her. She was blonde and exceptionally beautiful—and also extremely jealous. David looks more like her.

I remembered the first time I met that martinet of the ivories, Moshe Laski. I was five and he had recently immigrated to the U.S., with the not insubstantial help of my influential grandfather. Mr. Laski was a Polish Jew teaching piano at the Berlin Conservatory, and a thug by the name of Adolf Hitler was making some frightening promises concerning Jews in general and Moshe Laski in particular. How my grandfather managed to spirit him out of Germany is something I'll never know, for Mr. Laski promised he would never tell, and so far he never has.

Laski was my one and only piano teacher. He began preparing me, at the age of five, for the concert stage. He alternately begged and bullied, threatened and pleaded. He stormed and shouted and praised. I adored him. He tried to teach me how to play Chopin the way Laski thought Chopin would have played Chopin.

But my life wasn't confined to the piano bench. I went to an exclusive school for young ladies in northern Illinois, where I was given private tennis lessons and private riding lessons. Before I was ten years old Morrowitz Plastics had hit its peak and I had won two blue ribbons in my first horse show, competed in the Sedgewick-Kent Junior Tennis Cup (singles), and took second place in the Chicago Area Music Competition.

I was on top of the world when it started crumbling. Nazi tanks crossed the Polish border. My grandfather started making secret trips; he was often gone for weeks at a time. Although Morrowitz Plastics entered the war effort with a vengeance, my grandfather seemed to have a mission of his own that didn't include such mundane things as profits. Slowly, surreptitiously, my father started usurping Grandfather's authority under the guise of finally being willing to work for the company. Grandfather was too preoccupied with what was happening in Europe to really notice.

I was with my grandfather when he died. He had not been home long from one of his "business trips." He looked tired. Not just tired. He looked defeated, sick, and heartbroken. Stephan, his baby brother, had stayed in Poland despite all Grandfather's unrelenting attempts to get him out of the country. My great-uncle stayed, denouncing Hitler in the streets of Warsaw until the Gestapo caught him, threw him against the wall of the church where he worshiped, and executed him. The letter, which was somehow smuggled out of Poland by the Underground, was in my grandfather's hand. I saw him read it, then clutch his heart. I believe he was dead before he hit the ground. They found me there with him, just minutes later, begging him to get up. Someone pulled me away. It was Missouri Smith, my grandmother's colored maid and her most trusted friend and ally.

My grandmother was now the head of the business, but my father wrested the reins from her dainty hands and took over in actual fact. Grandfather had been bent on shipping whatever he could to England, but my father didn't believe there was much profit in doing that. He wanted to keep all European doors open. Hitler was expanding his empire daily, and it wouldn't do to offend him, or so my father reasoned. If Germany won the war in Europe, Hitler might remember who stayed neutral and do some favors of his own.

My grandmother was shocked, and many of our acquaintances disgusted. Society, which had accepted my grandparents, backed away from the Thorntons, who both firmly believed until Pearl Harbor, that America would stay out of the war.

Our fortunes started to decline. My father, who never wanted to start at the bottom and learn the business, was now at the top and running it swiftly into bankruptcy. Other companies who had always been happy in the past to work with Frederic Morrowitz refused to work with his upstart son-in-law. Morrowitz Plastics began losing customers. The government which had never hesitated doing business with my generous and patriotic grandfather would not renew its contract with my father, whose loyalty was in serious question. Most of the friends my parents had made deserted them. My grandmother, aged beyond her years by the sudden death of her beloved husband, was powerless against the will of my father. In short order the family assets were sold. The mansion on the lake went at auction. The servants, including Missouri Smith, were, of necessity, dismissed. Most of Grandmother's jewels were taken and sold. Most, but, as I was to discover later, not all.

We moved from the lake to an older section of the city that had, at the turn of the century, been the nice part of town. The once-grand Victorian homes were run down now, but the house we bought was big, and for the most part, livable.

June 1941, Ignace Paderewski died, and Mr. Laski went into mourning. He even attended some of the special masses held by the Chicago Polish community. Shortly after that I acquired a little brother. He was born on December 7. Needless to say, his birth was overshadowed by other events. He came unexpectedly, while my parents were in St. Louis trying to get backing for their failing business. They were out painting the town on a Saturday night when an infant of whose existence they were only vaguely suspicious decided to make his advent. An ambulance was called and mother had to spend some time in a St. Louis hospital. Premature babies seldom have an easy time coping with their new environment, and little David had a worse time than most.

My grandmother and I could hardly wait for the baby to come home. Missouri Smith, was willing to come back to us and work for expenses. Somehow she knew, without anyone having to tell her, that Grandmother was too old and frail to care for a baby, I was much too young, and my mother too uncaring. It was Missouri who named the little boy. My parents had reluctantly checked him out of the hospital without bothering about a name. Missouri and I were fixing up the nursery, and she was singing that old spiritual about Little David playing on his harp. We were both shouting "Hal-lay-loo!" when my mother and father walked in. Their dour expressions contrasted sharply with our jubilation. Missouri scooped the infant into her arms, and exclaimed, "Well, here's Li'l David, this verra minit."

So he became Little David, and when the St. Louis County Clerk contacted us, demanding a name for the birth certificate, that was what my father put down. He was a wrinkled and puny little baby with red blotches all over his thin body. I thought he was the most beautiful thing in the world.

Patrick and Camille Thornton seemed to feel he was a terrible mistake. I remembered a couple of times before when I had thought my mother was expecting, and then nothing had come of it. It made me wonder if I were a "mistake" too. A baby was a nuisance, too much trouble. Missouri, Grandmother and I conspired to keep David out of their way as much as possible.

Morrowitz Plastics, which had been tumbling downhill, finally hit bottom. The doors closed, and my father filed for bankruptcy. Rumors came to my ears that my father was speculating wildly, drinking heavily, and gambling uncontrollably. Grandmother still had two pieces of jewelry left. One was the simple gold wedding band a loving new husband had placed on her finger nearly forty years before. She had never taken it off. The other was her twenty-fifth anniversary gift—the Contessa Elena Fire Opal. A large fire opal, surrounded by sixteen perfectly matched pearls which were in turn surrounded by twenty diamonds, was set in a gold brooch with worked filigree in the design of a coat of arms of a prominent Spanish family of the seventeenth century. This lovely work of art had been commissioned for the bride of a wealthy count and had remained in his family until a descendant backed a very unpopular King Ferdinand VII in the early 1800's. The brooch was bandied about with the fluctuating fortunes of the Spanish nobles until Frederic Morrowitz purchased it.

Up to this point I had been only vaguely aware of the foibles and flaws of my parents. I had heard whispers about them, about their lifestyle. But my youth and my naiveté kept me from understanding all the innuendoes, and those few who loved me, like my grandparents, Moshe Laski, and Missouri Smith, protected me from the meaner aspects of their lives. But the day my father demanded my grandmother's two remaining pieces of jewelry was the day I finally realized just what my parents were.

I had heard arguments, muffled though they were, in the past few years. But on this particular day I inadvertently walked in on the nastiest scene I had ever witnessed.

Grandmother was in her small room, seated on her wooden rocker. Father was looming over her, and he was livid.

"They are mine," Grandmother said, "and I will not give them to you. I hope I have made myself perfectly clear, Patrick."

"We need the money," my father snarled, "and we need it now."

"Gambling debts, I assume. No, Patrick. I will not finance your vices any longer. In just a few short years you have managed to run through a fortune it took Frederic and me forty years to build. Because of you, I have very little I can leave to my grandchildren. But my wedding ring and my brooch are my legacy to Brittany. You will not—*ever*—get your hands on them."

My mother was in the room, sitting on the bed. Now it was her turn to be livid. She jumped at Grandmother grabbed her by the shoulder and shook her. "What do you mean by that?" she screamed. "Those pieces are mine. You have no right giving them to Brittany."

I ran into the room and grabbed my mother's hands and pulled her away. "Don't you touch her!" I cried.

Patrick Thornton jerked me around and swore at me. "How dare you handle your mother like that," he told me in a voice that froze my insides.

I swallowed, stepped back from him, and said in a scared little voice, "She was shaking Grandmother. She might have hurt her."

"This is none of your affair," he went on, as though I hadn't spoken. "This is between adults. You go and take care of that sickly brother of yours and don't worry about the old woman." With that he shoved me out of the room.

I stood outside the door for a few moments, but they were all talking low and I couldn't hear what was said. I was shaking violently and my stomach was turning over, but I didn't know what to do. Since there seemed to be no more threats to my grandmother, I left to see to David, who was indeed still having health problems. His first year on this earth had been touch-and-go, and if it hadn't been for Missouri Smith and my grandparents' doctor, Hiram Ableman, David would certainly have died.

Later that day, as Grandmother was napping, my mother slipped into her room, went through the little oak desk, and found

9

the combination to the small safe hidden in the paneling of the sitting room. I had seen her go into Grandmother's room and watched as she rifled through Grandmother's personal papers, and then I followed her downstairs and watched as she opened the safe and took out a sheaf of money, the spare cash Grandmother always kept "against a rainy day." Of the brooch there was no sign. And even Camille Thornton didn't have the nerve to pry the gold wedding ring off Grandmother's finger.

When Grandmother awoke from her nap, my mother approached her again about the Contessa Elena Fire Opal. "Tell me where it is," she demanded, "or so help me, Mother..."

"So," Grandmother said, "you stole the money from the safe. You are now a thief, on top of everything else."

Camille Thornton gave an ugly laugh. "It would be mine one day, anyway."

Grandmother sighed. "Let me tell you this, and it is the last word I intend to say on the subject: The brooch is where you cannot touch it. You can threaten and bully all you like, but you will not get your hands on it. You have the money. You will throw it away as you have everything else. But that brooch is mine, and it will be Brittany's, and that is final."

Although both of my parents hammered away at her for days, my grandmother never revealed where she had hidden the brooch. But Grandmother had now fully realized to what extent her daughter had turned on her, and it was the final blow. She didn't die suddenly like my grandfather. She just faded, like a delicate white rose. We buried her next to her husband in a little, unpretentious cemetery on the South Side. It was a sorry funeral, with only my parents, Missouri Smith, Moshe Laski, Dr. Ableman, my little brother David, and myself in attendance. David was barely two—too young to understand death or realize who it was in the grave, but he wept because Missouri and I were weeping. I held him, (he still didn't weigh much) and under the pretense of comforting him, I drew comfort from him. I was heartbroken. I felt I had lost my last true friend.

I was wrong. Mr. Laski continued to give me piano lessons, *gratis*. He was determined that I should go to Juliard. Missouri Smith continued to stay with the family, to care for David. Dr. Ableman was still on call any time David was sick. But few people would receive me socially now, even for my grandfather's sake, and I was beginning to feel all of the consequences of being my father's daughter.

In a couple of years the war ended. America was victorious and a euphoria flooded the land. I found some satisfaction in seeing my parents' "friends" so decisively ruined, but I couldn't work up the joy of those I saw dancing in the streets. The world was once more at peace, tenuous as that peace was, and soon we were looking at Russia again as enemy instead of friend. Our usefulness to Russia was over, and now she was the threat looming over us. But that had nothing to do with the fortunes of the Thorntons. In those two years we moved from the Victorian house to a small flat where Missouri Smith had to share David's room. From the flat we moved to an apartment where there was no room for her at all, and from that apartment to an even smaller one where I first started sleeping on the couch. Not only was the money from Grandfather's fortune completely gone, but my parents were deeply in debt.

David was five, so, small and thin as he was, he cheerfully started to school. I was sixteen, so I quit school. Not the girls' prep school I had attended when Grandfather was alive and paying the bills. I had long since had to leave that establishment. It was public school I quit, and I quit it to find a job.

Mr. Laski was furious. So was Missouri Smith.

"Yo's not to quit school," she stormed at me when I called and told her my plans.

"I don't have a choice, Missouri. My father can't keep a job, and my mother doesn't know how to do anything. That leaves me."

"Yore poor Granddaddy will go a'spinnin'," she said. "His li'l lamb out among the wolves."

"You know how frail David is. Doc Ableman takes very good care of him, but there is always medicine to buy, and he needs fresh fruit and vegetables."

"I got a little money…"

"And I want you to keep it. This is not your problem, Missouri. It's mine. If I were older I would kidnap David and go far away. One day I shall. But for that I need money. The only way I'll be able to get it is to earn it."

She fussed and scolded, but in the end I had my way. Mr. Laski was even more of an obstacle than Missouri. He offered money, although I knew that most of what he had earned here had gone to the refugees that poured into Palestine after the War. I asked only that he continue my lessons, and was reminded that he owed Frederic Morrowitz a debt that would be impossible to fully repay.

I read through all the help-wanted ads until finally I found one that just suited me. It was for a pianist at a restaurant.

I knocked on the door that was pointed out to me by a curious bartender. A gruff voice answered, "Come in."

I was nervous, as I always am around strangers, but I went in and found myself face-to-face with a man whose picture had been in the papers recently.

He was chewing on a fat cigar. He had a round face, a broken nose, and he was slightly balding. I recognized him instantly as Nick Costelli.

He, on the other hand, only saw a stammering kid in the doorway, and he wasn't too happy about it.

"Beat it," he said, and jerked his thumb in the general direction of the alley.

I swallowed hard, but stood my ground. "Your ad in the paper said you needed a pianist. Well, I'm a pianist."

"Hmph, well, I'd like one that's at least as old as my Scotch," he said, trying to hide a grin.

I fidgeted. "As long as your Scotch is sixteen."

He laughed outright at that. Then he sobered, because he could see I was on the verge of tears. He said kindly, "My dear girl, do you know what hours we keep here? You'd never get up in time for school."

"I've quit school," I said. Then I added, "Please, sir, I need the job. And I play, I really do. I can play anything."

Nick Costelli had been a small-time hood before the War. But according to the papers, he saw action in France, and was, in fact, among the first who hit the beaches at Normandy. His experiences in Europe did something to him, and when he came back to Chicago he wanted to become a legitimate businessman. He owned a saloon in the thirties and had his finger in gambling on the side, but now he had a fervent desire to run a class operation.

He led me to the piano in the empty restaurant. "Show me what you can do, kid."

So I played for him—jazz, ballads, the classics. And Nick hired me.

"You'll get ten bucks a day, plus tips," he told me. "We open at four in the afternoon, and we close at two in the morning. But until you're older, you quit at eleven. And you get one free meal. And," he pointed a stubby finger at me, "if anyone gets fresh, he'll have me to deal with."

Missouri Smith, staunch Baptist that she is, was appalled. "I been prayin' dat yo find yo'self a good job," she said through her tears.

"Well, it worked. Your God has led me to a fine job."

"He's yore God, too. An' I can 'most guarantee dat He didn't lead you dere."

"Second-guessing God, Missouri? Shame on you."

"But honey, God'll get you through dis. Ain't He always?"

"No, He ain't," I said. "He must have His mind on other things…if He exists."

Missouri used to take me to her little church when I was younger. I was the only white person there. I enjoyed the singing, and the Bible stories, and the kindness of those people who were—at least most of them—so poor, but so happy. But then Grandfather died, and I questioned God. When our fortune went and our friends deserted us, I pleaded with Him to tell me why. Finally, David's illness and the cruelty that caused Grandmother's death made me question God's involvement in the everyday lives of the humans He was supposed to have created.

Playing in a glorified night club on Chicago's near South Side, which had been, by the way, Al Capone's territory, didn't bother my conscience one little bit. I had bills to pay, and if there were a God, He would surely want me to pay off my creditors.

Only Missouri Smith and Moshe Laski knew where I was working. Mr. Laski was as unhappy about the situation as Missouri—until he met Nick Costelli.

I was just getting ready to play when Mr. Laski walked in. He walked right up to Nick and introduced himself. But before he could say another word, Nick said to him, "Yeah, I know you. You're the kid's piano teacher. She talks about you all the time."

Mr. Laski was disarmed. Then when Nick added, "Nobody bothers the kid. She's a decent girl, and if anybody gets fresh with her they'll have to deal with me," Mr. Laski was mollified.

Nick was very good to me. He used to send food home with me, ostensibly because he didn't want to throw it away, but he really knew I was having a rough time. After he met David, he would ask about him every day, and send some special treat specifically for "the kid." I couldn't let Nick see where we lived, so he used to come to dinner or for a visit at Missouri's apartment. Gradually he won her over. His speech was rough, but she could discern the kindness underneath. He gave David some German, French, and Belgian coins he had brought back from Europe. They weren't worth anything, but it was just the beginning. Nick kept adding to the collection, until Missouri worried that someone would steal the coins. When she objected to a particularly valuable half dollar, Nick whispered that someday David would need money for college. So Missouri put them in her safety deposit box.

Patrick Thornton was drinking more and more, and he was taking his wife with him to the seedier bars where he was still welcome. I told him at the outset that I wouldn't pay his bar tabs or any of his gambling debts. He was drunk at the time, and he dealt me a blow across my face that blackened an eye. I had to make up a story to tell Nick, because I was afraid of what he would do if he found out the truth.

Tips were good. I managed to save money, a little at a time. I kept the bank book in my little dressing room at the club so my parents couldn't run across it "accidentally." If they knew I was building a nest egg they would hound me for it. The rest of my earnings went for rent and food, and David's medical bills. I didn't really feel I was making a sacrifice—not when David would rush home from school in order to spend a half hour with me before I left for work. He would hurriedly pour out the day's news, watching my face to see the pride I would take in his good marks. He lived for me, just as I lived for him. On those rare occasions when there was bad news, I could tell before he opened the door. The two flights of stairs would not be echoing with his footsteps. It would take him an extra ten minutes to get to our apartment. How I hated to leave on those days.

Summers were much better. I'd take David to the playground, and we could both escape from the apartment, from the oppressive heat, and from...all the rest of it. When the vendors came around, we'd have a Coney or Polish sausage for lunch and Italian ice or a snowcone for dessert. In David's childish joys I found some of the fun I had missed.

Oh, memories that bless and burn.
O barren gain—and bitter loss.
—Robert Cameron Rogers

Chapter 2

Missouri finally informed me, when I turned nineteen, that it was time I got married, and she was praying for a nice Christian man to come and take me and David away from the life we were living.

The day after she told me this, I ran into Bryce Lansdowne. Bryce was a charming and handsome young man whose grandfather had been a personal friend and close business associate of my grandfather. I hadn't seen him for several years.

"I've been away at school, you know—Harvard. Then after graduation my parents sent me on a grand tour of Europe. I just got back yesterday."

"How wonderful! Europe!" I exclaimed. "Was it as exciting as it sounds?"

"It was fun. I especially enjoyed England. My mother is from there, you know."

How well I knew. His mother's family had been of the aristocracy. Even though impoverished by two wars, they were still titled, and Mrs. Lansdowne never let anyone forget it. I had seen her fairly recently, and she had cut me like a slice of bread. Naturally, I didn't tell Bryce.

He was scrutinizing my face. Finally he said, "You always were a very pretty girl, Brit, but you've grown into quite a beauty."

I could feel myself blushing. I never knew what to say to compliments.

17

But apparently he didn't expect a reply. "I...er...heard about the...er...bad luck your family has had. I'm sorry. I really liked your grandparents."

"Everyone did," I said. "But really, Bryce, I'd rather not talk about it. Gosh, it's good to see you. I don't see many of the old crowd anymore."

That was an understatement. I didn't see any of the old crowd any more.

Bryce and I began seeing each other. I was off on Sundays and Mondays, so on those nights we went out. I refused to tell him where I was working, and in his turn he didn't take me to places where his friends, and especially his family, might run into us.

It was Bryce who suggested taking David with us on our dates. I guess he could see how uncomfortable I was about leaving him, and how my mind was on him constantly. With David along, I could really relax. He was never any trouble. Unlike most eight or nine year-old boys, he was truly sensitive to others, and he'd give Bryce and me our space, even though he was never out of shouting range. We'd play a set of tennis then stroll through Lincoln Park; all of us loved the zoo. On rainy days there was the Field Museum. If we got tired of stuffed animals and mummies, there were live fish in the aquarium across the street. When the Cubs were home, we'd take in a Sunday afternoon double-header at Wrigley Field—my normally sedate grandparents had been rabid Cubs fans. Then Bryce would take us for dinner. Chicago has really great restaurants: Chinese, Polish, Greek, Italian, you name it. Our favorite was the Black Hawk in the Loop. Those were some of the happiest days David and I ever spent. And Bryce wasn't just being sweet. He seemed to enjoy the company of my beautiful honey-blonde little brother as much as I did.

On my twentieth birthday he proposed. I said yes. All I could think about was how David and I would finally have a chance at a real life.

Bryce's parents were furious. I knew they wouldn't be exactly jubilant, but I confess I wasn't prepared for their treatment of me when we went to tell them about our engagement. They let me know in no uncertain terms that Patrick Thornton's daughter wasn't good enough for their son, that Patrick Thornton's

18

reputation had damaged without repair the good name of Frederic Morrowitz.

They handled Bryce only slightly more subtly. They told him he would be ostracized by his friends, if he married me. They let gentle hints about wills and bonds and assets fall around him like soft snowflakes that can add up to a foot of snow if there are enough of them. Sylvia Bannister, of THE Bannisters, would make a much more suitable wife for a man going into the family law firm. Why, Bryce could possibly be a judge one day, and how would it look if his father-in-law were in jail?

I gave the ring back without a struggle. Missouri had been so happy at the news of my approaching marriage that she went to give thanks at church for answered prayers. Now I had the opportunity to tell her what I thought of her God. Sylvia Bannister, who had always disliked me because she couldn't beat me in tennis, or riding competition, or musical accomplishment, had beaten me now.

"So you can thank your God," I told Missouri.

But she would insist on seeing it differently. "Bryce jis' wun't the right man for yo, honey. God's got somebody better for yo. 'Member, He works in myster'ous ways."

"He must."

Then something happened to take my mind off Bryce Lansdowne. I came home after work and found David still awake and crying. He never did that.

"Sis," he pleaded, "please take me to Doc Ableman. Please." He had never asked before. He was sick—very, very sick. He said his head hurt and his neck. The moment I touched him, I felt the high fever. His little back was even arched to some degree. I was terribly worried—pardon me, that's a lie; I was scared silly.

I ran to my mother. "David's sick—really sick," I cried.

"David's always sick," she answered. "Your father's gone. He hasn't come home."

"Father's always gone," I countered. I can still feel the sting of her slap across my face.

"How dare you talk about your father like that," she shouted. "He may be hurt, lying somewhere."

"He's drunk, more than likely," I shouted back, stepping away from her reach. "You should be more concerned about your son."

"My first responsibility is to my husband. You would understand, if you ever managed to get one of your own."

I didn't let her see how that had hurt me. Instead I went to the telephone to call Missouri.

The line was dead. It had been disconnected. Then I remembered that I hadn't had enough to pay the bill.

I had to run down to the corner and make the call from the pay phone there. Missouri didn't waste time getting to the point. "Yo' git dat chile to Doc Ableman! I'll meet you dere in half an hour.

I didn't waste time either. I bundled David up, caught the "L" train, and took him to Children's Memorial.

They called Dr. Ableman, and he came in at once although it was now 3:30 a.m. After checking David over thoroughly, he told me he would like to keep him for observation. Of course, I agreed, but what could I do about that sinking feeling in my stomach?

The news was devastating; David had infantile paralysis. The scientific name is poliomyelitis, usually shortened to polio, the dread disease which attacks a child for no apparent reason, and a disease for which there was no known cure.

There was precious little David, fighting for his life inside that horrible iron lung. I swallowed my pride and prayed for a miracle. Nothing happened.

"He's not better," I told Missouri.

"He ain't worse. Honey, yo' gotta 'member dat miracles doan allus happen overnight. Sometimes dey take a while."

I decided to work this particular miracle myself. I found every book I could on the disease. I learned all I could about its treatment. Sister Elizabeth Kenny was an inspiration to me, even though Dr. Ableman warned me that her views were not accepted by the mainstream medical community.

I didn't care. I was willing to try anything. When David was allowed to come home, I applied hot packs to his legs. I massaged his legs for hours, and worked them up and down.

Dr. Ableman recommended a dog for David. He said it was the best therapy known to man. I went to the Humane Society and picked out the biggest, friendliest mutt they had. By the time I got him home he had somehow become "Napoleon." I was prepared for my parents' protests. I would buy his feed and walk him. David would keep him in his room. If anything happened to Napoleon, I warned them—if he should "accidentally" get out of the apartment and run away—I would stop paying the electric bill. They squealed in self-righteous fury at this invasion of their home, but they knew I meant it. It made me feel better about leaving David alone in the evenings. David was crazy about the dog. The two of them could play for hours, and Napoleon seemed to know just how rough he could be without hurting David.

School was out of the question for the time being. Missouri came up with a man by the name of Alexander Bergman. He was a brilliant historian working on his doctorate from the University of Chicago. His thesis, he said, was about the tutoring of invalids and it would be a tremendous favor if we would allow him to tutor David. I was so grateful, I didn't even think twice. The University, he assured me, paid him a fair amount for the classes he taught there; he couldn't possibly accept anything from me. The fact that he was Polish didn't register with me at the time. I took it at face value that we were doing him a favor.

Professor Bergman had some interesting ideas about education. "Vocabulary!" he would tell me over and over. "If the boy has a large enough vocabulary he can understand anything, and equally important he can express himself." That was when I made up a game to play with David. "Alliteration," I called it, and we would try to converse using the same initial over and over until we ran out of words and had to give up and start with a new initial. It made us both scour the dictionary and enlarge our vocabulary.

Now that he was spending so much time in bed, Missouri would bring his coins and let him study them. She usually came in the evenings when I was gone, but she never came when my parents were at the house. The coin collection was one more secret to be kept. Professor Bergman learned of them however, and agreed they were very educational. He had a few European coins he added, and then he seemed to always be coming across a rare or unusual coin "by chance." "Just a matter of knowing what to look for," he claimed. It was an ideal hobby for a crippled child, and

David delighted in it, unaware that anyone was planning for his future.

So David learned at home, in his small bedroom that overlooked a garbage-strewn and rat-infested alley three stories below, and I continued to work at Little Italy.

Now that I was older Nick decided to get me from behind the thin, filmy curtain at the back of his lounge. He built a stage in the center of the floor, decked me out in a gorgeous evening gown, bought a Steinway baby grand, and had me play requests. Moshe Laski came around to make sure I wasn't being molested and that I was sitting up straight and keeping my fingers arched.

My father eventually discovered where I worked and predictably he tried to borrow money from Nick. I could have saved him the trip. I could even have saved him being tossed out on his ear and threatened with mayhem. It wasn't that I had told Nick about my father. I was too ashamed to do that. It was all that I *hadn't* said. Nick was smart enough to fill in the omissions.

Several years passed. David would do better, then he would have a setback. When he had to spend more time in the hospital, Dr. Ableman managed to get Napoleon admitted too. A badge reading "physical therapist" was attached to his collar, but the nurses insisted he submit to daily baths. Professor Bergman said his thesis couldn't be delayed by these frequent hospitalizations, so he traveled daily to the hospital to continue David's schooling.

Those were the times I alternately prayed and cursed God. If David died, all my working and planning and saving would be wasted. I'd sit by his hospital bed, and pretend everything was just lovely. David would store up the jokes those wonderful nurses told him and repeat them for me. No matter how much pain he was in, he always had a smile, so I had to act happy too. Sometimes I felt the strain of faking cheerfulness was just too much on top of everything else. I'd go to my dressing room at Little Italy and sit there in a mood of black despair. Nick was understanding as always. He'd visit David himself at least once a week. That was more often than my parents did.

I went to several lawyers to try to get legal custody of my brother, but they were all discouraging. Even given the circumstances, it would have been virtually impossible to get David away from my parents. It just wasn't done. Besides, it would create another scandal, and another scandal was something I couldn't face. Reluctantly, I stayed with the family, for the sole purpose of taking care of David. I paid for medicine and hospitalization, though Dr. Abelman refused to take a penny for his own services. I brought home the groceries and paid most of the necessary bills while my father went from one job to another. Then he went from one bar to another, with my mother accompanying him.

～～～～～～～

That brought my reminiscing up to the present—to what had happened within the last week.

Friday night, while I was playing the piano on my stage at Little Italy, I saw a couple come in. Usually I didn't pay attention to the customers, but this particular customer wanted me to notice her. It was Sylvia Bannister, on the arm of Bryce Lansdowne.

Bryce looked at me then turned a bright red. Sylvia was gloating.

I smiled at them and nodded. Bryce was acutely uncomfortable. Sylvia, though, was in her element. Obviously, she had known I worked there. Just as obviously, Bryce hadn't.

When I went to my dressing room for my break, a little dinner was always there waiting for me. I was eating this when I heard a knock on my door. I knew who it was, but I invited her in anyway.

"Well, well," she said, "it's the little princess. Come down in the world a bit, haven't you."

I smiled at her. "I haven't stooped as low as you yet."

The smile froze on her face. "You should be nicer to me, you know. I'm about to do you a big favor."

"Sure," I said, "and your daddy's a Democrat."

"No, seriously." Her eyes narrowed. She looked like a Siamese cat sitting there, and practically purring. I happen not to be a cat lover. "It's about Bryce."

"Oh, really? Getting tired of him, are you?"

"Oh, no. Nothing like that. It's just that I've met...someone else—a cowboy."

"You don't say. With cows and horses and pigs and the lot?"

"Something like that." She smoothed the mink at her shoulder with a ring-laden hand. "I'm about to give old Bryce the brush-off. I thought I'd let you know. You can have him back. He'll be second-hand, of course, but," and she gave me a malicious grin, "you should be used to second-hand things by now."

I pushed my plate aside, coolly I thought, and told her with the sweetest smile I could muster, "I sincerely hope your cowboy takes a good look at your breeding."

I stood and walked casually to the door. She grabbed my arm and swung me around to face her. She was shorter than I, and on the plump side. That plumpness would turn to fat by the time she was thirty if she didn't quit indulging herself. I thought of that in the few seconds she stood glaring at me and it made me smile, which made her angrier.

"You think you're a regular wit, don't you," she spat at me. "Well, I'll have the last laugh. People need meat more than they need lawyers. My cowboy has a lot more money than Bryce will ever have. And I'll have fun spending it. Just remember that when you catch Bryce on the rebound."

"Sylvia, you're pathetic. I think I honestly feel sorry for you. But not as sorry as I feel for your cowboy. Excuse me, but some of us do have to work for our money. You know—work? Or, no, I guess you don't."

I left her still standing in my dressing room door and went back to my bench at the piano. I had been pretty catty myself, but I couldn't find any regret at the moment.

Bryce never came near me, but Sylvia still had some ammunition left and she had the parting shot. She had requested the "Tennessee Waltz," and after I played it she sauntered up to the piano and dropped a five-dollar bill onto my plate. On her arm was a silver bracelet, and from it dangled a diamond drop. She stilted her wrist several times so the diamond could catch the light. "I'm leaving the country tomorrow," she told me. "I'm going to Europe. Absence makes the heart grow fonder, as they say."

"Funny. I always heard 'out of sight, out of mind'. You better not be too clever. Like the dog with the bone who saw his reflection in the water. He ended up losing everything."

"Does this look like my cowboy will forget me?" She put her elbow on the piano and held her arm up, modeling the bracelet. "A going-away present—classy, tasteful, and very expensive."

Nick was making his way towards the piano. Customers were not allowed to pester me. If anyone wanted me to play a song he summoned his waiter and put the request on the silver plate along with an appropriate tip. If I didn't know the song, the customer got a free drink. Nick had to give away very few drinks. But under no circumstances was anyone allowed on my little stage.

"It's okay, Nick. I know this...er...lady." I turned to Sylvia. "Good luck. And good-bye."

She gave me a cold shoulder, and Nick a small smile, then went to join Bryce at the door. Nick muttered something under his breath. It was in no way a compliment to my recent guest.

Little Italy was always dark. Nick thought it gave his restaurant an aura of romance. I could barely see the two as they left. Funny. As I sat there playing "Harbor Lights" the only emotion I could feel was pity.

I played for the next few hours mechanically, my thoughts on things other than the ivory keys. Sylvia was a shallow, rich, spoiled brat like my mother. I wondered if she would make the same mistake in choosing a husband as Camille Morrowitz Thornton. Probably not. Sylvia had a hard, practical streak in her that would not allow her to blindly adore anyone.

Then I remembered a few nights back. I thought I had seen a familiar blonde at one of Nick's back, very private tables. Of course, I couldn't be sure it was my old nemesis. It was difficult to see the customers who dined at Little Italy. A spotlight was on me there on my platform in the middle of the dining room, but the rest of the place was dark, and the tables were more or less secluded. I seldom knew who requested specific tunes, but on that particular night I had a request to play, and sing, "Danny Boy". My voice wasn't bad, and I did a credible job. Then for three successive nights I had had the same request. But not tonight. No one came in and asked for the Irish ballad.

Shortly before closing, one of the waiters came up and handed me a note. It was from Bryce.

"Dear Brit," it read, "I'm terribly sorry we came here. I had no idea you were working for Nick Costelli. Sylvia did, though.

She told me so tonight. Apparently she has been here before, but I don't know with whom. Please believe it wasn't me. Please play and sing 'Lorena' for me, even though I won't be here to enjoy it. —Bryce."

Inside the note was a ten-dollar bill. I gave myself a mental shake, and had to smile. Poor Bryce. I played with a few keys, then struck the opening chord for the ballad that had been popular in the South during the Civil War.

"The sun's low down the sky, Lorena,
The frost gleams where the flowers have been;
The days creep slowly by, Lorena.
The snow is on the grass again.
The heart throbs on as warmly now,
As when the summer days were nigh.
Oh! the sun can never dip so low,
Adown affection's cloudless sky."

There was a slight catch in my throat, but I went on to the next verse.

"We loved each other then, Lorena.
More than we ever dared to tell;
And what we might have been, Lorena,
Had but our lovings prospered well,
But then—'tis past; the years are gone,
I'll not call up their shadowy forms;
I'll say to them, 'Lost years, sleep on!
Sleep on! Nor heed life's pelting storms.'"

Bryce must have remembered that my middle name is Lorena. I swallowed the lump in my throat, and thought back to the blonde of a few nights ago. The man with her was definitely not Bryce. Maybe Sylvia was there with her cowboy. But, no. If she were, she would have allowed me to see him, so she could gloat.

I consigned Sylvia to the fathomless deep, and Bryce along with her. He was weak, poor Bryce. I had some pity for him, but not much. If I really loved someone, I thought, I wouldn't let anything, anyone, or any circumstance stand in the way of that love. If Bryce could, he was not much of a man.

I left the restaurant that fateful Saturday morning at about two o'clock. I didn't want to miss the 2:10 bus; another one wouldn't come along for fifty minutes. I was walking fast. It had started to sleet, and the Chicago wind whipped around me and threw the sleet at me, stinging my face. The street was dark and fairly deserted, and suddenly I had a shiver of urgency. Something was wrong; something had happened. I knew it now. I had wanted to read the evening paper, but Nick told me he hadn't picked it up. That was ridiculous. Nick always picked up the paper. Politics and sports were Nick's favorite pastimes. And the policeman...yes, there had been a policeman in the club. He was in plain clothes, but Nick had taught me how to spot one, and I knew that this one had come into the lounge and that Nick had somehow got rid of him. And when I mentioned something about it in passing to Nick, he had casually brushed it off. Maybe too casually?

And then Nick had to leave, and told me not to go until he got back. But he hadn't come back, and I couldn't miss my bus.

I quickened my pace. Something was wrong. I felt I needed to see David at the clinic. Maybe something had happened to him. But, no...Nick would have told me.

I was fighting the wind and the sleet, hurrying as best I could, when a car roared up behind me. I turned, and saw my parents' old Ford. My father was at the wheel; he stopped the car beside me and rolled down his window.

"Get in," he said.

He was visibly drunk. He was having trouble focusing on me.

"What's wrong?" I shouted. "Is it David?" The wind carried my voice away.

"Isn't Dav-David," he slurred. Get in." My mother was sitting beside him. Her mouth had a disgusting, loose grin, and her eyes were watery. Fumes of alcohol through the partially-open window hit me full in the face.

"You're both drunk," I said. "You shouldn't be driving."

Patrick Thornton's bleary eyes opened. "Don't talk like that to me, girl. I'm sti-still your father. Get in!"

"Okay," I agreed, "but you've got to let me drive."

"Oh, aren't you the boshy one." my mother slurred. "Your precious grandparents let you get too big for your brish-brishes. Well, they're not here." She struggled up to a straighter position and said as sternly as she could, "Ish time you re-re-remembered whosh shtill bosh in this fam-family." A gurgling sound from deep in her body emitted through her wet mouth. "Your f-father and I are going to get David...and we are leaving the c-country."

"You're what!" I shouted. "Why? You know Doc said he wouldn't release David until..." I broke off. Dr. Abelman had told me privately that David was better than he had been in a long time, but he wouldn't release David until I could find a clean, comfortable, warm environment for the boy far away from the negative influence of his parents. No more rat-infested holes in the wall, no more cold-water flats, he had told me emphatically. No more drafty rooms, no more insufficient sunlight, no more climbing all those stairs, and no more being around lushes who didn't care about him or his illness. I had been working on the problem, but without much luck.

I swallowed, and took another tack. "Let me drive. We'll go get David."

My father shook his head. "Don't trust you, my li'l darlin'." The Irish lilt always became more pronounced as he got drunker. "Get in the back-back sheet, or we'll go without you."

In fact, he was already pulling away from the curb. I yanked open the back door and somehow managed to swing myself inside.

I was sitting right behind my father, with some wild idea of trying to grab the steering wheel. I realized, too late, that the possibility of doing that was remote. He was driving fast, much too fast for the weather. I sat on the edge of the seat planning to make a grab when an accident threatened. My mother, sensing my purpose, kept pushing me back. And all the while they told me their story. I began to understand, with a sickening thud of my heart, why Nick had kept the evening papers from me, and why he hadn't wanted me to leave the nightclub before he had a chance to talk to me.

Patrick Thornton owed a gambling debt. The bank where he was currently working—a job given to him by a sympathetic old friend for the sake of Frederic Morrowitz—was missing a substantial amount of money. My father rationalized that he could have paid the sum back with a little luck at the card table, and he grumbled about the twist of fate that had brought the bank examiners at this particular time. He became maudlin, something he always did when he got drunk, and started ranting about how the cards were stacked against him, about the kind of hand he had been dealt, saddled with a sickly son and an ungrateful daughter.

"How much did you steal?" I asked unkindly.

My mother turned on me like a vicious, spitting cat. "Your father didn't shteal, he borrowed. And don-don-don't you forget it."

I felt suddenly nauseous. This would be the final blow. I had had hopes of somehow bringing back the good name of Frederic and Sophia Morrowitz, but now they were dashed. This felony would put my father behind bars, and would forever follow my brother and me.

We raced through a red light. I shouted and made a futile grab for the steering wheel. My father threw up his right arm and hit me across the face. I fell back against the rear seat. I tried again, and the car made a sickening lurch onto the sidewalk. He slammed on the brakes and I fell forward. Then he hit the accelerator again and turned onto a side street, sideswiping a parked car and barely missing a lamppost.

I realized I should have gotten in the front seat. If I could reach the keys I could put an end to this insanity. I was yelling by now, and trying desperately to climb over the seat, but my mother was fighting me off. The car was hurtling along the center of the street and heading straight for another red light.

The Buick that crossed our path never had a chance. Our car hit it broadside and shoved it into a parked utility truck. Someone screamed, but whether it was me or my mother I don't know. The crunching sound of steel against steel seemed to go on forever. Somehow I ended up on the floor of the back seat, and I was bruised but not, apparently, badly injured. Every window on all three vehicles shattered, sending pieces of broken glass flying in all directions. My mother had gone clear through the windshield. Her body was on the hood of our old car, flung there like a lifeless rag doll. Blood was everywhere.

My father was still in the car, slumped over the steering wheel, his neck at a grotesque angle. His eyes were still open and staring out the shattered side window. Blood was trickling from his sagging mouth.

My door was jammed, so I climbed gingerly through the broken glass of the rear window, and slid off the trunk. My legs were wobbly, and I had cut myself in several places trying to get out of the car, but otherwise I was unhurt.

The Buick was crushed between our car and the parked utility truck. The driver's side was completely caved in, and the driver himself not visible. I had to see if anyone in the car could have survived, and was heading there when I heard the whimper. I smelled the gasoline at the same time.

The street was still deserted. No one had heard the crash and come to help, though probably not even a minute had passed. I climbed as quickly as I could onto the hood of the Buick, and there he was. The streetlamp, bent precariously over when the force of the impact rammed it, lit up the car like a bright stage. A boy, probably near David's age, was cradling a man's head in his lap. Blood was everywhere—all over the seat, all over the man, all over the boy. It was splattered over the interior of the door, the floor, even the top. The man's body had been crushed. There was nothing I could have done for him. Then there was the boy, and the mute appeal in his eyes, the question dying on his bloodless lips.

There was no time for explanations or sympathy. There was a spark, and a small flame, and I knew the vehicles would go up any second. The windshield was broken; I pulled at the glass with my bare hands, and thrust myself through the opening I had made. I made a desperate grab for the boy, but he shrank from me. He didn't want to leave his father. Crying pitifully, he kept shouting, "Dad. Get my dad. I won't leave him. I won't."

There was no time for gentleness. I was half in and half out of the car. Broken glass was digging at my ribs, and my hands were bleeding from deep cuts. Flames were spreading to the rear of the car. I grabbed the boy by his arm and was pulling at him. "Come on, kid," I shouted. "The car's going to explode any second."

I don't think he understood me. He tried to fight me until I dealt him a blow across his face. In my awkward position I couldn't have hit him too hard, but it was enough. In a trance-like state, he let me drag him through the shattered remains of the window, regardless now of the broken glass. As I pulled him off the hood of the Buick, a flame caught in his bulky coat. I threw him to the ground, and rolled him over several times, beating at the flames with my hands. Then somehow I managed to get us both to the other side of the street and behind a parked car just as the flames engulfed all three vehicles. There were several small explosions, and as the flames licked at the tangled steel, a small crowd started to gather. I left the boy, still dazed, sitting on the sidewalk and started to inch away from the scene. My clothes were in shreds, and I had blood all over me. I started to feel the pain of the deep cuts and burns, and took a look at my hands. My fingers looked like they had been torn to ribbons.

I surreptitiously took refuge in a deep doorway. When someone found the boy, I started walking swiftly away, aware that I was committing a crime: leaving the scene of an accident. Fortunately, the clinic was just a few blocks away.

He who chooses the beginning of a road
chooses the place it leads to.
It is the means that determine the end.
—Harry Emerson Fosdick

Chapter 3

I finally rose from the couch and went back to the window. The sleet was turning to a wet snow. I hoped it wouldn't keep me from leaving in the morning.

I turned back to the newspapers on the floor. The headlines literally screamed at me. "**$10,000 MISSING AT 1st UNION TRUST**." I glanced through the article again. Patrick Thornton had embezzled ten thousand dollars from the bank whose president had given him another chance to redeem his character. But one can't redeem a character one never had to begin with. After he had betrayed the trust of a friend of the family and been caught, he slunk away like the coward he was, to collect his wife and kids and make a run for it. In the process he killed a man—murdered him just as surely as if he had pointed a gun and shot it.

The story that should have made the headlines was relegated to the second page. There had been another robbery at another bank. The thieves had made off with more than half a million dollars, and had killed a guard and wounded another in their escape. But Cheyenne, Wyoming was too far away, especially when Patrick Thornton was making headlines again at home.

I bitterly resented the fact that the story made the front page, but at least the writer had enough compassion to leave David and me out of it. I suppose that someone who lived the kind of life my parents did deserved the recognition they were getting now. But it strengthened my resolve to get away from Chicago—the sooner, the better.

Sunday's headlines read: "**GOOD SAMARITAN DOCTOR KILLED IN FIERY CRASH**." I didn't want to read the article. I had asked Missouri to pick up the papers only to see if somehow I was in any of the pictures. A photograph of the accident scene was right under the picture. I had already seen it, but now I looked at it more carefully. My hand shook a little as I noticed something I had missed the first time. There, in the bottom right-hand corner, I saw myself, with my back to the camera. I know it was me. My hair was wild, the coat was torn, and there were stains darkening the pockets into which I had thrust my hands. I hoped no one else noticed it. With all the other spectators there at the scene, I was really very inconspicuous.

Missouri told me that she heard on the news that the boy insisted he was pulled from the wreck by a beautiful woman, and the police were asking for any witnesses to come forward. But since no one did—and surely someone who saved a life would admit to doing it—the police concluded that the boy was delirious.

Missouri, of course knew the truth. So did Dr. Abelman, Moshe Laski, and Nick Costelli. When I left the scene of the accident, I went straight to the clinic. Luckily, Dr. Abelman happened to be on duty, even though it was nearly three o'clock in the morning. I told him all that had happened, and he was very sympathetic. It was over and done with; he agreed that telling the authorities I was at the scene couldn't help anyone, and might even do me some harm.

He X-rayed my hands, painstakingly pulled out the dozens of bits of glass, and patiently stitched up my fingers. Then he brought Moshe Laski into the room. Dr. Abelman had notified Missouri Smith, Nick Costelli, and Mr. Laski while waiting for the novocaine to take effect, and they came immediately. Now Moshe Laski was there, his eyes swollen from crying.

"I wanted Moshe to be here with you when I gave you the news," Dr. Abelman told me.

I looked at my music teacher. Tears were rolling down his face. He picked up one bandaged hand. "Brittany, my poor darling. You...you..."

He looked at Dr. Abelman and shook his head. "I cannot say it, Hiram."

Dr. Abelman took a deep breath, then said, very kindly, "Brit, my dear. Your hands have been badly damaged. They have lost a lot of dexterity. Between the cuts and the burns, well, you will eventually be able to play the piano again, *if* you do everything I tell you to, but you will never play the concert circuit."

The blow was a heavy one. For twenty years I had worked and practiced, all towards this one end. Not only had it been my life's dream, but it was also the way for me to get David away from...

But they were gone now. I should have felt something. Pity, maybe? Sorrow? But, no, I didn't feel any of this, not even relief. All I felt was defeat. I lifted my bandaged hands and looked at them. But I wouldn't let myself cry. I would not shed one tear.

I walked out into the waiting room. Missouri Smith and Nick Costelli were there. Missouri had been crying; Nick was pacing up and down. When I came in, he came to me immediately. He looked at my bandaged hands, then he turned and ran out of the room.

Missouri was sobbing. "Yore po' han's, chile. Yo' po' han's."

I kicked at the wastepaper can that was by the door. "If your God has anything else planned for me I wish He would get it out of His system and then leave me alone."

"Oh, chile, doan tak on lak dat. De good Lord, He ain't to blame. Yo' gotta believe ole Missoura. He wouldn't nebber hurt yo'!"

"He allowed it. There's not much difference. Three people dead, and my hands...

"I should have insisted on driving. I should have done everything in my power to stop that car. I could have, if I would just have tried hard enough." My senses were getting dull. Aftereffects of the accident, I thought, or whatever pain medication Doc had given me. I saw Missouri from a long way off.

"I'm being punished—for being Patrick Thornton's daughter. For wanting to take David away from them. For not loving them. For not driving, oh, dear Lord, why wasn't I driving?"

I woke up hours later, on a couch in Doc's small, private office. He was sitting there, watching me.

I sat up and rubbed my eyes. The bandages scratched my face. That brought me to the present with a vengeance.

"What time is it?" I murmured.

He looked at his watch. "Nearly nine o'clock. In the morning. You've only been out for about five hours."

I stared at the floor. "I have funeral arrangements to make, I guess."

"Nick is making them. Listen, Brit, you didn't know this, but your grandfather took out a small funeral policy on your parents. It's not much, but it will bury them. The plot he bought has four more sites on it. None of this will have to come out of your pocket."

I looked up at the kindly old man. "Are you sure, Doc? Or is this some story you and Nick and Missouri and Moshe concocted, and you all are really footing the bill?"

"No, my dear. It's the truth. Here, I have the policy. Frederic entrusted it to me. Thank God he did."

He pulled out an official looking document. Sure enough, my farsighted grandfather had made funeral arrangements for my parents.

"I just want a few words said over them at the graveside," I told the doctor. "Nothing elaborate. I doubt anyone comes, anyway."

"Well, that's about all this covers." He sat, looking troubled. There was something else on his mind. I gave him a questioning look, and he smiled. "You might as well know," he went on, "that your father absconded with ten thousand dollars from the bank."

"I know he took some money. He told me. I'm so ashamed, Doc."

"The police came looking for you last night at Nick's, to see if you knew where your parents disappeared to."

"I knew a policeman walked in. I didn't know why."

"Well, that's why. Nick assured him that you couldn't possibly know anything about it. He went out looking for them himself."

"So that's where he was. I wondered why I was supposed to wait for him."

"Yes," Dr. Ableman squirmed uncomfortably, "Look, Brit, I know you, and I know what you think you ought to do. But really, you didn't steal that money, and you are not responsible for it."

"I didn't steal it, no. But if you think I won't pay it back, please think again."

"You need your money to take care of David."

"I'll take care of David, and I'll pay back the ten thousand dollars and leave Chicago as soon as possible."

The good doctor did agree with me on that point. David must be taken away from Chicago as quickly as humanly possible. It would do him severe harm, in his condition, if he were to find out all of the details concerning his parents' deaths. "I'll try to think of something, call a few friends. We'll work something out."

Finally, reluctantly, he gave me the other two policies. $5000 each, one on my father and one on my mother. "This is David's money as much as it is yours," he argued. "You should keep it for his sake."

"If David knew what our father did, he'd want me to pay the money back. It *is* for his sake, so that we can leave here free and clear."

I stayed at the clinic for a while, and told David the news of our parents' deaths. He cried, which was probably the natural thing for him to do. I was the one who was unnatural. I realized this, but couldn't do anything about it.

I knew I had to go home sooner or later. Missouri came with me. Somehow the police left us alone; apart from telling me officially about my parents' deaths they had nothing to say, or ask. Likewise, the press didn't hound me. I learned later that I had Nick Costelli to thank for this. He had more influence in the city than I had previously thought.

I called Horace Kint, Grandfather's old friend at the bank, and told him every penny would be paid back. I'd bring in the insurance policies Monday right after the funeral. He sounded relieved, but whether it was because he was getting his money back, or because he would no longer have to deal with Patrick Thornton, I didn't know.

Then I checked my own funds. I had barely six hundred dollars. It was hardly enough to start a new life, but it would have to do. The cold, wet, windy climate of Chicago replete with crowds, noises, and dirty air wasn't good for David. I would have to leave. But where would I go?

Nick came, and told me about the arrangements he had made. "They'll be laid out tomorrow afternoon. The graveside service will be Monday morning. They'll be laid in the same plot as your grandparents, and there is enough to pay for the funeral. But there isn't enough for a marker."

I shrugged. "A marker will have to wait, then. I can't afford one right now."

"I understand," Nick said. "To tell you the truth, I'd get pretty unhappy if you took any of your savings and wasted it on a stone. At least, right now."

"Well, don't worry, I won't. David's health is the most important thing." There was a knock. I kept fearing it would be strangers. "Missouri, Someone is at the door. Do you mind answering it?"

It was just Dr. Abelman, and he had some good news for me, he said. He had called a friend of his in a small town in the Sand Hills of Nebraska, a Dr. Levi Abrams. Dr. Abrams had specialized in polio patients; he would work with David.

"Nebraska?" I said, stunned. "Why Nebraska?"

"Because," Dr. Abelman patiently explained, "David needs a doctor who is knowledgeable about polio. He also needs fresh air, dry, clean air, and plenty of sunshine."

"Yes, I know. I thought about Florida."

Dr. Abelman shook his head. "No!" he said adamantly. "Not Florida. It is my opinion, and you must agree that it has merit, that tropical, even semi-tropical climates, breed the germs that cause this disease. The Sand Hills, where my old friend is practicing, are cold in the winter, but dry. The summers are hot, but not humid. This is where David will do the best, I know it."

"But I don't know anyone in Nebraska. And I never heard of the Sand Hills."

He put his hands on his hips. "So? You have all these friends in Florida?"

"Well, no, but…"

"No 'buts' about it. Levi is very good, and an old friend. I'll call and make arrangements. You leave right after the funeral. You should get there next Wednesday."

Argument was pointless. And Missouri agreed with him. Separately they were formidable; together they could have ruled the world.

Of course I knew nothing at all about Nebraska. It was lumped in my mind with Kansas, and all I knew of Kansas, like most of my generation, was that it wasn't Oz. It wasn't that land "over the rainbow…where troubles melt like lemon drops." I liked the song. Who didn't? I wasn't the only one looking for a "Never-Never Land" to escape to.

Moshe came by, but he couldn't stand looking at my hands. I told him my plans, and he realized that I had no choice but to leave. He promised to come to the funeral, and he left, crying once again.

Dr. Abelman had to get back to the clinic. He personally was making sure David would not hear any news about the theft or the accident. Nick followed him to the door, but came back for a moment. He cleared his throat and opened his mouth, but nothing came out. So he reached inside his jacket pocket and pulled out a sheaf of bills and mutely handed them to me.

I was deeply moved by the gesture, but I said, "Nick, I can't take this."

"It ain't for you," he told me. "It's for the kid. You ain't got the right to refuse it."

Then he hugged me, and left.

I was alone with Missouri when there was another knock on the door.

I got up from the floor and put aside Saturday's paper. "I don't want to see anyone," I told her, and went to David's room and gently shut the door.

A minute later Missouri tapped on the door and then came in. I was sitting on David's poor excuse for a bed, waiting for whoever had come to leave again.

She closed the door and whispered, "It's a Mr. John Ransom come to see yo'."

I literally sprang from the bed. "Who?" I gasped.

"De doctor's oldest boy. He come to ax you sumtin'."

"I'll just bet he has!" I took a turn around the small room. "I don't want to see him."

Missouri frowned at me. With her ample hands on her equally ample hips, she said, "I'd see him if'n I was yo'."

"Well, you're not me," I replied shortly. "Please, just get rid of him."

"Might not be so easy," she replied with a certain amount of satisfaction.

"I don't know why he's here."

"Yo' would if'n yo' ax him," she said reasonably.

"Well, I don't really care why he's here. Please, Missouri, don't you realize that I can't face him? Have you thought that he could take me to court, and has every right to?"

"Yo' is makin' one big mistake, honey."

"I've made them before—big ones. I'll probably make some again. Meantime, please get that man out of here."

Missouri left David's room somewhat in a huff, and was only gone a few brief moments. When she came back, she had that half-smile on her face that I never trusted. But she volunteered nothing, and as far as I was concerned, the case was closed.

But that didn't keep me from going to the window that overlooked the street. The light in our so-called living room was off. I pulled back the shabby curtain and watched for him to leave the building. It wasn't long before I saw his form: tall, his head bent as if he were in deep thought, his overcoat open and his hands thrust deep into his trouser pockets.

I went early to the funeral parlor. The caskets, naturally, had to be closed. Visitation was to be between two and four o'clock. I stood there for quite a while, alone with my thoughts. I had never wanted anything like this to happen. I had always longed for a family life, and I had wanted my parents to be loving and kind like my grandparents.

I was regretting not only the loss of life, but the loss of potential, the forfeiture of dreams. My parents could have been successful, respected. There was pity there, deep inside me, for lost character, and lost dignity. And there was deep sorrow, too, for I knew that if Missouri's God was real and there was a hell for sinners, my parents were suffering there right now.

Moshe Laski came, and sat with me for a while. Soon we were joined by Nick and Dr. Abelman. Doc said David was doing fine, but although he had pleaded to be with me, the good doctor told him the weather was much too bad for him to leave the clinic. Missouri came next. She told me that she had made some good chicken soup for me, and had packed a few of my things for the trip.

Several people came whom I didn't recognize but suspected were drinking buddies of my father's. Then Bryce Lansdowne came by.

"I thought you might want to...well, get away for a bit," he said kindly.

I looked at my few friends. They nodded in unison, and soon I found myself in Bryce's plush Lincoln. We went to a small but elegant restaurant, and he made me put something in my stomach.

I began the conversation by saying, "I hear Sylvia's in Europe."

He had the grace to look sheepish. "She left early yesterday morning."

"Well, at least you won't have to worry about her running into us."

He bristled a little. "That's not fair, Brit."

I was immediately sorry for baiting him. "I'm sorry, Bryce. It's just, well, everything happening. I'm not myself. Please disregard my bad mood."

He smiled. "You're quite a girl, Brit. Quite a girl. I...I...I want to tell you..."

I never let him finish. "I'm leaving Tuesday morning."

"Oh? Are you going on vacation?"

"No. I'm leaving for good and forever."

That surprised him. "You're kidding, aren't you?"

"I've never been more serious. I'm taking David and getting out of Chicago. With my tail between my legs, so to speak."

"But...this...has nothing to do with you, Brit."

"No? Well, a lot of people seemed to think that what my parents did—and were—rubbed off on me. Your folks included, if I remember correctly."

He shook his head but didn't reply. I guess there was nothing he could say.

We ate in silence for a few minutes, then he asked, "Where are you going?"

"To a place where people never heard of Patrick Thornton. In fact, they maybe never even heard of Chicago."

"In other words, you don't want to tell me."

"In other words, I don't want to tell anyone."

He cleared his throat. "I'll miss you."

I smiled at him. "No you won't. You'll be too busy defending crooks and wife-beaters to think much about me. But it was nice of you to say so. Anyway I'm happy for you that you escaped Sylvia."

Bryce nodded, "There's that to be thankful for at least."

All in all, it was an uncomfortable meal. I was glad when it was over. But in that brief hour Bryce Lansdowne was completely exorcised from my system. I knew now that any pang of regret I might have felt would never be. He left me off in front of the funeral parlor and I walked in without a backward glance.

Missouri was still there, and she hurried up to me, saying, "He was here—jus' a minit past."

"Who was?"

"Dat John Ransom. See? He signed de book."

I looked. In big black letters was the name John Ransom. His signature was large and decisive. I saw I had also missed Professor Bergman.

"Why on earth did he come here?"

"He say he gotta ax yo' sumtin. I wisht I knew what it was."

"I just wish he would stay away. I'm glad I wasn't here. I can imagine what he wants. If someone killed David I would have a lot of questions to ask, myself."

"I doan t'ink he wants to ax dose kinds of questions," Missouri argued.

"He does if he's any kind of son. He's angry and frustrated, and probably wants to vent his anger on someone. Well, he's not going to vent it on me. If he ever even suspected that I was in that car, and didn't keep my father from driving—can you imagine how he would feel? It's bad enough that my father...but it would be even worse if anyone knew I was..."

I couldn't finish. Tears were just under the surface. I was fighting to keep them and my voice under control. Missouri put her arms around me and patted my back, just like she did when I

42

was a child. "Dere, dere," she said, over and over, until I was calm again.

That night he came back again. Once more I refused to see him, but I watched him leave. Hatless, hands in pockets, he stood on the sidewalk as though he was trying to make up his mind about something. Apparently he made a decision, and that decision took him to his car. The motor came to instant life, and he was gone.

The funeral Monday was a sorry affair. The weather was cold and damp, and I was glad Dr. Abelman had refused to allow David to come.

A local minister said a few short words and led an even shorter prayer. There wasn't much to be said about people who lived—and died—like they did. It was over almost before it began. Moshe Laski and Nick Costelli were there, but I didn't want Missouri out in this weather, and Dr. Abelman had an emergency. Before I left the cemetery, I said good-bye to my grandparents. I felt that this would be the last time I would do so. I had brought some flowers and placed them on the graves. Then, with Nick on one side and Moshe Laski on the other, I left.

Missouri was at the apartment, packing up our few possessions. She greeted me with a big hug and a bowl of her famous chicken soup. I felt better after I ate. She had brought David's coin collection so that he could take them along. There was no question of selling any of the coins. They were for David's college fees. Then I told her of my decision to purchase a car.

"Nick found one for me. Used, of course, but in good condition, a '51 Chevy. They want four hundred dollars for it. Nick says it's a real buy. He's bringing it over this afternoon. Then I can start packing it."

That sent Missouri into a flood of tears. She kept crying, "My babies, my babies. Dey is leebin' me."

She kept that up off and on until Nick came with the car. It was difficult saying good-bye to my boss of nearly nine years. Nick had been very good to me. It was because of him that I had been able to save as much money as I had, for he had always paid generously.

It was hard for him to tell me good-bye, too. When he left he said he was going to the clinic, to say his farewells to David.

43

Moshe Laski came by later that day. He looked at my bandaged hands and started crying again. I honestly believe he was far more upset about them than I was.

It was time for me to finish packing. My bandages were a hindrance and I was grateful for Missouri's help. My few meager keepsakes were packed separately in a small box. My Shirley Temple doll, the framed photograph of my grandparents taken in happier times, my sheet music, the lovely sterling silver jewelry box Bryce had given me so long ago. I lifted the lid and listened to the tinkling notes of "The Music Box Dancer". I overcame a sudden urge to throw the box across the room. I knew I would regret it later if I succumbed to that impulse. I loved the delicately formed silver. Bryce had brought it from Italy and had given it to me on the day he proposed. It would be a reminder, I told myself, that at one time someone did want me. In the years ahead I would always have that.

That night he came back again. Missouri came softly into David's room, where I was finishing packing his few pieces of clothing. I had been so absorbed in what I was doing that I hadn't heard the knock on the front door.

I glanced up at her, and she whispered, "Dat Mr. Ransom is back ag'in, honey. He wants to talk to yo'. He say it's real 'portant."

I shook my head. "I don't know why he keeps coming. I can't imagine what we could possibly have to say to each other. Please, get rid of him."

"That ain' been so easy. He say he *gotta* talk to 'Miss Thornton'. An' I doan think he come for de reasons yo' suspects. He got kind eyes, dat man does. Real kind."

I looked up at her. "Missouri, I can't face him. I can't! I was there! He would know. How would I be able to explain these?" I held up my hands. "He would know I was with them, and didn't keep my father from driving." I was beginning to get quietly hysterical.

"Yo' saved his brudder's life. Yo' could tell him dat."

I shook my head. "I couldn't. I couldn't. I...just walked off and left. Like a coward. I didn't want anyone to know I was even near the accident. Police, questions, reporters. I couldn't face them. They would think I had known about the embezzlement. It

44

would be only natural. People might even think I was condoning their flight from the authorities. After all, I was with them. No, Missouri. He must never know—*no one* must ever know—that I was in that car. Please," I pleaded, "don't tell him. Don't ever tell a soul."

She looked at me, and a large tear slid down her face. "I won't," she promised. "But what am I gonna do 'bout him?" She jerked her head towards the closed door.

"Tell him I'm—I'm inconsolable, grief-stricken, heartbroken, anything you want, and that I'm in no fit condition to entertain strangers."

"I ain' gonna lie to dat po' boy," Missouri said huffily. "I'll jis' tell him yo' ain' receivin' visitors. But I still think yo' is makin' a mistake."

"I've made them before," I replied wearily. "And I'll make them again."

She gave a little snort, then was gone. I heard soft voices, but couldn't make out the words. The conversation went on for some time. I started fidgeting; there was no telling what Missouri Smith was telling this man who was so bent on seeing me.

I went to the door and put my ear to it, but it was no use. Whatever they were saying to each other was muffled. But finally he left, and Missouri came back into David's room. When she opened the door I was once more seated on the floor, ostensibly packing.

"Well, he's gone," she said unnecessarily.

"For good?"

"For good. His pappy's funeral is tomorrow. Imagine him comin' all de way here wif all he had to do tomorrow."

"Yes, imagine," I said flippantly. "What did he have to say?"

"Well, not much. Jis' dat he wanted to have a few words wif yo', an' dat he was sorry 'bout your folks. He wanted me to tell yo' dat. He say he gonna come back tomorrer night, an' he hopes yo' will take a few minutes to talk to him."

"And what did you say to that?"

Missouri pursed her lips. "I did not tell him yo' was leebin'. I promised yo' I wouldn't, and a promise is a promise. I jis' tol' him I doubted if'n yo' would see him tomorrer night, or any other time, and dat I hated him wastin' his time. Den he smiled at me an' tol'

45

me, he neber wasted his time, and dat he would keep comin' back till yo' give him a chance to talk to yo'. Den he left." She looked at me. "He's nice, honey. I really t'ink he's nice. Verra Christian, the way he treated me. Lak we was equals."

"You are equals," I said.

"Well, I knows dat, and yo' knows dat, but believe me, honey, not ever'body knows dat. Eben Mr. Bryce, he doan treat ol' Missouri lak she was much. But Mr. Johnny—'magine him askin' me to call him Johnny—why, he was so kind to dis ole colored lady. I laks him."

"I'm glad. You should have given him your address, then he can pester you after I'm gone from this place."

I stood up. My legs were stiff from sitting so long on the floor. I went out into the living room and turned off the lamp. Then I went to the window. For what I hoped would be the last time, I watched him as he stood in the dim glow of the street lamp, his dark hair glistening from the icy rain the sky was emptying, his hands thrust deep into his pockets. He turned once, and I stepped back, but not before I got a fairly good look at him. Missouri told me he had a kind face, but she forgot to mention how handsome.

He could not possibly have seen me. If he had he probably would have made his way back up those two long flights of stairs. But he pulled his keys from a pocket, got into his late-model Cadillac, and drove off. I breathed a sigh of relief. I was leaving in the morning, and I would never have to worry about the persistent Mr. John Ransom again.

I was sitting on the dilapidated sofa looking at my hands when Missouri came back into the room.

"You gonna be able to drive wif dem bandages?"

"When I go by the clinic to pick up David, Doc is going to take them off, change dressings, and reward them with less bulky tape. He thinks I'll be able to manage." I smiled at her. "I'm a good driver, you know."

"'Course yo' is. Yo' is good at anything yo' puts yo' mind to."

"Yeah. Right."

"Yo' should'a talked to dat po' boy,"

46

I threw up my hands. "I give up, Missouri. You have a one-track mind. And by the way, I have it on good authority that 'poor boy' is thirty-one."

Missouri smiled. "Int'rested, ain' yo'?"

"No. How could I be? I'm...just puzzled as to why he has been coming here for the past three nights. Curiosity and interest are not necessarily the same things, you know."

"He got such a kind face," she told me again. "But I t'ink I saw a stubb'n streak. He ain' de kind to give up so easy."

"Well, I have a stubborn streak, too."

She chuckled, a full, rich sound that came from deep within her. "Doan I know it," she said, still chuckling. "Doan I jis' know it."

In front, the sun climbs slow, how slowly,
but westward, look, the land is bright.
                                    —Arthur Hugh Clough

Chapter 4

The next morning brought little change in the weather. As early as I rose, Missouri was up before me. I would take her with me when I went to get David, and Dr. Abelman said he would see to it that she got home.

I gathered up the newspapers that were still scattered on the floor, and consigned them to the wastepaper basket. I still hadn't really read the articles about Dr. Samuel Ransom. It was enough that an innocent man of great personal worth had to die because of a fatal weakness in my father. The accident would haunt me the rest of my life. I knew enough; I certainly didn't need to add to my guilty conscience the personal life story of a man whose sole purpose in life seemed to be tending the poor and forgotten of Chicago's slums. Yet it was hard to keep from at least scanning the columns. I did learn that the family was wealthy, and that was a relief. Their insurance company certainly wouldn't collect anything from the Thorntons. The doctor's wife "had preceded him in death," as the newspaper put it. So there wasn't a grieving widow to haunt my imagination, but it meant the boy I had pulled from the car—his name was Richard and he was thirteen—had now lost his only parent. That hurt me deeply, and I wanted to believe all the good things Missouri was trying to tell me about John Ransom, because the boy would now be his responsibility.

I looked around. The apartment was as clean as that apartment would ever be. The few boxes—mostly books— and suitcases Missouri and I had packed were already in the trunk and between the seats. I closed the door and locked it, and for the last time in my life I descended the two flights of stairs.

I saw that Missouri was comfortable, got in the driver's side, pressed the starter button, put the car into gear, and pulled out into the traffic. I was leaving the city where I grew up, without a single regret.

I was still worried about our finances. I had a few hundred dollars left after I bought the car, but we had a trip of nearly a thousand miles to make and the expenses of settling into a new home. How long before I could find a job? What if we had to pay for a motel room while looking for a place to rent? I hoped rents would be cheaper than in Chicago.

As I pulled up to the clinic and was about to get out of the car, Missouri turned to me and said, "I got sumtin' fo' yo'."

For the first time my eyes filled with tears. "Oh, Missouri. You shouldn't have gotten anything for us. You can't afford it, and besides, we promised each other we would put any spare money aside so you could come to us as soon as possible."

Then her eyes filled with tears, too, but she said, "Dis ain' from me, honey. It's from yo' grandma. Here."

She handed me a packet. I looked inside, then I nearly dropped it. "What on earth!" I exclaimed.

"It's twelve t'ousan' dollars," she answered calmly. "It's from de sale of de Contessa what's-her-name's brooch."

I gaped at her. "You had it? You've had it all this time?"

She nodded. "Yo' grandma, she 'trusted it to me. 'For my babies', she tole me. When I heerd you was leebin' I took it to Nick and he done had it 'praised. 'Twelve t'ousan'' the man said. So I sol' it, 'n got the full 'mount. It's all dere."

I peeked inside the packet again. "Twelve thousand dollars. I can't believe it."

A tear crept down Missouri's cheek. "I knowed yo' would hate to part wif it, but I figgered yo' needed the money mor'n yo' needed a fancy piece of jew'ry. So..."

"You were right," I told her. "The money is worth more than the sentiment is—but Grandmother's Fire Opal..." I gave myself a mental shake. I hadn't seen it for years. I thought my mother had finally found it and sold it, and I resolved to forget about it. It wouldn't do for me to worry about Grandmother's most valuable keepsake, no matter how much I wanted it. Not because of its monetary value, but because of its value to her. Outside of the photograph, I had nothing that ever belonged to her.

I'm sure my face never changed expression when Missouri told me about the sale of the brooch, but she happens to know me extremely well.

"I knowed you wanted somethin' from yo' grandma. So here."

She opened her massive purse and pulled out a very small envelope. I opened it, and inside was Grandmother's gold wedding band. "She give it to me on her deafbed," Missouri told me. "She made me promise to give it to yo' when de time was right. Well, de time is right. Yo' needs dis."

I couldn't take the small ring from her hand. "Please put it in my purse, Missouri. I'll...I'll try it on later, when I can finally..." I held up my hands, and she nodded sympathetically.

So I was not to leave without something of my grandmother's after all. She had seen to it that I could begin the new life I had always wanted for myself and David. I hoped that whoever bought the Fire Opal would treasure it as my grandmother had.

Napoleon was in tearing spirits. I hoped he was a good traveler. I shoved him into the back seat, even before I carefully helped David into the front. He proved to be an excellent traveler. Perhaps he wanted to get away from the torments of Chicago's South Side as badly as I did.

David was finding it difficult to contain his excitement. It was his first trip away from Chicago, and he was acting half his age. All the way across Illinois he asked the question all kids ask when they go on a trip: "Are we almost there yet?"

When we stopped for dinner I gave him a map. "See? We still have Iowa to go through. And then, when we get to Nebraska, we have to go there."

"There" was a large section in western Nebraska that had very few towns and no cities whatsoever.

"Gosh," David said. "It doesn't look like there are very many people out there."

I suddenly felt a little worried. "Does that bother you?" I asked apprehensively.

"Gosh, no, Sis. I think I'll like it."

I smiled at him. "Me, too. Imagine, David: clean air, white snow, cows, horses…"

That got him. He sat straight up and squeaked, "Horses! Can I have one, do you think?"

"Well, we'll see." I answered vaguely.

His face fell. "That probably means no."

"Not necessarily. It means 'we'll see'."

We spent the first night somewhere in Iowa It was difficult finding a place that would take dogs, and Napoleon was more of a small pony. But we found a small motel whose proprietor took an instant liking to my little brother, who promised solemnly that Napoleon was a highly-trained animal with perfect manners. So we stayed the night, and the next morning found a restaurant with marvelous food. Then we headed west once again, the sun behind us and a brand new life ahead.

We got as far as Kearney the next evening. David had the Nebraska map spread out on his lap.

"There's a lake at Ogallala," he told me, struggling with the Indian name.

"I know. A lovely, large, lake and a lavish lodging place for the lame, so I've learned. If my labor can liquidate our lack, I'd like to leave you, lucky lad, in this locale for a languid, leisurely lull at least by late next summer." I had been working on this alliteration in my mind the whole drive. Now I couldn't help grinning at the surprise my announcement had caused.

David was left speechless for about five minutes. Finally he retorted, "Lord love you, as Missouri would say, I long to linger in this land." Then he took up his map-reading with even more enthusiasm.

"We can visit Chimney Rock, and Ash Hollow, and Scotts' Bluff, and…"

"Sure. We'll do all of that, just as soon as I get a job and save some money and find a house and get you completely well."

"It'll be a breeze," David grinned with all the naiveté of youth.

I had another surprise to share with him, "During December I dream of directing David in the discipline of driving."

"Sis!" he screamed at me. "Gosh! I'm only turning fourteen!"

"Out here people don't pay much attention to that. You're level-headed. I think you can be trusted."

"Gosh." he muttered again and sank down in the seat cushions.

So we spent the night in Kearney, and David was up at five thirty in the morning ready to head northwest.

"Lee's Corner," he said, looking it up on the map. "Here it is. It says the population is 298." He glanced at me from under his long, lashes.

I smiled at him. "So, we'll make it an even three hundred. And just remember, one of those 298 is Dr. Levi Abrams, a good friend of Dr. Abelman's. And Dr. Abelman told me he spent a lot of time working with polio victims."

The Sand Hills, our destination, are just what the name implies. Ahead of us and to the north lay gentle, rolling hills, golden in the rays of the sun. They seemed to stretch forever. Far to the west, I knew, they would become wild and more rugged as they joined the foothills of the Rocky Mountains. But here they were mellow and peaceful, with grazing cattle dotting them. We turned north for the last leg of our long journey. The road snaked through the hills and gradually narrowed until I feared it would disappear entirely. I kept following it, and eventually it turned out to be the main street of Lee's Corner.

"Look for Jefferson Street," I told David.

"We're on Jefferson, Sis. Look, there's a park."

"I see it. And Dr. Abrams is supposed to be right across the street from it. Yes, there's the clinic, and his house is next to it."

I parked on the street, which was surprisingly wide here, and went up to the door. A small sign told me the doctor would be back at four o'clock. David and I had a half hour to kill.

We drove on up Jefferson Street, which turned out to be the only paved street in the town. It ended at the town square, whose center was the county courthouse. We turned right, passed Kincaid County Bank, then turned left on Adams Avenue.

"Look! There's the school!" David shouted. "It's not very big."

"Are you disappointed," I asked.

"No! I think it will be easier to make friends in a smaller school."

We drove around the little town, which boasted, besides the rather impressive courthouse, a beautiful little Catholic church build out of white stone, a library that was fairly large for this small town, a Ben Franklin store that seemed to have everything including hardware, and all of it crowded in the window, a clothing and dry goods store, a movie theater, a newspaper office, and a grocery store. Off the main street there were also a beauty parlor, a barber shop, a charming Victorian boarding house, a mortuary, a dentist's office, a car dealership, a large fenced yard that held farm equipment, a gas station, and a sugar beet factory. The residential section seemed to be more on the east side of town, and I drove around there slowly to see if there were any houses for rent, or even for sale. Our excursion eventually took us back to the doctor's office, and an old Hudson that hadn't been there before was now parked in front. I parked behind it, then looked at David. I had been putting this off too long, but now I had to tell him.

He gave me that questioning look, his dark brown eyes wide and shadowed by his long lashes.

I looked at my hands. Doc had managed to wrap each finger, and although the tapes weren't as bulky as my first bandages, they were still thick and uncomfortable. And my hands were a reminder. They would always be a reminder...

I took a deep breath. "David, there is something I need to tell you. Our parents...there was some trouble."

He was still looking at me. This was going to be more difficult than I had first thought.

I tried again. "Our father, well, he embezzled some money from the bank where he worked. Do you know what embezzlement is?"

David nodded, his face grave. "He stole some money."

"Yes. He stole some money. But it has been all paid back, I want you to know that. But then there was the accident, and someone else besides our parents was killed."

David turned pale, but said calmly enough, "I thought something was terribly wrong. I wish people would tell me things, because when they don't I always imagine the worst. Of course, I guess this is the worst."

"Yes, this is the worst. Now, because of this, I feel it is necessary for us to change our names. I haven't had a chance to make it legal yet, but I will as soon as I can. Our last name will no longer be Thornton, it will be Morrow, which I shortened from Morrowitz. And you can keep David if you want, but I never did like the name Brittany."

"I don't like it much either," David confessed. "That's one reason I always called you 'Sis'."

I laughed, and ruffled his pale blonde hair.

I had thought about using one of my middle names. Grandmother had a love of poetry, and one of her favorite poems was Richard Lovelace's "To Lucasta, Going to the Wars". But Grandfather had been fascinated by the Civil War, and he knew just about all there was to know. He was even familiar with the songs of the era, his favorite being "Lorena", the popular bittersweet ballad the Confederate soldiers sang around their campfires all over the South. So my name was Brittany Lucasta Lorena Thornton.

"Which shall it be, David, Lucasta or Lorena?"

"I like Lucasta," he answered without hesitation, then quoted, "I could not love thee, Dear, so much, Loved I not honor more."

"Lucasta it is," I said cheerfully. "Lu for short. So here we are, Lu Morrow and her little brother David—starting over. Shall we go meet the doctor?"

He was waiting for us. By way of greeting he said, "Hiram called yesterday and told me he thought you would be pulling in sometime late this afternoon." He grinned and extended a hand.

David took it. "I'm very pleased to meet you, sir. I'm David Morrow, and this is my sister, Lu." Then my little brother looked at me and grinned, very well pleased with himself.

Dr. Abrams was rough and gruff, and very, very kind. He checked my hands first, then told me what I already knew. I would never play on a concert stage.

"The damage could have been a lot worse," he said, "but I'm not going to minimize the damage to your career. You will certainly be able to play the piano again, if you do faithfully—and I mean faithfully—the exercises prescribed by Hiram. And by me," he added, "because I'm going to give you a few more to do which will limber up those fingers. But even with the exercises and the daily applications of moist heat to your hands, you'll never be able to perform the 'Polonaise in A-Flat,' at least professionally."

"I realized that," I said. "At least you've told me I can play again. In the past few days I've come to realize that I would be grateful to be able to play Chopsticks if only David..."

"Yes, David." The doctor gently rubbed some salve on my hands and put a loose bandage around each finger, saying as he did so, "Hiram and I have been discussing David's case by phone for the last two days. He thinks very highly of the boy."

I smiled. "Everyone does."

Dr. Abrams' expression turned solemn. "I suppose he told you that whatever paralysis remains after a year is not likely to improve."

"Yes, he told me."

I said it very quietly, and Dr. Abrams looked up from the bandages and scrutinized my face. He saw the tears that were starting to form, and changed abruptly to a degree of cheerfulness.

"That's not to say we must give up fighting. David is walking, albeit with a limp. But he is walking. And we'll do everything we can to keep him walking. Right?"

I nodded.

"Now," he went on, "I'm finished. I'm going to write down everything I want you to do for these hands, and I want you to do it religiously. Or maybe I should rephrase that. I want you to do it on a regular basis. Hiram told me your views on religion."

I held up my hands. "Oh, I believe in a God, all right. Who else would have done this?"

The good doctor frowned. "Sometime, girl, you and I are going to have a talk, a serious talk. For now, send David in here."

His examination of my little brother was very thorough. David was underweight for a child of his age and a little anemic, Doctor Abrams said, looking at the inside of his eyelid. His blood pressure was a little low, but he had no temperature. He took a blood sample and urine sample to be checked later. He used calipers to measure the muscles in David's legs and wrote down the numbers. But mostly he went by his own touch. He ran his experienced hands all over David, and made him cough and breathe deeply and pant as he listened through his stethoscope. Finally David was sent back to the waiting room, and the good doctor turned to me.

"He needs fresh air more than anything," he told me. "And he'll get it out here. Let him go outside as much as he wants. Just make sure he stays warm and dry. He'll get an appetite and start putting on weight."

He had been sitting on a stool. Now he got up and looked out of the window. The sun was beginning to set behind the hills that stretched serenely westward. "I will lift up mine eyes unto the hills," he said softly, "From whence cometh my help."

"I beg your pardon?"

He chuckled. "Sorry, my dear. I was just quoting David."

"David?" I asked, puzzled.

"A different David. My mind was wandering a little. Forgive me. About David—your David—and this polio. I, along with many others, am of the opinion that warmer areas breed the virus that causes it. It spreads much more quickly in tropical and semi-tropical areas, and in places where sanitation is a problem."

I thought about the Chicago tenement district where we had been living for the past several years, and about the filth, the odor, the flies, the mosquitoes, and the perpetual blanket of dirty, smoky fog that not even the incessant wind could blow away.

"So I believe in a moderately cold climate," the doctor went on. "Don't get me wrong. It can get pretty hot here. But it's a good, dry heat that doesn't breed germs. Winters are cold, but not wet. Even the snow, and we get quite a lot of it, is dry. The important thing is to let David get all the fresh air he can. But do not, under any circumstances, let him get sick. At the first sign of a cough or fever, you call me immediately. I must warn you that an inflammation of the lungs could be fatal. I can't stress that enough."

I nodded. "I understand perfectly. Please rest assured that I will do everything in my power to see that David doesn't get so much as a sniffle."

The doctor rubbed his hands together. "Hiram has complete reliance in your ability to care for David. He...er...told me some of your background. About the accident, and the fact that David doesn't really know the details. He doesn't even know you pulled somebody from the wreck. So how, by the way, did you explain your hands?"

I felt my face go scarlet. "I told him I burned them trying to fix the oven."

"Oh, I see. You lied to him."

"I felt I had to. If anyone knew I was at the scene...I mean, if David thought I could have prevented it...I mean, I should have kept my father from driving. There surely must have been something I could have done."

I was beginning to pace, something I seemed to do every time I thought about the accident. The doctor put out a hand and grabbed my arm, and turned me around to face him.

"All of this fretting and foaming won't do you any good. From what Hiram said it would have happened whether you were there or not. And the fact that you were there made the difference between life and death for at least one person. I would think David would want to know. But don't worry. It's not my place to tell him anything you don't want him told. It's not my place to tell anyone. So don't worry. There is that in a doctor-patient relationship that makes all discussions confidential."

"Thank you. I appreciate it. I wouldn't want anyone here to know. I mean, embezzlement was bad enough. Can you imagine what people around here would think if they knew that the children of a...a...a thief, and a murderer had moved into their midst?"

"Well, most of the people here wouldn't hold it against you. But you'll have to find that out for yourself. The sins of the father are not to be visited upon the children. I'm paraphrasing, of course."

"Of course," I replied, a little uncertainly.

He went on. "And I've taken it upon myself to make arrangements for you to stay with a friend of mine for a few days while you get yourself oriented." His dark gray eyes twinkled. "A widow lady. We have a boarding house, but it's full right now, and my friend puts up people from time to time if there's no place else for them to stay. She'll help you get acquainted. You'll like her. I'll take you there now, if you're ready."

I breathed a sigh of pure relief. A burden seemed to be lifted off my shoulders. I wouldn't have to find myself a place to stay right away, and I would have the comfort and sympathy of a widow, a matron who had been through a bereavement of her own and could in part share some of the hurt and disappointment I was feeling at this particular time.

What I got was Marty Maguire, age twenty-eight. Instead of a plump, silver-haired, elderly woman in black bombazine, whatever that was, David and I were greeted by a perky, fresh-faced redhead of medium height and generous proportions dressed in a red-checkered shirt and denim jeans.

"I'm glad to meet you," she said, with a wide smile for us after Dr. Abrams introduced the Morrows. "Come in and make yourselves at home. Watch out for that truck! That child never puts away his toys. Takes after his father. As long as I knew Big Mike, which was forever, he never put anything away. At least, not where it belonged." She pumped my arm, and then David's.

My brother was in the process of thanking Dr. Abrams for all he had done. Marty let me thank him, too, then after she invited the doctor to supper and he politely refused, she turned back to us and said, "I'm putting you both upstairs. You can have it all to yourselves. Supper will be ready in a few minutes. Go on and wash up. The bathroom's down that hall. Watch out for the football! Just kick it out of the way. If he wants it he'll find it. Yes, there on the right, the door that's closed. We'll bring in your luggage later. I'll put the...Is that a dog? Yes, I suppose it must be. I'll put him in the yard. I hope you like stew. It's not as bad as everybody says it is. Use any towel that you can find."

David and I were standing at the end of the hall throughout this rather remarkable speech. When we heard the front door shut on the retreating doctor, we figured she had finished talking, so we took turns washing up and, finding no towels, wiped our hands on our shirts.

The food at least smelled good. A golden-haired little cherub was at the table, pouring water into his bowl of stew.

"Mikey, stop that this instant!" his mother demanded.

"But it hot," the little cherub replied.

"Well, blow on it. It will cool off. Not that hard, Mikey! I'll wipe that up, Miss Morrow. Sit here, David. You didn't even pray, I'll bet."

I glanced up and David stopped short in the act of taking his chair, but this had been addressed to Mikey.

"And in front of company, too," Marty Maguire added. "What will Jesus think?"

"Jesus loves the little children," Mikey sang.

"Of course He does. But He expects them to behave themselves." She sat down, folded her hands, and said a short blessing.

David and I glanced at each other uncomfortably while her head was bowed, then Mikey's eye caught David's. David winked at him and Mikey screwed up his face trying to wink back. So much, I thought, for the blessing.

The food smelled better than it tasted, but we two weary travelers ate with all the gusto of farm hands after haying.

"I'm not much of a cook," Marty said unnecessarily. "I'm not a bad seamstress, though. Where are you folks from?"

"I'm from St. Louis," David said quickly. That was true. He had been born there.

"Stan the Man!" the cherub piped up.

I glanced at my brother.

"Stan Musial," he said evenly. "My favorite player." This was also true. So far, neither of us was having to tell a lie.

"Mine, too," Mikey agreed.

"Many consider him the best player in the league," I added, though reserving my personal judgment.

"Oh, no!" Marty yelped.

I gave a little start, "Don't you like Stan Musial?"

"No! I mean, yes. Yes, I like him. But oh, no! I forgot the board meeting. I'm the church secretary. I have to take the minutes."

She jumped from her chair. "And they're discussing children's church tonight. I completely forgot about it. Can you watch Mikey? I won't be long—I hope."

She was pulling on her coat and heading toward the door when she suddenly wheeled back toward us. "Just look at me! If I walked into that church in blue jeans…"

60

She rushed past us, shaking her head and slammed the door on what I assumed was her own bedroom. I shook my head too. I was beginning to suspect that no one who knew Marty Maguire would be very shocked at anything she did.

In sixty seconds flat she emerged again in a green wool skirt that seemed a bit dressy for the checkered shirt, but she was struggling into a green cardigan that would pull the outfit together. As she ran past us again, she warned in a threatening tone, "And you better be good!" She glanced backwards, "I mean Mikey! I wasn't talking to you!" She was gone in a flash of flying red hair. So much for the motherly, widowed matron.

David and I looked at each other, then simultaneously turned to Mikey.

He gave us a gorgeous smile. "I'm that many," he said, and held up three sticky fingers.

Chapter 5

David washed the dishes and I dried them as best I could. The telephone rang several times that evening, each with a different ring. I answered it every time, and discovered that it was always for someone else. I realized that if one got a little bored during a long day he could listen in on the party line. I made up my mind then and there that we didn't need a phone. We could make our calls from someplace else, if we had any calls to make.

David took complete charge of Mikey. He gave the boy a bath, and during the course of that major event a lot of noise floated out to the living room, where I was trying to read one of the books I found in the huge, old bookcase.

Mrs. Maguire had a large, lovely home that dated back near the turn of the century. A big bay window looked out over the quiet street. Another bay window looked out at the garden of the rectory behind the little Catholic church. The garden area, neat even now, though the frost had finally killed the plants that had been there, separated the church from the rectory, which had been built out of the same white stone.

The name of the church was St. Peter's, a rather grand name for such a small church. I wondered momentarily if this were where Marty Maguire would be taking minutes. But there were no cars, and indeed the church was dark. The rectory had one light

63

shining in the window that faced me, and this went out even as I stood there and watched. A man came out of the door and got into an old coupe. The engine fired once, twice, then I heard the gears grind, and saw the headlights come to life. The car disappeared down the road.

Other lights dotted the little town, but no neon signs marred the velvety black of the night. Stars, possibly millions of them, winked down on the town. It seemed as though they were trying to send me a coded message, telling me that it was all right to go outside, to walk around, that there was no danger here, only peace.

"I'm going out for a bit," I called to David. "Will you be okay?"

David came into the living room. His shirt sleeves were rolled up past his elbows and he had obviously been splashed— several times—but he looked determined. "I'll be fine, even if I have to tie that kid up and hose him down!"

"Now you know what I went through," I laughed. "I won't be gone long."

I put on the black wool coat that had been my mother's, and David gritted his teeth and marched back to the bathroom with the determination of the U.S. Marines taking a beachhead.

Marty lived on the north edge of town, on the corner of Pine Street and Washington Avenue. I walked all the way to the south end of Washington, then took Hickory Street over to the quiet little park, and sat on one of the swings. I knew I was going to love it here. If only we could live quietly and forget the past. I couldn't see any reason to worry. It was as though we had come to another world. The railroad tracks ran just the other side of the park, into miles and miles of empty Sand Hills. I looked out into the black night. Occasionally I would see a light blink out there, somewhere among the hills. Otherwise, there was nothing.

I saw a house for sale in town, and it looked to be a nice one. It was just a block away from Marty's own Victorian-style home, and it would be convenient to the school. But for some reason I was drawn to those hills.

The wind whipped up and pushed the other swings into twisting action, but I remained where I was, just staring into the black night.

Finally I decided I had better go back. David might need reinforcements. But he was reading Mikey a bedtime story when I got back. It was about David and Goliath, and I wasn't sure which of the boys was enjoying it more.

I picked up the book I had found and was reading it when David finally came from Mikey's room.

"I'll bring in the overnight bags," he told me, "then I'm off to bed."

After he made sure Napoleon was bedded down for the night, he went to the room Marty had prepared for him. I decided to wait up for my hostess. Besides, I wasn't really tired; I was too excited to sleep.

Marty Maguire got home sometime after midnight.

"Whew! What a night," she said, kicking off her shoes. "All that fuss about light bulbs. 40 watts or 60 watts? At midnight, who cares?"

"Since the discussion did last until midnight, apparently somebody does," I answered. "Was the issue resolved?"

"No. It was tabled. Can you beat that? Two of our deacons are out of town, so there really couldn't be a vote. After all of that. It seems that 40 watt bulbs are cheaper to operate, at least according to the president of the board. But you can't see. Our halls are dim anyway, and it's really bad at night. But our illustrious chairman—a good man, don't get me wrong—is a bit of a tightwad, and he had one other vote with him. So it was deadlocked."

"How do you think the absent members will vote?"

She laughed. "They'll want 100 watt bulbs, then it will be split three ways. As if there aren't more important things to decide. Like whether we should try a children's church."

"What's a children's church?" I asked.

She gave me a sidelong glance. "A lot of the big city churches have them."

"I'm not acquainted with the practices of big city churches," I told her woodenly.

She gave me a look of incredulity. "You're not? Did you go to a small church, then?"

"I didn't go to any church at all."

She bit her lip. I was to learn that whenever Marty Maguire was at a loss for words—which I was also to learn wasn't often—she bit her lower lip.

She finally said, "Oh, I see. Well, we'd like you to try ours. It's very friendly, and most all of the Protestants around here go there—Grace Community Church. It's non-denominational. We'd be very happy to have you and David visit us."

I sat there looking non-committal, and after a brief pause, she went on, "Well, anyway, children's church is a place for kids, say under the age of eight or ten, who get bored with the adult services. Not that I mean they're boring," she assured me quickly, even a little guiltily. "But kids tend to think so. I remember that I sure did. Anyway, they could have their own service, one where they could get a Bible story, kid's version, and they could get up from their chairs without being frowned back down, and they could have games and refreshments. I think it would help our attendance, and I also think it would really benefit the kids. And, in the long run I think those who are against it now would see that they would enjoy church much more if there weren't a lot of fidgety kids attracting attention and disrupting the service."

"Makes sense to me," I agreed.

"Oh, well. It's really my project. Mikey can be such a handful in church, especially if Rev. Hurst is longwinded—not that he usually is—but just every once in a while he forgets to look at the clock that one of the board members thoughtfully placed at the back of the sanctuary. Where is Mikey, anyway?"

"In bed. Sound asleep."

"Really?" She seemed amazed. "What did you have to bribe him with?"

"Bribery is David's department. I believe he read him a bedtime story."

She smiled. Marty Maguire has an exceptionally sweet smile. It seems to light up her whole face.

"David seems like such a nice kid," she said. "Too bad about the polio, but he seems to be getting around pretty well."

"How did you know it was polio?" I wondered.

"Well, when Dr. Abrams brings a kid out here for treatment that's what it is. He's made polio practically an industry in this town."

66

I hadn't thought of that, but I realized it must be true. An important doctor doesn't move to the middle of nowhere in order to give up his practice, but to improve it. "So there are other children here undergoing treatment?"

"Only a couple right now. It's been a real thrill to see some of them come here and make so much improvement they can go home again. Though we kind of get attached to them too."

"That's encouraging. I think David's going to do very well out here."

"Oh, he will. This is a marvelous place. I can't imagine living anywhere else. When Big Mike was killed—he died in Korea—I thought I couldn't bear to stay here. So many memories. We went to school together; I knew him all my life. But then I realized that this is where he would have wanted me to raise our child, so I stayed, and I've never been sorry. But enough about me. You'll hear it all anyway. Small town, you know. And I forgot to warn you about the phone. I'm two long rings. So tell me, what do you do?"

"For a living? Well, I did play the piano."

She glanced at my hands. "Doc said you burned them. Do you think you can still play? After the dressings come off, I mean?"

"I sincerely hope so."

Her face brightened. "That's wonderful. Like manna from heaven! We need a pianist at church."

"I hope you find one," I replied, amused to think of myself as being heaven-sent.

"It's a Steinway," she added.

"I'm impressed."

"It's used, though."

"They're the best kind."

She bit her lip. Finally she said, "I'm sure Rev. Hurst wouldn't mind if you ever wanted to play it. Oh, and you did the dishes, too. How sweet. I hope you didn't hurt your hands."

"David washed. I only dried."

She bit her lip again. "If you're worried about people staring, don't...I mean...you could play... Why, we could even turn the piano so that it faces the congregation, and no one..."

"I'm not worried about people staring. I'm just not a church person."

She bit her lower lip. "Well, not everybody is." She looked like she wanted to say more, then changed her mind. "I hope Mikey remembered to say his prayers. He forgets, sometimes. I'll bet you're exhausted, and here I am, talking your arm off. And we have a busy day tomorrow."

"We do?"

"Oh, yes, first we must get David enrolled in school. What grade is he in?"

I hesitated a moment, then finally said, "David's illness…has kept him from going to school for a while. He's had a private tutor for some time now." Then I was struck with a disturbing thought. "Will he need any records to get into school?"

Marty Maguire shook her head. "I doubt it. Mr. Stoker, the principal, will probably just give him a test. If he does well, he'll be put with his age group. We're not too formal here. But we insist on our kids getting a good education. You'll like our principal. Doc did say 'Miss Morrow,' didn't he?"

"Very single," I assured her, "and content to stay that way."

"Too bad. Mr. Stoker is single."

"And he's probably content to stay that way, too."

"Most men are, until we prove them differently," she said. "We have several eligible bachelors around here. Maybe…"

"And maybe not." I laughed. "Please don't try to get me married off. I have enough problems as it is."

I didn't want to add that I had seen enough of married life not to want to take a chance on it. And I had seen enough of men…

So I excused myself, after thanking Mrs. Maguire, who insisted that she be called Marty, for a lovely dinner, and went to the room opposite David's. I could hear his gentle breathing and knew he was sleeping well, and, I hoped, dreamlessly.

David was up well before I was. He was, I discovered, still on Central time.

Marty was fixing breakfast. She even managed to burn the toast. She was scraping it when I came down.

"David and Napoleon are out exploring our little town. Don't worry. He can't get into much trouble. He seemed fascinated by the fact that we have only one paved street. The rest are still gravel. I made sure he was dressed warm before he left, and told him to be back by 7:30 for breakfast. Do you drink coffee?"

"I prefer tea, but if you don't have any, I'll take coffee."

"I have tea somewhere," and she started pulling out the contents of her cabinet. "Yes, here it is. One bag, and I can't guarantee how old it is. Big Mike's great aunt liked tea, and so we kept it here for her. She's been gone, let's see, six or seven...no, eight! Eight years! I better let it steep for a while."

I decided it was better than no tea at all.

"Are you needing a job?" Marty asked as she poured hot water over the bag.

"Yes. The sooner the better."

The cup overflowed a little. "Sorry about that," she said, bringing me the cup that was full to the brim. "Pete needs a waitress. It's not fancy, but the tips should be good." She pulled out a chair and sat across from me. "Or you can go to Scottsbluff if you're looking for office work. But that's a far piece to drive."

"I'd like to stay around here if I could. With David going to school I'd like to be close by."

"Then I'll take you to Pete's about ten o'clock, after the breakfast rush but before the dinner crowd gets there. But first we'll take David to the school. We'll do that right after breakfast. He can start Monday, after you get settled in. It'll be a short week, of course, with Thanksgiving. I think he'll like the kids. I grew up with most of their parents or older brothers and sisters."

Breakfast was memorable only because Mikey dumped his lumpy oatmeal on the floor and Marty slipped in it as she was bringing a platter of sunny-side-up eggs to the table. The eggs slid from the platter and splattered everywhere, like oozing yellow paint. David, invigorated from his walk, burst into laughter. It took all of us—including Napoleon—to clean up the mess. David offered to eat some of the oatmeal that was left over from Mikey's breakfast; I declined anything, saying I wasn't really very hungry. Marty insisted I eat something, so I settled for the scraped pieces of toast.

I dressed up in my best suit, my only suit. It was navy blue; the jacket had wide lapels and the skirt was pleated at the bottom. It was a shade too big for me, but it didn't look bad, though it was several years out of fashion. I wore a white blouse, and slipped my feet into the only pair of high heels I possessed, which were red. I was passable, even patriotic, if not in vogue, and I hoped I would make a good impression on Pete, whose surname I didn't know.

I offered to do the driving, but Marty told me she was used to the roads and so was her car. It was a monster of a Packard, a little beat up, but we got in, and were off on our new adventure.

Marty parked in front of the school then led us to the principal's office. After introducing us to Frank Stoker she excused herself and took off on an errand of her own, promising she would return in an hour.

Mr. Stoker was polite and personable and not bad-looking. I could see no reason for him to remain a bachelor except that he chose to. He gave David several tests in his office while I sat in the hall and fidgeted. I had stressed to David how important it was that our past life be kept as secret as possible, and he had accepted it without question, leading me to wonder what he had known or guessed about the outrageous Thorntons.

But I didn't want him to lie outright, and I squirmed a little, thinking what information an intelligent person might be able to glean from my naive little brother.

But apparently it wasn't anything earthshaking. Mr. Stocker told me David was a fine young man and that he would be a member of the Freshman Class.

"You'll want to meet Karen," he told us both. "She's a junior."

I looked at him blankly. Who was Karen that we should especially want to meet her?

He smiled—he had a very nice smile—and explained. "Karen Hempstead is another of Dr. Abrams' patients. She's been here almost four years now, but she's from St. Louis too."

A cold chill passed over me. I did not want to meet Karen Hempstead. I did not want David to have to meet her. Her first question would probably be "What part of St. Louis are you from?"

I mumbled something about David looking forward to meeting all the students, and we hurried out.

David was thrilled almost beyond tolerance. He would start school—high school!—Monday.

As we waited for Marty on the school steps, he told me that in high school you were permitted to take electives—as though I had never been to high school. He had wanted to sign up for band, but you had to be able to march, so he had signed up for art, and he was going to be in a painting class! I was amazed and pleased to see him so thrilled about it. Before long the Packard pulled up.

"I dropped Mikey off at Aggie's. She loves him to death, just like she did Big Mike when he was a kid, and when I told her how much we had to do today she offered to keep him. Which is just how I planned it." And she grinned at me.

We dropped David off at Marty's then headed for Pete's Diner. It was located right across from the courthouse.

He had a few customers, early lunches I assumed, for Pete was standing at the grill flipping hamburgers. Several men were throwing him friendly insults, which he tossed back in kind.

Marty went to the counter. "Pete, this is Lu Morrow."

Pete turned around. His face was shiny with sweat. He was a big man, tall and bulky. He pointed a stubby finger at me. "That her?" he asked Marty.

"Yep," Marty answered.

"When can she start?"

"Not before Monday a week," Marty answered him. "She's not even settled in yet."

"Couldn't start today, could she?"

Marty answered, "Nope," firmly. I wondered why I was even there.

Pete grumbled, but said, "Get her here a week from Monday, then. Six o'clock sharp. She'll have to buy her own uniform."

"Oh?" one of the customers said. "A uniform! Pete, you gettin' fancy on us all of a sudden?"

"Yeah," someone else said. "Probably gonna raise his prices now that he's gettin' uniformed help."

"And we ain't gettin' our money's worth now," said a third. "Hey, Marty, that the new gal in town?"

"Yes, it is. Everybody, this is Lu Morrow, from St. Louis. Lu," she said, turning to me, "if any of these fellows was worth knowing I'd introduce you to them."

There was a lot of good-natured laughter, and I, who was wanting to keep a low profile, was wondering how I was going to do it. It was apparent that David and I, being newcomers to this small community, were, for the time being, the talk of the town.

"What kind of uniform?" Marty inquired.

"I dunno. Work something out with Marge."

Marty turned me toward the door. "Thanks, Pete, see you Sunday."

"Just make sure she's here at six o'clock sharp," Pete said, getting in the last word as we were leaving.

I hadn't said a word the entire time I was in his little diner, and now I looked at Marty skeptically.

She laughed at my expression. "Pete takes some getting used to. Woman-hater, is our Pete. A woman has to earn his respect. Don't worry, you'll get along fine. Come on. We'll hunt up David. He told me he might go exploring again. When we find him we'll go home for dinner."

"Who's Marge?" I wondered.

"Marge and Joe Gaitlyn own the dry goods store. She'll probably have to order something for you."

Next we went to Aggie's to pick up Mikey. This was the sympathetic, elderly friend I had expected in Marty. She was one of those who couldn't do enough for people.

"I'm so sorry Freddy's not home from school yet. He is thrilled over David's coming, and his parents want to meet you, but they are both working days."

I felt a warning twinge. "Why would they want to meet us?" I hoped my voice wasn't as unfriendly as the thoughts going through my head.

"Oh, they're staying with me while Dr. Abrams treats Freddy. They're from Chicago, but they're not gangsters—not at all!"

Chicago! I could feel my pulse racing. And of course, anyone from Chicago was bound to be a gangster. Wasn't that the way the movies portrayed us? Calm down, I told myself. Chicago is a big town and I didn't really know that many people. But what if Freddy had been treated in the polio ward at Children's Memorial?

72

This was even worse than Karen Hempstead. I was glad for Mikey's distraction to cover my nervousness. I was glad we were in a rush.

David was not going to be hard to find. He had made his way to the park, and at the back of the park ran the railroad tracks. There a small crowd had gathered, with David in the middle of it.

"What on earth!" I exclaimed.

Marty was still in the act of parking the car when I jumped out and ran up to the crowd. A young and very pretty woman was hugging a small child and David at the same time, and several people were lavishing kind attention on Napoleon.

David managed to free himself from the embrace of the woman and came rushing up to me.

"You should have seen it, Sis!" he said, breathless from excitement.

"Are you all right?" I asked, taking him by the shoulders and examining his flushed face.

"Am I all right? I'm terrific. You know what happened?"

But then the young woman and Marty joined us at about the same time.

"You must be Lu," the woman said, tears streaming down her face. "I'm Marsha Retting. This is my daughter, Suzanne."

She thrust the child at me, and I automatically held out my arms and took her. She was, I judged, about Mikey's age.

"What's going on, Marsha?" Marty asked.

"This boy," Marsha answered, and put her arms around David again. "And that wonderful dog of his." Then she burst into a new spasm of crying.

I looked at David. "If someone doesn't tell me this instant..."

A man joined us. "I'm Jeb Truman, the deputy sheriff. Hi, Marty."

Marty smiled at him. "Lu Morrow, Jeb. And I guess you have already met David."

"We've all met David." He turned to me. "It seems that somehow Suzanne got away from her mama here and decided it might be fun to play on the railroad tracks. She didn't see the train coming. David did, though, and started running."

"Trying to run," David amended.

"And he was yelling at the top of his lungs, too," Marsha said, "But I was too far away to do anything!" and she broke into fresh sobs.

"I knew I wouldn't make it in time," David continued. "Then, all of a sudden, here comes Napoleon, and he grabs the little girl by the coat and pulls her off the tracks just as the engine goes by!"

It was a good thing there was a park bench handy. I fumbled for it and managed to sit down. Marsha Retting was still bawling, and Jeb Truman was trying to get her to stop. A number of people were coming up to David and me, congratulating us for having such a wonderful animal. The owner of the newspaper came by and took a picture of David, Napoleon, and Suzanne.

So much, I thought, for keeping a low profile. We hadn't been in town twenty-four hours and already David was a hero. As I sat there, dazed, people were shaking my hand—very carefully—and introducing themselves. They were hugging David, petting Napoleon, and trying to comfort poor Marsha. But Marsha, I knew, wouldn't get over this terrible fright in a hurry, and if she wanted to cry I wished they would let her.

Suddenly I was confronted by a small, elderly woman whom David had taken by the hand and brought to me.

"Sis, this is Mrs. Lassiter. She invited us over to supper tonight. Mrs. Lassiter, this is my sister Br...Lucasta."

"How do you do," I said politely.

"How nice to meet you, my dear," she said in a soft, cultured voice. "What excitement! And Marty, how is that scamp of a son of yours?"

"Fine," Marty answered.

"You must not let him take his marbles to church. They make such a noise when they are dropped on the floor during the middle of prayer."

"I've already taken them away from him. I hope you know that I wasn't aware he had them. He sneaked them into his pockets."

Mrs. Lassiter gave her a gentle, knowing smile. "I remember how little boys are. I had one, too."

Marty cleared her throat. I think she did it to keep from smiling. "Yes, we all know Owen."

Mrs. Lassiter turned to me. "I was so pleased to meet your charming brother." She bestowed on David a motherly smile. "I do hope you will join me for supper. I live just over there," and she pointed to a pretty, little, white frame home facing the park. "It won't be a fancy meal, but I enjoy company so. And you have such a lovely, fresh face. Your brother tells me you play the piano. When you get your bandages taken off I hope you'll play for me. I have a spinet, but I don't play anymore. Arthritis, you know."

I hardly knew what to say. This certainly wasn't like living in the city. Who in Chicago, on first acquaintance, would ask someone home to dinner?

But Marty said, "Go ahead, Lu. Mrs. Lassiter's a great cook. Better than I am. But then, who isn't? And I have a call to make tonight, anyway." She turned to the older lady. "Old Man Nottleman. The boy rode to town to give me a message."

Mrs. Lassiter shook her head. "Those poor children, being raised by that man." She moved closer to me and confided, "You know, most people around here think he was in on that Lanning bank robbery, back in '97. Think that was when he was shot in the leg, and not by a drunken Sioux, like he says."

"Well, I do feel sorry for the kids," Marty nodded. "We've tried to get them away from there, but nobody will take all three, and they refuse to be split up. Besides, the old man threatened Rev. Hurst with a shotgun the last time he went out there."

Mrs. Lassiter patted Marty's arm. "Well, you be careful, dear."

"I will."

"And you and David be at my house at six o'clock," Mrs. Lassiter said to me. "Fried chicken." And she winked at David, then held out her arms to Suzanne.

Suzanne must have known her a lot better than I did, because she went to her gladly and the two of them walked away. Then I turned to my brother, who had the grace to blush.

"I didn't know she was going to ask us for dinner, Sis, honestly I didn't. When I mentioned fried chicken was my favorite..."

Marty laughed. "She would have invited you anyway," she told us.

"Why?" I asked. "Small town hospitality?"

"Perhaps. Partly. Oh, you'll find out. Come on, it's time to eat. All of this excitement has made me hungry."

We managed to extricate ourselves from the crowd, retrieve Napoleon, and head back to Marty's.

He is the happiest, be he king or peasant,
who finds peace in his home.
—Johann Wolfgang von Goethe

Chapter 6

I was curious about Mr. Nottleman. It seemed to me this suspected bank robber was still living under a cloud of distrust after more than fifty years, and it warned me how we would be regarded if the truth ever came out. I asked Marty about him while we ate. It helped me take my mind off the food.

"He came here sometime in the late 1890s," she said. "Twenty years later he grabbed a young bride when her intended went off to the War. They had several children, so I heard, but only one survived, a daughter, Rose. Rose ran off with some scoundrel, according to the story. They say it killed her mom. Rose's husband was apparently shot over a gambling debt down south somewhere, but not before he fathered three children. Rose tried to raise them, but she got pneumonia. She was delicate to begin with. So sick, and broke, she came crawling back to her father. The old man took them all in, grudgingly. Rose died not long afterwards, and he's had the kids ever since. Josh and Kate, both teenagers now, and Jack, who's about ten."

"Do they go to school here?" David asked.

"Oh, no. There's a one-room schoolhouse back in the hills for the kids who live too far to come to town. There are nine or ten students between the first and twelfth grades. They've got a decent teacher, a man who ranches out there. That's all open range, and people are few and far between."

"What's 'open range?'" I asked.

Marty laughed. "If you hit a cow, it's your fault. There are no fences. I'll drive you up there sometime."

So Aggie kept Mikey for the night, and Marty went back into the hills to see what Old Man Nottleman wanted. While we were getting ready to go to Mrs. Lassiter's, someone knocked on Marty's door. When I opened it, a handsome young man stuck his hand toward me and introduced himself.

"Hi, I'm Dave Retting. I had to come over and..."

Napoleon pushed past me as if he knew this visitor was for him. Mr. Retting began petting the dog enthusiastically.

"David," I called, "it's someone to see you."

Suzanne's father couldn't express his appreciation enough. I was glad David was the recipient of all that effusive gratitude and not me.

We were a little late getting to Mrs. Lassiter's. I immediately and rather shockingly discovered why Mrs. Lassiter had invited me to dine with her. That sweet, frail little frame hid the heart of a wily, cold-blooded matchmaker. Her son Owen "just happened" to be dining there, too. Neither of us knew the other was coming. All in all, it was a delicious but decidedly uncomfortable meal.

Owen was a widower, Mrs. Lassiter pointed out. Several times. He had a big spread to take care of and a daughter to raise. I fidgeted uneasily. So did Owen. His home was large, his mother told me, and comfortable, but it needed a woman's touch. I suggested, sweetly and with the best of intentions, that it would be nice if Mother Lassiter could move in, and got an anguished look from the mother and a pained frown from the son.

"I couldn't," she gasped.

"No, she couldn't," her son agreed. "Her heart."

"My nerves," Mrs. Lassiter corrected, then caught herself, and added, "not on a big place like that, with all those hired hands to contend with."

"And Cynthia," Owen added wickedly. "My daughter," he explained to me. "A very pretty, very wild, little filly."

"Who only needs a mother's kind but firm hand," Mrs. Lassiter added.

"Ha!" Owen chortled.

Mrs. Lassiter's little play had gone awry. Only David seemed to enjoy the party. He ate five pieces of Mrs. Lassiter's fried chicken.

"I knew it!" Marty laughed after I closed the front door on Owen, who had kindly walked David and me home. "She's been trying to get him married off for five years. Even tried me, after Big Mike died. Poor Owen."

"He's very nice," I remarked noncommittally.

"He is. But headstrong. Bossy. Except when it comes to Cynthia. She knows how to handle him."

"So I gather. What is he, about thirty-five?"

"About," Marty answered. "Letta died, oh some six years ago. Cynthia would have been about nine. Mrs. Lassiter moved out there for a year. Tried to help. But she and Cindy are like oil and water. Cindy's headstrong, just like her father. Mrs. Lassiter finally gave up and moved back to town. She's been trying to get him married off ever since."

"Well, I like him," David announced. "And he has horses. Lots of them. And cattle, and hogs, too." He gave me a significant look.

"Good for him," I said. "But horses or no, I'll choose my own husband, thank you—if I ever decide I need one. What I don't need are mothers and brothers pushing me where I don't want to go."

Old Man Nottleman, it turned out, needed a doctor. Marty told me she had brought him to town, to see Doc Abrams, and Doc had immediately sent him on to the hospital in Scottsbluff. She had been in the process of packing a few things when Owen brought me home. She asked me if I minded if she went up to the Nottleman place to stay with the kids for a few days.

"Because I hate the thought of them being alone up there. Not that they can't handle it. I'm sure they can. But I'm taking some groceries up to them—the church keeps a fund for emergencies like this—and I'll stay long enough for them to get adjusted to being by themselves. You and David can stay here, and please make yourselves at home. I'm taking Mikey with me. Aggie said she'd keep him, but with four boarders she has her hands full, and I'd rather have him with me, anyway. You're sure you don't mind my leaving?"

I assured her that I didn't, that I thought it was very nice of her to be so concerned. I told her that David and I would be searching for a place to live, anyway, but she said that if I waited until she got back she would help me look.

She left us then, in a flurry, and I watched her drive away, her headlights arcing the sky as the Packard went up a distant hill and then disappeared over it.

I found that I really liked the Widow Maguire.

Saturday was full. I went to the local grocer, whose wife sold real estate on the side. Mrs. Makepeace took me to several houses, none of which was on the paved street. But I didn't care for any of them. For some reason I was drawn to those hills which climbed gently up and away from this sleepy little town.

Mrs. Makepeace told me, "You won't find nothin' back there. All big ranches and farms, and nobody's selling."

But somebody was selling. He caught up with me at the tiny post office.

"My name's Slim Rhodes," he said without preamble, " Y'er the new gal what's stayin' over to Marty's."

I nodded. "Yes, I'm Lu Morrow."

"I hear you been lookin' fer a place to live."

Small town, I kept telling myself. "Yes. I've been all over."

"I know. Well, I got a quarter section 'bout three miles north of here, as the crow flies. Good house, too. Built by my ol' man. And," he added with pride, "I installed indoor plumbing."

We made our way to a quiet corner of the building. The postmistress was eyeing us curiously and straining to hear our conversation. I put the letter, addressed to Missouri Smith in Chicago, back into my purse. I would mail it later from Scottsbluff.

"Mrs. Makepeace told me there was nothing available in the country," I said.

"She would. They don't none of them want me to sell except to that Calhoun bunch." He sounded thoroughly disgusted. "Why,

80

I wouldn't sell to them horse thieves if they give me all the money they got, which is considerable."

He reached into his shirt pocket and pulled out a can of chewing tobacco. He flipped it open and picked out a big wad. Some of the tobacco spilled down the front of his wool shirt.

He shoved the tobacco into his cheek. He was a grizzled old man who hadn't shaved in days. His clothes were wrinkled and not particularly clean, and were way too big for him. He smelled like he had been cleaning out the hen house. Quite recently. I shuddered to think what his house must look like, but I felt I had to take a look at it, just out of curiosity.

"Why would people expect you to sell out to a bunch of…horse thieves, did you call them?"

He looked around. A boxholder came and picked up his mail. The postmistress was still feigning disinterest.

"Because for some strange reason most people around here like 'em, and my quarter section sits right square in the middle of their land. Which is also considerable."

I looked around too, then whispered, "What is a quarter section?"

His eyes popped open. "Don't they teach you nuthin' in them fancy big-city schools? A quarter section is 160 acres, a half mile by a half mile."

"Oh," I said a little breathlessly. That sounded like a lot of land.

"I know it ain't much," he went on. "But it's got an artesian well on it." He waited for the expected question. I refused to ask it. If I bought his property I was sure I would eventually discover what an artesian well is.

"Can I see it? Today?" I asked.

He grinned. Two top teeth were missing. "Why, shore. Jist git in yer car and follow me."

David was off somewhere with Napoleon, probably making new friends, so I didn't take time to look for him.

Slim Rhodes was obviously in a hurry. At least, he drove like he was. I followed the dust he left swirling in his wake as he raced over the dirt road that wound through the hills. We passed two houses and a lot of cows.

The third house stood back from the road several hundred feet. Pine trees that had been planted years ago guarded the house from winter's wind on the north and west sides.

I followed Mr. Rhodes up the drive. Yes, there was the chicken coop. And a barn. And a story-and-a-half white frame house that looked as though it had been recently re-painted.

The house may not have been particularly impressive, but the view certainly was. I got out of my car, shaded my eyes, and scanned the countryside.

"That's Courthouse Rock," Mr. Rhodes said as he walked up to me. "Actually Jailhouse Rock is just this side of it, but from here they sorta blend together."

"Magnificent! Like a fortress guarding the Plains. How far is it?"

"As the crow flies, Forty miles. Maybe more."

"That far?"

"Oh. yeah. It's big. Kinda fools you. You drive to Bridgeport and you think you're almost to the Rock. But you still have about six miles to go. You need to climb it sometime. Not durin' snake season, though."

"Snake season?" I grimaced. "There would be snakes, of course. I never thought about that."

Mr. Rhodes shook his head. "City folks! Of course there's snakes. Rattlers! But usually they won't bother you if you don't bother them."

"A load off my mind," I said dryly.

"So. That's the barn, and the hen coop. And that," he said, pointing towards a tiny unpainted building leaning precariously, "is the outhouse, but...Say, you do know what an outhouse is, don't you?"

This obnoxious little man was beginning to annoy me. The only satisfaction I could feel was in the knowledge that he would be just as ignorant in the city as I was here. I said, "I've heard of them."

He looked a little sour. "Well, you probably have. But anyway, you don't need to worry 'bout it, 'cause I have indoor plumbing."

The wind was kicking up a little, and it was turning colder. I pulled my coat tighter around me, and was grateful for the bandages that were keeping my hands warm.

I followed him into the house, which was in very good repair. The screened porch, which was on the south side, was large and ran the whole width of the house. We entered the kitchen from the porch. It was large but not modern. It had a sink, and a gas stove that was fueled by a propane tank in the yard. He showed me how to turn it on and regulate the flames. I was relieved that the oven worked. There was an electric refrigerator instead of an ice box, and a big pantry that held probably a six-month supply of groceries. There were a few cabinets, all wood, that Mr. Rhodes told me he had built. There was a large wooden table in the center, built by his father.

From the kitchen we went to the dining room. The oak furniture probably dated back to the Civil War. The table was large and heavy, and Mr. Rhodes obviously took great pride in it because it was polished to a bright sheen. So was the massive sideboard that matched it. Eight chairs surrounded the table, one at each end and three on each side. In my mind I was tearing down the awful puce draperies and replacing them with something bright and airy.

Down a short hall was the bedroom, also furnished in old oak. There were a four-poster bed, a chest, a high-boy, and two night stands. The draperies were a sickly shade of yellow, but the pale blue walls perfectly matched the blue of the lovely flowered rug that all but hid a wood floor.

The bathroom was just off the hall between the bedroom and the dining room. Mr. Rhodes explained he had built it in what once was a very large closet. It was quite modern, having been installed only a few years before. He was very proud of it.

The bedroom not only opened onto the hall, but it also opened into the 'parlor'. That room, also a spacious one, had an overstuffed couch, a chair to match, and two end tables. A small oak desk was near the window, and an oil stove against the inside wall. Next to the stove sat an ornately-carved wooden rocker.

Mr. Rhodes explained how to use the stove and promised me that the house would not get cold, even in sub-zero temperatures. I believed him. The house was marvelously warm.

A stairwell rose to the second floor from the parlor; we went past it and back into the kitchen. The first floor went around in a complete circle.

Mr. Rhodes let me meander through the house while he fixed a pot of coffee. I went upstairs. There were two bedrooms, each with two dormer windows. There were also two large closets, and a small storage room. One of the bedrooms looked out over the neighbor's land, and the other faced Courthouse Rock, high on the distant Plains.

The house was clean and neat, and I thought to myself that Mr. Rhodes would be so much more appealing if he would keep himself as well-groomed.

The coffee smelled stronger that Mr. Rhodes did, so I told him that I seldom drank coffee, and asked him instead if he had any tea.

His lips twisted sourly and he muttered something about "city folks" under his breath and, grudgingly, I thought, put a kettle on to boil.

When it whistled, he gave me a tea bag and a cup of hot water, and we sat down at the round wooden table there in his homey kitchen.

I came right to the point. "How much do you want for the place?"

"A right nice place to raise a young'un."

I knew that. That was why I wanted it. So I asked again, "How much are you asking?"

"Not far from town," he said, as though he hadn't heard me. "Leastways, not too far. Good view, sturdy buildin's."

I agreed. Several times. He was worse than Mrs. Makepeace. I tried again. "I would like to buy it, Mr. Rhodes, but I really need to know how much to pay you."

"The milk cow comes with it. You know how to milk a cow?"

"I'll learn. HOW MUCH?"

He rubbed his stubbly chin with a gnarled thumb, and seemed to be making a decision about something. He glanced at me once, and I could see that something was bothering him.

Finally he said, "Cantankerous neighbors. Can't let a little lady like you git into a situation like this without warnin' you.

Tough, both of them." His eyes shifted from mine, then back again. "One of them's an Injun. Thought I better tell you."

I shrugged my shoulders. "Has he massacred anybody lately? Taken any scalps?"

He gave me the scathing look he thought I deserved. "'Course not. Don't be ridiculous! But he's an Injun jist the same. I don't hold with them varmints livin' like a white man, as though he had a right to."

I was puzzled. "Well, doesn't he?"

Slim Rhodes slammed a fist down on the table, and I was glad it was well-built. "No, he don't! Not in my book. And there's other folks around here who feel the same way. Not enough, but some."

"And how far is this...er...Injun neighbor?"

"Not even two miles. See them trees down there?" He pointed out of one of the kitchen windows. "That's their place. It's a big house, but you can't see it for the trees. But at night, if the yard light's on, you can see its shape, sort of. They call it Calhoun House." He made another sour face. "Sounds like some fancy hotel or somethin', don't it? Took him in, they did. A dirty Injun. Treated him like a son. Cheated a poor honest white man out of his land till all I had left was this quarter section, but made him a member of the family."

His voice had risen passionately and he turned an alarming shade of purple, but he collected himself, took a few moments to calm down, and said, "Jist thought I'd warn you. Don't want it said I took advantage of a greenhorn, and a female one at that."

"Well, I certainly appreciate your honesty." He didn't notice the irony in my voice. "But what I don't quite understand is that if you didn't want to live so close to this...er...Injun, why on earth didn't you sell out to that Calhoun bunch?"

"Because I didn't want ta give 'em the satisfaction," he said fiercely. Then he chuckled. "Boy, wouldn't I like to see their faces when they git back and find I've sold the place right from under their noses."

"You haven't sold it yet," I pointed out. "You still haven't told me how much you want for it."

"Thirteen thousand dollars," he said. "That's for everythin', includin' the furniture, the chickens, and Betty Lou."

I gave him a questioning look.

"The milk cow," he explained. "And pots and pans and dishes. Even the bedding. The whole works, except for the rocking chair and a few books. Those I'll take to my brother's with me. He's been after me to come and live with him now that his wife's gone, and he's got a nice place in Sydney. Thirteen thousand. It's a bargain."

I did some mental arithmetic. I still had the twelve thousand, cash, from the sale of Grandmother's fire opal. I also had about two hundred dollars left from my savings account. Since I didn't know how my job with Pete would work out, I thought I had better save something for Grandmother's inevitable "rainy day."

"Eleven thousand, cash," I said.

He thought for a moment, a long moment. He was doing some mental calculations, too. I knew, from what he had told me, that he would have trouble selling to almost anyone else around here. He also knew, because my face is usually a dead giveaway, that I really wanted this place.

He seemed to come to a decision. "Twelve thousand, and I'll throw in my rifle and the separator. It separates the milk from the cream," he added quickly.

Twelve thousand was the exact amount Missouri got for the Opal. It seemed only fair. I would get a legacy from my grandparents after all.

"Sold!" I said.

And Mr. Rhodes said, "When can I get the money?"

"As soon as I get the deed."

"Monday, then. We'll go to the courthouse and close the deal. Too bad the boys aren't gettin' back until Wednesday, or so I heard. Don't even know the reason they had to go away. But I'll be gone by then. I was goin' to my brother's for Thanksgivin', anyway, so now I jist won't come back." He thought for a moment more. "Say, you'd best not tell any of the folks around here that you're buyin' my place. Those boys might hear 'bout it and come high-tailin' it home early, and we don't want that. Mighty popular with most of the folks in these parts." He shook his head. "Never could understand it, myself."

I promised not to tell even David all of the details. Marty, either, if she got home.

Mr. Rhodes looked a little alarmed. "Especially Marty," he said.

Marty Maguire seemed to be the hub around which her little church spun, and if Marty knew anything, like me buying a place from under the noses of some very influential and well-liked people, she would be sure to tell someone, and I wanted to settle in before I brought recriminations down on my head.

So I left Mr. Rhodes packing his few belongings, and went back to town.

I eventually caught up with David, who had been very busy himself. Napoleon had apparently wanted chicken for his main meal, and consequently David made the acquaintance of several of the townspeople who raised chickens in their backyards and weren't inclined to look upon the dog as the town hero.

Now safely tied to Marty's clothespole, Napoleon was polishing off a can of dog food purchased at the grocer's, whose chickens were among those Napoleon had been terrorizing.

"And then Mrs. Makepeace invited me to church tomorrow. After she saw how harmless Napoleon really is, and that I really tried to keep him away from her chickens, she was real nice. She sells the eggs in her store. She said I'd really like it at the church, that there are a lot of kids from the high school who go there. Like the Melroses, and the Abners and the Lynches, and the Forrests, and the Mathiesons. She said the Mathieson kids are all nice, and their mother, too. But she said some things about the father. 'Scooter,' she called him. Told me to watch out for him. Said he's mean as a bear. Can I go, Sis?"

I hesitated. It was, after all, David's life. He would need to make his own decisions. But I remembered my experiences with God. It seemed like whatever I prayed for, I got just the opposite. I wanted my grandfather to live, but he died. I prayed for David to get better; instead, he was stricken with polio. I begged God not to let Grandmother die and leave me virtually alone in the world. But she died. I prayed that my parents would stop drinking—I wanted a family life so desperately, for myself and especially for David. I wanted a kind husband who could care for David and me. But Bryce had feet of clay. Finally I asked for a career, one I had worked for all of my life, and one that would eventually free me and my little brother. I looked at my hands. That was what came from listening to Missouri go on and on about her God. I didn't want David to have to face that kind of disillusionment. He had had enough to bear in his young life.

"You can do what you want, of course," I told him, "but I have some news for you. I bought us a house—out in the country."

I've never seen a kid's face light up like his did. Church was forgotten.

"Can I see it? Now? What's it like? Is there a lot of land? Do you think I could have a horse?" The questions tumbled out in one long breath.

"You can see it tomorrow. The man I bought it from said we could start moving our things in then. It's not a huge house, but it has three bedrooms and indoor plumbing. It's very clean, though not very modern. The furniture comes with it, although I do want to buy a rocking chair. It has a marvelous view because it sets high in the hills. It is on a quarter section, which is one hundred and sixty acres. And yes, one day you may have a horse. I'll teach you how to ride. But for the present, you must not tell a soul about it, especially Marty, if she comes back. The man who is selling it to us doesn't want any complications to arise and upset the deal. It seems his neighbors, who are out of town at the moment, might do something to see the sale doesn't go through. That seems to be the only drawback—our neighbors. Mr. Rhodes, the person selling us the place, doesn't seem to think too highly of the 'Calhoun bunch'. He told me they cheated quite a few farmers and ranchers out of their land during the Depression. But we really won't have to have anything to do with them. They are, after all, nearly two miles away, even though their land surrounds ours. All we have to do is mind our own business, and we shouldn't have any trouble."

So David and I packed our belongings and took them to our new home. When we arrived there early Sunday morning Mr. Rhodes had already packed his clothes and those gaudy knick-knacks that seemed to clutter every table. He helped us clean out our packed car, stacking everything on the porch for the time being.

Then he took us over the property in his little truck. Glancing at the sky, he said, "There'll be snow by mornin'. You should always have a big supply of food stored in case you get snowed in. Which happens, though not usually this early. But January, and

February, and into March, be careful. December, too, sometimes. We 'most always have a white Christmas.

"See them fences? That's my propi'ty line. Anything on the other side belongs to that Calhoun bunch. You'll want to keep off their land. An' especially you need to watch that dog." He had been looking askance at Napoleon since we arrived. "Ranchers'll shoot a strange dog on sight."

I was delighted to see that the meandering creek cut through a corner of the property. But Mr. Rhodes declared it was a drawback. "You'll have more trouble keepin' up them water gates than the hull rest of the fence combined. Remember, it's their cattle, so jest let them worry about keepin' 'em in."

Along the creek were the dry, brushy skeletons of trees. They looked rather unattractive to me. "Them's cottonwoods," Mr. Rhodes informed us. "You'd think they was dead, but next summer you'll wanta have a picnic down here in their shade. There's no sound so soothin' to the mind as what the cottonwoods make. When there don't even seem to be a breeze, all their leaves'll be a flutterin' and whisperin' like the sound of runnin' water."

"Why, Mr. Rhodes," I was surprised, "you are rather eloquent concerning these trees."

"All westerners love cottonwoods. They grow wherever there's a bit of water, and have led many a thirsty soul to a life-savin' drink."

Yes, I thought, I'll be here next summer when the leaves grow again, and my life that looks so barren now will put out new growth too. The lifeless trees gave me new hope.

We drove back across the empty pasture. He had been forced by circumstances to sell his own cattle he explained. Then he took us to the barn. Betty Lou was there, waiting to be milked. He told David that after the tour he would show him how to do it. "It's got to be done morning and night. Won't hurt you to learn how to do it too, missy."

I told him I would give it my best shot.

From the barn we went to the chicken coop. About thirty hens were milling around the yard, and a lone rooster was doing his strut.

"You'll want to make real sure they're all shut in good 'n tight every night, and when it's cold, really cold, there's a kerosene heater. But that's only for weather that's dangerous. And be careful not to set the place on fire. Always make sure the door is closed tight. Them sneakin' coyotes come out of the hills when they're good 'n hungry and try to git at 'em. You'll hear the hens squawk plenty then, but by the time you git to your rifle, the thieving' coward'll be gone. Without his meal, too, if you locked them all in like yer sposed to. But count 'em when you put 'em to bed for the night, 'cause if you leave one out, it's a goner."

I cleared my throat. "Will coyotes attack a person?"

He let out a hoarse guffaw. "If you city folks don't beat all! You'll be lucky ever to see a coyote, much less git close enough to git attacked by one. They stay as far away from humans as possible. You'll hear 'em howl, and that's about as close as you'll ever git."

The milking lesson was hilarious—to me if not to David. My hands, fortunately, precluded me from milking, so I was able to stand back and watch as David tugged and yanked. Betty Lou was patient, turning her head occasionally to see what was going on, but for the most part she seemed to regard David with cynical amusement.

Finally David seemed to get the hang of it. He was very proud of himself. For my part, I was delighted that we would have fresh milk everyday, and cream too. Mr. Rhodes showed us how to pour the milk into the separator, and turn the crank, and we watched fascinated as foamy cream flowed into its own container. Then there was the chore of disassembling and washing the separator. I hoped we could get it together again.

It took us the better part of the day to get Mr. Rhodes' things moved out. All three of us cleaned, moved furniture around to suit me, and then David and I put our own things away. Mr. Rhodes went through everything again to make sure he had what he needed to finish out his life at his brother's in Sydney. He would spend one last night in his home, and meet me at the courthouse the next afternoon.

As dusk fell David and I made one more swing around the farm, bedded down the chickens for the night, said good-bye to Betty Lou, and headed for Lee's Corner.

Marty still wasn't home. On Monday morning I cleaned her house. Then I went to the grocery store and bought supplies for David and myself, and some for Marty. I also bought her an automatic toaster from the Ben Franklin store, where I met Jeb Truman's parents (who proceeded to invite me to church), and then I went to the courthouse.

Mr. Rhodes was there ahead of me. He handed me the notarized deed, and I handed him twelve thousand dollars, all in hundred-dollar bills.

I heard Mr. Stuart, the recorder, say to Mr. Rhodes, when he thought I was out of ear shot, "They're not going to like this."

Mr. Rhodes said something rather rustic about that 'Calhoun bunch', but I had bought the property, it was in my name, and I mentally snapped my fingers and said, "That for the Calhouns."

I went to Scottsbluff, which is a unique town, though compared to Lee's Corner it's a thriving metropolis. But I didn't have time to climb the famous bluff. I wanted paint and wallpaper, and material for curtains, and Lee's Corner didn't have much of a selection. Scottsbluff wasn't exactly Chicago either, but it had a Sears & Roebucks so if there were anything I couldn't find locally, I could order it. I also rented a post office box and mailed my letter to Missouri Smith, to which I had added another page describing our new home.

By the time I got back David was out of school and excited about his new friends. I heard about them all the way home, which was three miles as the crow flies but nearly eight miles for anything on wheels.

I discovered there was no such thing as a school bus, so I took David to school on Tuesday and picked him up Tuesday afternoon. When I approached the front door, I saw David was talking to a small dark boy. The short aluminum crutches tipped me off that this was Freddy.

"Sis," he introduced me, "this is Freddy D'Angelo. He's in fourth grade and he and his parents live at the boarding house."

"I'm glad to meet you, Freddy," I told him sincerely. Very glad that you're a complete stranger, I added to myself. But he was Italian. Had his parents ever visited Little Italy? Again I was seized by that urge to get away from there. Was it possible to live in a small town without becoming intimately acquainted with every person in it?

By Wednesday David had made a friend who lived northwest of us and who offered to pick him up for school and bring him home. So I painted and papered and waited for Marty to get home from the Nottleman's so she could help me make curtains and matching bedspreads. On Wednesday I also bought a big turkey and all the trimmings. For the first time in years we would celebrate Thanksgiving. Because for the first time in years we had something for which to be thankful.

What must be shall be; and that which
is a necessity to him that struggles,
is little more than choice
to him that is willing.
—Seneca

Chapter 7

It had snowed Sunday night, just as Mr. Rhodes had predicted. It was a gentle snow that fell like soft petals of a delicate white flower, and it covered the ground with large flakes. Monday and Tuesday there had been another three inches or so, but here on Wednesday the sky was clear and pale blue. I was waiting for David to come in on that fateful evening before Thanksgiving. He had gone to milk Betty Lou, and put up the chickens, (to whom Napoleon had thankfully taken an instant aversion,) securely in their cozy coop. Then he told me he and Napoleon were going to explore, and I asked him to be home by dark.

I glanced at my hands, something I had been doing far too often ever since Dr. Abrams had taken off the dressings that afternoon. The fingers were horribly scarred, the palms still red and swollen. The stitches were out, and the doctor had mentioned something about skin grafts later on, but we both knew that nothing would bring back the dexterity I needed for the concert stage. Now I still seemed to see the scars and redness right through the thin layer of gauze bandages.

A pot of stew was bubbling on the stove. I had just turned down the burner; I was having trouble getting used to propane. The turkey was in its roasting pan ready to be stuffed. It would be just David and me tomorrow; Marty still wasn't back, and Doc had been invited to dinner at the home of Marty's pastor, the Hursts. David and I had been invited to Mrs. Lassiter's, but I made some polite excuse. I wasn't ready to go through that again.

I was proud of our little house. David loved it, as I knew he would. He had chosen the upstairs bedroom that overlooked the rolling hills with Courthouse Rock far in the distance and the North Platte flowing east past it, carrying the waters of the Wyoming mountains to the mighty Missouri.

The cheerful yellow wallpaper had given new life to the dining room, and I did the "parlor" in a mint green that matched the upholstery in the lovely old sofa. The rocker I had purchased at a second-hand shop in Scottsbluff was next to the oil stove, whose pipes went to every room of the house, giving it a special warmth.

I went to the rocker and settled down comfortably with one of the westerns Mr. Rhodes had left, but the book lay open in my lap, and I stared out the window at some distant ghost.

I hadn't had the nightmare for the past two nights. For two nights in a row I hadn't seen the Buick cross our path, hadn't heard the screams that, in my nightmare, were endless. I hadn't heard the deafening crash, hadn't seen the bodies tangled in grotesque shapes trapped in the spreading flames, or the blood splattered over the seats, the hoods, the floor. For the past two mornings I hadn't awakened to look at my hands, to see if the blood was still on them. Perhaps I wouldn't dream it again. Perhaps I could gradually build a new life without memories of the past.

For two nights I had been free of the nightmare, but it still haunted me through the days. I wondered if I could ever be able to bring myself to tell David the truth. That our father killed an innocent man...and that I was there and should have prevented it. Maybe, when he was older he would understand. But now? No, I couldn't tell him now. He was looking and feeling so much better, I couldn't do anything to upset that.

The book was still open on my lap. It was the hammering at the front door that brought me back to the present. Perhaps Marty had come home and come out to check on me. I laid the book on the end table beside me, and stood up. As I did so, a premonition, something so tangible it almost kept me from moving, struck me so forcibly that I didn't want to answer that peremptory knock. I knew it was not Marty. I walked slowly to the door, and hesitated before I opened it. I remember shivering.

I turned the knob. A blast of wind took the door out of my hand and threw it open. The sun was setting in the west, and it lit up Courthouse Rock in a blaze of golden glory. He was standing there, his back to me, watching the spectacular sunset. But in that split second before he turned, I knew who he was. I had seen that lithe, tall figure, that coal-black hair, and that same stance, hands deep in pockets. I knew who he was even before he turned to me with that same sweet smile that had won Missouri's heart. His leather jacket was open and he was not wearing a hat.

A flicker of surprise came and went so quickly in those deep blue eyes of his that I wondered if I had imagined it. He said, "Miss Morrow? I'm your neighbor, John Ransom." And he held out his hand.

I stood there, my heart in my throat, and I held on to the door post to keep from toppling over. From a distance he was handsome; at three feet he was devastating. There was a smile lurking in those electric blue eyes.

My dismay—or was it despair?—must have shown in my face. He raised one eyebrow a fraction and added, "but my friends call me Johnny."

I tried to gather my wits, and finally managed in a shaky voice, "How...how do you do?"

He stood there a few moments more, while those last few days in Chicago flooded me once again with painful memories and bitter shame.

"May I come in?" he finally dropped his hand.

I stood aside, reluctantly. "Of course," I answered woodenly. "Please do."

He walked past me into the parlor, colder now because of the length of time the front door had remained open, and went straight to the little stove.

I tried to regain my composure. "We've just moved in. Please excuse..."

But he said smoothly, "The place looks very nice. I see you've moved the furniture around. And old Slim would never have thought of wallpaper. A nice touch, Miss Morrow." I suddenly wondered why I had chosen Morrow. It should have been Smith or Jones, something that wouldn't have associated me with the past.

"Call me Lu," I said mechanically. "Everyone does." But he had never seen me. He didn't know me. His casual remarks were proof of that. And I must act natural, as if I were meeting a new neighbor.

His hands warm now, he made his way unhesitatingly to the kitchen. "I see you've painted the cabinets. And a tablecloth. Very…er…feminine. Do you mind if I take off my coat?"

My heart sank as I helplessly watched him pull off his expensive leather jacket. He went back to the parlor and I followed mutely. I sat back in my rocker and motioned for him to take the chair opposite. He picked up the book I had been reading and flipped through its pages. "*Western Union*. It's a pretty good book. Old Slim had quite a collection of books. I guess he left most of them?"

I nodded my head.

"I didn't think he would take them. Never was much of a reader, old Slim. Most of those books belonged to his brother. The one who died, not the one he went to live with."

I sat there, my hands in my lap. Whether he didn't notice them or was making a point not to notice them I couldn't tell. I know I was trying to make them as inconspicuous as possible. I was also going to let him set the tone of the conversation. My mind was still reeling, and I didn't know anything to say. I couldn't believe this. John Ransom was in Chicago. How could he be my next-door-neighbor in the Nebraska Sand Hills? In my imagination I saw God laughing uproariously at His little joke.

So we sat in silence for a few moments. His appeared to be a contented silence, but mine was an agitated one, and I never could hide my feelings.

Finally he said, "A gentleman by the name of Napoleon paid us a visit."

I groaned outwardly, but inwardly I was grateful for someone else to talk about even if it was our dog, "Oh, dear. That mutt."

His eyes danced. "Not a mutt! A genuine Transylvanian Alpine Sheephound. I, of course, recognized it as one the instant I laid eyes on it. They are known by their rather distinctive...er...coloring and their predilection for chasing cattle."

I was not in the mood for jokes, "You met David?" I asked apprehensively.

"I did. Hot on the heels of that mutt...er...sheephound. We asked him to stay for supper—David, not Napoleon. He said it was up to you, and since you don't have a phone, I came to ask you in person."

I was terribly, and probably visibly, upset. I saw all I had planned and hoped for crumbling before my eyes. This fantastic coincidence could turn on me and cause me, and especially David, acute and painful grief. This was another strong case for Fate, which had me once more in its grip, and against God, who must have been having a field day.

"You say you're our neighbor, Mr. Ransom?" I'm afraid it sounded like a challenge, as if I could make it false, even make him disappear. "I thought we were surrounded by the Calhoun place."

"You mean 'That Calhoun Bunch, those conniving horse thieves,' don't you?"

I cleared my throat. "Well, Mr. Rhodes, I mean..." My voice faltered.

"I know what you mean. I've known Slim Rhodes all my life. Probably led you to believe my grandfather swindled him out of his land, save this piece."

"Not exactly 'swindled.' Look, I don't want to get mixed up in a range war. I only wanted a place for my brother..." My voice faltered again.

He smiled at me. Black hair, blue eyes, and that smile. "I know. David was telling us all about it. A fount of information, that boy."

Terror-stricken, I searched his face for a deeper meaning, but there had been no irony in his voice, nor was his expression anything but friendly.

"Told us all about St. Louis," John Ransom went on, "and the Cardinals, and Stan the Man, and the big brewery, and the barges on the Mississippi."

Another thought, unpleasant in its inception, burst into my mind. Had I, who abhorred lying, made my brother into a prevaricator? It was one thing, I reasoned, to try to protect ourselves against malicious gossip, but it was quite another to deliberately deceive when it wasn't necessary. But then again, maybe this was one of those times when it was necessary. But "what a tangled web we weave." I would have to talk to my little brother.

But meanwhile I would have to talk to John Ransom, and I didn't know in the least what to say.

"Did you...did you get the impression he was missing..." I almost said St. Louis, but there was no sense lying when I could avoid it. I caught myself just in time, and finished with, "...the city?"

"Not at all. He loves it here. And if old Slim had to sell this place to somebody other than me—which he apparently did feel he had to do—I'm glad he sold it to you." And again he smiled.

I felt hot color creeping up my face. He saw it, too. I always wished my face didn't give me away. But all my life, try though I might, I could never achieve a totally impassive expression. And as he smiled, I saw once more the headlines: **GOOD SAMARITAN DOCTOR KILLED**...

I cleared my throat. "It was kind of you to invite David for dinner."

"Supper," he corrected. "Here we have breakfast, dinner, and supper."

"Supper, then. But..."

"Please let him stay. We'd love to have him. I have a brother about his age and I really miss him. So does Coy. Coy's my adopted brother, but Slim would have told you all about that—or his version of it. Anyway, Rick's my brother's name. He's in Chicago now, with an aunt, but he's moving back here when the school year is over. I'm glad he'll have a friend close by. And meanwhile, we'd like to get to know David better. He'll brighten up our dreary lives. In fact, he already has. It's been a while since a kid has visited us two old bachelors."

I was feeling too weak to argue, "Of course, if he wants to stay, he may." And I wondered if the other bachelor—the adopted brother—was Mr. Rhodes' "Injun".

John Ransom added, "The invitation to supper also extends to you."

I answered, "No," a little too quickly. Then I added, in a belated attempt at courtesy, "Thank you, but I have a lot to do."

"Are you sure? It's been a long time since a lovely lady has graced our table, and Coy's a tolerable cook."

"Thank you, but I really can't." I waved a hand in the general direction of some boxes that still needed unpacking, but he looked pointedly at the book lying open on the table.

"I understand," he said, his voice dry. "I'll bring David and Napoleon back early. Especially Napoleon, who is at the present locked in our barn. And thank you for letting us borrow him. David, I mean." Again that smile.

I handed him his jacket and he shrugged himself into it. I walked him to the front door. The wind had kicked up and was blowing even colder.

"We'll have more snow by morning," he told me as I opened the door. "And by the way," he added, with a decidedly wicked gleam in his eyes, "David said you were fixing a big turkey tomorrow, and I saw for myself how big it is. He invited us to share it."

My mouth fell open as panic swept over me. I teetered on my feet and reached out a hand for the door jamb.

He took my elbow to steady me, but of course it had the opposite effect. I tried to say something but nothing came out.

"Mighty nice of you," he went on. "Right neighborly. David said about five. Is that all right?"

I nodded my head, "Quite all right," I said hoarsely. The swirling cold wind carried my voice away.

"Then we'll see you tomorrow."

He took his hand from my elbow, bestowed on me one more smile, and left. I somehow managed to get inside, and the wind slammed the front door shut.

I went to the window and watched him get into his pickup, and wondered with irrelevancy where the Cadillac was. He waved, put the truck into gear, and roared down the drive. It seemed to me everyone out here drove as if they were in the Indy 500.

I went back to my rocker, but only looked at the book lying where he had left it. I couldn't stop shaking. My nightmare, suddenly and without warning, had burst into life. How could I keep our secret now? What would I tell Missouri? I had already told her I had a job and there was an extra bedroom in the house, and now I couldn't let her come. When school let out in June and his brother came home, my little game might be over anyway.

~~~~~~~~~~

John Ransom brought David and Napoleon home earlier than I thought he would, so I was not prepared for the three of them when they walked in on me. I was deeply absorbed in my own troubled thoughts, so much so that I didn't notice the lights coming up the drive or hear the back door open and then close.

I know my look showed surprise; I hoped it didn't show the utter consternation I felt.

"We've racketed her respite," John Ransom said to my brother.

"Regrettable," David said.

"Will there be repercussions?" Mr. Ransom asked.

"Righteous resentment," David answered quickly.

"Really?"

"Oh, enough," I broke in sharply. I'm not sure if I was irritated because they walked in on me unawares or because David had apparently taught John Ransom our little game.

"I'm completely contrite," Mr. Ransom told me with a formal bow, a smile lurking just behind his blue eyes and playing at the corners of his mouth.

"I'm not convinced you have the capacity to be completely contrite, Mr. Ransom," I said, and meant it.

"It's not conceivable!"

"On the contrary..." I replied, then stopped myself. How did I end up playing games with John Ransom? I gathered myself together and said in a calmer voice, "But enough of this. I must thank you for having my brother for din...supper."

"His appreciation was properly profuse," John Ransom said.

David looked from one to the other of us and grinned. "I'm tired," he said. I think I'll turn in." He smiled at our guest. "Thank you again for a wonderful evening. I'll see you tomorrow."

I had a feeling David would be "asleep" before I could have a chance to talk to him about Thanksgiving dinner—or supper.

John Ransom, instead of leaving, walked over to one of the boxes I had not yet unpacked, and picked up a book. "From Zane Grey to Victor Hugo. I'm impressed."

I had risen to my feet when they came in, and I still stood there, as self-conscious as a school girl while he flipped through the book. "I like to read," I finally said, almost defiantly.

He glanced once more at the book before he put it back in the box. "You must," he said, the dry tone very pronounced.

I still stood there, my hands clasped together behind my back, and he gave me that wicked grin again. He seemed to be enjoying himself very much.

"David left us alone on purpose, you know," he told me.

I felt my face grow warm. "I know. But you don't have to stay just because of that. I mean..."

"I know what you mean." His voice was as dry as autumn leaves. "I need to get back, anyway. Coy wanted me to ask you if we needed to bring anything tomorrow. He's the cook since our last one left us."

"Nothing I can think of." My voice was stilted, even hostile. "Just be here at five."

I walked him to the door and said what I hoped was a pleasant good-bye. And a few minutes later, when I walked into David's room, he did indeed appear to be sleeping. I couldn't be sure, so I tiptoed out. Whatever I wanted to say could wait until morning. That night my dream of the accident returned.

When I went into the kitchen on Thanksgiving morning David was already there ahead of me.

Before I could even open my mouth, he blurted out, "Did you like Johnny?"

I put my hands on my hips, "Where do you get off calling him 'Johnny'?"

"He asked me to. And Coy is short for Black Coyote. His father was Howling Coyote. Coy is a full-blooded Sioux, but he calls it Lakota. And you should see his horse! Big and black. Do you like Johnny?"

"I don't know 'Johnny'. And I don't know why you invited two perfect strangers to Thanksgiving dinner!"

"Oh, Sis, they're our nearest neighbors! Besides what could I do? Johnny's dad died last week and they just got back from the funeral yesterday. It was somewhere back East. And they didn't tell anyone in town, because they were afraid people would try to travel in this weather for the funeral. So they're going to have a memorial service for him a week from Sunday. But nobody knows about it yet, so don't say anything to anybody."

"Not even Marty?"

"Especially not Marty. At least that's what Johnny told me. They don't want to ruin anyone's holiday. I think they're both terrific. Dr. Ransom sounded pretty terrific, too. He was real popular when he practiced medicine here. At least that's what Coy said."

"Well, if no one is supposed to know about this funeral, how come they told you?"

David sat at his place at the kitchen table. He put his elbows on the table and rested his chin in his hands. "Well, it's kind of a long story."

I was making pancake batter. I brought the bowl to the table, sat down opposite my little brother, and said as I stirred the batter, "Well, I seem to have nothing but time today. How did you happen to meet them, and why did they tell you something no one else is supposed to know?"

He squirmed a little. "Well," he finally said. "It was kind of Napoleon's fault. He ran off from me. When I caught up with him he was chasing the Ransom's cows. I couldn't catch him, and I yelled and yelled for him to stop and come home. You know he usually minds me, but he was having too good a time. Then I saw someone come riding really fast. He chased Napoleon down and managed to grab his collar. By the time I got to them, the man was off the horse and had tied a rope around Napoleon's collar. I introduced myself, and he told me his name was John Ransom."

David looked at me and grinned. I kept mixing the batter.

"So then what happened?" I asked.

"Well, by that time we were a lot closer to his house than we were to ours. He asked if I wanted to go home with him and he'd get the truck and bring us both home. So I said sure, and he got on his horse—Captain is his name—and pulled me up behind him, and we went to his place. He showed me how to bed down a horse, then we locked Napoleon in a small room. Then he showed me Coy's stallion, Seneca. I thought he was named for the Indian tribe, but Johnny said Coy named him after some famous Roman. And I saw the new horse Johnny is training. He's a beauty! You should see him, dark brown with...

"You're straying from the point, little brother."

"Oh,...yeah. Well, he asked if I'd like to meet a real full-blooded Indian, and I said of course I would, so he took me inside. He yelled for Coy, and Coy answered from the back of the house that he was on the telephone with the funeral director and that they needed to know if the stone should have the actual date or just the year when Dad died. Johnny told him he'd be right there, and excused himself. I heard him say something to Coy, and then Coy came out. He told me Johnny needed to talk to the man on the telephone but that he'd be right back. I asked Coy who died, and he told me their dad did, a few days ago. But he didn't seem to want to talk about it, and when Johnny came back into the room I naturally said I was sorry, but I didn't ask any more questions. Honest I didn't!" David looked at me pleadingly and crossed his heart.

"Then Johnny smiled at me and told me that no one else knew, and would I please not tell anybody, because their Dad was well-liked and they wouldn't want to ruin anybody's Thanksgiving by mourning for him. Then they changed the subject, and that was that."

I looked at my batter. I had been mixing it so hard there were no lumps. Pancake batter is supposed to be slightly lumpy. I cleared my throat, and asked as casually as I could, "What else did you find out about our neighbors?"

"Well, Johnny has a little brother, Rick, who lived with their Dad back East. Rick is really his half-brother. Several years after Johnny's mother died his dad remarried a woman he met in New York. She moved out here, but she hated the country. So eventually he gave up his practice here to Dr. Abrams and set up one back East, I guess in New York. But Rick's mother has been dead for a while too. Rick was born here and really loves the ranch, so now he'll be moving back when the school year is over. Johnny thinks I'll really like him. Anyway, Johnny was visiting his dad when he died, and then Coy flew back for the funeral, and they drove home together."

I went to the stove and took my time lighting the burner. "Did they tell you what happened?" I asked, my back to my brother.

"No. And I didn't want to ask. I mean, I wouldn't have even blurted out 'who died?' if I had been thinking. And they seemed shook up about it, but, well, not really sad. Johnny told me his dad was in a better place than any of us could possibly imagine, and while they will mourn his passing they won't mourn him. I wish I knew what he meant."

"Well, as long as you didn't pry. It's not polite to ask too many questions."

"I just told them I was real sorry. I mean, I guess they felt they had to tell me something, because of what I had heard. And it's not like it's a secret. I mean, after today everyone will know anyway."

The stove lit, I took out a frying pan and put butter in it. As I watched it start to sizzle, I asked, I hoped nonchalantly, "Did you...tell them...about..."

"No. Not a thing. And, funny, but they didn't ask any questions about us. I told them we were born in St. Louis, and I guess they took it for granted that that's where we're from."

I turned to him, and he glanced sideways at me through his dark lashes. "I hated lying to them," he said.

"You didn't lie to them."

"Letting people draw the wrong conclusions is not exactly telling the truth."

I poured the batter into the pan. "The conclusion they choose to draw is their own responsibility. Go get the milk. I'll need cream for the pumpkin pies."

His mind was instantly off ethics. "Custard, too?"

"Yes, brat, custard, too. I need eight eggs. See if we have that many this morning."

He was off in a flash. I watched through the window as he made his way across the sparkling snow to the barn, and wondered how in the world I was going to get through an entire meal with those three males.

When David came back with the milk, the cream, and the eggs, I had somehow collected my scattered wits. In spite of all my efforts, my life was getting more complicated by the day, but now the complications arose from a different and infinitely more dangerous source. I wondered, however briefly, about selling the place. But I couldn't do that to David. He was happy, now, and if I could just keep those two long miles between myself and my neighbor...

If.

But not today. David was full of Johnny and Coy.

"Coy saved Johnny's life. Years ago. He had been living on the reservation. Johnny said it's a miserable place. I don't know what I thought a reservation would look like, but it certainly shouldn't look like scattered slums. But that was the way Johnny described it. He said the government has done very badly by the Indians. Coy told me that when he was born, in March, 1924, Indians still hadn't been given their citizenship. Isn't that terrible? I mean, I thought anyone born in the United States was automatically a citizen."

I was interested in spite of myself. "Not citizens?"

David shook his fair head. "Not until June of that year. And even then they couldn't vote. That didn't happen until fifteen years later. Johnny says that's why Coy is a Democrat. I think they must argue about politics a lot, because Coy told him, 'Not in front of the boy.'"

I relaxed enough to laugh, "And what did you contribute to the conversation?"

Again I got that sidelong glance, "I told them you were single."

"Thank you very much," I glared at him. "I need another match-maker."

David said, "You're welcome," a little uncertainly, then asked again, "Do you like him?"

"Who?"

"Johnny!"

"I don't know him. And I don't want any pushes or pulls from you. Understand? Men are made uncomfortable by pushy females—and their little brothers."

"Johnny told me he thought you were nice," he went doggedly on, "and very pretty."

"What was he supposed to say? 'Your relative is really rather repulsive.' I can hear him now."

David laughed, "Johnny wouldn't have dared be so deplorable, but I would have defended your dignity to my dying day. But I digress. Come on, Sis, tell me you think he's nice."

"All right. You think he's nice." I started cracking eggs into a bowl. I didn't want to have to look at my little brother. "Listen, David dear, I don't mind that you asked them over for dinner, or supper, or whatever they want to call it, just for today. But I'm going to be very busy when I start work next Monday, so it might be a good idea for you to check with me before you invite friends over for a meal." Especially those friends, I added to myself.

So David reluctantly agreed, and while he was outside romping with Napoleon, I outdid myself preparing the Thanksgiving meal. I felt I was prepared also; I wouldn't let this throw me.

My guests arrived an hour early, laden with several large packages—beef, in every imaginable form: hamburger, steaks, roast, ribs, and, to David's disgust, liver. It more than filled the freezer part of the refrigerator. And had I needed anything to complete the dinner, they would gladly have gone back for it. Since I didn't need anything, they set about helping me.

Coy was a tall, bronze Indian with the proud hawk-like features and coal-black hair of his race. He was certainly a beautiful specimen, and stood about two inches taller even than his brother. Where John Ransom had the lithe figure of a distance runner, Coy was muscular, maybe a shot-putter. His strength was a visible thing, but I was sure John's was there below the surface, out of sight, but just as potent.

When John made the introductions I realized that big, tough, and aggressive though he might look, Coy was on the shy side. But he made himself useful in the kitchen, while John and David more or less got in the way.

At last it was time to eat. For this special occasion we would eat in the dining room. John held out a chair for me, and no one sat until I was seated. John sat to my right, Coy to my left, and David across from me, looking immensely pleased with himself.

Then came a rather embarrassing moment. John gently took my right hand, and Coy my left, then they bowed their heads and waited. I threw a questioning look at David, whose hands were also held captive.

John glanced at me. "Don't you ask the blessing?"

I blinked. "The blessing? Oh, the blessing. I, well, I... Why don't one of you?" It was a plea.

"Well, then I suppose the honor should go to the oldest. That would be you, Coy."

Coy grinned. "By three months."

So we bowed our heads, and Coy administered the blessing. I was glad he was the tall, silent type. Or maybe he was just hungry. He asked that the hands that prepared the food be blessed, but thanked the wrong Person for providing it. When he said a soft 'Amen' and John echoed it, the moment was over. I pulled my hands free and made rather a hard job of carving the turkey. John suggested that that honor should also go to Coy, who grinned and said something to the effect that he hadn't used a knife in that way for years. I assumed it was some private joke.

On this shrunken globe,
men can no longer live as strangers.
—Adlai E. Stevenson

Chapter 8

All through that dinner-supper I waited for the inevitable questions. Where are you from? What do you do for a living? Where did you go to school? What are your hobbies? Do you have any family? What happened to your hands?

They didn't ask. I know David hadn't told them our life story. He told them about his struggle with polio, and we talked a little about Dr. Jonas Salk and what his discovery could mean to thousands of kids. I told them only that our parents had died, and that I wanted to get David away from the city."

"A big, noisy place, St. Louis," Coy said.

"Isn't it, though?" I agreed.

David had already told them I was single, but he repeated it that evening for good measure. We talked, mostly about trivial things, and we ate, and I worried the whole time that either David or I would make a fatal slip.

But we didn't, and as the north wind howled through the trees that stood on two sides of our house I cleared the plates from the table. John helped me while David showed Coy his coin collection.

I stacked the dishes in the rack as Johnny washed, rinsed and handed them to me. I felt his eyes on me, but I didn't dare look at him.

My hands made me feel especially conspicuous, but he wasn't like Marty, who blurted questions. He never said a word, not even when our respective roles with the dishes seemed to invite comment.

Finally he said, "You're as nervous as a cat tonight, Lucasta."

My hand jerked a little, and I almost dropped a plate. "That's ridiculous," I said. "Why should I be nervous?"

"That's what I'd like to know. I hope it's not because of Coy and me."

"Nonsense. I'm glad to have you. David seems to like the two of you very much, and it's been a long time since he's..." I stopped short.

He waited for me to finish. "Since he's..." he prompted.

"Had any real friends." I finished.

"I understand he spent quite a lot of time in the hospital."

"Quite a lot."

"Which one?"

"Several," I answered coolly. "He was in Children's for a while." That was true; he was born there. "That's part of Washington University in St. Louis. One of the best research facilities in the country."

"I know. I've been there. It's by Forest Park and the St. Louis Zoo. The heart and soul of St. Louis."

He handed me the last plate. I set it in the rack and tried to remove my apron, but my fingers couldn't quite cope with the knot.

Deftly, he untied my sash, and I gave him a gruff "thanks," then brought the pies to the kitchen table. I heard laughter from the parlor. David said something, and Coy answered in kind, and I wondered what they were talking about.

I cut the pies, with John sitting in a chair watching my face. I stole a glance at him, and he smiled.

"I think I'm flattered," he said. "I've never known anyone to be afraid of me before."

"I'm not afraid of you!"

"No? I'm delighted to hear it. Perhaps, then, you will allow me to take you out for supper Saturday night. Or maybe I should have asked before you picked up that knife."

I did look at him then. There was no doubt about it. He was handsome. Dark curly hair, blue eyes, a sweet, lazy smile. Then I looked at the pumpkin pie I was slicing. It looked as though I had attacked it with one of Coy's tomahawks. I suppose the Sioux used tomahawks.

"Maybe you'd prefer pecan?" was all I could manage to say.

He, too, gave the pumpkin pie a long, wistful look. "Definitely."

I sliced the pecan pie as gently as I could, and put a big piece on a dessert plate. "David likes custard. Do you know what Coy would like?"

"A little of each. Even the pulverized pumpkin."

I took the whipped cream out of the refrigerator, then put everything on a tray and took it to the parlor, where we had decided to have our dessert. Then I went back for the coffee. David had fresh milk from Betty Lou, and I had my usual cup of tea. But no pie for me. I had lost my appetite.

After I sat down in my rocker, John said, "You didn't answer my question, you know."

I felt the color rush to my face. And David sat there looking at me, a question in his eyes.

"No, I don't think so," I managed to say. "Thank you anyway."

"No, what?" my little brother asked.

"None of your business, squirt," John Ransom answered with a smile.

Then deftly, before David could pursue the matter, he turned the subject to his brother.

For the next hour I was fascinated as Coy, tentatively at first, then gradually with more ease, told us a little personal history of America's overlooked, bypassed, and generally forgotten natives.

"I grew up on the reservation," he told us, "just across the border in South Dakota. My grandfather was eighteen years old and with Crazy Horse when his braves met up with Custer. After the Battle of the Little Big Horn my grandfather fled north with Sitting Bull."

"Wow!" David said, his eyes as big as the dessert plates.

Coy gave him a shy smile. "Sounds heroic, doesn't it. Even a little romantic. But actually it was very grim. My grandfather, Gray Hawk, didn't spare me any of the details about their sojourn in Canada. And he was also very…graphic…when he talked about General George Armstrong Custer. 'Yellow Hair' Custer. A lot has been said about him, that he was a hero, even a martyr. But the Indians called him 'Woman Killer'. He had a reputation—not that he was the only one—for killing unarmed Indians, and the very old, and the very young. And women.

"Well, my people knew this, and they set a trap for him. Indians always left their women and children in the village when they went into battle. This time they used them as bait. They knew Custer would head straight for the helpless in the village. He had no more compunction about shooting them than he did buffalo. The more Indians he killed the more votes he thought he'd get when he ran for president. My grandfather was sure Custer wanted to be the Great White Father."

I admit I was mesmerized. This was certainly a different point of view than the one in the history books.

"Crazy Horse set the trap," Coy went on. "It made it much easier for the band when Custer split his troops. Custer thought he couldn't lose. But then Custer had never come across Crazy Horse's strategy or Sitting Bull's medicine."

"What do you mean, 'Sitting Bull's medicine?'" David asked before I could.

"Sitting Bull, according to my grandfather, wasn't actually at the battle. He wasn't a war chief. He was more of a priest, or medicine man. My grandfather said he was in the mountains making medicine. Offerings to the Great Spirit, I guess."

"It worked," I said.

Coy shrugged. "The Battle of the Little Bighorn was certainly the Sioux's greatest victory. It was ultimately, though, their most devastating defeat. When Custer and his column were killed, soldiers came by the thousands. Sitting Bull fled into Canada. Crazy Horse stayed in the United States but went on the run. He was killed a year later. My grandfather said he came under a flag of truce to get medical aid for his wife. He was murdered. There's no other word for it."

"What happened to Sitting Bull and your grandfather?" This from David, who hadn't moved a muscle during Coy's story.

"Well, life in Canada was difficult. The Red Coats—Mounted Police—treated them better than the United States soldiers did, but couldn't feed them. Game was scarce, and the winters were harder than they were used to. Many died. Finally Sitting Bull brought them back."

"What happened to your grandfather?" I asked, completely forgetting my resolve not to be inquisitive.

"He married. Morning Wind was her name. She bore him two children. She was very beautiful. A soldier wanted to marry her, but she married Gray Hawk instead. The soldier even tried to buy her. He offered ten horses. That was quite a lot. An Indian's wealth is judged partly by how many horses he has. But my grandfather loved her very much. The white men never understood how 'savages' could love, but they loved as fiercely as they fought. There was a chief named Man-Afraid-Of-His-Horses. My grandfather got the name Man-Who-Would-Not-Trade-For-Horses."

"What happened to your grandmother? Do you remember her?" David asked, and I was immediately struck by the fear that Coy's and John's questions could get just as personal.

Coy shook his head. "She was killed shortly after my mother was born. At Wounded Knee. Ever hear of it?"

David shook his head, but I remembered something. "There was a massacre, wasn't there?"

"Yes. A band of unarmed Indians were gunned down by the Seventh Cavalry, Custer's old unit."

"Why?" David asked.

"Well, it seems as though some Indian agents who were unfamiliar with their responsibilities learned about a wave of religious ceremonies that were centered around a so-called 'Ghost Dance.' They misinterpreted this religious revival as insurrection and sent troops to the Pine Ridge Agency in South Dakota. The frightened Sioux were driven into the Badlands. Then a group of Sioux in government service shot Sitting Bull, who was a prisoner at the Standing Rock Agency, and a fight broke out that cost twelve more Sioux their lives. In the hysteria that followed, other clashes occurred. The most serious took place at Wounded Knee Creek, northeast of Pine Ridge. Three hundred and fifty-six Sioux, who had already surrendered to the troops and were unarmed, were attacked in their camp. Over two hundred of them were slaughtered. My grandmother fell on top of her baby, my mother. My grandfather found her there after the blizzard hit. There was nothing he could do for her. Most of those who had only been wounded froze to death before help came. For three days they laid there, in the deep snow. When help finally did arrive, the surviving wounded were taken to a church. It was December twenty-ninth. Across the altar was a big banner that said 'Peace on Earth - Goodwill Towards Men'. My grandfather, who could read, said he would never forget that banner as long as he lived. He buried my grandmother's bullet-ridden body, took my mother home to her older brother, and then did something widowed Indians seldom do. He stayed widowed. He refused to marry again. He always said that had he sold Morning Wind to the white soldier she never would have died like that. The Ghost Dance War was the last major Indian uprising."

"That happened the same year William Jennings Bryan was first elected to Congress," John put in. "It was also the same year the Sherman Antitrust Act was passed. And on the day Gray Hawk buried his wife, the first ever Army-Navy football game was played."

"Yes," Coy said. "1890. A time when America was supposed to be civilized. Anyway, my grandfather hated the soldiers after she was killed. He and a few others danced the Ghost Dance in secret after that, even though it had been banned after the war."

David's brow puckered. "Ghost Dance? I've never heard of it. War Dance, and Rain Dance, but never Ghost Dance."

Coy, a faraway look in his eyes, began to explain. "A prophet—Messianic, if you want to call him that—from a western tribe, claimed the messiah was coming to the Indians. I'm sure there were several versions, but they were, in principle, the same. Of course, I grew up on my grandfather's personal version. Jesus the Christ had been mistreated by the White Man. So He would come back to earth as an Indian, and the Red Man would treat Him with all the respect He was due. He would make the Red Man strong again. The White race would gradually die out because he would be poisoned by the water and streams, air and land he was polluting, and would ultimately starve because he was killing game for pleasure and overgrazing the land. The Red Man would then once again be masters of the country that was theirs to begin with. The buffalo would come back, and the Sioux would once again be allowed to wash in the tears of the Great Spirit."

"The rivers and streams of the Black Hills, "John explained. "The Black Hills are sacred to the Sioux. And the Great White Father—Andrew Johnson this time—promised that as long as the sun rose and the grass grew, the Sioux could keep the *Paha-Sapa*, the Black Hills."

"What's one broken promise?" Coy asked.

I could only shake my head. "So your grandfather belonged to this religion?"

"Yes. He believed in it right up to the end. He thought the white men would consume themselves with greed."

"He may yet prove to be right," I said. "We're certainly polluting everything we touch."

"True," Coy agreed. "But my grandfather's bitterness consumed him. He raised me to hate the white man, to never trust him. See, my parents died when a scarlet fever epidemic swept through the reservation. I was about three-and-a-half. My uncle had already been killed in France, in the Great War. I never knew my grandmother or my uncle, and I don't remember my parents. All I had was an old brave named Gray Hawk. He taught me the ancient customs, rituals, chants, dances, so I would be prepared for the Messiah, this cross between Christ and Moses, when He came to free His people from the bondage of the White Man. Grandfather let me quit the reservation school when I was ten. I had gone for about five years, which is about average for an Indian on a reservation. Not too many whites were overly concerned about educating us. He let me run wild, like a deer. He said that is how the Indian should be—free as the game we used to hunt. I hunted deer and antelope and squirrel, in season or out, it didn't matter to me, and when there was no game I jumped the reservation and stole chickens from the white farmers. I was even known to take a calf or two." His face got a little red. He went on apologetically, "You must understand that I was raised to believe that it was perfectly all right, even necessary, to steal from the white man. because he had stolen so much from us."

"And we did, too," John said. "Everything from their land to their dignity."

"So then what happened?" David asked, still spellbound.

"Grandfather had his source of whiskey. Indians, for some reason, can't tolerate alcohol, even as well as the average white alcoholic. In fact, up until two years ago it was illegal for an Indian to have, or be sold, alcoholic beverages."

"I never realized," I said.

"Most people don't. I wish it were still illegal. Indians on the reservations can now drink themselves to death with the approval of the United States Congress. My grandfather drank himself to death before it was legal to do so. I was twelve when he died. I kept out of the way of the agent, the missionaries, the teachers. I took my grandfather's Ghost Shirt—I'll show it to you sometime; it's really a work of art—and I left the reservation whenever I wanted to. I roamed the *Paha-Sapa*, lived off the land more or less, just as I thought I was meant to. Then the Ransoms entered my picture."

"Actually, he entered our picture," John amended. "Dad and I were camping in the Black Hills—then off limits, by the way, to my friend here. Dad wanted to teach me some geology, so that was our excuse for the trip. Mom decided to stay home. She didn't like doing without the creature-comforts, like hot running-water or electricity."

"And she didn't like missing her soap operas on the radio," Coy broke in. "Our Gal Sunday, Helen Trent, Ma Perkins..."

John smiled. "Many was the time we would walk in on her just sobbing over one of the programs. Anyway, Dad and I pitched our tent far away from any modern conveniences. We roasted our meat over an open fire and cooked our beans in a pot set in the ashes. I thought it was great."

Coy laughed, "That's because you didn't *have* to live that way."

"True." John laughed also. "On this particular day a summer storm was brewing, and we were going to stay put. Storms in the mountains can be something. But a hiker had fallen, and the rangers knew where to find Dad, so he had to go. He told me to stay in camp and get dinner ready while he was gone. I offered to go with him but he told me he'd need his dinner more than he'd need me where fifty people were probably already there to get in his way.

"But I got bored. I went on a hike, not very far. I went to the edge of a bluff. Ever been to the Black Hills?"

David and I shook our heads.

116

"Well, they're not hills, but fairly high mountains. And I was so intent on watching an eagle circling its nest on the peak across from me that I got too near the edge of a cliff. The loose ground gave way under me, and I fell. I landed on a ledge some fifteen feet down. Below me was a straight drop of maybe three hundred feet.

"Then the storm kicked up in earnest. Nothing can quite compare to lightning in the mountains. It was bursting all around me. I was terrified, and on top of that I had broken my arm. There was no way I could climb back up, even if I had wanted to try.

"But then I saw a face peering at me from above. A boy about my age, with a dark face, long black hair, and thirty-two teeth. I saw them all, from flat on my back on the ledge. He was grinning like the proverbial Cheshire cat. I'll never forget the first words he said to me. 'White Boy in heap big trouble. Need help. Me riskum life if White Boy give plenty wampum.'"

I laughed. "You really didn't talk like that, did you, Coy?"

Coy gave a shame-faced grin, and John assured me, "Oh, Coy here could quote Shakespeare even then, education or no. But he would have his little jokes. Anyway, his face disappeared, and I thought I had imagined it. The skies picked that particular time to open, and I think they dumped most of their contents directly on me. On top of that I was starting to feel sick. Suddenly the end of a rope hit me in the face, and he slithered down it. There we were, the two of us, on that small ledge, with a death-drop inches away. Somehow Coy got us both up that cliff. I'll never know how, because when he first moved me a pain shot through my arm, and I passed out cold. I came to for a few moments. I was half lying across the neck of a pony, and my rescuer was sitting behind me, trying to keep me from falling."

"He started to squirm," Coy added, "so I put him back to sleep. One gentle crack to the back of the neck."

"Gentle my eye" John said. "I must have been out for the better part of an hour."

"You were lucky," Coy retorted. "I had to put up with your sagging weight, the heavy rain, a horse that wanted to bolt every time he heard a clap of thunder, and the dread that the White Boy would die of his injury or pneumonia or both and that I would get blamed. I wish I could have been out."

"Maybe I'll oblige you sometime," John told him sweetly. "Anyway, when I came to I was in a small room, neat and very clean. I was warm and dry. Sore and stiff, too, but at least I was safe. My eyes finally focused, and I found myself looking into the black eyes of the cutest little Indian girl I had ever seen. She was sitting on a chair by the bed. Her elbows were propped up on my pillow and her chin was in her hands.

"Her first words were, 'I thought you'd never wake up. And I'm s'posed to tell Mama when you do'. She scampered off then, and pretty soon a tall, slender woman came into the room, followed by my rescuer.

"He said, 'Ah, White Boy lives. Him lucky'. And the woman said, 'Coy, behave yourself. He's in enough agony as it is. He doesn't need some red-skinned ham tormenting him'.

"Coy grinned at me then. He had brought me to the house of Yellow Star. She had changed her name to Alice because she had read *Alice in Wonderland*, and she said she felt something like Alice in the White Man's world. Coy—Black Coyote was his tribal name—told me Yellow Star was a woman of medicine. I thought he meant that she was a nurse, but he told me she was better than a nurse. She was a woman of medicine.

"She made me drink an herb tea and some meat broth, then made me eat a special paste she had made from dried berries and nuts and something I didn't want to ask about. She had set my arm in a splint while I was still unconscious, and since it was my left arm—I'm left handed—she had to help me eat. Coy stood there watching and probably enjoying my helplessness, and all the while the little girl's eyes went from Coy to me to Coy again, those snapping black eyes."

John paused here to give Coy a significant look. Coy smiled ruefully.

"I see Coy has nothing to add at this point, so I'll say here that the little girl introduced herself as Mary and confided that she was going to marry Black Coyote when she grew up."

I looked at Coy, who was getting red at the throat. "And has she grown up?" I asked.

Coy cleared his throat. "She was seven at the time. A mere child."

"She's twenty-five now, and still single," John answered.

Coy squirmed. "She was a kid. She had a crush."

"I don't know about that. All I know is that when you and Alice left and Mary sat down to keep her vigil over me, she told me she'd love Black Coyote till the day she died."

"That was eighteen years ago," Coy protested. "Besides, if she said that to you in confidence you shouldn't have repeated it."

"She said it to the Indian agent, the policeman, and the outraged farmer who caught you stealing his chickens."

John turned to me. "You should have seen it! Dad had discovered where I was and came to fetch me. He was very impressed with Alice's work. Coy had already disappeared, and Alice told us she had known him for years; that he was like the wind, coming and going and blowing hot and cold, however he pleased.

"After a few days of Alice's tender care I was released into the not-so-gentle ministrations of my father (I had disobeyed him, after all) and we went off to find, or try to find, Black Coyote. Word drifted to us that an Indian boy had been caught stealing chickens. We went to a crude jail, and there he was. Tall, defiant, and putting on his best Indian act, pretending he knew very little English, and speaking mostly in Lakota.

"Dad stepped forward and offered to pay for the chickens. The farmer wanted more than those scrawny chickens were worth, but Dad paid for them anyway, and for Coy's freedom, too. The police chief wasn't at first willing to let Coy go. It seems he was on the Ten-Most-Wanted-From-The-Reservation list. But the illustrious chief wasn't beyond bribery, and Coy was freed. Dad chased everyone else out of the jailhouse, then walked up to Coy and said, 'Well, my boy. It seems we have bought you. What do you suggest we do with you?'

"Coy, in Indian sign language, told my father to let him go in peace to the *Paha Sapa*, so he could once more hunt the mighty game. Then Dad, also in Indian sign, told Coy something to the effect that if he considered skinny chickens mighty game then the future of the Sioux Nation was in serious jeopardy." John laughed. "That is the one and only time I've seen Coy completely stunned. But he recovered and said, "*Wakan Tanka* give back hunting ground to Sioux. Many buffalo will come, and Sioux and Cheyenne will once more be free to roam land'. Dad said he hoped so, but meantime maybe Black Coyote would like to live with us and roam Ransom Creek. Alice had told us that his folks were dead and that he had no family left."

"What is the *Wakan Tanka*?" David asked.

"The Sioux name for the creator and controller of the universe," Coy answered.

"What did Coy think about living with you?" David wanted to know.

John extended his arm, and said in what was a fairly good imitation of Coy, "Gray Hawk and Morning Wind and Howling Coyote all crossed Sky Trail (their name for the Milky Way) and gone to Happy Hunting Ground. Biting Bear killed in Great War. Black Coyote can take care of Black Coyote."

Coy laughed. "Not bad, Johnny." Then he turned to David, who was thoroughly and completely engrossed, and said, "Then Dad told me, 'Black Coyote heap big hunter. Get caught stealing skinny chickens'. I was caught and knew it. It took some doing, but Dad finally got me off the reservation—cut through a lot of red tape…" (I chuckled at that.) "…and brought me to his ranch."

"We got him enrolled in school," John continued. "At first some of the people here didn't approve."

"Some still don't," Coy broke in, and I thought of Slim Rhodes.

But everything finally settled down to near normal. I learned that though he hadn't gone to school for a while, Coy had read extensively. Dad told him he needed an education to help his race, that the Sioux Nation needed some healthy and intelligent young blood. Coy adopted the name Youngblood."

"What did your mother have to say about all of this?" I asked John.

"She was pleased. Said I had needed a brother for a long time. And Dad needed more help on the ranch. See, part of the ranch was handed down to Dad, but part of it had been in Mom's family. Together they had nearly 400 sections. With Dad being a doctor, he had to rely on farm hands to do most of the work on the place. Mom left her share—130 sections—to Coy."

"Talk about the coyote among the chickens," Coy said. "An Indian owning land. Good land. There are still a few smarting over that one."

"It was your land to begin with," John told him. "So we thought it was only fair. Besides, Mom believed in poetic justice." He turned back to David and me. "See, it's rather complicated, but after the Civil War, a number of ex-Confederate soldiers who had fought under Lee came west to find a corner where they would not be harassed by Reconstruction. This is where they ended up, and that's how Lee's Corner got its name. But a northerner by the name of Jeremy Ransom had also moved here. He named this creek, and a little town to the north. It's not much, mainly a small post office and a general store. When my mother, a Calhoun and a direct descendent of John C. Calhoun, married my father, her father disinherited her. He was a hater—he hated northerners, Indians, Catholics, Jews, Mormons, Quakers, Eastern Europeans. But Mom didn't have any siblings, so when her father died all his land went to his younger brother, who never married. He left my mother the land she should have gotten in the first place. So she left it to Coy." He grinned at me. "She had a peculiar sense of humor, and I bet she's up in heaven having herself a good laugh. She used to call certain people around here bigots. She was never one to pull any punches."

"Mendacious, conniving bigots," Coy amended. "I'll never forget when Mom and Dad went to court to make me their legal ward. I thought it was going to be Wounded Knee all over again. She rounded on Scooter Mathieson like *Iya*—what my people call a cyclone—when he told the packed courtroom that the Ransoms were taking in a dirty Indian while decent white folks were going hungry, She called him a...er...a...well, never mind what she called him. It made 'mendacious, conniving bigot' sound like a compliment."

"I've heard of Scooter Mathieson," I said. "Marty says he hangs around the sheriff quite a bit. Not that Marty came right out and said anything, but I could tell she doesn't care much for the two of them. Doesn't Scooter Mathieson work?"

"Hardly ever," John answered. "He and Carter have been as thick as thieves—and that could be literal—ever since Harley Stone had a stroke and Carter, through somebody's gross negligence, was named as acting sheriff. A few of us are watching that situation until the special election. I can almost guarantee that

Carter won't get voted into office. Most people around here don't cotton much to him."

"He does have his following," Coy said. "Most everybody who has ever resented my being here is backing him."

"That's not enough, though, "John said. "Jeb Truman is a decent, honest fellow, conscientious, likable, a fine Christian. He'll win by a landslide."

"Jeb is the young deputy." I remembered.

John nodded. "Friend of the family, a cousin of Marty's, member of our church."

"Single," Coy added. "You left that out."

"So I did," John admitted.

David, though, wasn't interested in politics or other dark, devious innuendoes floating through our conversation. "What happened to Alice and Mary Star?" he asked.

"Alice has been battling cancer for some time now," John answered, his quiet voice holding a hint of sadness. "This could well be her last winter. Mary wanted to take care of her full-time—she finished nursing school two years ago—but Alice insisted she was needed more on the reservation. So Mary is working for a doctor, a Sioux, on the reservation. He has a fairly large practice, including some whites. And he," John finished, "is also single. By the way, Coy, when was the last time you saw Mary?"

Coy pulled at his collar. I'm sure it was an unconscious gesture. "I went to visit Alice two weeks ago, while you were on vacation."

"Yes, you told me you went to visit her when you went to buy that roan mare."

Coy pulled at his collar again. "Mary was there, too," he mumbled.

"Imagine you leaving that out," John said. "And how is our little Mary?"

"Five feet ten in her stocking feet. That's how 'our little Mary' is. I think it's time to go home."

John looked at his watch, and rose immediately. "Yes, it is. I didn't know it was so late. I guess I was too comfortable and the company too good." He smiled at David. "Besides, Indians don't like to be outside after midnight. The *Wakan Tanka*," he explained, "wouldn't be able to find him if he should...er...expire in the dark."

"You just might expire in the dark," Coy said to John.

David was looking from one to the other. "Is that true?" he asked Coy, "about Indians?"

"Only about Apaches," Coy answered straight-faced. "The Sioux aren't afraid of the dark. Or anything else."

"Except five foot ten Indian maidens," John said.

Coy pulled him out the door. I waved good-bye, and they shouted their thanks even though they had thanked me often throughout the din-supper. Then, as the pickup backed up, turned, and sped on its way, I shut the door and turned to my little brother. "Well, David my love, it seems our neighbors have taken to you, and vice-versa."

"I think they're terrific!" David said enthusiastically. "Don't you think they're terrific?"

"A very interesting pair. And don't go believing everything they said. Half the time they had their tongues in their cheeks."

"What does that mean?"

"That they were teasing us. Having a little fun with the greenhorns. Ghost Dances indeed! A trip up the Milky Way. Tears of the *Wakan Tanka*. Coy was probably making it up as he went along."

A sad tale's best for winter.
—Shakespeare

Chapter 9

Our guests had stayed until midnight. I had gone through a few difficult moments but had come out more or less unscathed, and ended up actually enjoying the evening when I wasn't remembering who John Ransom was or who my father had been...

Mr. Ransom, gentleman that he was, didn't press the invitation to din-supper, for which I was grateful. But they did ask if David and I would like to go to church with them. I refused, of course, but David said he'd like to try it. It was David's life, I told myself, and I had to let David lead it.

So Sunday came, and they picked David up at the house in the Cadillac and drove off down the snowy road and eventually disappeared into the hills.

It was after two o'clock when they got back. I heard the door on the screened porch slam and I ran to the kitchen. David was stomping the snow from his boots. John Ransom was with him. They both shed their outer clothing and came into the warmth of the kitchen.

"We took him to dinner in Bridgeport," Mr. Ransom explained. "I hope you don't mind."

"Of course not, Mr. Ransom. Please come in and warm yourself." An unnecessary invitation, since he was in the process of doing just that. "Would you care for some coffee or tea?"

"Coffee, thanks. It's nine degrees outside. We dropped Coy off on the way here. He's checking the spread."

"In this weather?" I asked.

"Especially in this weather. We don't want to lose any of our cows. They're going to have calves in a few months, so we need to keep them content and fed. Today it's Coy's turn to check up on everybody."

"Everybody?"

"Our ranch hands," he explained. "We have them spread out in their own homes all over these hills. A lot of them are Indians. They like the freedom. It beats being stuck on a reservation. Each hand is responsible for ten sections. Today Coy is responsible for each hand."

I was making the coffee. David had disappeared up the stairs, and I wondered what he was doing.

I knew what John Ransom was doing; he was making himself right at home. He pulled out a chair and sat at the kitchen table...and watched me.

"You must have quite a lot of cattle," I said without thinking, then winced. That could be construed as a bit personal.

"Quite a lot," he answered.

I filled a cup and took it to him. I needed to say something. David had told me about Samuel Ransom, and John would expect me to say something, I'm sure. We had gone through an entire Thanksgiving meal without mentioning his death. It was almost like a forbidden subject. But I couldn't avoid the subject forever, and Mr. Ransom might think it a bit odd, if not downright callous, if I didn't mention his father now. So I plunged into waters I was afraid might prove to be too deep, but only because I felt I had to.

"David...told me about the death of your father. He said your...loss...was very recent. He told me Thursday but said you didn't want anyone to know, so I didn't mention it. I was hoping that maybe the din-supper might have taken your mind off your bereavement, even for a short while. But now everyone must have heard, so I want to tell you I am very sorry." I didn't add: you'll never know how sorry.

There. I had said it. I had actually brought up Dr. Samuel Ransom. I stole a glance at my uninvited guest. He was looking into the deep, dark liquid in his cup.

He said, without looking up, "Dad was a terrific guy. He will be missed." Then he looked at me. "He was killed in an automobile accident, you know. My brother was with him. Rick wants to be a doctor too, and he often went with Dad on his calls if there were no school the next day."

I went to the sink. I had to do something. Had he told David it was an auto accident I wondered? I started peeling the potatoes I would boil for din-supper. I thought, irrelevantly, that I would never get used to calling the evening meal supper. Supper was something one had at midnight, after a show or concert. Dinner was what one ate at six o'clock in the evening, not at noon. Well, at least they got breakfast right.

John had quit speaking. I turned and stole a quick glance at him. He was pulling the cream pitcher towards himself. It was empty.

"Here, I'll get you some," I said.

"No, don't bother. I can drink it black."

"Nonsense. If you can take David out to eat, I can surely swing a little cream for your coffee."

I took it to him, and he poured some into his cup. Then, not particularly wanting to offend him by going back to the potatoes, I sat down across from him and put my hands in my lap.

I watched him stir the coffee, now a few shades lighter. He was a little pale also. "The cars caught on fire," he went on, but I think he forgot I was there. He was going over again, what had happened two weeks before on a deserted Chicago street. He must have relived the horror so many times. I know I had. I always would. It was there, in front of me every waking moment. I glanced down at my hands. Yes, every waking moment. And when I slept, the horrible nightmares, frightening in their realism.

"Rick was inside," he was saying, and I brought myself back to the cozy little kitchen. "He would have died too. Then someone came along and pulled him out. We never found out who it was. All Rick could tell us was that it was a beautiful woman in a green coat. She saved his life." He smiled a little. "If I didn't know Rick better I'd say he was imagining things. Especially since no one came forward. But if Rick said a beautiful woman pulled him out of the burning car, then a beautiful woman pulled him out of the car…"

I started to shake, at least inwardly. When Rick came home would he recognize me? Surely not! It had been traumatic, and after more than six months he wouldn't remember…Not like I

127

remembered. I was seeing it again: the cars, the blood, the boy whose coat was being consumed by flames…I could have had this boy's death on my conscience as well. I cleared my throat and said, "Please believe me when I say how terribly sorry I am—about everything."

He looked at me. A corner of his mouth went up. "I believe you."

I waited, for bitterness or anger or even hate to come to the surface. but it didn't. It hadn't Thursday, either. Whatever John Ransom was feeling about the death of his father, it wasn't any of those emotions.

I was beginning to wonder, in the uncomfortable silence, where my little brother was. I could certainly have used him to fill the long voids in the conversation I was, and wasn't, having with John Ransom.

"I can't imagine what's keeping David," I said finally.

"Oh, he's probably upstairs taking a nap. He wanted to go back to church with us tonight. With your permission, of course."

"Oh. Oh, I see. I thought…" I stopped, and felt the betraying crimson creep up my face.

John Ransom's eyes started dancing. "That he left us alone on purpose again," he finished.

I felt the color drain suddenly. "That's not what I was going to say," I said lamely.

"Little liar," he said without heat.

I glanced at him, then down at my hands. They were lying motionless in my lap, the swollen fingers with the ugly red scars and white blotches where dead skin would never come back to life. I almost wished for the bandages again.

"I loved my father very much," John Ransom said finally, breaking into my thoughts, "and I'm going to miss him. But God doesn't make mistakes. For some reason I can't even begin to fathom, it was time for Dad to go home. Dad's death had a purpose, and that's why I haven't questioned it. I'm comforted by the knowledge that Dad is much better off where he is. You see, Lu, death's not the end, it's the beginning, if you're a Christian."

I got up and went to the window that looked out at the barn. "I'm glad you have that comfort."

"Yes. I sleep well at night." He got up and came to stand behind me. "But enough about Dad's death. I'd like to tell you sometime about his life, if you'll let me. For now, though, I've got chores to do."

"I'll get your coat." I turned. John stood there for a moment, looking at me. then he stepped aside, and the uneasy moment was over.

As he was pulling on his cashmere overcoat I thanked him once again for taking David to church.

"You're quite welcome. Tell him we'll pick him up at six thirty tonight. That is, if it's all right with you."

"Sure," I said lightly. "Why not? If he wants to go."

John grinned. "Oh, he wants to go. Six-thirty. Sharp!"

~~~~~~~~~~

David got home at about ten thirty that night full of the wonderful things the kids did at church. After the service someone opened the high school gym. One of the mothers had made doughnuts; another mother brought punch. They played a rough and ready game of basketball, and because David couldn't participate they let him referee. Then they played charades, which David thoroughly enjoyed, and when the ping pong table was set up David managed to play a credible game. "Because I don't really have to move around that much," he explained.

He went on to tell me that Johnny and Coy were among the chaperones, and I somehow got the feeling that they had set the whole thing up for David's benefit.

But while I was grateful for their evident interest in my brother, I questioned their motives and was apprehensive about the final results. I didn't want them to become so enmeshed in David's life that I would get tangled up, too. If it had only been anyone else. But no, it had to be John Ransom. And if he found out about the accident...Oh, he might make fine speeches about how his father is better off where he is, but I thought that if Mr. Ransom were ever to come face to face with the person who could have prevented the accident, recriminations would be heaped, and the life I was trying to build for David would crumble. We would be left worse off than we would have been had we stayed in Chicago.

I went to work that Monday morning after a rather restless night. I was full of apprehension, about the past, which might catch up with me, and about the future if it did.

But Pete Jones fully intended to take care of my present. He kept me busy all through the breakfast rush hour, and it wasn't until nearly ten o'clock that I was able to take a break.

I wore lightweight cotton gloves under yellow rubber ones to hide as well as protect my hands. They were a little bulky but I knew that in time I would get used to them.

I pulled them off now as I sat down in a little booth with a cup of tea. Pete came out with a plate and said gruffly, "Veal cutlet. I forgot to tell you that you get one free meal. But it's got to be whatever I have the most of."

"Veal cutlet sounds wonderful."

He handed me the plate then said, "Eat it out front at one of the tables by the window. I want everyone to get a good look at my pretty new waitress."

"Oh, I... oh," I stammered. "Really, oh, thank you, Mr. Jones." I knew I was blushing furiously. "What can I say?"

"Call me Pete," he said gruffly. "And don't go thankin' me fer tellin' the truth. It ain't no coincidence that I had one of the biggest crowds here today that I've ever had. No coincidence atall. Didn't you notice them fellers come in all clean and shaved as though they hadn't been up workin' since dawn?"

"Oh, well, I'm really not used to...I mean, oh Pete! What can I say? Everyone was a perfect gentleman."

"Which is another thing," he said, "'cause most of 'em ain't. They jist put on their Sunday manners for the new gal in town."

I sighed. I wondered if I would ever get used to living in a small town.

I took my lunch, or rather "dinner," to a quiet booth near the front and was enjoying it heartily when a shadow fell across the table. I looked up.

"May I join you?" John Ransom asked, then proceeded to do just that.

"Well, I'm still working. Technically." I tried to sound discouraging.

"Oh, don't bother about Pete. He never worries much about technicalities."

"Then by all means, Mr. Ransom, please join me." A moot statement, since he was already seated.

Pete bustled out with a cup of coffee. "Nice to see you, Johnny."

John smiled at him. "I just saw you yesterday, Pete. You know, at church, but then you were sleeping, so maybe you didn't see me."

Pete glanced at me in embarrassment, "I wasn't sleepin.' I was prayin'."

"Oh? Well, I'm afraid your snores may have drowned out your prayers, so you'd better repeat them."

Pete turned beet-red and bristled. "Now, Johnny, I was goin' to church 'fore you was born. Every Sunday, Sunday night, Wednesday night."

John laughed. "So I guess you're entitled to get tired of it every once in a while. Only do me a favor. Sit on the other side, next time. Way in the back. That way I'll at least be able to hear the choir."

Pete grinned at that. "You really want to hear the choir, Johnny? Our choir?"

"You've got a point. What's good for dessert?"

"Everything," Pete said simply. "How about some pumpkin pie?"

John looked up at him. "Did you slice it?"

Pete looked puzzled. "Sure I did."

"Then I'll have some."

Pete frowned and shrugged then went off for the pie.

I went on eating. Mr. Ransom had joined me uninvited, so he could start the conversation.

Instead, he leaned back against the booth, folded his arms behind his head, and watched me. The ugly scars on my hands seemed to loom large in front of me.

I finally said, "Did you want anything in particular, Mr. Ransom?"

"Please, call me John. Or Johnny. And yes. I wanted a piece of pumpkin pie. Something that through no fault of my own was denied me on Thanksgiving day."

"If that's all, I can have Pete wrap it up and send it home with you."

"Pretty, and thoughtful too," he said. "No, I'll eat it here. I wanted to ask you for a favor."

"Sure," I said with a little asperity. "How much do you need?"

He laughed outright at that. "How much of your time, do you mean? A few hours, at least. I would like you—and David, of course—to attend Friday night's basketball game with me."

I wiped my lips with my napkin, then replied, "I'm terribly sorry, but I—and David, of course—have other plans."

"Oh," he said, "I'm sorry to hear that. I thought you might enjoy the game."

I stood and picked up my plate. "I intend to," I told him firmly. "Is there anything else I can do for you?"

He smiled. "Offhand, I can think of several things. But for the present, you might keep that...er...Alpine Sheepdog of yours away from our cattle. He spooks them, and that's not really good for expectant mothers."

"I'll tell David," I promised. "We'll keep him at home. You'd think he would find enough to do on our hundred and sixty acres."

"Oh, I don't know," John Ransom said. "It's not all that much room, after all. But if you can keep him from running our cows into a frenzy I would be most obliged."

"I will. Now if you'll excuse me..."

He stood, as I left the table and made for the nether regions of the diner. He was Pete's customer. Let Pete take care of him.

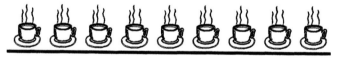

I worked hard that week. Business was brisk and I made adequate money. Tips were better than I thought they would be, and the hours, once I could get used to them, were much better than the hours I kept at Little Italy.

Pete's other waitress was Carol McFarland, a good-natured, middle-aged lady whose kids were grown and, as she put it, "flown." Her shift started at eleven when business began to pick up for dinner, and she worked until Pete closed at seven p.m. then mopped before going home. I could leave at two p.m. which gave me a nice long afternoon and evening to myself.

Monday after work I went to see Marty Maguire, who had finally returned from the Nottleman place. And Tuesday I dropped in on Mrs. Lassiter. Her son was there, and I played some slower Chopin pieces which they both seemed to enjoy.

David went back to church on Wednesday night and I used the time to catch up with my reading.

On Thursday afternoon, just as I was leaving the diner, a man who could have passed for a leprechaun walked in. His clothing as well as his general manner announced him as the parish priest.

Pete came out smiling to greet him personally.

"I didn't come here to see you, Pete," he said. "I have come to meet the lassie."

The door had already closed behind me when Pete called me back. He introduced me to the priest with all the pride he might have had in a well-behaved puppy.

Arm around me, he propelled me forward. "This is Lu Morrow, Father. Lu, meet Father O'Brien." And he literally beamed.

The priest took my hand, to shake it. My woolen mittens were on, so he didn't see. He squeezed hard, and I winced. He dropped it immediately, and said, "Oh, I'm sorry, lass. I knew you had cut your hands, or burned them, but I forgot."

"You...forgot?"

"Well, yes. You know how it is in a small town. One hears things, and when a new person moves here...I mean, most people who move around here are movin' out. So, what really did you do to your hands."

I must have gaped at him for a full five seconds. Then I gathered my wits and answered without inflection, "I burned them trying to fix our oven."

"In St. Louis?"

"That's where I'm from."

He searched my face, for what I don't know. "I see," was all he said. "Well, I'm from County Cork. But I haven't been home for years. Not since before the War. The Second one. I suppose Ireland's changed."

"I believe everything does," I said, just to be saying something.

"Even St. Louis. I couldn't understand them letting the Browns go. And without a struggle."

I searched frantically through my brain. The Browns? Who on earth were the Browns?

"Moved to Baltimore, they did, and call themselves the Orioles now," he told Pete. "Imagine. Naming a team after a little bitty bird."

Oh, I thought, the American League. I felt like a pure ignoramus. I wanted to tell them that Ernie Banks had hit forty-four homeruns this season including five grand-slams for a new major league record. "Well," I said, trying to fortify my position of having come from St. Louis, "the Cardinals are named for a little bird, and they were outdrawing them."

The priest shook his head. "I know, lass, I know. No one seems to know the meanin' of the word loyalty any more. But I didn't come here to talk about baseball. I wanted to see the new gal in town who has most of the single men here in a tizzy—even Sean McMichaels, and he's going into the priesthood." He looked at me, and added, "Maybe."

I turned scarlet, and Pete said to the priest, "She don't like compliments, Father. Why, she doesn't even notice them guys makin' sheep eyes at her all through breakfast and dinner."

He laughed. "Fair enough. No more compliments. I just wanted to tell her that we have an organ and anytime she would like to practice on it she's welcome." He turned to me. "The church is over by Marty's, and it's never locked. Just make yourself at home any time." He searched my face again, and finally asked, "You're not by any chance Catholic, are you?"

I shook my head. "No. I'm afraid not. My grandparents were good Catholics, but I guess I've strayed from the faith."

"Would you like to come back?"

I smiled. "I don't think so. But thanks for asking."

He smiled back. "Well, we allow Protestants to play the organ, too."

I didn't tell him that I didn't consider myself a Protestant either. I just excused myself and went home. Napoleon had broken loose again and met me clear at the end of the drive.

*The difference between
perseverance and obstinacy is,
that one often comes from a strong will,
and the other from a strong won't.*
—Henry Ward Beecher

Chapter 10

When I said I expected to enjoy Friday night's basketball game I could never have guessed what was in store for me. David said he needed to get to school early, and that Cody Forrest would pick him up. Cody was the center, David explained.

So David left, and I was alone in the house when Mr. Stoker picked me up for our date. He had asked me that first Tuesday when I drove David to school, and now I was thankful he had.

"David went early," I told him as we were leaving. "I wonder why?"

Lance Stoker smiled. "He has a bit of a surprise for you," he said. "I think you'll be pleased."

So we went to the gymnasium and I tried to ignore the stares and knowing looks we received as we made our way to the top of the bleachers.

Mr. Stoker's presence seemed to put a damper on the enthusiasm displayed by those of the student body who were seated in our immediate vicinity. Gradually most of them moved, and adults, whose enthusiasm was of a less demonstrative kind, took their places.

The principal was not unaware of the damping effect he had on the raucous behavior of some of the students. "It's the home opener," he explained. "For some reason a lot of the students think it's a reason for acting like wild animals."

"Oh, I see. Well, I don't think they're behaving too badly."

Mr. Stoker grinned. "Not at the moment anyway."

The cheerleaders were running around the floor doing cartwheels and yelling, and the band struck up a few notes. Then it began playing in earnest, and the crowd rose to its feet in unison and began singing what I thought must be the school song. Then someone led the Pledge of Allegiance, and Father O'Brien said a short prayer. No sooner had he said his 'Amen' than the crowd started making wild noises again.

We sat back down. Mr. Stoker asked me if I wanted anything to eat or drink, but I told him I didn't, so we settled down to what conversation we could manage amidst the roar of the crowd. I kept wondering where David was. I noticed a tall, thin girl wearing the leg braces that so often identified polio victims. I turned to Mr. Stoker, and he nodded.

"Yes, that's Karen. Shall I invite her up here?"

"No," I said too quickly. "I mean, I don't want her to climb all the way up here. I can meet her later." I watched her laughing with other students. Large round glasses accentuated the thinness of her face. Her hair was long and sandy-colored; it was the only attractive thing about her. Her arms like her face were too thin and decorated with an abundance of freckles. I was tempted to feel pity, but she didn't seem to feel any for herself. On the contrary she seemed to be enjoying her friends, and if they were conscious of her handicap they hid it very well.

Finally the captain of the cheerleading squad went up to the microphone that was set up on the gym floor. She tapped it a few times. The crowd immediately became silent.

"Welcome to the home opener," she said. Her voice blasted through the gym. Someone stepped up and turned the volume down a shade or two.

The girl giggled. "Welcome to the home opener," she repeated. "Tonight we are hosting the Lions of Appleton Crossing." She then proceeded to name the players, who ran out as she did so. There was general applause from both sides of the gym floor.

136

Then she announced, "And now I would like to introduce the Lee's Corner Bulldogs." A roar shook the rafters. "At center, Cody Forrest."

A tall, lean young man ran out to the center of the court. The applause was thunderous.

"At guard, Danny Mercer."

Another boy ran out on the court and stood beside Cody Forrest. There was more applause.

She went on to announce Roy Parnell, the forward, the other guard, Denny Mercer, who was the exact copy of his twin brother. The other forward was Billy Parnell, Roy's younger brother. As I watched these fine, healthy young men, in uniform from their crew-cuts down, I felt a pang that David could never be part of this group. But he was making friends with them, and I was grateful for that. Thus I was lost in my own thoughts as she named off the second string players and paused briefly.

"And our trainer, David Morrow."

I came back to the gymnasium with a start. I gasped, and turned to Mr. Stoker. He was grinning.

David came out and stood with the players. There was more applause. Someone from the stands yelled, "Where's Napoleon?", and David laughed.

"And finally, our coach, Mr. Wayne Voyle," the cheerleader concluded.

A tall, loose-limbed young man walked out and stood beside David. He was obviously very popular. The roar of the crowd was deafening.

Then finally everyone settled down and the game began. As much as I always liked basketball, tonight I spent most of the time watching my little brother. The disease that kept him from participating in sports was not interfering in his obvious enjoyment of being team manager, ready with water, towels, and anything else the players needed. He was also available for anything the coach needed, and he worked hard that night. I've never seen David happier.

It was about midway through the first quarter when I saw John Ransom. He had come into the gym and was looking over the crowd. For whom? I wondered with dread. I turned away so all he could see was the back of my head, but finally he spotted me. As he made his way up the rows of bleachers, it amazed me how the seated fans cheerfully moved a little left or right to make a path for him. Most of them spoke a word or two and he responded in kind with a laugh or a smile or an answer to a question. But at last he arrived at the top.

"Evening, Miss Morrow. Lance," he said. "Is there room for me?"

Lance and I moved over, and John took the space beside me. He leaned over me and said to my companion, "How come Harry didn't start?"

"He came down with the measles yesterday," Lance answered.

"Oh, brother. That means the whole family will probably get them." To me, he explained, "Harry Fitzpatrick is one of the forwards. He is the oldest of eight children."

And to Lance, he said, "Billy Parnell is doing a credible job, though." Then he looked back at me. "Billy is only a freshman."

I heard him, but I was paying more attention to the interested glances we were getting—all three of us—at the top of the bleachers.

The game was an exciting one, and I was determined to enjoy it. And I was also determined to enjoy myself with Mr. Lance Stoker. Most of my comments were directed towards him, and if John Ransom chose to think I was ignoring him, that was his affair.

Mr. Stoker didn't particularly want to ignore him though, and spoke often to him over the course of the game. I was to learn later that they were good friends. At half-time, Mr. Stoker went to get us pop and popcorn, and I was left with John Ransom.

But not for long. Soon the little priest joined us. I made such a point of welcoming him that he asked me again if I was sure I wasn't Catholic.

"So, how have you been, Father O'Brien?" John asked politely.

He rubbed his hands together. "Fine, fine. No need to ask how you're doing. Of all the young bucks, you're the one who gets to squire the prettiest girl in town to the first home basketball game."

I felt myself turning bright red.

John said easily, "Not quite. I did ask her, but I was a little late. She's here with Lance."

The priest's eyes twinkled. "Ah. I see. And you, Johnny, of course you couldn't find any other place to sit."

"No, I couldn't," he grinned.

"Not that you tried overmuch." He looked at me. "So how do you like sitting between the two best-looking bachelors in the county?"

I smiled at him. "But I'm not sitting by you, Father," I said.

At that, he burst into laughter. "What a diplomat you are, lass. And what a comeback. Well, here comes Lance. What do they say, Four's a crowd? Hello, Lance."

"Hello, Father. Enjoying the game?"

"I'd enjoy it more if I had a...er...better seat. But all the ones up here are taken. So I better go back to the Forrests. They're savin' my seat for me. But I would much rather be up here." And he winked at me.

"What was that all about?" Lance asked after the priest left.

"You know how we Irish are," John answered. "Everything is high drama."

So we watched the second half, and I stayed crushed between the two men. Once Lance had to go and quiet some young fans who were getting a little too rowdy, and once he had to quell an argument. On those two occasions I was left with John Ransom, and on neither occasion did I have anything to say. He didn't either. Once I gave him a quick glance, and caught him absorbed in some thought of his own. Then I remembered his recent loss, and wondered if he were thinking about the accident, about Chicago. There was a slight frown on his brow, and he seemed to be somewhere other than at a noisy, crowded basketball game.

After the game a very excited David sought me out and grabbed my arm. "Excuse us, Mr. Stoker," he said, "but I'd like Sis to meet a few of my friends."

So Mr. Stoker said he had to make sure everyone's exit from the auditorium was without incident, and I was left hurrying in my brother's wake.

That night I met the entire team, save Harry Fitzpatrick, along with their parents, and learned how popular my brother had become in just a short while. Of course the article in last week's

Kincaid County Chronicle about him and Napoleon didn't hurt him.

But it was with mixed emotions that I watched how rapidly he was becoming involved in the life of this little town. His picture would be in the paper again, this time accompanying an article about the team. It seemed that the more I wanted us to be away from the limelight, the more the limelight sought us out.

Then, when we were looking for Lance Stoker, David asked, "Did you see Johnny?"

"Why, yes, as a matter of fact I did get a glimpse or two of him tonight. Why?"

"Well, I need to thank him."

I opened my eyes wide. "Thank him? For what?"

"Well, he's the one who talked to the coach about letting me be manager."

"Did Mr. Ransom tell you that?"

"Gosh, no. I don't think I'm really supposed to know. But Danny Mercer—or was it Denny, they look exactly alike—told me he overheard Johnny ask Coach to think about some way I could get involved with the team, and the two of them came up with this. And I get a varsity letter just like the players!"

I took a deep breath. "He's around here somewhere, I think. Thank him if you feel you must, but I think that since he didn't tell you himself but apparently wanted to keep it a secret, you might embarrass him by thanking him."

"Well, I think I should thank him, Sis. That was awfully nice for him to bother."

I thought so, myself. If, that is, he didn't have any ulterior motives.

Then Lance Stoker came up to me and asked if I would like to go out for a hamburger.

"In Lee's Corner?" I asked. "I didn't think there was a hamburger joint within miles of here."

"There isn't. There's a good one in Scottsbluff, though."

I was just about to refuse with the excuse that I had to work on the following day when David came up to us, and I said to him, "You had better get home. We both have a busy day tomorrow."

His face fell.

"What's wrong?" I asked.

140

"The kids all go to the Burger Barn in Scottsbluff whenever they win a home game on a Friday night," he said in one breath.

We were standing outside. I looked up at the stars. "Who's driving?"

"Well, Sally Maples, the captain of the cheerleading squad. And Danny Mercer or Denny, anyway, one of the twins. And Jonathan Tindle, he's president of the student body. And Sharon Lassiter, she has her own car. She's vice president of the Junior class. And Miss Lynch, she's the librarian and the sponsor of the Student Council. And Coach Voyle..."

"Okay, okay. The whole school's going I take it," so I gave him a dollar and told him he could go, and he gave me a big hug and was off.

Mr. Stoker looked at me. "We don't have to go to the Burger Barn. There are other places in Scottsbluff."

I was really a bit tired. "I don't mean this to sound coy, but why don't you come to my place for some coffee and home-made sweet potato pie. I would love to go to Scottsbluff, but I have to be at work at six o'clock in the morning, and even if we left this instant," and I looked at my watch, "we wouldn't get back until well after midnight."

"Sweet potato pie sounds wonderful. I haven't had any for quite a while."

So we went to my little house in the country and Lance Stoker had a piece of sweet potato pie and two cups of coffee, and we sat and talked until the clock on the wall in the parlor chimed eleven o'clock. He left, reluctantly, and I went in to wash the dishes.

When I heard the knock on the front door I wondered how David could be back so soon. I had lived so long in the seamier part of Chicago that I automatically locked the doors even though I had discovered that the people out here seldom did.

But when I opened the door, John Ransom stood there.

"I met Lance on my way home and thought you might still be up," he said without preamble.

"I'm still up. But not for long."

He didn't take the not-too-subtle hint. "I thought I might keep you company until David comes home."

"Thank you. You're very kind. But I have to get up early."

He looked down at me and grinned. "You can't make me believe you'll get any sleep before David gets home." It was true. This was the first time David had gone anywhere with a bunch of kids, and I wouldn't be able to rest until he got back. So I opened the door wider and allowed John Ransom to come in.

He went straight to the easy chair that stood on one side of the oil-burning stove. I watched helplessly as he seemed to settle in for the duration.

"Would you like a piece of sweet potato pie?" I asked. It sounded grudging, even to my ears.

"Yes, that would be very nice."

I cut him a piece, and took it to him with a cup of coffee, with cream, then sat opposite him in my comfortable rocking chair.

He smiled at me and made some complimentary remark about the pie, but I wasn't paying much attention to what he was saying. My thoughts were in turmoil.

Finally I blurted out, "Why are you here?"

One eyebrow raised fractionally. "To keep you company until David gets home," he answered. "And to find out how you enjoyed the game."

"I enjoyed it very much, thank you. And I know how tired you must be. David is not your responsibility and you must not feel you need to wait up for him."

"I'm not in the least tired. And my motives are mostly pure. I thought, with Coy at the north ranch and David in Scottsbluff and Lance on his way back to town that you and I might take this opportunity to get to know one another better. After all, I am your nearest neighbor. And you are my nearest neighbor."

He would be suspicious if I were rude. After all, he hadn't done anything to deserve it. On the other hand, why would he want to pursue a friendship? I hadn't done anything to deserve that.

So it was with the intention of keeping the conversation impersonal that I said, "I thoroughly enjoyed the basketball game. The gymnasium is quite large for such a small school."

"It is, isn't it. And the school is very well-equipped. And the town is nice too, and the people are wonderful." His eyes mirrored the smile in his voice. "Come on, Lu, I didn't come here to talk commonplaces. I came because I'd like to get to know my neighbors."

"There's not much to know," I finally managed to say. "Our parents are dead, and because of David's...health...I wanted to leave the city and take him someplace where there was fresh air." And I had to come here of all places, I added to myself.

"How did you happen to pick Lee's Corner?"

I looked at the flame that lit up the belly of the oil stove. "I had heard of Dr. Abrams. That he had some experience working with polio patients."

"He's a good doctor. Did you ever hear how he managed to come to the States?"

I shook my head. The conversation had somehow taken a wrong turn, but I didn't know how to get it back on a safe course.

"Of course, I don't know all of the details. He would never reveal them. But I do know that he was living in Poland when the Nazis invaded. For years he had been very vocal against Hitler, and tried to warn his countrymen against the Third Reich. When Hitler's heavy tanks rolled across the Polish border, the only resistance was an army still on horseback." He shook his head. "Dr. Abrams' wife and children were executed in front of his eyes."

I gasped. He looked at me. "Yes. And he was imprisoned. He didn't care. He wanted to die. He begged God to let him die."

"What a compassionate God, to be sure," I said sarcastically.

"He is," John said quietly. "He really is. See, there was a purpose for the good doctor to stay alive. A Polish underground group was being financed by someone here in the States, and they managed to get Dr. Abrams out of the prison camp and eventually out of Poland. He started out by working with polio victims. He was working at a hospital in Chicago, but he wanted a private practice in a climate that would be healthier for his patients. My father wanted to move to Chicago, so they made a swap."

I suddenly felt caught in a web. So it was not just unbelievably bad luck that I had ended up in the same town with John Ransom. Dr. Abrams had known my grandfather. That was at least one person in this town who knew all my secrets. I was willing to bet that Dr. Ableman had been a friend of Dr. Ransom as well. My oldest, dearest friend, I thought sarcastically, and he set me up. The only way to escape the past was to have no friends at all.

"If the Salk vaccine lives up to its promise, Dr. Abrams' polio will soon be eradicated. So he has turned his attention to the Indians. He spends a lot of his time on the reservations."

"I didn't know that," I murmured, not really hearing him.

John smiled at me. "So. What did old Slim tell you about us?"

The question caught me off guard. "Why, nothing much," I stammered.

"You're being...what did Father O'Brien call it?...diplomatic."

"Well, he did say something—look, It's not really important."

"It is if you believe it," John Ransom said seriously. "Even if you believe just a little of it."

I fidgeted. "Only that somehow he was cheated out of his place."

John nodded. "I thought that might be it. He's been telling that story to anyone who would listen. My grandfather bought a lot of places around here during the Depression from families who were struggling financially. He promised to sell them back—at the price he paid for them—to anybody who wanted to move back. Some folks did, most didn't. Slim had the same chance as anyone else. Granddad bought all but this quarter section from him. But Slim didn't know how to manage money. He never could buy the property back. Of course, Slim didn't mind all that so much, until we took in Coy."

"Yes, he didn't try to hide the fact that he doesn't like Coy."

"There are a few around here who don't. It...worries me sometimes."

That last was less a statement to me than it was an unpleasant thought put into words. I don't think he even realized he had said it.

I was going to say something, I'm not sure what, when I heard a car door slam, and in seconds David burst through the door.

"I thought Johnny was here. Hi!"

John looked at his watch. "Well, it's not even midnight yet. I thought you'd be out much later." David shook his head. "I went with Sharon and she had to be home by midnight. Most of the kids will be out much later."

I stifled a yawn. "I have to be up in five hours," I reminded them.

"And so do I," John said. He looked at David. "I just thought I'd keep your sister company while you were gone."

"Oh," he said innocently. "I thought maybe Mr. Stoker might have done that."

I felt myself blushing. "Mr. Stoker...had to leave early," I said, "and apparently Mr. Ransom didn't."

"Gosh, you leave with one guy and end up with another. What am I going to do with you, Sis?"

John thought that was funny. At least, he laughed. All I wanted to do was strangle my little brother.

After John reminded David to keep his dog at home, or at any event away from the Ransom Creek Ranch cattle, he left, and I was alone with David. "Did you have a good time?" I asked.

"Yes. Did you?"

"Of course."

"Did you have a better time with Mr. Stoker, or with Johnny Ransom?"

"Actually," I said, "the best company I had all evening was Father O'Brien. Now get to bed. You have chores to do in the morning, and I need to get some sleep," I thought to myself—if I can.

The weak can never forgive.
Forgiveness is the attribute of the strong.
—Mahatma Gandhi

Chapter 11

Sunday John and Coy picked David up for church again. When they brought him back about half past noon I was out in the barn watering Betty Lou.

Coy was driving. He waved as he turned the truck around, and I waved back. John waved, too.

David came up to me and said, "This afternoon is the memorial service for their father. They want to know if I can go."

I looked at the men in the pickup. Coy had put the truck in neutral and was obviously waiting for David to go back and give them an answer.

I suddenly had a vision of what might be said at the service—how and where Dr. Ransom had died, and the circumstances that surrounded the accident, of Rick, who had been spared, and possibly even the names of the two that had caused and been killed in the same accident.

I shuddered, and David asked, "Are you cold?"

"No!" I answered curtly, and then said, "I mean, yes. David, I'm not feeling too well, and there are things I need to get done today, and I really don't feel up to doing them. I was hoping you would be here this afternoon to help, so I could rest."

David was visibly disappointed. "Like what?" he asked.

I looked around. "Oh, like getting this barn in better shape, and bringing in some more hay for Betty Lou. And fixing the latch on the door of the chicken coop." I coughed. "I'm afraid if I get to feeling much worse I won't be able to go in to work tomorrow, and I really can't afford to miss."

"But I can do that stuff tomorrow after school," he protested.

The men sat in the truck and watched us.

"You have basketball practice or a game every single school night and you don't get home until past dark," I pointed out, "and these chores can't be put off until next weekend."

He glinted at me through his long lashes. "You don't want me to go," he said accusingly.

"That's ridiculous," I said a little too loudly. "But you can't do just everything David. You have certain responsibilities here which you promised you would shoulder and..."

"But they've been so good to me," he protested.

"And I haven't?" I asked, my voice rising.

I glanced at the truck. John and Coy were watching with some interest although I knew they couldn't hear us. But David and I were upset and I knew they could see that, so I forced myself to calm down before I spoke again.

David stood there looking at the ground. "You've been terrific," he answered in a small voice. "I'll tell them I can't go." He glanced up at me. "But I don't know what Johnny will think."

"He's been raised on a ranch. He'll know that chores come first."

"Marty Maguire is coming all the way back from Nottleman's for the service," he told me.

"Well, after all, she's known John Ransom all her life. She knew Dr. Ransom, too. You've known Mr. Ransom for barely a week and a half, and you never met his father at all."

"I feel I've know Johnny all my life," David replied with some asperity. "But I won't go. Excuse me, please," he said with emphasized politeness.

He went to the truck and said something to the men. They both smiled at him and nodded as though they understood, then Coy put the truck in gear and they sped off down the long drive.

David watched until the truck disappeared over a draw then he came back to me, his chin dragging.

If I was supposed to be getting sick I thought I'd better act the part. I coughed again then told him I was going inside to take some aspirin and a nap. I asked him to please make sure the manger was full of hay and the latch on the chicken coop fixed. Then I went inside, feeling guilty for a duplicity which I had never before used on my trusting little brother.

Work at the diner was welcome, because I was kept hustling, too busy to think. But business this Monday was unusually slow. Then Scooter Mathieson came in about a quarter to eleven. He was already roaring drunk.

My only customer was Coy, and I had just served him a sandwich and gone back behind the counter. He was eating it and reading the Scottsbluff paper when Scooter staggered in.

"Whatcha doin' here?" Scooter demanded, pointing at Coy.

Coy ignored him and kept on eating. Scooter walked up to him on unsteady legs and punched him on the arm.

"I asked a question, you dirty Injun," he said.

I yelled for Pete. He came out of the kitchen like a shot from a pistol, and grabbed the collar of Scooter Mathieson's shirt. I followed him.

"You're drunk," Pete roared. "Git outa here before I throw you out!"

Scooter, who was much smaller and lighter than either of the two men, rounded on Pete like an angry bull. "Kickin' out a decent white man while you let this Injun stay and eat. Dirty Injun, who's got plenty of land, while I have to work hard jist to keep my section, with a wife 'n five kids to su-su-support."

"You never supported your wife 'n kids. They've always supported you!" Pete pushed him toward the door.

Scooter took a swing at him. Pete ducked easily out of reach.

"You're ash bad as he ish," Scooter said thickly. "Ever'body allus sides with him and Ransom." Then he got a sly look on his face. "Ever'body but my friends." He swayed, and Pete grabbed and steadied him. "My friends," he said again. "Sheriff Carter and Joe." Scooter tapped Pete's chest with a knobby finger. "Bet you didn't know the sheriff was my friend. Well, he ish. An' me'n my friends, we're gonna have lots of money." He jerked his thumb at Coy, who was still calmly eating, and added nastily, "Then we'll get rid o' the likes of him, Ransom or no Ransom. Send him back to the reshervashun, him and that Sioux b…"

He never finished the word. Coy, with lightening speed, was out of his chair and had Scooter by the throat in one fluid move.

Pete was already getting between the two men when Sheriff Carter walked in. "Take your hands off him," he snapped at Coy.

Coy dropped his hands instantly, and Scooter slithered to the floor.

Carter sauntered up to Coy. "You causin' trouble, Indian?"

Pete bristled, and I said, "He was not, sheriff."

Carter waved a hand at me. "Ain't askin' you, lady. I'm askin' him," and he pointed a finger in Coy's face.

"No, I'm not causing trouble, sheriff," Coy answered quietly. "In fact, I was just leaving."

"You're not leavin' if this man wants to charge you with assault!" the sheriff snarled.

"Don't be a bigger fool than God made you, Carter," Pete said through his teeth. "Scooter is drunk, in case you haven't noticed. In my place, again if you haven't noticed. He ain't supposed to come in my place when he's been drinking. I've told him a hundred times. So he comes in today with a snootfull and bothers a paying customer. If there are any charges to be made, I'll make them—against him," and he pointed to Scooter. "And I will, too, if you don't get him outa here pronto!"

The sheriff blustered a little, but grabbed Scooter and pulled him out of the diner. I stared at them, speechless. But not for long.

I turned to Coy and demanded, "What was that all about?"

Coy, typically, had little to say. He just shrugged.

So Pete answered me. "Scooter Mathieson is nothing but trouble. Don't know why Annie Simpson ever married him. Doesn't take care of his farm or his family. Buddy, buddy with the sheriff all of a sudden. Don't like him, neither. Comin' up fer election soon, thank goodness."

"But what's he got against Coy?"

Coy had moved back a few paces, listening to our conversation but not participating in it.

"Not too many years back a lot of restaurants wouldn't serve Indians. Some still don't. They weren't allowed on public transportation, and those who lived off the reservation weren't encouraged to go to school."

"The boys told me, but I never really could comprehend..."

"Most people don't," Pete said. "A few people around here— not many, but still too many—are jealous of Coy. He's one-third owner of one of the biggest ranches in Nebraska. Some say he's got no right to it. People like Scooter Mathieson. Besides," and Pete shot Coy a grin, "Coy here has one of the prettiest gals around here—Mary Star."

Coy actually blushed.

Pete went on, grinning wickedly, "A real looker she is. And crazy about Coy. But Coy, here, won't come to the point."

Coy decided that now was a good time to leave. But as I watched him go I had the uncomfortable feeling, that not only were Sheriff Carter and Scooter Mathieson not to be trusted, but that Coy could possibly be in danger from them.

~~~~~~~~~~

I ordered David's Christmas present later that day—a letterman's jacket two sizes too big for him because he'd eventually grow into it, and I was hoping soon. He was still thin, but he looked healthier than he had ever looked in his life.

After I ordered it I went home. The weather was still cold; none of the snow had melted even though the sun had been out all day. The wind picked up the dry snow and deposited it along the fences in four-foot drifts.

John Ransom was waiting for me. He was sitting in his red pickup. As soon as he saw me turn into the drive he turned off his motor and let himself out into the cold.

"What is it?" I asked when he opened the door to my car and helped me out. His face shocked me.

"I'll tell you inside," he said, and took my elbow.

I pulled away from him. "Did something happen to David?" I had to know.

He shook his head, then took hold of my elbow again and guided me to the house.

We went in and shed our coats. I automatically put hot water on the stove. "I'm out of coffee. Would you care for tea?" I asked, intent on lighting the burner.

"Tea's fine."

I could tell by his voice as well as by his expression that something was dreadfully wrong. But he would tell me in his own good time. As long as David was all right I could face anything.

151

I had baked a chocolate cake the night before. I cut two pieces, put them carefully on my good china, and carried them to the table. I brought the hot water and poured it over the tea bags in the cups. He watched me the whole time.

When finally I sat down, he said, "I don't know quite how to tell you this. God knows I wish I didn't have to. I...I ran over Napoleon with my pickup."

My breath caught in my throat.

For the first time since I had known him, John Ransom looked at me with genuine anguish, and without a shred of his usual self-confidence. "I'm sorry. You can't know how much."

"Is he...dead?" My own soul screamed with pain, as I thought of how David loved the dog.

John swallowed hard. "I...shot him. I had to. There was nothing else I could have done."

"I see." I was looking into the steam floating up from my cup. "Well, at least he won't run the fat off your cattle anymore," I said dully.

He leaped to his feet, "Are you suggesting I did it on purpose?"

Of course I knew he didn't. But if he thought I did, he might keep his distance in the future. So I said, by way of answer, "You have been complaining about him."

He pushed his plate away, the cake uneaten. "I know you can't possibly believe I would do anything that drastic. Or maybe you can?"

He thrust his fingers through his dark, curly hair and stood up. "I ran over Napoleon when he was chasing me down my driveway. He hit an icy spot and slid right under my wheel. There was no way I could have avoided hitting him. His...his back was broken. He was in agony. I had no choice but to shoot him. It was one of the hardest things I've ever had to do. David..."

"Don't worry about David," I broke in, and rose from my chair. My voice was completely without expression. "I'll tell him. I'll tell him I found him on the road, that someone must have hit him. He...thinks a lot of you. I won't tell him you did it. One heartbreak at a time is enough to handle."

The look John Ransom gave me was pure granite. Those blue eyes smoldered to gray. He reached out to me, then dropped his hand. "I'm sorry," he said softly. "About everything."

He left me. I never heard one sound as he closed my front door, got into his truck, and sped down the drive. All I could hear was my own heart pounding while my emotions argued with my judgment. In the end, judgment won. I had wanted him out of my life. Well, now maybe he would stay out, if he thought I despised him. Of course I knew it was an accident, but the end justifies the means, or so I told myself, and if that was what it took to get John Ransom out of my life, then I would let him think I believed he killed Napoleon to keep him away from his precious cattle.

But I loved my brother, and my brother loved John Ransom. I felt I could keep Mr. Ransom out of my life but still in my brother's, so I decided I would tell David that I found Napoleon on the road. That way David at least would still have Mr. Ransom, and I had a inexplicable confidence that whatever I did, John Ransom would always be David's friend.

So when David came home from basketball practice later that afternoon, I was prepared to tell him my little falsehood.

But when he walked through the door his eyes were red. I thought at first that it must be from the cold, but closer observation told me he had been crying.

"I know. Napoleon's dead," he said, before I could open my mouth.

"How did you find out?" I managed to ask.

"Johnny told me." He sniffed, and drew his hand across his nose. "He picked me up from school and told me on the way home. He said he did it, that it was an accident, that Napoleon slid under the wheel of his truck and that his back got broke. He told me he had to shoot him to get him out of his misery. He…He asked me to forgive him."

"And…did you?"

David looked at me through watery eyes. "Of course," he said, and turned and ran up the stairs.

I let him cry it out. It wouldn't do for me to go up and try to comfort him. David was at the in-between age, not a boy any longer, but not yet a man, and I couldn't embarrass him by watching him cry.

After about an hour, David went out to do his chores. He appeared to be taking this heartbreak with the same stoic dignity with which he had met all the others.

More composed now, he told me, "Johnny took me to Napoleon, and we buried him in the little pet cemetery behind their barn. Johnny showed me where the dog he had as a kid is buried. Johnny said he just showed up late one night in the middle of winter, so Johnny named him Nicodemus." David gave me a fleeting glance. "Something to do with the Bible," he explained.

"Oh," I replied, a little uncertainly.

"Well, anyway," David continued, "the dog was part Collie and part German Shepherd. Johnny was about eight years old when Nicodemus came, and a few years later, Nick, which is what they called him, saved his life. Killed a rattler that was going to bite Johnny. But Nick got bit and was real sick for a long time. Johnny told me that one day during the War, Nick, who was very old by then, started howling. He kept it up all day. No one could figure out why. They found out later that that was the day Johnny was wounded in France."

"I hear dogs have some special radar when it comes to people they love," I said.

"They're smart," David said emphatically. "Just like when Napoleon saved little Suzanne from the railroad tracks." A tear started trickling down his cheek. He brushed it away quickly. "And so anyway," he continued after he regained his composure, "we buried Napoleon right next to Nick. Nick died before Johnny came home from the War. There's a marker there, and for Coy's dog Joe, too. Coy named him after Chief Joseph."

"Oh, I remember," I said. "The one who said 'I will fight no more forever. '"

"Yes, that's him. And there are a few cats, and John's mother's dogs. She used to go and find strays and bring them home. There's even a dog buried there that belonged to John's great-grandfather who fought in the Civil War. Its name was Jeb."

"After Jeb Stuart, I suppose."

"Yes. I think it was the ancestor who fought for the South. But Johnny has ancestors who fought for the North, too. He even said he had one who couldn't make up his mind and so fought on both sides."

I smiled. "I would have thought he'd have stayed out of the war completely."

"That's what I said, too, but Johnny told me that the Ransoms loved to fight, and they didn't always need a reason."

But this modern-day Ransom, I thought to myself, would need a strong reason to fight. And I didn't doubt the outcome should John Ransom ever find himself in a situation where he was forced to use his fists. I also knew, I don't know why, that John Ransom would never fight on his own behalf; it would have to be for someone else. My thoughts turned suddenly to Coy Youngblood, and I wondered what measures John would take if the bigotry aimed at his brother turned violent.

I wouldn't put my thoughts into words. Maybe my imagination was suddenly becoming overactive, and what I had seen at the diner was just a harmless drunk trying to pick a fight.

I shook myself from the nebulous flight of fancy and said to my brother, "Well, it was nice of Mr. Ransom to go to the trouble of helping you bury Napoleon."

"I know." He tried to control his voice, and the tears that were starting to fill his eyes again. "But I'm going to miss him so much."

I put my arms around him. "So am I," I said soothingly. "But one day we'll get another dog, and you'll love him too."

David sniffed. "Not as much as Napoleon," he said.

"No, of course not."

~~~~~~~~~

Tuesday and Wednesday I found myself waiting, in vain, for John Ransom to come by for his daily pie and coffee. Trying to manage my tangled affairs I had cost Pete a customer.

I was too busy to worry about it. I was getting ready for a very special day.

I arranged with Pete to use his diner for David's birthday party. I held it on Wednesday night after church. Marty Maguire helped me get everything ready and was on hand to introduce me to people whom I hadn't already met either at the diner or at the basketball game.

Coy and John both came, the one reserved but helpful, the other courteous but distant. I could only be grateful for both the courtesy and the distance.

We had sandwiches, cake, ice cream, and punch. And presents piled on the front table as the guests poured in.

The party was a boisterous affair but everyone seemed to be enjoying themselves. I was shocked at the number of people who came and was grateful that Marty had coaxed me to buy extra food. Not only did the Grace congregation come, apparently *in toto*, but others from the school showed up as well as members of St. Peter's Parish including the D'Angelo family.

I avoided them by spending most of the time in the kitchen with Pete and Carol, fixing sandwiches and making more punch. Karen Hempstead came in and insisted on helping. But finally it was time for David to open his presents.

I had seldom seen him so excited. The only other times were when I told him we were leaving Chicago, and when I showed him the home I had bought for us.

There he stood, the Birthday Boy, opening presents at the very first party he had ever been given. I turned and walked to the back of the kitchen, and forced myself not to cry.

From the cheerleaders he got a sweatshirt with the school's bulldog on the front and his name on the back above the number 14. The basketball players had chipped in and bought a huge picture of the team, which everyone autographed. Pete gave him a cowboy hat—an expensive one. Marty had made him a western shirt, and Mikey gave him a picture of Stan Musial. Suzanne Retting didn't forget him, either. She gave him a beautifully-tooled leather belt with a large silver buckle. Even Father O'Brien brought a gift. It was a plaque with a bronze relief of Christ on the cross, and underneath , also in bronze, the words, "He was wounded for our iniquities. Isaias 53."

The party was a huge success. Marty and Pete stayed and helped me clean up the mess, which really didn't take too long. It was barely ten o'clock when we finally left, and it wasn't until David and I were almost home that it registered with me that Coy and John hadn't given a gift. I admitted I was a little surprised, but relieved. Our obligation to them seemed always increasing.

156

I took my time over the snow-covered road. The wind was coming up and clouds raced past the crescent moon. Few stars winked at us as we traveled west, and the hills were only looming shadows, dark against an even darker night. I knew by now what it meant—we would have more snow by morning.

David talked non-stop from the moment we left the diner. The trunk and back seat of the Chevy were full of presents, and it wasn't until this night that I realized how popular my little brother had become.

"That was great, Sis," he kept repeating all the way home. Forgotten was the misunderstanding that had marred the previous Sunday. David was not one to hold a grudge—unlike his older sister.

He proceeded to tell me a little something about everyone who was at the party, then he went over the gifts he had received.

We turned off the main road and drove up our long drive, the headlights making an arc over our field. When I turned again towards the barn, those same lights caught something in their glare.

I hit the brakes and said, "What on earth?"

But David was out of the car even before it came to a full stop. I left the lights on so I could see to make my way to the barn, and when I finally caught up with David he was already at the open barn door.

My breath caught in my throat. "What a beautiful animal!" I finally managed to say.

"It's Johnny's new horse," David told me, "He's named Goliath, cause Johnny said he's smaller than Captain or Seneca and he didn't want him to get an inferiority complex. He's two years old, and Johnny's been training him. I wonder what he's doing here?"

The horse couldn't have been less concerned; he was chomping lazily at some hay. There was a white envelope attached to the post to which Goliath was tied. David pulled it off and ripped it open.

"What is it?" I asked; David had suddenly become speechless.

He mutely handed me the envelope. Inside it was one of those comical birthday cards, clever and unsentimental. Under the printed message was a written note. It said: "A dark horse for a bright kid. Happy birthday." The signature was written with the same strong flourish I had seen on the register at the funeral parlor.

"Wow!" David whooped. "A horse! For me! Wow!"

I walked carefully around the animal. It wasn't just a cow pony. It had all the qualities of a champion. If I knew it, John Ransom knew it. Yet he had so casually given it to David, a boy he hardly knew.

"You'll teach me how to ride, won't you, Sis?"

I was on the verge of telling him that of course I would, when it dawned on me that some might think it strange that a girl brought up in the city could ride as well as I could. So I said instead, "I would love to teach you, but I bet Mr. Ransom would be pleased if you asked him to teach you."

"Do you think so?"

"Yes, I think so. Anyway you'll want to learn to ride western style, and I'm not very knowledgeable about that. Come on, let's get him bedded down for the night, and then I'll drive you over to their house and you can thank him."

But there was something we had overlooked in the excitement, and I nearly tripped over it as we left the barn. There, on the floor, was a finely tooled western saddle—Coy's gift to David.

"My cup runneth over," David said, quoting a David of a much earlier era.

As we pulled up to the big ranch house, I told David, "Don't tell them I know how to ride." I searched for a good reason, then came up with what, to my ears, sounded like a feeble one. But it was, I thought, better than nothing. "They might wonder why I'm not teaching you myself."

David was too excited not to accept this flimsy excuse. He jumped out of the car and went up the steps as fast as his lameness allowed. I stayed where I was, and John Ransom didn't make any attempt to invite me in. I told myself I wasn't disappointed, that things were much better this way. By four o'clock in the morning I had myself nearly convinced.

Every evening after that David rode over to the Ransom Creek Ranch and got a lesson. His horse was on the small side, a bay gelding with a white stocking on his off rear leg. I left it up to John and Coy to explain what a gelding is.

My little brother proved to be a good pupil, and soon he was riding out on his own, galloping across the landscape as though he had been doing it for years instead of mere days. David confided that John had trained Goliath to jump, and when he was sure David was ready, he would coach him in the same skill. I remembered the exhilaration I used to feel, flying through the air. To a boy who had never been able to run, this kind of freedom had to be special. I got a lump in my throat every time after that when I saw him riding across the pasture on his way home. He was growing healthier and more sure of himself every day.

Bigotry has no head and cannot think,
no heart and cannot feel.
When she moves it is in wrath.
—Daniel O'Connell

Chapter 12

Every afternoon when I came home from work I would see either John or Coy riding around their land, tending their cattle and checking the fences. Even though John's mount was a sorrel quarter-horse and Coy's was a black Arabian stallion, from this distance it was hard to tell them apart. All I could see was a rider silhouetted against the backdrop of an endless sky.

I never waved. I doubt if they could have seen me if I did. But as I climbed my porch steps I always stood and watched for a moment the solitary rider on the open plain and rolling hills. It was a scene that must have been repeated daily for the past eighty years.

That's what I was doing on that crisp wintry day in mid-December, watching the rider follow the herd.

Suddenly the horse stopped and the rider slumped over. Even as I put my hand to my eyes to shield them from the sun so as to get a clearer look, I heard the crack of a rifle.

I screamed for David who happened to be home early because it was a game night. He came out of the house as fast as he could, but I was already running towards the barn.

I snatched up the bridle, but didn't bother putting David's saddle on Goliath. I was on his back in an instant.

"Take the car and go to the ranch. Get whoever's there to call the doctor, then get back as soon as you can. One of the boys has been shot! If no one's home, call Doc yourself. And hurry!"

I didn't wait to see him jump in the car. I knew he could drive—hadn't I been teaching him since we moved out here?—and I knew he would keep his head on his shoulders and not take any chances. I wheeled Goliath around and headed for the Ransom's land. I took the two fences between myself and the rider easily; the old familiar thrill brought a smile even at this time of stress. The gelding could jump all right.

My heart was in my throat. I hoped I wouldn't be too late, then I wondered what I would do when I got there. He was still in the saddle but slumped over the horse's neck and hanging on to its mane.

Distances can fool a person, especially out in these hills; the horse and rider were farther than they looked. Or maybe it just seemed farther.

It was the big, black horse. I slowed and approached cautiously for fear of spooking him. Thankfully the horse remained motionless, and Coy was still in the saddle, but it was costing him an effort.

I sidled up to Coy, who was barely conscious and bleeding badly. The bullet had ripped through the heavy cowhide of his jacket and grazed his back emerging under his left arm then re-entering the underside of his upper arm. "Easy boy, easy," I spoke soothingly and gently patted the rangy black. He seemed to understand that something unusual had happened and he must remain calm. Seneca allowed me to slip onto his back and I got my arms around Coy and somehow managed to hang onto him as I turned the horse and headed for my place, which was much closer than the big ranch house. Seneca was used to opening gates, and waited while I leaned over to slip the latches.

I took Seneca right up to the front porch, then slid off his broad back. I tried to help Coy down, but he was too heavy, and he knocked me down as he fell from his horse. He had finally passed out. I ran inside and got the quilt and blankets from my bed and a carving knife and some clean white towels, which I ripped into long strips. I hated to cut the expensive jacket but it had three bullet holes now anyway, and it was much easier than trying to pry it off his unresponsive body.

The wounds were bleeding profusely. I slapped a handful of clean snow into the awful hole under his arm and watched it turn crimson and disappear as I quickly rolled one of the strips into a compress and bound it to his upper arm as tightly as I could. The bullet had plowed a furrow four inches long in his back, then entering the thick triceps muscle it had lodged somewhere inside, probably at the bone. I packed more snow and rags into the gouge on his back. Then I covered Coy, trying to get at least part of the bedding under him.

The Chevy was coming fast up the drive. John was at the wheel. The car slid a little on the snow as John brought it to an abrupt halt, and he was out of the door before the engine had sputtered to a full stop.

"I tried to get him inside," I said as he came rushing up to us, "but he couldn't make it."

John bent over his brother. Coy's breathing was shallow, but between the cold and my tight tourniquet at least the bleeding had slowed. It was still oozing out of the wound, but barely.

"I'll help you get him inside," I told John, but he bent over Coy and with a strength I had only previously suspected, he somehow managed to get the bigger man across his shoulder and lift him off the frozen ground.

I threw open the door and led John to my room, where he laid him as gently as he could on my sheets.

"I'll get some ice," I said. "I don't want him to start bleeding again."

David came in as I finished filling the ice bag. His face was ashen even though he had been out in the bitter weather.

"I put Seneca in the barn," he told me, "and then Goliath came home and I put him up, too."

"Good man," I said. "Here, take this to John and tell him to get it on Coy's wound. The cold will slow up the flow of blood. Tell him I'm making coffee. Is Doc coming?"

"He's on his way. I called him while Johnny was getting ready." He took the ice and was gone.

I made the coffee strong and took it in to John Ransom. He was pale, but when I handed him the cup he managed a smile. "Thank you," he whispered. He looked at Coy, then back at me. "What on earth happened?"

I shrugged my shoulders. "I'm not sure. I was watching him when all of a sudden he fell forward, and I was wondering why when I heard the shot." I motioned towards the bed in a helpless gesture. "He was only barely conscious when I got to him. He saw me, but he never spoke. By the time I got him here he had passed out. Do you—think he's lost too much blood?"

John shook his head. "I don't know. I wish Doc would get here."

"Maybe we should have taken him to town," I said.

He shook his head again. "I'm sure he's better off here, lying down." He sipped the hot, strong coffee. "You say you saw him fall, and then heard the shot?"

I nodded. "There's no doubt about that. It was only a matter of a split second, but as I told you, for that brief instant I wondered why he had so suddenly fallen forward."

"So Coy was probably between you and whoever shot at him."

I gaped at John Ransom. "Shot at him? Surely you don't mean that! It had to be a stray bullet, somebody out hunting."

But John shook his head. "Nobody out here would shoot into a herd. No, Lu, somebody deliberately shot Coy."

"No," I said, not wanting to believe him. "You're wrong. Who would want to..."

My voice trailed off as John sat on my little vanity stool and watched me. I was remembering the recent nasty little scene at the diner, and the slant the sheriff wanted to put on it. And I was remembering, too, Slim Rhodes, who expressed the sentiments of some of the people in this part of the state. A small minority of the people, but enough, as John had phrased it, to matter.

I suddenly felt the need to do something. John looked uncomfortable sitting on my small stool, so I left the room and came back with my rocker.

He gave me a wan smile, and said, "Thank you." Then he turned his attention back to his brother, and I tiptoed out of the room.

David joined John, and the two of them knelt by the bedside and prayed. I needed to do something, too, only I needed to do something that would actually help. I decided that what everyone would need when the next harrowing hour was over was hot soup, so I set about making some. It was simmering on the stove when Doc finally arrived.

He went to work immediately. The bullet had to come out, and Doc didn't stand around discussing the pros and cons of doing it in my bedroom.

The men didn't need me. At least I hoped they didn't. Nothing could have made me stay in that room.

But David, scuttling between the bedroom and the kitchen, kept me informed of every move the doctor made. The bullet missed an artery, barely, but was pressing on a nerve. The pain had to have been unbearable, and was probably the reason why Coy had passed out, and not from the loss of blood as I first had feared.

Finally it was over. Doc came into the kitchen. He had scrubbed his hands in the bathroom sink and was drying them on one of my new towels. I was sitting at the table drinking a cup of tea.

"He's under," Doc told me. "He'll be under for some time. Nasty wound. You say you saw how it happened?"

I shook my head. "I only saw him fall forward just a split second before I heard a shot." I looked at the doctor, whose face held a thoughtful expression. "It...it had to be an accident?" I meant it to be a statement, but it came out as a question.

But Doc shook his head. "Everyone around here knows how to handle a gun. I don't know of anybody who's fool enough to shoot towards a herd. No, I agree with Johnny. Whoever shot at Coy intended to shoot him."

He sat down opposite me. I got up and poured a cup of coffee and brought it to him. He poured some sugar into the rich brown liquid and stirred it absently. "I don't like the feel of this," he finally said. "Neither does Johnny. It's all over town that Coy and Scooter Mathieson had a quarrel, a rumor spread for some reason by our hardworking sheriff."

"I was there," I told him, "and there was no quarrel. Scooter tried to pick one, but Coy walked away. It was only when Scooter was on the verge of saying something vile about Coy's friend, Mary Star, that Coy grabbed him. And he didn't really hurt him, although I admit I was kind of wishing that he would."

"I don't know of a meaner man than Scooter Mathieson, especially when he's got a bellyful of whiskey. Why Annie Simpson...but it's over and done with, and she won't leave him, poor soul. It's a very sad case."

"Yes. I've met her and her kids. They're very nice."

Doc finished his coffee. I poured him some more and then put a bowl of hot soup in front of him. He dug into it with relish, then said, "Johnny would probably like some, too. I couldn't get him to leave Coy. He and David are still in there praying. Maybe you wouldn't mind taking some into him later?"

"Of course not. As soon as they're...finished."

Doc emptied his bowl and turned down the offer of more. Then, pushing his plate aside he said to me, "Coy can't be moved for a few days. I'm sorry, but it can't be helped. I don't want to risk opening the wound."

"Naturally Coy can stay here for as long as necessary."

"Johnny, too?" Doc asked.

I looked at him. Those dark eyes which had shown fatigue and worry now sparked to life.

"What do you mean, 'Johnny, too?'" I asked, feeling a slight tremor of panic.

"Well, someone has to stay with Coy. You have to go to work, and David's in school. That leaves Johnny."

"I could get Marty..." I began, my composure slowly slipping.

But Doc shook his head. "Mikey's got the measles. Besides, no one could drag Johnny away from Coy right now."

I let out a long breath. "I guess not," I finally admitted.

He smiled, and rose to leave. "I'll take a look at my patient before I go, and I want to tell you that your quick actions probably saved Coy's life. If you hadn't seen it happen, I doubt Coy would have had a chance. The law requires me to report gunshot wounds, so our dutiful acting-sheriff will probably be out to ask you some questions when he gets around to it. Meanwhile, just try to keep the patient quiet. I'll be back tomorrow to check on him."

I didn't know quite what to do. I fidgeted around the kitchen while Doc went back to my room and gave some quiet instructions to John. Then I heard the front door open and close, and the doctor's old reliable Hudson start up. I put a steaming bowl of soup, a few pieces of homemade bread, and some more coffee on a tray and took it in to John.

David was sitting on the stool on one side of the bed, and John was in the rocker on the other side. They were carrying on a quiet conversation across Coy, whose breathing was more even now, but John jumped to his feet the moment I stepped into the room.

"That looks good," he whispered as he came towards me. "Here, let me."

He took the tray from my hands and set it on the dressing table, after which he said a brief, quiet blessing. Then he dove into the soup as though he hadn't eaten for days.

I glanced at Coy. "He's still sleeping," I said unnecessarily.

"Yes. probably for several more hours," David replied.

They had managed to undress Coy and wash him off. Now he was sleeping comfortably under my clean sheets and warm comforter. I smoothed the comforter, an automatic gesture, and pulled my new curtains a little tighter across the window. Then I told David he had better get his chores done and get ready for the game.

"Ah, Sis. Do I have to? I mean, after I called Doc I called Forrests and told Cody not to come by for me."

I put my hands on my hips. "Why did you do that?" I asked quietly.

"Well, because what if Coy needs something? Johnny can't leave him alone, and we don't have a phone." I could see some sense in that. One of us should stay home. I didn't really want to spend the evening with John Ransom and his unconscious brother. And I had no way to tell Lance Stoker not to come after me.

"Oh, all right. Stay and help Mr. Ransom. But don't get any ideas about missing school tomorrow. Coy should be stable by then." I turned to John Ransom. "Is there anything you need before I leave."

He smiled at me. "I think you have done a good day's work already."

It was a way of thanking me. I didn't want any thanks. I had always had difficulty accepting appreciation with any semblance of graciousness.

I got out of the room as quickly as I could, and as I went to clean up the kitchen I raised my eyes to heaven. "Thanks a lot," I said sarcastically. "Just when I think I've gotten rid of him, You find a way to move him into my house."

By the time we arrived at the game the whole town had heard about the incident. Most people liked the soft-spoken Sioux and were not only shocked that there had been a shooting but that it was Coy Youngblood who had been shot. But then, having once recovered from surprise, everyone seemed to think Scooter Mathieson had done it.

I made up my mind I wouldn't answer any questions posed by the curious citizens of Kincaid County. After all, what did I know? Nothing, really. I saw no one, and heard nothing but the shot.

At home, Lance Stoker came in to tell David about the game and how he was missed. He went in to see Coy who was still sleeping, and he stared at the cot John Ransom had set up next to the bed. I felt furious, but John seemed rather amused.

"Hi, Lance," he drawled. "Nasty business. Coy hasn't come to yet, but I want to be right here when he does."

"Of course," Lance agreed. "Well, David, I'll see you in the morning. Maybe you'll have more news then."

I sent David downstairs with extra bedding, and then spent a very uneasy night.

I got up even earlier than usual, but John was already in the kitchen making breakfast when I came downstairs.

"It snowed last night," he told me. "I'm driving you into town. No, don't look at me like that. I said it wrong. May I please drive you into town? I need to pick up a few things and Doc is giving me extra pain medication for Coy."

"I can drive in snow. Even David can, as you saw yesterday. I've been doing it for quite some time. It snows...in St. Louis, too, you know. I'll be glad to pick up whatever you need from town."

"That's kind of you—I hope you like your eggs scrambled— but I really need to go myself. Coy will be all right for a few hours."

So John drove us into town, and I was glad he did although I didn't want to admit it to him. He drove expertly through the foot of new snow that had fallen during the night. It was dry and light, easily moved by the heavy winds, which carried it to fences and the sides of houses and deposited it in high drifts.

I had little to say during that drive. David and John carried on a conversation in which I did not participate. It was mostly about the church and the people who went there. I recognized the names, but somehow felt left out of the discussion. It was, of course, of my own choosing, but it felt a little awkward not being a part of something that interested my little brother. It was the first time that had happened since he was born. I sat there in the cab of the truck, sandwiched between the two males, and looked straight ahead out the windshield at the totally white landscape.

The diner had more business than usual. Everyone wanted to know what had happened, and most hoped that Scooter Mathieson would be paid back in full when Coy got back on his feet, although there was some speculation that Johnny Ransom might not wait that long. Several times I overheard the phrase, "back-shooter." I gathered it was a kind of unpardonable sin. Rumors spread and grew, and by the end of the day I felt the Sioux and the Seventh Cavalry would have one more go at it.

Lance Stoker came in to ask how I was doing. Then he asked me if I would care to go to a movie with him in Scottsbluff. I told him I would love to, but would have to take a rain check, and he said he understood. But the way he said it made me want to ask him just exactly what it was that he understood. He inquired about Coy, and I told him only that I thought he was out of danger.

Then I went to the little grocery store to buy enough groceries to get the four of us through the week, and fended off the questions thrown at me by the Makepeaces. At four o'clock John picked me up. He had spent the rest of the day with Coy.

"He wanted books," John told me, "so I spent the better part of an hour at the library this morning trying to pick out a few he hasn't already read."

"I have boxes of books. I wish you'd have said something."

John laughed. "I've seen what you read. Coy isn't into westerns—or *Les Miserables*."

"I have mysteries, poetry, Shakespeare, historical novels, biographies, classics…"

"I could have saved an hour, then. By the way, David has practice tonight and was invited to spend the night with the twins. I told him that if I didn't come back for him by four-thirty that it was okay with you."

"But he hasn't any clothes!"

"Oh, don't worry. With as many boys as the Mercers have, they're bound to have some clothes that will fit him. Is it all right with you if he stays?"

I looked at him uncertainly.

He said, accurately reading my mind, "Coy is still there to act as chaperone." His voice was as smooth as cream.

I wish I didn't blush. It was something I should have outgrown years ago.

"Perhaps I should stay with Marty tonight," I finally said. "That will save you from feeling you have to bring me to work tomorrow."

"Marty wouldn't have any clothes that fit you," he said. "Besides, I'm not going that way." As if it were twenty miles out of his way instead of two blocks.

So we drove home through the snow, as the sun, far to the southwest at the winter solstice, slowly slipped behind Courthouse Rock. I stole a glance at my companion, and remarked to myself once again that ever since I had made the resolve to keep Mr. John Ransom at arm's length I found myself, through a series of strange circumstances, almost constantly in his company. I resolved to make a very special telephone call the next morning—early.

Sheriff Carter was waiting for me when I got home. John carried the groceries in and Carter sat down at my kitchen table and took out a little notebook and the stub of a pencil.

"So," he said, "You're the little lady who saw the whole thing."

Little lady? I thought. At five foot eight I had an inch or two on him. What was he trying to pull? He was friendly and jovial, and something else, too. Maybe a little too friendly and jovial? Something didn't quite ring true, like a man playing Santa who didn't like kids. Instinct warned me to be wary of this chubby little man with the face of a cherub. I hadn't liked him the first time I saw him at the diner. I didn't trust him, either. Now it was more.

I sat down at the table. "All I saw was Coy fall forward on his horse. Then I heard a shot. But I didn't see anything or anybody."

He jotted all of this down. "I talked to your brother at school. He tells me you jumped on his horse and headed straight for the victim."

"Yes," I answered warily.

He looked at me and grinned. John was standing behind him, leaning against the counter, his arms folded in front of him. He was smiling to himself, as though something were amusing him.

"There's two fences between here and where the Indian was shot," the sheriff pointed out, disbelief in his round face.

"The Indian has a name," John said softly.

The sheriff turned to him, and John Ransom smiled sweetly.

Carter forced a laugh, and said a shade too heartily, "Of course, of course. I didn't mean nothin' by it." He turned back to me. "But my point is, little lady…"

"She has a name, too," John said.

The sheriff turned beet red. "Of course she does. Miss Morrow, naturally. But my point is—Miss Morrow—what did you do about them fences?"

I saw myself caught. If I denied jumping them, Coy, David, and probably John would know I was lying, and maybe the sheriff too. "I couldn't control the horse. He saw his friend Seneca, and probably sensed something was wrong, and he took a direct route."

The sheriff's eyes narrowed to little slits. "That's mighty fancy ridin' for a city gal."

"You wouldn't say that if you'd have seen me," I said evenly, "hanging on for dear life."

The sheriff gave me a hard look. "You could have let the boy—David," and he glanced back at John, "go for him, seein' that Johnny here has been teachin' him how to ride."

"The thought never even entered my mind," I told him. "Not with someone out there who didn't seem to be too particular what he was shooting at."

"Just what do you mean by that?" the sheriff growled, stripping himself of all pretense of amiability. "You sayin' someone did that on purpose?"

"I think 'not particular' implies the opposite of 'on purpose,'" I said emphatically. "You're the one jumping to conclusions."

He snapped his notebook shut. "Well, just be mighty careful how you phrase things," he warned. "Won't do to have some newcomer makin' crazy accusations."

That wiped the smile from John Ransom's face. He stepped forward and blocked the sheriff's exit. "Don't be a fool, Carter," he said in a quiet voice which made my blood run cold. "No one *but you* said anything about its being deliberate. Now if you have the information you need…"

"I do, for now." He frowned at me and pointed a stubby finger in the direction of my chin. "And you watch out what you say."

John grabbed the offending finger. "And you watch out where you point that thing!" He proceeded to propel the sheriff out the door.

I was a little shaky when John came back in from seeing Carter off the premises.

"Don't mind Carter," he told me. "He's harmless."

"Do you really believe that?" I asked.

He gave me a wry grin. "Well, I couldn't prove anything if I didn't."

I started putting away the groceries. "How's Coy?"

"Sore. But grateful. Very, very grateful."

I felt my cheeks grow warm. I couldn't look at John Ransom. I stammered a little, and it finally came out as, "I'm glad he's feeling better."

John chuckled.. "I didn't say he was feeling better. In fact, he's been sick the better part of the day."

John came and stood behind me. He was so close I could feel his warm breath on my hair. I cleared my throat. "So, have you had din-supper yet?"

"I polished off your soup at dinner. It was delicious. I even managed to get some down Coy."

"And it made him sick."

"No. Doc's pain medication made him sick. He was very grateful for the hot soup. He thought it was delicious, too."

I shrugged.

"But then," he went on, "you don't especially appreciate compliments. Like you don't especially appreciate thanks. But I reserve the right to thank you anyway."

I dropped my hands. My back was still turned to him. "No need," I said lightly.

He put his hands on my shoulders and turned me around. I had a good look at the top button of his shirt.

"Look at me, Lu."

I raised my eyes. He was smiling gently.

"Coy was able to give me a fairly accurate account of what happened. He thought that was mighty fancy riding, too. He saw you coming towards him like one of the Valkyries. At least, that's how he described it. He was conscious, you know, until he fell off Seneca."

"Beginner's luck," I said, my throat dry.

"Not likely. Where did you learn to ride like that?"

"Summer camp," I answered, and then added, before he could ask any more questions, "Did he happen to have an educated guess about where the shot came from?"

"He thought it was from the west. It was a .30-.30. He was just turning to look westward when the shot struck him. The angle saved him."

He picked up the remains of Coy's jacket and stuck his finger through the first hole. It was over the left shoulder blade. "If it had struck him square that bullet would have gone through his heart. The jacket helped too. By the time the bullet had penetrated the cowhide three times it was nearly spent or it might have shattered the bone.

"Of course, just about everyone around here owns a deer rifle—even you." And he nodded towards the rifle mounted on the wall above the door to the porch.

I looked at the Winchester Rhodes had left me. "It's for coyotes," I said defensively.

He laughed. "You're going to shoot coyotes? My dear girl!" And he laughed again, then asked, "Do you have any idea how to use that thing?"

I pulled away from him. "I'll learn," I said. "Excuse me. I want to look in on Coy."

He pulled me back. "Coy is sleeping. Just what are you running from, Lu?"

"Who says I'm running from anything?"

"I do. I'm suspicious you're running from a lot of things, maybe—most importantly—from God."

Why couldn't he mind his own business? "Once and for all, I am not running from anything!" I replied defensively, conscious that I was becoming a chronic liar.

"Not even from me?"

"Not even from you," I said, with no inflection whatsoever in my voice.

"Then why do I always get the impression that you are constantly avoiding me?"

"I told you once..."

"And I didn't believe you. You're nice to Coy, you kid around with the customers at the diner. You have David's principal eating out of your hand..."

"That's a particularly obnoxious idea," I broke in, trying for lightness.

He pulled me a little closer. "Beauty, wit, and courage—a lethal combination." He kissed me on the forehead and let me go.

I practically ran to the stove. "Din-supper will be ready in about an hour." I made a production out of lighting the burner. Anything, just so I wouldn't have to turn around and face him.

He left the kitchen, and I breathed a sigh of...was it really relief?

I made some chicken broth for Coy, and some weak tea, and jello for dessert. He gave me a smile that was as weak as the tea, but it was a smile nevertheless, and I was grateful for it.

"You're looking better than the last time I saw you," I told him.

"I could return the compliment," he said, with another small smile. "At least your hair is combed now."

In a strictly feminine gesture I self-consciously patted my hair.

Then he sobered. "Actually the last time I saw you, you looked better to me than any human I've ever seen. I can't thank you enough..."

"Nonsense," I said briskly, tucking his sheets and fluffing his pillow. "You've done so much for us—all that beef you brought, taking David to church, the horse..."

"Johnny gave the horse."

I smiled at him. "John gave the horse, but you gave the saddle."

"Which *you* didn't need."

I looked him straight in the eyes. "Which I didn't need," I said. "Eat your broth."

While I sat with Coy, John ate the better part of a stewing hen and all the dumplings. He did the dishes while I did a load of bloody bedding in the old wringer washing machine. Then I excused myself early and went upstairs to the spare room across from David's. That night I rummaged through all my books and the ones Slim Rhodes had left and came up with a variety I thought the men might like. Then I fell into bed and slept the sleep of exhaustion.

I loved to choose and see my path;
but now Lead Thou me on!
I loved the garish day, and,
spite of fears, pride ruled my will:
—John Henry Newman

Chapter 13

As soon as John dropped me off at work the next morning, I was on the telephone, and that afternoon I left work a little early. I told Pete to inform John that I had found a ride home, and when I walked in on Coy I had a surprise for him.

He sat straight up in bed. "Mary!"

She laughed. "Coy!" she mimicked. "What mess have you gotten yourself into now?"

He squirmed a little under her intense regard. "I'm not quite sure," he finally answered.

"Well, whatever it is I hope it gets resolved pretty fast. The whole town is talking about it, and if this were still the Old West I'd say there was a lynching party in the making."

"If this were still the Old West," Coy retorted, "they'd be pinning a medal on whoever shot an Indian."

Mary opened her bag and pulled out a thermometer. "Fiddlesticks!" she said. "Now open your mouth wide, there's a good boy."

Coy obeyed her, then watched her warily as she took his pulse, straightened the covers, and smoothed the hair back that had fallen across his forehead.

She took the thermometer from his compressed lips and said with a professional air, "No fever, thank the Lord."

"I could have told you that," he said.

"Now, Coy, don't be sulky. Be a good boy for Nurse and you can have some ice cream after supper."

I had to laugh. Coy frowned at me. "If this is your idea of a joke…"

Mary sobered suddenly. "This is no joke, Coy. This is serious. You've been shot, and the only conclusion we can come to is that it was deliberate."

"Nonsense!" he snapped. "Why you and Johnny must persist in believing somebody actually took a pot shot at me…"

"We're not the only ones who think that," Mary snapped back, her hands on her hips. She shook a finger at him. "You had better watch yourself, Coy Youngblood. Johnny's not one to worry unnecessarily, but he's worried now."

"How do you know? Have you seen him yet?"

"Well, no," she admitted. "But Lu told me…"

That drew another frown from Coy. "I know Mary has an overactive imagination," he said to me, "but I didn't think you had one, too."

"It's not my imagination that you were shot. And it wasn't my imagination that Scooter Mathieson tried to pick a fight with you. Or that Sheriff Carter was bent on taking his side against you."

Mary turned to me. "Scooter tried to pick a fight with Coy?"

"I…I forgot to tell you. Maybe I shouldn't have told you now." The look Coy gave me affirmed this. But, having once started, I went doggedly on. "And then there was Slim Rhodes. He resents Coy, too, and told me there were a few others around here who do. And I agree with John. I don't like the feel of this, either."

"It was an accident," Coy insisted.

"I thought so at first, too," I said. "But the more I think about it, and the more I learn from people around here who know about guns and rifles and how to use them, well, now I'm not so sure."

"Well, however it happened," Mary said crisply, "the first thing of major importance is that we get you well and out of Lu's hair. Then we'll try to sort the whole thing out."

I left them then, and went to make supper. Coy had been living on soup and jello and the like. Tonight I thought he could handle something more substantial, so I was in the process of putting a roast into the oven when John Ransom walked in.

178

"I went by to pick you up," he said. "But Pete told me you left early. Who brought you home?"

"I did," Mary said, coming into the kitchen.

John gave me a wry grin, then went and took both of Mary's hands in his. "How kind of you to come," he told her. Then he turned to me. "And how kind of you to invite her."

"Take your tongue out of your cheek, Johnny," Mary ordered. "The poor girl needed reinforcements. One of you is a handful, but the two of you together could send one into an early grave. Lu, where should I put my gear?"

I wiped my hands on my apron. "Upstairs, the room on the left. There are twin beds. I'm using the one by the window."

She bestowed on me a smile of thanks and on John one of pure mischief.

When she had gone I turned to face John. He was giving me his lazy smile.

"Reinforcements, indeed," he said.

I thought I read that look accurately. "I'm not worried about my reputation," I snapped. "If I needed a chaperone, which I don't, David's presence in the house is sufficient. I'm worried about Coy. You're not exactly the stuff of which ministering angels are made, and I was beginning to be afraid that even though the bullet didn't kill him, your well-intentioned but maladroit nursing just might."

"And with a registered nurse here, I could move back home knowing that Coy is in good hands."

"That, too," I said, a little defiantly.

He smiled kindly at me, and said, his voice soft and gentle, "I know this hasn't been easy on you, Lu. Working a full-time job, then taking care of a houseful of men. I can't tell you enough how much I...we...appreciate all you've done. Especially since I somehow—through absolutely no fault of my own, I might add— seem to make you tense and nervous. And I do appreciate the fact that you invited Mary to come, whatever your motives were in doing so. I admit it hasn't been easy on me, either, being here, with you, and I admit, too, that it will be best for me to move back to the ranch. I knew last night that I needed to go, but I honestly didn't want to leave Coy here by himself all day, and I didn't want

179

you to have to worry about him all night. Mary will take care of both those concerns."

So John Ransom moved back to his ranch, and Mary stayed for three more days looking after Coy, and in that space of time I learned to like and respect this young lady who was caring so assiduously for her friend.

Finally, on Saturday morning, we were able to bundle Coy into John's comfortable Cadillac and send him home. Mary was going to stay with him until Monday morning, then she was going to go back to work.

The house felt suddenly very empty, even with David there, chattering about school and basketball and church. Even though John Ransom had moved back home, he had still been coming every evening for a few hours to give Mary a breather and keep his friend company. Now there was once again just David and me.

David was on the floor doing his homework. I was sitting in my rocking chair, reading.

Suddenly David looked up at me. "Miss them, don't you?" he asked with a certain relish, even though it could have been construed as more of a statement.

"I miss Mary," I answered.

"Ha!"

"What do you mean by 'ha!'?"

"Only that you can fool some of the people all of the time, and all of the people some of the time, but you can't fool me."

"Studying Lincoln, are you, little brother?"

He nodded. "The Civil War. And don't change the subject. You like John, don't you?" Again, it was more a statement than a question.

I closed my book with a snap. "David, dear, there are some things a fourteen year-old cannot possibly understand. Not even you, smart kid that you are. I can't fall in love with John Ransom just because you want me to. The…chemistry just isn't there."

David put the pencil he was holding carefully on the floor, and smiled slightly. Almost the way John Ransom smiled. "Sis, I know you too well. I've seen you around men. The way you look at Johnny—well, I've never seen you look at anyone else quite that way."

180

I stood up. The room was suddenly stuffy. "I make it a point not to look at him," I managed to say.

David grinned. "That's what I mean."

I groaned. "I'm going to check on the animals before I go to bed."

"You don't need to. I already did, when I shut the chickens in for the night."

"Well, I'm going to anyway."

I pulled on my boots, threw my coat on and donned a knit cap. I stuffed my hands into my warm woolen mittens then left the house in an agitated state of mind. I should have moved the instant I found out who our closest neighbor was. Or, having decided that for David's sake I would stay, I should have kept that neighbor at arm's length. Or further. Now I was in a mess, and it didn't help my state of mind that it was a mess of my own making.

I walked around the yard. There were contented clucking sounds from the chicken coop. I went into the barn. Goliath was standing in his stall, peacefully eating his oats. Betty Lou eyed me curiously.

I left the barn and walked down the drive. A hazy quarter moon was throwing dim light from behind shadowy clouds racing across the sky. There were a few pinpoints of light in the heavens, but the Milky Way, Coy's Sky Trail, could not be seen.

I walked briskly down the long drive to the road. Perhaps, I thought, I should tell David the truth. All of it. He was growing up. He might understand.

I stopped short. Understand what? That after our father stole money from the bank where he worked, he had gone on a rip-roaring drunk and killed—murdered—a highly-respected doctor? And that that doctor was John Ransom's father? And that I was in the car, and if I had only tried hard enough could surely have prevented the accident?

No, I told myself. I couldn't tell David. It would shatter his newly-found confidence. He would be unhappy for the rest of his life, especially loving John Ransom the way he did.

I walked back through the cold night air. The hills around me were ghostly shadows, the pine trees that lined the drive made a rushing sound as the wind flew past them and propelled me towards my house.

181

I glanced towards the Ransom place. A single light shone through their own trees. From that distance it looked as remote as the few stars that had braved the clouds.

I heard the mournful howl of a coyote. That is probably the most lonesome sound on earth. It reverberated against the hills and whipped around me like the wind. Then it died, slowly, and once more the night was silent. I suddenly felt very lonely myself.

I quickly went back to the warmth of our home. David was still on the floor doing his homework.

He looked up and grinned. "Any loose livestock lying around lackadaisically?"

"No, the wolves won't win any windfalls with you on watch."

He went back to his homework.

"Algebra?" I asked.

"Yes. It's a snap. We have one of the best math teachers— she's been here for years. Had Johnny and Coy and Big Mike Maguire when they were my age. So did a lot of my other teachers."

"How interesting. And since you again bring up the subject of John Ransom, I'd like to say something to you."

He put his pencil down again and folded his hands and gave me a limpid look while he patiently waited for me to begin.

I sat back down on my rocker, then ran my tongue over my dry lips. This, I thought, was going to be difficult. "It's like this, David," I began, then didn't quite know where to go from there. I tried again. "It's like this. I had a few friends in Chicago—not many, I grant you, but a few—but I never expected you to feel the same way about them as I did. Now you have quite a few friends of your own, and you have your own reasons for liking them. But it would be unfair to me if you expect me to like them as much, and for the same reasons, as you do."

He started to interrupt, but I motioned for him to be still and continued, "I realize you like John Ransom. I'm sure you'd like him for a brother, and I'm equally sure he would make a fine one. But I'm not going to marry just to give you a big brother. You'll be out on your own in a few years and I'd be stuck. So you be friends with Mr. Ransom, but don't expect me to be. You're embarrassing us both with your not-too-gentle hints. No David!

182

Don't say a word! Not one! I love you and I will do everything in my power to make you happy—except marry. I'd rather not be around John Ransom, for reasons of my own, so please don't create, or even encourage, situations that would force me to be."

He waited until he was sure I was finished, then he said, "You know, not once did you actually say you don't like him."

~~~~~~~~~

Sunday was a lonely day. David generally didn't get home from church until well after two o'clock, and then he took a nap so he could go back to church that night. Mary was still with Coy, so John Ransom was by himself when he came to get David for church.

I always waited up for him, and sometimes I had to stay up fairly late because more often than not someone had the teens over for a snack after the evening service.

On this particular Sunday night I was so engrossed with my book that I didn't notice the car lights coming up the drive or hear the slam of its door. Just all of a sudden David was standing in front of me, his eyes shining.

"Well?" I said. "You're full of news. What is it?"

He took the chair on the other side of the stove. "I…I…I gave my heart to Jesus tonight!"

I gaped at him, then slowly put my book down. "You what?"

He swallowed, then said, quietly and with dignity, "I gave my heart to Jesus tonight."

"Oh. I see. And what is Jesus going to do with it?"

He looked disappointed. I guessed he wanted me to be as excited as he was. But as I sat there, looking at his flushed face, all I could think of was the disillusionment he was letting himself in for. What, after all, had God done for us? I automatically looked at my hands. The ugly scars were a constant reminder of vanished hopes and dreams, of sorrow and death, of what could have been but would never be.

As I sat there looking at the only living relative I have on this earth, I could only wonder why he had made this decision.

"You know," he said slowly, "there is something I want to tell you, but I don't quite know how. It's just that, well, I went up after the altar call, and prayed, and Johnny was there praying with me, and Rev. Hurst, and Marty, and a lot of my friends. And I asked for forgiveness of all my sins."

"David, you're barely fourteen years-old! How many sins could you possibly have?"

He grinned then, "What you don't know! Pride is probably the biggest. I mean, I don't know if pride is always a sin, but when you think maybe you're better than somebody else. Like my art. My teacher has been so encouraging, I got to thinking that I was just about the best artist around.

"And then there's this boy at school who gives me a rough time about me being...well, crippled. I was getting to really dislike him even though Karen tried to talk to me about it. She said he was more crippled than we were, but I couldn't see it. But now I understand what she meant, and I don't resent him anymore, because we're supposed to love our enemies. Why," he said on a note of wonderment, "Jesus even forgave the soldiers who nailed Him to the cross."

"That's all well and good, David, but..."

"But here's the part I want to tell you," he went on as though I hadn't spoken, "something really wonderful happened! I...I all of a sudden didn't mind being crippled anymore! I mean, well, it's always bothered me that I couldn't do certain things, like run and play sports, and then I get tired so easily. But you know, I can ride a horse really well, and I can paint and draw, and I'm the team manager and the guys say I can wrap their ankles better than Coach. And I have so many friends, and I have the greatest sister in the world!" he put his arms around me and squeezed.

Tears were stinging the back of my eyes. I would not allow them to fall. I waited until I knew I had a firm grip on my voice, then said, "David, I never realized how you felt about your...condition."

"Do you think I would tell you, with everything else you have to worry about? Yes, I can say it now. It really used to bother me. But it doesn't any more. I realized how happy I am, and then on the way home Johnny and I talked about it, and he told me that everybody is crippled in one way or another, just that it's not always noticeable."

"Oh?" I said weakly.

David nodded his head. "He said that Marty gets real lonesome for Big Mike and goes through some rough times, especially around the holidays. And Coy is very shy and seldom stands up for himself. And Johnny told me he has a temper and has a real struggle keeping it under control, and that a temper can cripple a person's character just like polio can cripple his legs."

"Oh," I said again. "But, David. Are you ready for this kind of commitment?"

"I think so. Tonight it might seem easy being a real Christian, and tomorrow I may find out how really hard it is. But I'm going to be one. When I gave my heart to Jesus, all of a sudden I felt so wonderful. I…didn't hurt anymore."

He went to bed on that, and left me alone in my parlor with my frantic thoughts. I only had David, and now he was moving away from me, little by little, ever since we came here. Of course I was happy to see him developing independence. I had seen enough of smothering, obsessive "love" in my mother to hate it. I wanted David to have a life of his own, and I knew that meant I had to let go and have a life of my own. I thought I was doing that when I'd spend an evening with Marty or go on a date. But growing up didn't have to mean growing apart, did it? Couldn't David and I always be close? He "gave his heart to Jesus." Did that mean there was no part left for me? What more could God do to me? Was I going to lose David too?

~~~~~~~~~

Monday evening, Marty Maguire came to visit me after I got home from work.

"Oh!" she squealed. "The place looks beautiful. Those curtains look terrific, too, even if I do say so myself."

I smiled. "Thank you. And thank you again for making them."

She handed Mikey to me. "I've got something in the car for David."

She rushed back outside while I stood there holding the little bundle of energy.

"Know what?" Mikey asked me.

"What?"

185

"Santa is bwinging me a twicycle."

"He is?"

He nodded, and his blonde curls bounced enthusiastically. "A wed one. Wif a beepew."

"A what?"

"A beepew. Honk, honk! A beepew."

"Oh. A beeper. A horn. You must have been a very good boy this year."

He nodded again, then looked at me thoughtfully and decided to come clean. "Well, I bwoke Mommy's vase."

"You did?"

The golden curls bounced. "Yep. But Mommy said it was awight, 'cause she didn't like it, anyway. Mrs. Finkle gave it to Mommy and Daddy when they got mawied, and she didn't even like it then."

"Oh, I see."

"Did you know my daddy?"

I shook my head with genuine regret.

He looked thoughtful. "I didn't, too. My daddy's in heaven."

"Oh," I said again.

"Whew is yo daddy?"

It caught me by surprise. I stammered a little, then put him down and said, "Wow, Mikey. You're heavy. Getting to be a really big boy."

"I *am* a big boy," he agreed. "Whew is yo..."

"Mikey! Stop being so nosy!" Marty told him from the doorway. Then to me she said, "I'm sorry, Lu. The boy never stops asking questions."

She handed me the package she brought in. "For David. I hope he likes it."

I took the gaily-wrapped package from her. "I'm sure he will. How thoughtful of you."

"Oh, it's nothing, really. David has been so sweet to Mikey. Completely takes him over in church.

She stopped for a second as though she didn't quite want to tell me something. She told me anyway. "Did you know David's singing a solo at church Christmas Eve?"

I was surprised. David hadn't said a word to me about it. "He has a sweet voice," was all I could manage to say.

"Oh, I know he does." Marty Maguire is the most consistently optimistic person I have ever met. "I was...I mean...we all were hoping you would come hear him."

"Of course I will," I said as though it were a foregone conclusion. "I wouldn't dream of missing it."

"Oh, good. We'll all be delighted." She bit her lower lip. Marty's face is an open book. She wanted to ask me something but wasn't sure of my reaction. Finally she said, "Do you know 'The Lord's Prayer?'"

"I know the music, if that's what you're asking."

She dimpled. "That's wonderful."

I looked at her warily. "Why?"

"We-ell. I was wondering if you could play it Christmas Eve. Aggie can barely get through 'Silent Night', and that after years of practice, and I can read music all right as long as it's not fancy. But David said you're good. Really good."

"David would." I tried to smile. "It's...been a long time, and I have nowhere to practice."

Her face lit up. "You can practice at church. We have a..."

"Steinway," I finished for her. "I know. You told me. But I really don't have time..."

"Oh, sure you do. Mikey, put that book down!"

I turned around. Mikey was in the process of losing my place in *Kitty Foyle*. "Don't got pictews," he said with a note of disgust.

Marty ran to pick up the book. "Sorry, Lu. This child is book-crazy. And picture-crazy ever since David's been drawing for him."

"Drawing for him?"

"Oh, yes. All sorts of pictures. Dogs, cats, horses. Clever cartoon types. You know."

I really didn't, but I wouldn't say so. I was beginning to discover that there were aspects of my little brother's life about which I knew absolutely nothing.

"How about some coffee or tea?" I asked my red-headed friend. "And cookies—chocolate chip."

"I like cookies," Mikey piped. "And coffee."

I patted his fair head. "You'll drink milk, my little man," I told him. "Fresh from Betty Lou."

I served them at the kitchen table while Marty kept up a steady flow of conversation. Very informative, is Marty Maguire. She talked a lot about her husband, and his best friends, Johnny Ransom and Coy Youngblood.

"Inseparable," she told me, "and did they ever get into a lot of trouble! The three of them formed a club—The Secret Society of Sportsmen—Triple S. In order to get in you had to be male, naturally, and involved in at least one sport. And you had to do something unusual or daring and at least two other members of the club had to witness you doing it."

"Sounds rather…juvenile," I commented.

She laughed. "It was. But of course that's what they were, juveniles. And really, some of the things were hilarious."

"Well, what did your husband have to do."

"Oh, brother. Johnny and Coy got their heads together and really thought of something. Big Mike had to hot-wire Mr. Finkle's old tractor and drive it all the way to the park and then back again without being caught."

"And did he do it?"

Marty went off into peals of laughter, a light silvery sound like bells in the wind. "He drove it, all right. All the way to town and around the park. But on his way back he got a flat tire. He went running back to town and caught up with Johnny and Coy, and the three of them were up all night trying to fix it. When Mike finally got it back to the Finkles, old Mr. Finkle was there waiting for him. Boy, did he catch it!"

I laughed, too. "What did the other two have to do?"

She shrugged her shoulders. "Mike never told me what he and Johnny thought up for Coy, or what he and Coy planned for Johnny. But whatever it was, all three were the charter members of the Triple S. Johnny was the president, of course. Johnny was always the president. Or the captain. Or the spokesman. But nobody ever minded. Everybody loved him. Still do. He's a great guy." She darted me a look, her green eyes flashing through her thick lashes.

"Not you, too, Marty!" I said. "And here I thought I could at least count on you."

"Well, I worry about Johnny," she explained. "He needs a wife."

"Then you marry him."

She went off into more peals of laughter. "I wouldn't want marriage to spoil our friendship. No, Johnny and me, never!"

"Well, that's too bad, him being the great guy you say he is. Tell me more about this Triple S." I wanted her to get her mind off matchmaking.

"It's only open to high school boys involved in sports. The president is traditionally a senior. Each boy takes an oath that he will not divulge what the members do for their initiation."

"Definitely juvenile," I said.

"To us, now. But to a high school boy, it's very important. It's an elite group. I mean, the boys have to maintain a 'B' average, with nothing less than a 'C' on their grade cards. And what they do must be daring but not dangerous, and it can't involve breaking the law. I mean, Big Mike didn't steal the tractor, he just borrowed it."

"Do you know of any other exploits?"

Another of her laughs. "Oh, a lot of mischievous things that happen around town are blamed on the boys, but I think a lot are just things that happen in any community. But I do know of two instances which can't be explained any other way."

I refilled Marty's cup and got myself another tea bag. Mikey was shoveling down cookies, and he had a big milk mustache over his little bow-shaped mouth.

"Here's a napkin," Marty told him. "Wipe that mustache off and drink your milk like a gentleman."

"Don't wanna be a genman," Mikey told her, his mouth full of cookies.

"I don't care. You're going to be one, whether you like it or not."

"Wanna be a sojur, like my daddy."

Marty shook her head. "People around here still miss Big Mike. He was going to take over the church when Rev. Hurst retired. Everybody still talks about him—the way he lived." She was quiet for a moment, then added in a far-away voice, "The way he died." She gave herself a mental shake, then went on in her normal, friendly voice. "Mikey doesn't miss a thing." She smiled fondly at her son. "Big Mike was awarded the Congressional

Medal of Honor. Posthumously. They say he saved the lives of eight men, including his captain. But he was killed in the attempt."

I watched the steam rise from my cup of tea. "I'm so sorry," I told Marty. "To win the Medal, and then not even know..."

"Oh, he knows, all right," Marty assured me. "And he knows about Mikey, too, even though the letter I sent him telling him we were going to have a baby came back unopened. Oh, well, let's see. I was going to tell you, oh yes. The Triple S. You've met Father O'Brien?"

I nodded. Marty was back to her garrulous self.

"Well, there's a wooden sign on his door that says 'St. Peter's Rectory' in big block letters. One day—this was just over a year ago—when he left the rectory to hold morning mass at the church, some of his parishioners gathered in his yard and were gaping at the sign. During the night someone had replaced it with another wooden sign, also carved in big block letters, that said 'Home for Unwed Fathers.'"

Marty finished on a gurgle of laughter, and I joined in.

When I finally stopped I asked what the good priest thought about it.

"Oh, he thought it was hilarious. He didn't take it down. Of course, he didn't know the bishop was paying him a surprise visit later that day, and unfortunately his sense of humor was not as well-developed as Father O'Brien's."

And you don't know who did it?"

"Not a clue. Of course, it almost had to be one of the boys who attends his church. But that's not the best one. Have you met Mr. Peabody?"

I wrinkled up my nose.

"That's the one," Marty said. "He is the president of our church board. But this happened to his father, old Zeb Peabody. He was one of those self-righteous individuals who give Christians a bad name. You know the kind."

I certainly did.

"And on top of that, he was terribly cranky," Marty went on. "No one could ever do anything right. But he liked to donate to good causes, especially to the church. However, he wanted people to know about his good works, A Pharisee, you might say."

I didn't know a Pharisee from a Republican, but I listened anyway. It was getting good.

"Well, a few years before he passed away he donated the organ to our church. Of course the Bible says our right hand is not supposed to know what our left hand is doing. I think old Zeb put his own interpretation on that. So he went down to the paper and told Jesse Renshaw what he had done, and that he'd like something in the paper about it. He even told Jess what to write. The article was three paragraphs long, telling all about Zeb and the organ he donated. I'll never forget it. It was supposed to end with, 'as First Corinthians chapter 9, verse 7, says: 'For God loveth a cheerful giver.'

"Jess always sets his type on Tuesday night so he can get up first thing on Wednesday morning and run off the papers. He never suspected." Marty shook her head and I was afraid she was going to start laughing and not finish the story. "Well, he printed his papers, and they went all over the county. But someone, that Tuesday night after Jess set his type and went home, had managed to get into the office and add a line to the galley. The article ended with: 'For God loveth a cheerful giver, *but He also accepteth from a grouch.*'" And she went off into peals of laughter again.

It was the best laugh I had had in ages.

She finally stopped and wiped her eyes. "You should have seen old Zeb. He was livid. He stormed into Jesse's shop and really read him the riot act. And at church that Sunday morning, every time the organ was played there were giggles everywhere. Old Zeb always sat in the front pew, and that day he kept his face looking straight ahead. It was red as a cherry. Some of us were in the choir, looking back at him. It was hard to keep a straight face. I held my hymn book as high as I dared so I couldn't see him, and he couldn't see me." She started laughing again. "There were a few boys who worked on the school paper, but Zeb could never pin any of them down. Neither could Jesse. On the day of Zeb's funeral, when Mrs. Hurst started playing the organ, I mean, some of us couldn't help ourselves. One person even said it would make an appropriate epitaph. Oh, I don't mean to sound unfeeling. But it was funny."

I thought it was funny, too. And I didn't even know old Zeb Peabody, although I was acquainted with his son, who had made it a point to let me know he was president of the church board, as though it were a count in his favor.

Marty and I spent a very pleasant afternoon. Then before she left she came to the point of her visit, which was not, as I discovered, merely to ask me to play the piano on Christmas Eve.

"One of my friends from college—I went a year, believe it or not—is getting married Friday night in Scottsbluff and I was wondering if you would go with me. David said he'd watch Mikey"—she gave her son a fond look—"and you and I could get away for a few hours, maybe do some last-minute shopping while we're there."

"Why, I'd love to go. I'll need to pick up a present."

"Oh, that's sweet, but you don't know her, and I'm taking one. Her name is Sandy Carl. She was my roommate. She asked me to be in it, but I wasn't sure I'd be here. I wanted to visit my mom for Christmas, and she lives near Denver. But I couldn't get away after all. So I should at least go to the wedding, and you and I both need some time off. Could you be ready about five o'clock next Friday evening?"

"I'll take my suit to work and change there."

"Good. Then I'll pick you up at Pete's."

*Music is the only language in which
you cannot say a mean or sarcastic thing.*
—Lord Erskine

Chapter 14

Friday Marty showed up about a half hour late. I jumped in the Packard and we roared off. I had on my serviceable suit, my one and only suit. And I had decided to take a little gift, after all.

"That was sweet of you," Marty told me. "You'll like her family. I met them when big Mike was still in Europe. He and Johnny and Coy all decided to join together, right from high school. They were able to stick together too, and all saw action in Africa, Italy, and France." She shuddered. "Johnny got wounded, but I guess you've already heard about that."

"No, actually I haven't."

She looked a little surprised. "I thought everyone knew. Big Mike told the story. Coy was trapped, got his foot caught or something. The Germans were all over the place, but Johnny went looking for him, and found him, too. He helped Coy get loose, and they shot their way out. Johnny got wounded, but they made it back to the others. Johnny and Coy don't talk much about it, but Coy did say that Johnny more than evened the score. I guess you heard how the two of them met?"

I nodded. "They told me, and David has repeated it several times, for good measure. Seems like John should have won some kind of medal for rescuing Coy?"

Marty threw her head back and laughed her inimitable laugh. "Well, he was given a Purple Heart since he was wounded. But he came closer to being court-martialed than decorated. His lieutenant had forbidden him to attempt the rescue; he was sure it was completely hopeless. Johnny just went AWOL at the front, but he didn't exactly qualify as a deserter, so when they got back he got chewed out, but everybody was pretty busy at the moment and they never took any other action. The interesting part was that Johnny found him by imitating a screech owl. Coy said he knew there were no screech owls in France, but he hoped the Jerrys didn't know it."

I had to laugh too, but it made me see again how senseless war is: grown men playing children's games for the highest possible stakes.

"My," Marty continued, shaking her head, "I've never seen Coy and Johnny take to a kid like they have to David. They treat him almost the same way they treat their own brother Rick. David is such a sweet kid."

"Thanks."

"And he seems to be getting better. His color's good and he's putting on weight."

"Yes," I agreed. "This move has been good for him. The air in...St. Louis...didn't help." This was perfectly true.

"I think it's an advantage for a kid to grow up in the country. Say, by the way, did you hear the sheriff's verdict on the shooting?"

"Yes. He says it was an accident."

"But what do you think, Lu?" She was suddenly tense.

"I don't know what to think. I mean, at first I thought it had to be—that it couldn't be anything else. But I'm not so sure, now that I've had time to think about it. I saw hate—real hate—in Scooter Mathieson's eyes that day at the diner. I think that at that point, had he had a gun, he would have shot Coy on the spot instead of just insulting him."

"A lot of townsfolk think that Sheriff Carter has told a few key people not to point their fingers at Scooter for the express purpose of keeping things stirred up. Some of us think the sheriff would like to see Coy try to even the score so he'll have a reason for arresting him."

"I can't see Coy picking a fight with anyone."

"Of course not," Marty agreed. "Johnny's the one with the temper. But I agree with you. I think Scooter is capable of pointing a gun and pulling the trigger. I wouldn't tell anyone else that, but you're no gossip and I know it won't go any farther."

It had bothered me, that shooting. I didn't like Scooter Mathieson, and I didn't trust Sheriff Carter. But it was over, and I think Coy Youngblood had shrugged it off as an accident, so, as far as he was concerned, the matter was settled.

"Scooter Mathieson is trouble," Marty went on. "He has the sweetest wife, always at church with her five kids. Mark's the oldest—seventeen. He loves sports but he can't play because he has to take care of their place, and he does it almost single-handed. Scooter doesn't lift a finger, and if it weren't for Mark they'd lose everything. The four girls pitch in every way they can, but it seems like whenever they get a little bit ahead Scooter blows it."

Marty's talk brought back some unpleasant memories of my own youth.

"If we have a town drunk, it's Scooter." Marty said, breaking into my thoughts. "I'll never understand comedy sketches about alcoholics. There's nothing funny about it. It's sad, heart-breaking."

How well I knew. "I think it's all blown over." I wanted to change the subject, so I asked, "What do you think about the ICC's order to end racial segregation on trains and buses?"

"It's about time," she answered, and talk turned to politics and stayed there until Marty pulled into Scottsbluff.

"What church are we looking for?" I asked.

"Trinity," she said. "There. That must be it. See all the decorated cars? Mike and I got married in the spring. I don't know why anyone would get married in the winter, and at Christmas, too."

We had to park two blocks away and slide to church. It was small and crowded, and we were obviously late. A slightly overweight soprano was already singing 'I Love You Truly' about half-a-key off tune when we walked in.

There was a large table for gifts in the vestibule, and we set our presents with the rest. An usher came up to us and whispered, "Friends of the bride, or groom?"

"Bride," Marty answered.

We scooted down a side aisle and nearly to the front, where there were still a few vacant seats. We stepped over half-a-dozen pairs of feet to the last stanza of the song and squeezed into the empty places.

Marty looked around. "I don't see a soul I know," she said "I guess our other friends from college couldn't make it because of the weather. And I don't recognize any of the family members. That could be her cousin Harry. She told me he had a big nose and red hair. Wanted to fix me up with him once. Glad I didn't let her!"

The music started. Mendelssohn.

"Her mother's gained weight," Marty whispered as an usher led the woman to her place on the front row. "A lot of weight."

Then came the attendants. Marty leaned towards me once again. "I would have thought Mary Sue Michaels—but maybe she's maid of honor."

She wasn't.

"Sandy's made some new friends since college," Marty remarked.

Then the first few strains of Wagner's wedding march were played, and on cue the bride, on her father's arm, appeared at the back of the church.

Marty gave an audible groan. "That's not Sandy! Come on. We've got to get out of here."

I had always carefully avoided embarrassing situations. I wanted to stay right where I was.

But Marty was tugging at me, so as soon as the bride took her place in front of the minister, we stepped over those same pairs of feet and excused ourselves as graciously as we could under the circumstances.

But getting out of the pew proved to be the easy part. We had to rummage through the pile of gifts on the table to retrieve ours.

"That one's mine. Here, Lu, this one's yours."

She handed me a package and we left as quickly as we could, while at least half of the congregation craned their necks to watch what we were doing.

We were standing outside in front of the church as the bitter wind whipped around and through us, and Marty kept saying, "Trinity Lutheran, I know that's...no! Wait! Trinity Methodist! That's it! How could I have forgotten that Sandy's dad is a Methodist minister!"

So we slipped and slid back to Marty's car.

"You're sure? It's not Trinity Church of God, nor Trinity Baptist?"

"No, no. It's Trinity Methodist."

We took off to find Trinity Methodist. When we finally arrived the ceremony was nearly over. I let Marty go in first to make sure she recognized someone, and when she motioned to me that she did, I went in, too. We scurried as quickly and quietly as we could to a place in the very back row.

The groom kissed his bride, and they marched back up the aisle, arm in arm and obviously very happy. Marty was crying.

"I always do, at weddings," she said, blowing her nose. "I cry more at weddings than I do at funerals."

The reception was in the basement. Marty and I had kept our gifts, and still had them when Marty introduced me to her former room-mate, who in turn introduced us both to her new husband. Since we were the last to go through the reception line, Sandy and her husband and Marty and I all strolled over to the table loaded with the gifts. All the other two hundred or so guests gathered around, and Sandy told everyone who we were, and we were met with smiles and friendly greetings.

Marty, bless her heart, took my present out of my hands and handed it to her friend. "It's good luck if your gift is the first one the bride opens," she explained to me.

So Sandy thanked me and opened the present I had so carefully wrapped. Then she opened the box, and pulled out, not the silver vase I had picked out, but something entirely different. She gave me a crooked, uncertain smile as she displayed the present. I could feel everyone's eyes on me. This Methodist minister's daughter was holding in her hand a delicately carved and obviously expensive beer stein.

Marty leaned over to me and whispered, "It's beautiful, Lu, it really is. But Sandy doesn't drink. Wesleyan background, you know. I should have told you."

I said out of the corner of my mouth, "I didn't buy that. You picked up the wrong gift at the other church."

"But the wrapping…"

"Is the same. I can see that. Same paper, same size box. Oh brother."

197

So Marty, good sport that she is, stopped the opening of the gifts to explain to the guests what had happened.

Everyone had a good laugh, and later, before she left the church, Sandy came over to me and said, "One day I'll tell you what Marty did to me. I can see she hasn't changed one bit!"

~~~~~~~~

On the trip to Scottsbluff I had picked up mail, and I'm afraid I shed a few private tears over the Christmas cards from Chicago. Dr. Ableman had been in touch with Dr. Abrams and was so joyful over David's progress, I sensed as never before the real love that had motivated all his kindness through the years. It is humbling to realize you're loved, especially when you've done nothing to deserve it. I said that to David as I shared the letter with him, and he said that was the way God loved us. I wished people wouldn't keep filling his head with these simplistic ideas.

There was a kind note from Professor Bergman too, although he and Mr. Laski wouldn't send a Christmas card of course. But Moshe sent a package of sheet music as a gift for me, and for both David and me, the kindest, sweetest gift we would ever receive, a small scrap book of memories he had kept: some notes and letters my grandparents had sent him, some newspaper clippings of happier times, a photo of me at the piano with a huge bow in my hair and my proud grandparents and piano teacher standing behind me, some awards I had won, and handmade birthday cards I had made for him. His birthday was easy to remember, February 22; he said the whole United States celebrated with him. I determined I would make another card this coming year.

Nick had sent money; I was not surprised, but it made me uncomfortable, although it was earmarked, "Give the kid a good Christmas for once in his life." Missouri, of course, had written a long letter, full of good wishes and probably equally good advice, though as always, I was not receptive to it. She also shared that Nick had visited her church with her one Sunday, then decided he needed to start attending mass on a regular basis. She was praying for him, as, needless to say, she was for David and me. David had already sent her a lengthy letter about his experiences at church, but they must have crossed in the mail.

For myself, I hadn't been able to write her—not since I found out who my next-door neighbor was. I'm sure David told her his name, so she must have figured it out by now. I could just picture her glee, and I was sure the next letter would be full of "I told you! I told you so."

Those last few days before Christmas were busy. Pete always closed his diner two days before and two days after Christmas, giving me a nice little vacation. It was made even nicer by the fact that he still paid me.

I was able to go shopping with David for tree ornaments and other decorations we would put around the house. We went out and cut a pine—the first tree we had since David could remember—and we went through the process of stringing popcorn and cranberries and then draping the hand-made garland around the sweet-smelling evergreen. I filled the rest of the house with pine boughs, and sprinkled them with artificial snow.

I spent those last two days before Christmas baking, and practicing "The Lord's Prayer." The melody, I had to admit, was beautiful. I was to play it through once, then John Ransom would sing it. I didn't know that until the first time I went to the church to practice. Marty had conveniently forgotten to tell me that little detail.

He had been coming to the diner every afternoon for his pie and coffee, and always left me his usual quarter tip, which was too much for a thirty-cent piece of pie and a ten-cent cup of coffee. We only exchanged commonplaces, and if Pete noticed that I was cool and aloof to a customer he never mentioned it.

John noticed it, though, even though he never said anything about it. He just placed his order and left his tip, always with that sweet smile.

Now as I was removing my wraps in the church vestibule, he walked in. I said in an attempt to be polite but distant, "Hello, John. It's nice to see you."

He gave me a devilish grin. "You're in church, you know."

"I recognized it by its steeple."

Marty had the grace to look a little sheepish. "Johnny's going to sing it." she told me apologetically as she handed me the sheet music. "You'll play it through once first though."

I glanced at the music, and then at John Ransom. "What key?" I asked him.

He smiled and shrugged. "I don't know. Just don't make it too high."

I went to the bench and sat down. The Steinway was gleaming with a fresh coat of polish. I opened the lid and gingerly touched the ivory keys, then ran some chords. The tones were beautiful.

"It's a lovely instrument," I told them both.

"Yes, we're proud of it," Marty said, coming to stand next to it. "The senator's wife donated it when she got her new one. She's sorry, though. She said if she had to do it all over again, she would keep this one and donate the new one." She glanced at her watch. "Oh, dear! It's past two o'clock. I've got to get Mikey from Aggie's." She was gone on the words. Her "I'll see you two later" was caught by the wind and carried away as she flew through the door.

John looked at me, those flashing blue eyes daring me to think of some excuse to flee the church.

But I just smiled up at him as sweetly as I could, then looked through the music. The familiar keyboard, where I had spent so many hours of my life, soothed the edginess I always felt when John Ransom was around. I played the song through once, softly. My fingers felt stiff and awkward, but I knew that only a professional would notice what I heard so plainly. I was thankful that Moshe Laski was far away. It would have broken his heart. But I was profoundly grateful it was no worse. With time and practice I could improve.

John stood right behind me, watching. I could feel his presence as though it were tangible—warm and comforting, and safe. And something I had no right to.

"You can play it in that key at first," he told me, "but you'll have to lower it for me."

He sang it beautifully, and I wondered if his fine baritone voice had been trained. I added a few touches of my own to the score and he remarked that he was sure Schubert would have approved.

"Thank you. I like Schubert."

I started to get up, but he put his hand gently on my shoulder and pushed me back down. "Please go on playing," he asked.

So I played. An etude, a waltz, a nocturne, then "Grande Fantasie," and the sun wheeled, and its rays came like arrows of flame through the stained glass window, throwing our shadows against the white plaster wall.

"Will you sing for me?"

"Oh, I'm not a singer. I've never had a lesson."

"Please sing something," he asked quietly.

I cleared my throat. He was entirely too close. I needed air, breathing room. "What...what would you like?"

"You pick it."

Remembering that I had done pretty well with it those last nights at Little Italy, I chose the familiar Irish ballad.

"Oh Danny Boy, the pipes, the pipes, are calling, From glen to glen and down the mountain side. The summer's gone..."

And on I sang, carried away by the poignant words and melody. When I finished I looked at him, and was startled. I thought I saw tears in those blue eyes. His hand had never left my shoulder.

"That was...wonderful," he told me softly.

"I must go," I said, and tried to rise.

"Must you?"

"Yes, I...David..."

"You're always running away from me. Why, Lu?"

I opened my mouth to disclaim, or explain, or say something, when another voice, boisterously Irish, intruded.

"Wonderful! Beautiful! I heartily agree." said Father O'Brien. "I just ran into Marty—almost literally—and she told me you were here, Lucasta dear."

He walked down the aisle towards us. I was so grateful to him I bubbled over with enthusiasm. "Oh, Father O'Brien. It's so good to see you. I haven't seen you in ages. You're looking well; of course you always do." I stopped for breath. Then I thought to myself, Good grief, you sound just like Marty.

Both men looked at me in some surprise, then Father O'Brien turned to my companion, grinned wickedly, and said, "And you, Johnny my boy, are you glad to see me too?"

"Of course I am," John said evenly. "As always."

"Liar. I've interrupted something." The priest winked at me.

"No, Father. Though any earlier, and you would have interrupted our practice session," I told him. My face was burning.

"That's why I came."

"To interrupt our practice session?" John asked blandly.

"No, no. I didn't mean to interrupt...er...anything. But I've come to ask Lucasta a favor."

"Ask away," I said. "While I'm in the Christmas spirit."

"Ah," he said, rubbing his chubby hands together. "Would you happen to be acquainted with Schubert's work?"

"Yes," I replied hesitantly, "some of it."

"Good. Then after you've played 'The Lord's Prayer' here, I was wonderin' if you could play the 'Ave Maria' at Midnight Mass."

I stole a glance at John Ransom. Those eyes! Now they were dancing like sunlight on a clear blue lake.

"Get me the sheet music, Father. I wouldn't want it said around town that I carried a religious prejudice. Maybe for Hanukkah I could play 'Hava Nagila.'"

He laughed. "Hanukkah is over. But you can play it for me and Levi Abrams sometime. Just come over to the church when you're done doin'...whatever it is you're doin.'" He turned and went out as cheerfully as he had come.

"Barry Fitzgerald, *Going My Way*. Ever see it?" I said to John.

"Yes, in New York, when I got back from France. It's a great movie, but...I'm surprised you've seen it."

"Oh, I have nothing against religious films. They're kind of sweet and gentle. Gets one away from the real world."

He frowned. "I can't agree. But then my religion—or, rather, my faith in Christ—is my real world."

I put the lid down carefully over the ivory keys and folded my sheet music.

"What's your reality, Lu?"

"David," I answered quickly. "He's all that matters." I wasn't looking at him when I answered.

He took me by the shoulders and turned me around to face him. "Isn't there room for anyone else in your world?"

I swallowed hard. "No. I don't think so. I...no, there isn't."

"Lu, you're making an idol of David, and God has a way of destroying our idols. Don't force Him…"

I broke away from his near-embrace and fled the church.

Marty was at St. Peter's when I got there. "Father told me you would play 'Ave Maria' for him," she said by way of greeting. "That's sweet. A lot of us come here after our Christmas Eve service. His Midnight Masses are beautiful. Here she is, Father."

Mikey held his arms out to me and I took him. "Did you have a nice time at Aggie's?" I asked.

He nodded his head, and his golden curls danced.

Father O'Brien was just rising from his prayers, and Marty said, "Still praying that the British will be driven from Northern Ireland?"

He winked at her. "That would be treasonous, darlin' girl. The English have done wonders for us. Given us kings and queens to rule us, soldiers to guard us, taxes to break our backs. Why on earth would I want the English out of my country?"

Marty laughed. "Come on, Mikey. Say good-bye to Lu and Father O'Brien."

She took her son back, and he said a charming good-bye to me, and then asked his mother, "Is he my daddy?"

Marty stared blankly at her son. "Wha…what did you say?"

Mikey pointed at the priest. "I said, is he my daddy?"

Father O'Brien broke into loud guffaws "You called me 'father,' Marty. You had better explain to the boy. I'm in enough trouble with my bishop as it is."

"I'll try. Come on Mikey. We'll go home and make some cookies." She threw Father O'Brien a smile over her shoulder. "I'll bring you some," she promised.

"Saints preserve me!" the priest exclaimed when she had gone. "The last time she brought me cookies I chipped a tooth on one. She needs to get married—to someone who can afford the dental work. How's Johnny?"

The sudden shift in conversation caught me off-guard. "You should know," I stammered. You just saw him."

"And none too happy he seemed."

"Well, I'm not acquainted with him well enough to know his moods. Where's your music?" He gave me a piercing look. I gave him one right back, so he didn't press the issue. He went through a small door and came back with some yellowed and worn sheet music. He handed it to me as though he were giving me the secret code of the Irish Republican Army.

"I'll take care of it," I promised him.

"The organ is up there, in the loft at the back. Everyone will hear you but no one will be able to see you. Sort of gives the impression that the music is comin' from heaven. And speakin' of heaven, you're an angel to do this for me."

"Think nothing of it."

He showed me the steps to the loft. I played the song through several times. The sweet notes of the organ floated to every corner of the small but beautiful church.

When I went back down to join Father O'Brien, his pale blue eyes were filled with tears. "I haven't heard it played so beautifully in years. I don't suppose...but no, you're not Catholic."

"No. I'm not Catholic. But any time you want a song played for a special occasion, let me know."

"Ah, you're a lamb, a sweet lamb. Of course, I wouldn't want to put Mrs. Flaherty's nose out of joint—not that it would be an easy task, mind you—but there are times, like now when she's out of town, and I'd need someone to play."

"Just call on me."

"I will, lass. I will."

On Christmas Eve I donned my same blue suit. I wore a bright red blouse with it, and David presented me with a beautiful Christmas corsage of small red carnations. We drove into town behind John and Coy. John was at my car door when I parked, opening it for me and helping me out even before the engine stopped sputtering.

I was a little breathless. I blamed it on the icy night air.

The four of us walked into church together. Most heads turned towards us as we entered the sanctuary, and a few even nodded knowingly. If John Ransom didn't seem to notice, I certainly did. By the time we found a partially empty pew, my face, I was sure, was as red as a Christmas Poinsettia.

I found myself, quite without wanting to, between John and David. Though I didn't know many of the songs in the hymnal, I did know the Christmas carols, and since David seemed to want to share his hymn book with Coy, I had no choice but to share mine with John. I'm sure everyone thought we were a cozy foursome.

The children sang a few songs, several had short pieces to say, and then David sang 'O Holy Night' with simple organ accompaniment. He had a sweet, clear voice, and I marveled, not for the first time, at the surprises of which David seemed to be full.

Rev. Hurst proved to be a mediocre speaker with a voice that cracked like dry pine needles. Fortunately he wasn't long-winded, at least not on this night, and soon it was time for "The Lord's Prayer."

I took my place at the piano, and John stood behind me. I played it through once, and then hit John's opening note.

And for the first time in my life I found myself actually listening to the words as John sang them.

"Our Father, which art in heaven, hallowed be Thy name, Thy kingdom come, Thy will be done, on earth as it is in heaven. Give us this day our daily bread, and forgive us our debts as we forgive our debtors. And lead us not into temptation, but deliver us from evil, For Thine is the kingdom, and the power, and the glory, forever. Amen."

My fingers played over the last few notes again, then the clear tones died slowly in the absolute silence of the church.

I peeked at the stilled congregation. Some heads were bowed, and other faces were lifted heavenward with a look of rapture. I looked at John, and he smiled at me.

A number of us went to St. Peter's after the Christmas party at the community church. A lot of Protestants were, I discovered, quite fond of the priest.

I went to the loft immediately. There would be no more sharing of a hymnal with John Ransom.

The service was about forty-five minutes long. I played all of the songs; it seemed the absent Miss Flaherty was the only Catholic who could play an organ.

The "Ave Maria" was the final song, and no one sang it. It turned out that no one knew the Latin words except Father O'Brien, and he couldn't carry a tune.

The good priest thanked me after the Mass, and several of his flock approached me about joining the church.

I thanked them politely, gave them some double-talk, and left with David.

It was a beautiful night, clear and crisp. We wound our way through the hills that were glistening silver under the light of the white December moon, David and I each lost in our own private thoughts.

Finally I glanced over at him, and he gave me that look.

"What did you do now?" I asked.

His eyes, sparkling under his long lashes, slid towards me and then slid away. "Well...," he started, then bit his lower lip.

"You might as well come clean. I'll find out sooner or later."

"Actually, you'll find out sooner," he said. "I...well, they miss Rick, you know, and they said Christmas is no fun without kids, so..."

I moaned. "So you invited John and Coy for Christmas dinner."

The eyes slid towards me again. "Well, no. I didn't think you'd want me to do that and I remembered you said we were eating out."

I breathed a long, relieved sigh.

"I invited them over for tonight, instead," he finished with a rush.

"Tonight!" I lost my grip for a split second and the car swerved on the snow. I waited until I got it—and myself—completely under control before I allowed myself to say anything. "It's after midnight, David!"

He grinned. "It's Christmas Day, Sis. 'Peace on earth...'"

"'Good will towards men.' I know. But why these particular men, and all the time?"

"I like them," he said simply.

A coward is incapable of exhibiting love;
it is the prerogative of the brave.
—Mahatma Gandhi

Chapter 15

They drove up not fifteen minutes after we got home. They were loaded down with presents.

I saw them from the window over the sink. "They're bearing gifts, Brother Dear," I called to David, "and we don't..."

"Oh yes we do!" And David came into the kitchen carrying two inexpertly-wrapped presents. "For them, from us."

I put my hands on my hips. "David, you're getting entirely out of hand. You used to be such a straight-forward, predictable child."

"Well, I'm not a child anymore," he informed me. "I'll put them under the tree."

He was gone, leaving me to answer the knock. Their opening remarks indicated that David had led them to believe that the invitation came from both of us. But I was well aware of the fact that John Ransom knew better.

I took their coats and invited them into the parlor. David was plugging in the tree, and there were a number of presents already underneath.

My foresighted and optimistic little brother had also hung mistletoe in the doorway, which I didn't notice, but our guests did. So there I stood, rather stupidly, I admit, and got kissed on the cheek first by a very shy Coy Youngblood, and then more thoroughly by John Ransom.

I fled back into the kitchen to catch my breath and give my hands a chance to steady themselves.

But John followed. He came to me, his arms ready to grasp me once again, but I forestalled him by handing him a platter of candies, cookies, and the nut roll Nick Costelli's chef had taught me to make.

"Would you please take this into the parlor?" I asked him.

He gave me a wry smile, obediently took the platter from my hands, and left. He didn't come back. I made the coffee and tea in peace and told myself I was glad, while laughter from the parlor floated gently to my ears.

I carried the steaming cups in on a tray and John took it from me and set it on the end table.

"We've been telling David about the Triple S," he said to me. "It seems he already knew what happened to Big Mike Maguire."

"Marty told me, and I told David. I hope I didn't breach some code of ethics."

Coy and John both laughed. "The whole town knew by the next afternoon. Mr. Finkle was ready to spit nails. Poor Mike. He had to haul hay for Mr. Finkle for a solid week, with no pay."

I sat down in my rocker. John took the comfortable chair opposite me. Coy had the sofa all to himself because David was sitting, cross-legged on the floor by the tree.

"What did you have to do?" David asked Coy.

Coy glanced at John, who smiled and said, "Go ahead, Coy. We were kids then. They'll understand that we didn't have much sense in those days."

"Only if you tell them what you did," Coy shot at him.

John Ransom actually turned a little scarlet. "That they might not understand," he murmured.

Coy laughed. Coy, I thought to myself, should laugh more often, and then I wished the personable Mary Star were here, sharing this night with us.

He looked once more at his good friend, then turned to David, with only occasional glances at me. "Well the old senator—the present senator's uncle, as a matter of fact—built the mansion on the north edge of town and lived there when he wasn't in Washington. He was a dyed-in-the-wool Republican, like most were here in those days." He gave John a sardonic look.

"Or still are," John replied smoothly, and my brother laughed.

"Well, anyway," Coy continued, "Senator Billingsworth was a great debater, a filibustering fool, you could never get a word in edgewise."

"Much like our present senator," John added.

Coy nodded. "And he was a great friend of Wendell Willkie, and really helped catapult him to the top of the Republican Party's ticket in 1940. Some even say Billingsworth had a lot to do with Willkie changing his party affiliation from the Democrats to the Republicans. Willkie ran a brilliant campaign. He was energetic, frank, likable, witty, and gave Roosevelt a few bad moments.

Well, the senator was home for a few days during the campaign to rest. I sat on Indian Mound—you remember, David, where I told you we might have found an Indian burial ground—with my binoculars and waited up half the night for Senator Billingsworth to retire for the evening. The light in his study was on until well past two o'clock in the morning. He must have been working on a speech. I got cramped, cold, and tired, but finally the light went off. I waited another fifteen minutes, and then I made my way to the mansion. I thought I'd had it when one of his dogs started barking, but I managed to make friends with the beast, and he let me go about my business. I put Roosevelt signs all over his barn, his front door, and his car when I discovered the garage wasn't locked. Then I decided to be more daring. I mean, who locks their doors here? So I sneaked into the house, went to the coat rack, and put Roosevelt buttons on every coat and jacket that was hanging there."

"Goodness! Did he ever discover who did it?"

Coy laughed, and John answered. "No, but he had his suspicions. Everyone knew Coy, here, was a Democrat—I'm sorry, Coy, is a Democrat—and that he was really tired in church the next day, but no one could prove a thing. Only Mike and I knew, and we would never give Coy away."

"Anyhow the Senator showed up in church the next morning before he left for the campaign trail, and he had a Roosevelt button on his jacket. He sure got ribbed," Coy went on. "And he completely missed the bumper sticker on the back of his Lincoln. Mrs. Billingsworth said they were clear to Washington before it was discovered by—of all people—Wendell Willkie."

"Who was reported to have said," John added, "'If you're going to display that name, the hind end of anything is the place to do it.'"

"But," Coy put in, "he didn't...er...say it quite like that."

I laughed, but sobered immediately, and asked my little brother, "So, David, now that you're involved in basketball, are you planning on joining this club?"

David was slightly embarrassed. "I couldn't tell you, Sis. It's a code, you know."

"Like honor among thieves? Great. Now I get to worry that you'll hop a train, or grab a rattlesnake by its tail, or hitch-hike to Wyoming."

"Well," David mumbled. "it's not supposed to be dangerous." Then he turned to John. "Go on, tell us what you did. I bet it wasn't dangerous."

"We-ll," John replied, "that's a matter of opinion. See, we had a librarian...Now, please, take into consideration the fact that I was a boy and prone just like any boy to do some of the crazy things boys do."

I nodded and said I would definitely take that into consideration before I made my final judgement.

"Well, this librarian was a maiden lady, tall and thin, horn-rimmed glasses, a long, thin nose that twitched with distaste at anything out of the ordinary. You know the type—ready to believe the worst about anybody, and repeat it. Very prim and proper was our good librarian. She was one of those people who never does anything wrong and is the first to cast a stone at anybody who does."

"Like in the Bible," David explained to me. "When Jesus said that whoever was without sin should..."

"I understand the allusion," I said, a little sharply. Did my kid brother think I was totally ignorant?

John cleared his throat. "Well, she was really hard on kids who...well, who showed a...shall we say certain amount of natural affection for the opposite sex?"

"Yes." Coy added, "you should have seen her when she caught Johnny and Corrine Parker kissing in the library."

"Never mind," John told him, frowning, "that's neither here nor there."

"No," agreed Coy, "it was behind the shelves in the poetry section."

John's eyes rolled towards the ceiling. "My past is catching up with me. Anyway—may I continue, Coy, or are there any more revelations you would like to make?"

"I think I've said enough," Coy answered, then looked at John's face and added, "probably more than enough."

"Well, Miss Peabody—Oh, I see you're already familiar with that name. Miss Peabody was a sister of old Zeb."

"Aunt Elvira to our present Mr. Peabody," Coy put in.

John nodded. "This happened because I was emptying the trash, picking out some papers to start a fire in the stove. I found a catalog that had been torn in two and discarded. It was addressed to my mother, and I shouldn't have been so curious, but I flipped through the pages and got the shock of my young life."

Coy started to laugh, and John continued, "It was a lingerie catalog. Now I wasn't that easy to shock. I had read—and looked—through all Dad's medical books, and at one time even toyed with the idea of going into medicine myself."

"Until he found out how much work all those college classes would be," Coy told us.

"I'm not going to have any reputation left, Coy, if you don't stop telling tales about me. Are you going to let me finish this?"

Coy immediately treated John to his most dead-pan expression, and John went on with his story. "To make a long story short (if Coy will keep his mouth shut), I behaved like any adolescent boy, and instead of burning the catalog, I showed it to Coy. Then the two of us showed it to Mike. We could hardly focus on a page, we were so embarrassed, but it gave us an idea. We decided to send for the most scandalous thing we could find in the book and have it mailed to the library."

Coy shook his head and hid his face. He was *still* embarrassed. "We picked out a black lace thing—they called it a 'teddy'—with...uh..." he choked.

John's face was flaming, "Never mind! That's sufficient description. I'm sure Lu has an imagination.

"It was to be my stunt, so I paid for it and sent off the order blank. It said allow two weeks for delivery, so after about ten days we started haunting the library when the postman was due.

Luckily, the library was way at the end of his route, so we spread the word, and most of the guys from high school were there every afternoon when he made his rounds. Several days went by, and one afternoon I saw old Zeb come in with some of his friends, including old Rafe Michaelson, the only bachelor who ever showed any interest in Elvira Peabody."

"We all looked at each other and had the same thought," Coy admitted. "If only it could come today."

"The mailman left a small brown box, but it looked just like a book, so we didn't have much hope. Still we were all watching out of the corners of our eyes. Miss Peabody, on the other hand, wasn't paying much attention to the package she was opening. She was watching Rafe out of the corner of her eye. Then we saw a look of puzzlement come into her face, and she snatched at the box...and held up the contents..."

John went into spasms, so Coy picked up the story, "If by any chance there had been anyone in the library who wasn't already watching, she gave a tiny shriek that got their attention."

"Then," John continued, "she just sort of melted. That's the best I can describe it. Her hands slowly lowered, but her head and shoulders disappeared behind the counter too. I guess she just sat down, but I really thought she had fainted, and it kind of scared me. I jumped up to see if she was all right.

"She jumped up too, and our eyes met. Either she guessed intuitively that I was responsible or else she just had to blame someone, and I had unintentionally offered myself. She snatched her coat and purse and was out of that library like a shot," John said, between bouts of his own laughter.

"Ran past Mike and me, her face livid with rage," Coy started laughing again. "It did us a lot of good to see her paid back in her own coin, even if it wasn't a very nice trick to play. But, like I said, we were kids. The enormity of what we had done didn't hit home for a while."

"I disagree," John said. "It hit me pretty fast."

"Why? What happened?" my little brother, who was trying to follow this but was not fully understanding the implications, asked John.

"When my mother heard the story—and of course it was all over town by nightfall—she remembered the catalog she had discarded, and she asked me so pointedly I couldn't deny it. She and Dad were both furious. He confined me to my room—for life. But then he settled down after a few days, and put me in solitary confinement for a month. I could only go to school and church."

"Luckily it was between basketball and baseball, or we wouldn't have had our shortstop," Coy put in.

John nodded. "Yes, I timed it right, anyway. Although I did miss a week of baseball practice. But Dad was hopping mad, and at that point I don't think he cared if I ever played sports again. He made me apologize to Miss Peabody. I think that was harder than being confined to my room."

I said, "Talk about a Christian witness!"

He was still laughing. "If anybody tells you Christians don't have their faults, don't you believe it. I admit it was wrong of me to get even with her for all the unkind things she had said and done over the years. But I paid a price. Not only did I get pretty sick of my own company, but because I missed a week of baseball practice I was not eligible to play in the first game. I was edged out of the conference triple batting crown by a player from Bridgeport because he had one more homerun than I did on the season. I was averaging about two per game, so I probably would have beaten him. Sin," he concluded, "does not pay."

"Well..." Coy grinned, "there was one more little thing." He waited for John to finish the tale.

"Yes, although we have no proof that there was any connection, it was about three weeks later that Elvira and Rafe announced their engagement."

I joined in the hilarity. I laughed until tears were streaming down my face.

After that, talk became more general until the two men realized how late it was getting. John reached under the tree and handed David the present he had brought him. "It's technically Christmas, so go ahead and open it."

David looked at him shyly then tore off the wrapping paper. Inside was a box. David opened it gently. There it was: a Bible, bound in rich dark brown leather. The inscription on the front was in gold italic lettering, "David Morrow." And underneath it, "Christmas, 1955."

David picked it up gingerly, and fingered the leather. "Ohhh...," he breathed. "Thank you so much."

He opened it and reverently turned the pages. "It's got pictures...and look, in the back, a concordance, and a dictionary...and here, special notes on the life of Jesus."

He was showing me all of its features. I knew it was expensive. I glanced up at John. He was watching my expression, not David's.

"Yes, it's very nice," I said to him, with the same inflection I would have used had I been remarking about any other expensive and beautifully-bound book. "I'm sure David will take good care of it. It was very thoughtful of you."

"You're welcome," John said to David, "Here, open Coy's present."

He handed David another present from under the tree. It was bigger than John's gift to him. David tore into it, and gasped. A pair of cowboy boots, black hand-tooled leather, lay in the box.

"Now you're the real thing," Coy told him.

David was speechless. Coy took this, appropriately enough, as a very special thank you.

David took them from the box, pulled off his slippers, and tried them on. They fit perfectly. "Wow!" he finally managed.

Then he took them off and put them under the tree next to his Bible. He pulled out the two flat presents he had wrapped and handed them to the men.

"David, how thoughtful. Coy and I never expected..."

"I know you didn't, I mean, you wouldn't. Not you two. But, well, you've been so nice to me. And they're not much, really." He sat back, his face a little flushed from his brief, naive speech.

The look John Ransom gave my little brother made my heart turn over. "Anything you gave us would be of great personal value," he said softly, and carefully unwrapped his gift.

My breath caught in my throat. It was a painting. I had no idea David was even working on it. It was the view from our porch, with Courthouse Rock standing like a gold-rimmed fortress guarding the plains far below and the mellow amber hills rolling gently towards it. The sun was in the process of setting behind it, and David had managed to give the impression of distance and light. Cattle were sprinkled over the hills, and a lone rider was sitting on his sorrel horse and gazing at something far off. The rider had to be John Ransom. Only he could sit so easily in the saddle, with an apparently careless hold on the reins.

"You painted this?" John asked David, his voice filled with wonder.

He nodded shyly. "And I made the frame in shop."

"That's you and Captain," Coy said when John handed him the painting. Then to David he said, "I never realized how good an artist you are."

"Open your gift, Coy."

Coy obeyed. It was another painting, this time of Seneca. Again Courthouse Rock stood in the background, but Coy's beautiful black stallion dominated the picture. David had managed to capture the spirit and proud heritage of the horse. He was standing on his hind legs, his front hoofs pawing at the sky, his mane flying in the wind.

Coy was touched by David's gesture. "I'll treasure it the rest of my life," he told my brother, and no one could ever doubt Coy Youngblood's sincerity.

I started to rise, but Coy stopped me. "Hey, do you think I'd forget the young lady God used to save my life?" He handed me a gift, a book from the size and feel.

Why hadn't I anticipated this? I should have known and had a return gift prepared.

"You...you shouldn't have felt you needed to...I just happened to be there," I was growing red in the face.

Coy smiled warmly, "I don't believe anything ever 'just happens.' God is taking care of me and of course he uses people— Johnny when I was in France, you the other day. Anyway it's just a book. You have that coming for all the books you loaned me."

As he talked I had removed the wrapping. "George Mueller?" I read.

"I know you like biographies," he murmured shyly. "I liked this one, so I hoped you would too."

I had never heard of George Mueller, "Is he famous?"

"Well, he was well-known in England in his own day, which was the last century, but he is famous in Heaven which is what counts."

The life story of some Christian, I thought. I was disappointed in Coy. Somehow I didn't think he would be trying to convert me too. Nevertheless I thanked him politely.

I went to the kitchen to wrap up some cookies and pastries for them to take home. That would be some return at least. John followed me into the kitchen.

"I have something for you too," he said, and pulled a little package from his pocket.

"I couldn't," I stammered. "I...appreciate...but I couldn't. It...it wouldn't be...and anyway I don't have one..."

He gently picked up my scarred right hand, held it for only a moment, then pressed the small gift into it. "It's Christmas," he said softly. "Humor me."

"But..."

He put a finger on my lips. "Open it."

I opened it. Inside the box was an exquisitely carved ivory grand piano.

"It's...lovely," I said weakly. The word sounded, and was, inadequate. The smallest details on the ivory were sharp. Someone had used delicate strokes to carve the piano, and it had taken a long time. I knew it was expensive. "Thank you."

"You're welcome," he said, his eyes a muted blue now, like the azure haze that covers the Smoky Mountains. "And thank you."

I looked at him. "For what?"

"For this," and he swept me into his arms and kissed me.

Short though the kiss was, it left me breathless. I nearly dropped the ivory piano that was still in my hand.

He held me from him, and took in my burning face and wet eyelashes in one gentle glance, then pulled me to him again.

When he finally let me go, he said, somewhat breathless himself, "Well, I've proven one thing, at least."

I took a step back choking. "And what's that?" I asked with as much cool indignation as I could muster.

"Only that you're not as indifferent to me as you would like me to think you are."

That cool indignation started to warm. "I've never tried to make you think anything. Actually, I haven't thought much about you one way or the other." My ears and scalp were on fire.

He put his finger under my chin and tipped my face up towards him. "We are going to have to break this habit of lying."

Whatever denial I was going to make died in my throat. When he gave me a third kiss, quick but gentle, I pulled away, and tried to think of something sarcastic to say, but any response I would have made was cut off by the arrival of my young but very discerning little brother.

"Coy is waiting for Johnny," he said as he walked in on us. But then he stopped in mid-stride, looked from my flushed face to John's lazy smile, and said, with a knowing, annoying little grin on his face, "But he can wait a little longer. He doesn't mind. Go on doing...whatever it was you were doing. And don't mind me. I'm leaving."

"So am I," I said, and grabbed the box of goodies I had wrapped. I shot past John Ransom, and went as quickly as decorum permitted into my little parlor. I handed Coy the wrapped package, and thanked him for everything.

John had followed me into the parlor and was in the process of putting on his overcoat. He asked, grinning wickedly, "Are you going to thank me for everything, too?"

David gave me a bright look and Coy gave John a questioning one. I tried to look as noncommittal as is possible for me, but all I managed was to just look guilty. And I hadn't done anything.

I was in an untenable situation. I felt I had to do something, and do it quickly. God was getting out of hand with this little joke. All right, so I had moved from the smoke and jumped feet-first into the fire. How was I supposed to know that the only person I had ever tried to avoid in my life would show up a thousand miles away and turn out to be my nearest neighbor? And when I tried to keep him at arm's length, that he would end up living in my house? And when I treated him as indifferently as I could, David would love him like a favorite brother? And that when I ignored him to the point of rudeness, he would kiss me, and shake me to the root of my being?

And there he was, smiling at me as though he could read my mind, and looking at me like he wished we were alone, just the two of us, without the inquisitive stares of David and Coy.

217

I asked God silently if He was happy at this turn of events, if He really wanted to do this to David. For the time had come for me to make a decision. Either David and I would have to move away from here, or I would have to tell both David and John the whole truth, or I would have to be so hateful to my nearest neighbor that he would never want to come near me again.

I didn't like any of the options. It looked like heartbreak for David whichever way I chose. David was doing so well—better than he had ever done in his young and unhappy life—that I hated to drag him off somewhere against his will, away from Dr. Abrams and the first real home we had ever had, with only a slim chance that things would work out as happily again. If I told David the truth that would surely break his heart, and might even cause a serious setback physically. John, knowing the truth about my parents, and especially about my part in the tragedy, would never, and understandably so, want to have anything more to do with us. That would crush David.

The third option I had already been trying as far—no, further, than decency permitted. I had returned curt ingratitude for all John's kindness, rudeness to his unfailing courtesy, and for reasons neither he nor my brother could possibly guess.

I was already ashamed of that and of the lies I had told. I doubted I could go much further without hating myself. And worse—I could even turn David against me. But in spite of all I had done, I had failed to convince either of them. On this particular night I was afraid I had proved him right. I wasn't indifferent.

All this was going through my head as I mechanically wished them a Merry Christmas, thanked them for the gifts, and waved at them until they were speeding down the drive.

Yes, I thought to myself, God was having a field day with me. And everything He had done, as I analyzed my life up to this point, brought me every day more steadily into the sphere of John Ransom.

I needed to talk to someone, to get some advice. To have someone tell me that this was all nonsense, that I had an overactive imagination, that God was too busy to be playing practical jokes on me.

But my closest friend here was Marty Maguire, and I couldn't very well tell her my life story. She had loved the doctor, and she grew up with the doctor's family, and if she knew what had happened in Chicago only what?—only a little over a month ago? No, I couldn't talk to Marty. The same held true for Mary Star. She was too close to the family. What about Aggie? There was a kind soul who I was sure wouldn't hold anything against me. But she had been a close personal friend of the good doctor and his wife, his first wife. How could I know in what manner she would take the news that his death could have been avoided? What about Pete? He was a man and would tend not to be too sentimental. But there again, he was close to the family. No, I had no one here. I had no one back in Chicago, either. No one that I could talk to about this, anyway. And what on earth could I say? How could I define the problem to them when I couldn't even get it clear to myself. It was not something I could put my finger on, this feeling of growing panic.

Missouri Smith had always been my confidante, as she had been my grandmother's, and she had a lot of hard common sense—when she wasn't letting it get sidetracked by her religious views. But I knew how she would view this: I could just hear her telling me that all things worked together for good, and that God sent me here, and this is where I should be, and that everything was going to turn out for the best, because this was His master plan. No, I couldn't talk to Missouri, either. And I could picture the enormous satisfaction she would get from the fact that I had refused to see John Ransom in Chicago, against her advice, and now I was in a position where through the auspices of my little brother he had become an integral part of my life. No, pride wouldn't allow me to talk to Missouri Smith.

I could feign interest in other men. Lance Stoker and I went out occasionally, and Wayne Voyle had asked me out. Owen Lassiter was showing some interest, and there were a few others who were, too. But leading them on would be dishonesty of the worst kind, and I had a feeling that John Ransom would see through the ploy anyway.

It was a problem. I was still trying to work it out when I saw that the sky outside my window was turning gray.

A man's own folly ruins his life—
yet his heart rages against the Lord
Proverbs 19:3

Chapter 16

Christmas Day was to provide yet another shock. David and I got up as the sky was changing from charcoal gray to light pearl, and the hills seemed to change from floating ghostly shapes into something more substantial. We had a hearty breakfast of sausage and eggs, and fresh milk and cream, and then went into the parlor to enjoy the quiet of our first Christmas away from the intrusive noises of Chicago.

I handed David a large box wrapped with colorful paper. "For you, kiddo."

He tore it open with more enthusiasm than I had ever seen him show for a present. When he pulled out the black and gold lettermen's jacket, his mouth moved up and down for a few seconds but nothing came out. All he could do was look at me.

It was too large; I bought it that way on purpose, an act of faith so to speak. I still owed on it, but the kind owner of the clothing store, Mr. Gaitlyn, let me bring it home anyway.

The bulldog mascot was on the back, just below the name of the school, and underneath was our new last name. On the front, in embroidery, was the name "David," and room for the varsity letter he would receive when basketball season was over.

Then he handed me my gift from him. I opened it, and there was another painting. It was of our house, and barn, with the hills that surrounded it covered with pure white snow, and Courthouse Rock barely perceptible on the far horizon. I studied the picture closely. David had somehow managed to paint contentment and peace into the landscape, and the special beauty that was unique to this part of the country. The sun reflected on the snow, and David had captured the glistening rainbow colors. The trees that lined Ransom Creek were slightly bent from the weight of the snow, and drifts all but hid the line of fence that separated our property from our neighbor's.

"That's only part of your gift," David explained. "I'm going to do one for each season."

"David, I love it. I had no idea you had so much artistic ability. Have you thought of making a career in art?"

David gave me one of his fleeting glances from under his long, thick lashes.

"What was that for?" I asked him.

"Oh, nothing. It's just that...well, I'm not sure about it, so maybe I ought to wait to tell you."

"And leave me in suspense? Not on your life, little brother. What is going through that remarkable brain of yours now?" An uncomfortable thought came into my head. "You didn't invite those two over for today, did you?"

He shook his head emphatically, and I breathed a little easier. "No, nothing like that. They were going to spend the day with Mary Star and her mother. It's just that I, well, I'm thinking about..." he glanced at me again, then finished with a rush, "...going into the ministry."

"The what!?" I practically yelled.

"I knew you'd take it like that. That's why I haven't said anything. But, you know, I owe God so much, and I'd like to repay him."

"What do you owe God?" I asked ferociously. "You're crippled."

"But I'm alive."

"And our parents were worthless—no parents at all."

"But you've been mother and father to me. And I can't remember Grandmother, but nobody could have a better grandmother than Missouri."

I looked at my hands. "And, my dreams were shattered by a...by a stupid accident."

"But you can still play," he cried. "You can play better with those hands than most people who study and practice for a lifetime. Maybe you weren't supposed to go on the concert circuit. Maybe God has something better in store for you. Look at me. I'm crippled, but I'm still getting a varsity letter. And I can't run, but I can ride. Johnny says I'm a natural. And I can paint. Maybe God has taken away what we think is best for ourselves in order to give us what He knows is best for us."

I looked at him aghast, "But David—*you*—a minister!"

He gave me a crooked grin. "Yeah, it's pretty shocking, I imagine. But I want to serve Him in some way, and right now I think this is the way. Maybe later He'll show me something different. But one thing is for sure, I've never been happier, and I'd like to do something to repay Him."

I was a little resentful. No, I was a lot resentful. David was happier because of me, because of what I had gone through to get us here. I got up and went to the kitchen and made a big task out of doing the dishes. Presently David came in to dry them. He was sensitive enough to read my reaction as jealousy.

"You know, there's room in my life for both you and God," he told me soberly. The statement startled me; it echoed so nearly the words with which John Ransom had challenged me three days earlier.

"I suppose so. Look, David, let's not talk about it right now. Not today. We have a lot of things to do. We have gifts for Pete, and Doc, and Father O'Brien, and Marty and Mikey, and we need to get going. You're just a freshman. You have plenty of time to decide your future."

So we finished the dishes, packed the car, and headed for town. I went to the diner and read while David went to church, and after church we went on our rounds.

We stopped at the rectory first. Father O'Brien greeted us cheerfully. Dr. Abrams was already there.

The good doctor rose as we entered the small living room. "Terence and I always spend Christmas afternoon playing backgammon," he explained.

"Been doin' it for years, ever since Levi moved to town. A tradition, you might say," the little priest added. "Come in, sit down. Oh, a gift. How kind. Have some cookies. Well, the red ones Marty baked. Eat them at your own risk. Mrs. O'Banyon made the chocolate ones, and I would recommend those. How about some tea, or milk?"

I took the tea and David drank some milk, and we wanted to be loyal to our friend so we ate some of the red cookies, and immediately understood Father's point.

David went back to the car to get Doc's present, and the two men opened the gifts and exclaimed, one at the ornate pipe and the other at the painting of the beautiful little Catholic church.

Our next stop was Marty's. Mikey proudly displayed his red tricycle, then hopped on it to show off his skill as a driver. He ran into Marty's end table before any of us could stop him. The lamp teetered, and I managed to grab it just before it fell. I couldn't save the platter of cookies, though, and it crashed to the floor, sending cookies in every direction. It was brought quietly to my attention by my little brother that while the glass platter broke into several pieces, not one cookie so much as even chipped.

I handed Marty a small package, and she mumbled something about not getting me anything. But I told her that was nonsense, that she had made my curtains and wouldn't take a penny for her work, so I wanted to do something for her. Actually, I admitted to myself, I preferred being on the giving end. It was less awkward.

Marty opened the gift, and inside were three beautifully embroidered fine linen handkerchiefs edged with delicate lace. She exclaimed over them, and impulsively kissed me on the cheek.

Then David handed Mikey his gift. We had bought the child a fireman's hat. He donned it and went screeching through the house on his tricycle.

Our next stop was Aggie's. She was in the process of making Christmas dinner for her boarders, and invited us to stay. Marty, she told us, was coming. But we had more stops to make, and then David and I were going to Scottsbluff for dinner and a movie.

We went to Pete's, who had been invited to share Christmas dinner with the Hursts. We gave him a really colorful necktie. He had a good laugh over it, especially when my brother told him wickedly, "It's loud enough to keep you awake in church."

Then David and I took off for Scottsbluff and a rather expensive restaurant that was open on Christmas afternoon. This was Nick's treat, bless his heart.

We didn't get back until late that evening. Because it was Christmas and many of the congregation were spending the day with relatives, there was no evening church service. So David and I spent a contented evening playing Monopoly, and went to bed as the waxing moon sent its mellow light through our front window.

The week between Christmas and New Year's was hectic. I spent Monday and Tuesday painting the upstairs bedrooms and started refinishing an old but well-made wooden vanity I found in a room in the barn. There were other things in there too—old newspapers moldy with age, a rusty kid's wagon, tools, a broken doll I was going to try to mend, a box of mementos from the turn of the century, a few Roosevelt buttons, and a myriad of other things that would be fun to look through some stormy day.

John and Coy came back from their visit with Mary Star on Monday, but didn't make an effort to visit us. I could only be relieved. Tuesday came and went without either of them making an appearance. But on Wednesday John was once more in the diner, getting his pie and coffee.

I was busy, even at mid-afternoon. When John finally got my attention, he placed his order, and then invited me out for New Year's Eve.

"I'm sorry," I said briskly. "I have other plans. Would you like pumpkin pie, or pecan?"

"Pecan. With whom?"

I raised my eyebrows. "If I thought it was any of your business, I'd tell you."

He smiled. "How about Friday night, then?"

I shook my head. "I have plans then, too. And tomorrow night. And of course you go to church on Wednesday evenings. Last night I was free, though."

"And of course you would have joined me for supper,"

"Now you'll never know," I said. "Excuse me, I do have other tables."

Unfortunately, Wayne Voyle picked that time to come in, and he joined John at the front table. When I brought John's pie and coffee out to him, Wayne looked up at me and said, "I just found out that the high school at Scottsbluff is putting on *Carousel*. I thought you might like to go there instead of ice skating. If you would, I can get the tickets today."

225

My face started to grow warm. I couldn't—wouldn't—look at John Ransom. "Of course! I love Richard Rodgers' music. We can always go ice skating some other time."

"Good enough. I'll see you tomorrow night. Let's see, we'd better leave no later than five, so I'll pick you up about a quarter to."

He excused himself from me and then John, and left. I plopped the plate down in front of John, who never said a word. Nor did he say anything when I refilled his cup of coffee. But he left his usual tip.

I didn't really enjoy the play; of course I already knew the more popular songs and I knew Rodgers and Hammerstein tended to be overly sentimental, but I wasn't prepared for the heavy-handed religiosity. But Wayne Voyle proved to be an enjoyable companion. Riding home I started humming the lilting "Carousel Waltz" almost involuntarily. We ended up singing and laughing all the way home, "June is bustin' out all over," and finally "This was a real nice clambake...and we all had a real good time." But the song that kept running through the back of my mind was one I hadn't heard before that night—"The Highest Judge of All."

At home in bed I lay awake thinking of the silly plot: a woman falls in love with a scoundrel who turns into a thief and then, trying to escape, he's killed, leaving their daughter a legacy of shame and poverty. That part was realistic all right, but the disgusting thing was the happy ending—life could turn around and be beautiful if you only realized that "you'll never walk alone." I started planning a letter to Oscar Hammerstein. But...well, maybe he wasn't wrong exactly, maybe it did work like that for some people. Billy, the carousel barker, was a lot like my father, vain, arrogant, immature, except—I remembered his soliloquy, "My little girl..." If my father had wanted me, if he had loved me, maybe everything would have been different. It had been a long time since I felt so much hurt. Why had they named the musical *Carousel*? Was it supposed to be a metaphor for life?

Surprisingly my brother, who seemed so eager to get me married off, wasn't too happy about my seeing his coach, and was even less enthused about my date with Lance Stoker on Friday night.

"I don't choose your friends, David," I pointed out to him as I put on the finishing touches to my new dress which I had purchased for the party to which David's principal was taking me.

"I know, but..."

"No, don't say a word. You've been pushing me at John Ransom ever since we moved here, and it's not fair. I told you once before, I'll choose my own friends, and my own husband, and I'm *getting a little tired* of your interference."

I had never spoken to my little brother in that tone before, and he was more than a little hurt. I looked at his downcast expression and felt ashamed. I added more kindly, "Now you go and have fun at the Mercers, and don't worry about me. And here, I got a letter from Missouri today, and she enclosed this for you." I handed him the sheets of paper. "So read it, and write her back, and I can drop it off on my way to Scottsbluff this evening, if you'd like."

He took stationery, and said sulkily, "I'll read it. And I'll write her. And I'll mail it myself."

"That'll teach me," I said, my tongue in my cheek.

David never stayed angry for long. He gave me a reluctant grin, told me impishly that he hoped I really didn't enjoy myself, and left to get ready for his evening with the twins.

I had a fair time with Lance Stoker—pleasant but not outstanding. A lot better than the time I had with Evan Weber, a young widower who took me to his parents' for New Year's Eve.

The Weber's were wonderful people, pleasant and homey types. But they had dearly loved Evan's wife Rosemary, who had died young and tragically in an accident several years earlier, and I spent the entire evening listening to their reminiscences. Rosemary Weber had been tiny and dainty, blonde and fair, shy and dependent—everything, in fact, that I'm not. Listening to them extol the virtues of a woman dead these eight years made me almost wish I had accepted John Ransom's invitation, whatever the consequences.

My thoughts turned against my will to John Ransom, and what he was doing on this last night of 1955. I wondered how he was spending New Year's Eve. Certainly not being maudlin about the past, even the recent past which saw the tragic demise of his father. No, John Ransom was never a prisoner of melancholia.

I had little to say as we made our way back to my home, and Evan had even less. He bid me an absent goodnight when he walked me to the door, and I, without a pang of regret, watched him leave still deep in thought about his little blonde wife.

David was spending the night at the church. The youth group was having an all-night party, with games and a movie the church had rented called *The Robe*. I knew he was having a good time, and I reflected that I would have had a better time had I been home in bed...with a toothache.

I always left the lamp on in the parlor. It was on now, its dim, honeyed light barely reaching to the dark corners of the room. I took off my coat and threw it in the general direction of the sofa.

"Don't scream," came a voice from the kitchen—a voice I knew only too well. He poked his head around the corner. "It's only me."

"What are you doing here?" I asked sharply.

"Borrowing a cup of sugar. No, honestly." He held up a cup, and indeed it did have sugar in it. "Coy went shopping today and forgot to buy some, and you know me, I can't drink my coffee without it."

I looked at my watch. It was nearly eleven o'clock. "You shouldn't be drinking coffee at this hour."

"I have to. It's the only way I can stay up until midnight. By the way, I'm glad you have accepted the country custom of leaving your doors unlocked."

"Not any more," I said with some asperity.

He gave me a sardonic look. "You're home awfully early. Have a good time at the Webers?"

"Lovely," I snapped.

He laughed softly. "I told you not to lie to me. I can tell you exactly what you did tonight. Evan picked you up early. He was in a pensive mood. He took you to his parents' home. They greeted you with gentle but plaintive kindness, and then the three of them proceeded to talk about Rosemary the entire evening. Am I close?"

"My evening with Evan is none of your business. How did you know I was with him, anyway?"

"David, of course. And he wasn't too happy about it, either."

"David is taking his role as man of the house a little too seriously," I said curtly. "And you're carrying this business about being neighborly a little too far. What makes you think you can break into my house and demand to know how I spent my evening?"

"Your door was unlocked, and I never make demands."

"Well, you have your sugar, so you can leave."

He put the cup down on the table and took a step nearer to me. He held out his hand but never touched me. Finally he let it drop. I took a step backwards and bumped into the end table.

"Don't look so frightened," he said. "A kiss didn't hurt you."

I fumbled my way to the sofa and sat down. He had read my mind, and it made me angry. "I'm never frightened," I told him. "And I have been kissed before."

He grinned. "But not, I bet, by Evan Weber."

"My osculatory history is none of your business, either." I absently started plucking at the loose threads on the sofa. "You act as if you had some claim on me."

"I saw you first," he grinned.

That really upset me. What did he mean by that? "You're mistaken. Actually Doc saw me first if you want to know."

He chose the chair facing me rather than the place next to me on the sofa, and sat down. "I'll leave, Lu. But not until we get a few things straightened out."

"For instance?"

"You, for instance. As in you and me. Lu, my dear, why do you keep avoiding me?"

I still plucked at the threads. "I don't..."

He held up a hand. "Yes, you do. You like me—no, don't bother denying that, either. You kissed me back, you know."

I looked at him. My face was hot. "I didn't."

He smiled. I wished he wouldn't smile at me like that. "You did. Don't you think I can tell? Maybe you like me more than you want to. Why you wouldn't want to is what I can't understand."

I had ripped several threads of the lovely upholstery. I looked at my handiwork instead of at him.

He waited for me to say something, but words couldn't get past the lump in my throat.

"Maybe I'm not saying this right," he finally said. "I guess I haven't had any experience."

I did glance at him then. "Corrine of the Library," and gave him a tight smile.

He laughed. "I was seventeen. She's married now, with four children. I saw her last year. All two hundred pounds of her."

He leaned back in the chair, his long legs stretched out in front of him and crossed at the ankles. He was completely relaxed.

I pulled a few more threads.

"You're...well, you're a mystery," he went on. "Maybe that's the attraction. Or part of the attraction, anyway. You're a beautiful woman, intelligent, capable."

"Thank you," I mumbled.

I could feel his eyes on me, but I still couldn't bring myself to look at him.

"And sweet," he added as he got to his feet. "At least, to everyone but me and Sheriff Carter. I can understand your attitude towards our illustrious sheriff, but why you have lumped me in with him is something I don't understand."

He came to me, and taking my hands, lifted me to my feet. I pulled my hands away, but he put an arm around me and with his free hand pushed my head onto his shoulder.

"Whatever it is, Lu, we can work it out," he whispered. "We can, Lu."

I shook my head. My face was buried in his soft camel-hair sweater. I felt tears well up in my eyes. Tears he must never see.

"Is that final?' he asked.

I didn't move. I couldn't speak.

"Then it's not final. Lu, listen. I'm here for you. I'll always be here for you. There's nothing you can tell me that I wouldn't understand—and there's nothing I wouldn't do for you."

I pushed him away and turned from him. I could see our reflections in the window I was facing. He was just behind me, his breath warm on my hair. "You better go," I whispered. I hoped he didn't hear the catch in my voice.

There was a brief silence. The wind whipped suddenly through the trees and snow cascaded to the already white ground as the moon lit up the landscape. I heard the distant sad wail of a coyote. It sounded as lost, as lonely, as I felt at that moment.

"I'll go," he said finally. "And I won't come back until you want me to—until you need me to. The next move is yours, Lu."

I felt his warm presence leave me. He paused only to say, "Happy New Year, Lu. And God bless you."

He was gone. The room felt suddenly cold. A gust of wind played with the electric lines outside, and my lamp flickered. The room was thrown into grotesque shadows, and then darkness obliterated even them. The only light was the hazy moon, shining intermittently through racing dark clouds.

The pervasive gloom seemed to match my mood. At that moment, I believed in my heart that I would have done better to have stayed in Chicago, and possibly died there.

~~~~~~~~~

The following week brought with it some semblance of normalcy. Christmas decorations were packed away, school was back in session, and I was back at work. The main topic of my customers was the Orange Bowl, which Oklahoma had won quite handily over Maryland, and the preceding year's tragic Orange Bowl, which Nebraska lost to Duke.

The basketball season was in full swing, and I attended as many games as I could. On those occasions when I saw John Ransom, he would nod politely or wave, but he never went out of his way to speak to me.

He didn't come for his daily pie and coffee, either, and when they picked David up for church and brought him back, he never made any attempt to come inside the house.

I felt David watching me closely, but he never brought up the subject of John Ransom. That he was disappointed in the way things worked out was something I deeply regretted.

Marty invited me to supper on that Saturday of the second week of January. I accepted because I was a little lonely and needed some feminine chit-chat, and Marty could take a person's mind off of anything.

And she did, for a while, manage to take my mind off my troubling if incoherent thoughts. Of course, she started off the evening by inviting me to church again.

"You might like it," she said. "And the people, most of them anyway, are really very nice. Rev. Hurst is retiring in April, and we have no idea who we'll get to take his place, but for now we're enjoying Rev. Hurst's last days with us."

I burst out laughing. "Marty! You better rephrase that. You made it sound like you're glad he's leaving."

She reddened. "I'm not, of course. That's not to say we couldn't do with a younger man, one who would be good for the teens."

"You know, you actually sound disloyal."

"Do I? I don't mean to. It's just that this isn't the Thirties anymore. America has changed. We've been through two wars in a very short time, and it's matured us. Even made us a little cynical. When Rev. Hurst came to us thirty-five years ago he carried his belongings in a horse-drawn wagon. Now we're flying at the speed of sound. Everything is happening faster. And a new morality—which is really the old immorality—is slowly creeping into our society, and Rev. Hurst can't cope with it. We need someone young and strong who is better equipped to fight the devil. Rev. Hurst is just too naive to be able to relate to the adults of the next generation. He doesn't fully comprehend what kids are facing today, and I think it's going to get worse unless Christians get off their..." She stopped short. "I'm sorry, Lu. I didn't mean to preach. I'm beginning to sound like Johnny."

I didn't bat an eye.

She darted a not-very-subtle look at me, but I remained passive.

She bit her lower lip. "You know," she said, twirling her spoon in her coffee, "Coy is worried about Johnny."

She gave me another sideways glance. I sipped my tea.

"There's a girl who's been chasing him. Pretty pushy, from what Coy says," she went on. "Oh, I mean Coy doesn't actually say anything derogatory. But it's his looks. You know how Coy is."

"I know how Coy is," I said woodenly.

"Well, Johnny seems to have met this girl..."

"Listen, dear," I told Marty, "I don't mean to interrupt—check that, I do mean to interrupt—but John Ransom's business is his own. And if you think anyone can push him where he doesn't want to go, then you don't know him as well as you've tried to convince me you do."

She gasped, "Why, Lu Morrow! I've never heard you talk like that. I believe you have a temper."

"I'm beginning to believe it myself. Look, Marty, I'm sorry, but I am just a little sick of everybody trying to keep me up-to-date on John Ransom's every move. I'm sorry if I sound cross, but..."

"I understand. I should learn to keep my mouth shut and mind my own business. But it's just that Coy's so unhappy about it."

"Well, it isn't Coy's business any more than it's yours, mine, or anybody else's. If you don't mind, I'll have another piece of cherry pie."

Marty was so pleased that someone actually asked for seconds of something she made that she instantly dropped the subject of John Ransom and his phantom girlfriend.

I took the long way home, up north past the Kerry's place, then over to the Lesters and the Tates, then across the creek and south again past my nearest neighbors.

The yard light was on, and it lit up the barn, the house, and the chicken coop. I could see a man walking from the barn. It had to be Coy Youngblood. John, I knew had gone to Cheyenne to purchase some farm machinery and would be gone for a few days.

And possibly to meet with this girl who's been chasing him? Well, why not? I said to myself. It's his business.

So nigh is grandeur to our dust,
So near is God to man,
When duty whispers low, "Thou must,"
The youth replies, "I can."
—Ralph Waldo Emerson

Chapter 17

The next day was Sunday, and it brought disturbing news: Scooter Mathieson had been found stabbed to death.

John Ransom was still in Cheyenne. Coy took David to church, and it wasn't until he got home that Sunday afternoon that I heard all about it. It was the talk of the whole little town. Murder was all it could have been. The first murder in the county since 1922, when Clancy Wells killed that nice Scott boy over a woman. The day slipped by slowly and uneasily. The town grew quiet, and its citizens eyed each other suspiciously, wanting to talk about the murder but hesitating to put private opinions into public words. There were a lot of people in town who didn't like the unkempt, hateful alcoholic, but no one could think of anyone who disliked him enough to murder him.

No one except Sheriff Carter. On Monday everything came to a head. Coy Youngblood was arrested for the murder of Carl "Scooter" Mathieson.

By Monday night John Ransom was back in town and demanding from the sheriff what proof he had.

I had to tell David that night at supper.

David was shocked. "He couldn't have done it. He couldn't have!" he cried, his eyes bright with unshed tears.

"I know that. And so does practically everyone else."

235

"Except the sheriff. And I don't know what 'proof' he has, but Coy didn't kill anybody."

"Of course he didn't. And no jury will convict him."

But my teenage brother put a lot of store in what a lawman said, and the word "sheriff" conjured up a lot of romantic tales of the Old West. In David's young eyes, if the sheriff had evidence, no matter how circumstantial, Coy was convicted already.

"The hearing is tomorrow morning," I said. "Coy will get a chance to speak in his own defense."

Tuesday morning came, and most of the men in town and a good many of the women crowded into the small courthouse. Even Slim Rhodes came to town for this all the way from Sydney. Pete went to court, but I stayed in the diner. I knew we wouldn't get any business, but I couldn't bear to see a man I considered a close friend stand in handcuffs before the judge.

When the court recessed for dinner Pete and Carol came back to the diner. Pete's feet were dragging, "The sheriff says it was Coy's knife. And Coy himself admitted that the knife is his."

I took a deep breath. "It doesn't look good for Coy, does it." It was a statement. I didn't expect an answer.

Pete shook his head.

Then I perked up. "What time was the body discovered? I saw Coy at about ten o'clock Saturday night..."

But my employer shook his head again. The body was discovered shortly after two o'clock Sunday morning—by the sheriff. He was hauling Harley Bishop to jail for being drunk and disorderly at the Night Hawk. Found the body behind the barber shop."

"The barber shop isn't on the way from the tavern to the jail," I objected.

"No, it's not. But Carter said he needed to stop off at his house for some medicine he's been taking and saw Coy's jeep drive off. Harley said it was Coy's jeep, too. The sheriff said that Coy was driving fast, and he got suspicious and decided to investigate."

I sat down on a chair and put my head in my hands. The diner was starting to fill up, but neither Pete nor I took any notice of the customers. They seemed to want only to talk about the recent developments anyway, so we let them. Carol finally started around with coffee cups.

I eventually made myself get up and serve coffee, but Pete said he didn't feel like cooking anything, which was all right because everyone seemed to have lost his appetite.

At two o'clock everyone went back to the hearing, but fifteen minutes hadn't passed before Pete came running back to the diner.

"Lu! You better come quick!" Pete was yelling at me from the door. "David's in the courtroom and demanding to be heard!"

"What! David?" I ripped off my apron and ran to Pete, who was panting from the exertion of running in freezing weather. I grabbed the collar of his coat. "What did you say? David is there?"

Pete nodded. "He came barging in," he huffed. "Said Coy...couldn't have...killed anybody. You'd...better come."

But I was out the door before Pete could even finish. Coatless, I ran across to the courthouse, disregarding the ice and snow and the freezing temperature.

David was standing on a chair, shouting to be heard. Sheriff Carter was trying to reach him but was being prevented by a group of men standing around David and holding the fat sheriff at bay. The judge was pounding his gavel but at the moment no one could hear it. I took in all of this in one brief glance.

I stepped into the room and tried to fight my way to my brother. But John Ransom beat me to him, and shouted loudly enough to be heard over the melee. "If he's got something to say, let him say it. This is a hearing, not a hanging."

There was general agreement, most of the men nodding and saying that the kid had a right to be heard.

"What could he possibly have to say?" the sheriff snarled.

"We won't know until he says it," John replied.

"But I have proof!"

"And it's all circumstantial," John said, his famous temper beginning to surface. "Just what are you afraid of, Carter?"

The blustering sheriff backed down, and even managed a small, if insincere, smile. "Why, nothing, Johnny. Nothing. It's just that he's underage, and everyone knows he's a friend of the accused..."

"Which is a point in David's favor," someone shouted.

Finally the gavel was heard. Almost in unison everyone turned to the wizened little judge.

"Order in this court!" he yelled. "This is not a wrestling match. I'll have quiet or I'll throw every last one of you out!" He pointed his gavel at David. "Boy, you'll have a chance to speak as soon as the sheriff finishes his testimony."

The spectators made their way back to their seats, and I ran to my brother, who was now nestled safely in the crook of John Ransom's arm.

"David," I whispered. What on earth is this all about?"

He was a trifle shamefaced; his ears were bright red. "I'll tell it to the court," he mumbled.

I looked across him to John Ransom. He shrugged his shoulders. It was apparent that he didn't have any idea as to what David was going to say.

The sheriff had a final piece of evidence which might have given Coy Youngblood a sound motive for killing Scooter Mathieson. A Marlin .30-.30 was found at the Mathieson home. Ballistics proved that it was the same rifle that fired the bullet dug out of Coy's arm.

With testimony now over, those few present who bore a grudge against Coy because of the land he owned nodded to each other, judging him guilty before any trial would be held. I shuddered when the thought came to me that some of these same men might be on the jury.

But now it was David's turn to speak. He was scared but determined. The clerk swore him in, and the judge, with a gruff kindness, told him to tell his story.

David looked far away and completely alone as he sat in the witness stand. "Well," he started, his young voice a little shaky, "Coy couldn't have killed Scooter, or anybody else."

"The kid's a friend of the redskin," somebody with a coarse voice called out. "Naturally he'd say that."

The judge rapped his gavel and called for order. Then he pointed it at the man who had just spoken and said, "Any more out of you, Joe Fletcher, and you'll be in jail for contempt." Then he turned to David and said gently, "Now, boy, go on. Do you have a reason for saying this?"

"Y-yes, sir," David stammered. "See, I was in the barn at the Ransom Creek Ranch. I got there a little before midnight."

The judge raised his eyebrows. "What were you doing in the barn at that hour?"

David squirmed, then bowed his head and mumbled, "I was going to ride Seneca." Then he glanced at Coy, who hadn't changed his stoic expression.

"Going to ride Seneca? That wild stallion?" the judge asked incredulously.

Some of the men in the room started chuckling. My little brother raised his head and stared hard at the crowd. "I did it, too!" he shouted, and the laughter abruptly ceased.

"I hid in the barn," he went on. "I had already gone and got Coy's Ghost Shirt, and had it on. I was just getting ready to put a bridle on Seneca when I heard a car come." He pointed at Coy. "It was his Jeep, and he was driving. I dove behind some bales of hay, and hid. Coy was whistling. He came into the barn and fed Seneca some oats."

David gained confidence as he spoke. "Then he left. I watched him go into the house. I saw the kitchen light go on, and then a few minutes later go off again. Then I thought I better wait some more, because I wanted him sleeping so he couldn't hear me take off with Seneca."

The judge broke in at this point. "Why was it that you were so determined to ride that renegade?"

David squirmed some more, his face turning a bright scarlet. "I'm not supposed to tell," he finally said.

A number of the men looked at each other knowingly. The judge cleared his throat and said, "Hrumph. Yes, I think I understand. That...hmmm...club. Okay, so you had to ride Seneca."

David nodded his head. "And...some of the guys...were waiting for me at the seven-mile junction. I...had to ride Seneca there and back." He glanced apprehensively at Coy.

The defendant's expression was as impassive as ever.

"Weren't you a little afraid?" Judge Kincaid asked.

"I was scared to death!" David answered. "Of Seneca, and of Coy if he ever caught me."

There was general laughter, which died down immediately when the judge brought his bushy gray eyebrows together and glared at the crowd.

"Go on," he told David when the courtroom was quiet.

"Well, I put the saddle and bridle on Seneca and was just getting ready to mount when I saw the Jeep take off. I never heard anybody come, and I guess my heart was pounding too hard for me to hear it start up. But there it went, down the drive. It didn't have its headlights on, and I didn't know who was driving it, only that it was somebody tall."

"You don't think it could have been Coy?" the judge asked kindly.

"No, sir. You see, I saw him later. I suppose you're wondering why I didn't go get Coy. I guess now that I should have. But I really didn't think the man was stealing the Jeep. I mean, it could have been someone in trouble, or...or something. And under the circumstances I was afraid to wake up Coy."

"So you let the man and the Jeep get away."

David nodded again. "Then I took off on Seneca, and for some reason he let me ride him. And I saw that when the Jeep got to the road, the headlights came on, and I tried to keep the lights in sight as long as I could. The Jeep drove to town. The...guys...hiding at the junction were waiting for me. I asked them if they noticed the Jeep when it came by, and they told me that they had been there long enough to see half the county drive by. They were just getting ready to come looking for me because I had taken so long. they were afraid Seneca might have thrown me." He took a deep breath. "Anyway, I asked them if they recognized the Jeep, and they all said it was Coy Youngblood's. Then I asked if they recognized the driver, and none of them did. So I showed them the Ghost Shirt, and made up my mind to tell Coy about his Jeep when I got back to the ranch. I had already put the saddle and bridle up and was rubbing Seneca down when the Jeep came back. I went to the barn door and watched. It came back up the drive with its lights off, and the driver parked it exactly where Coy had left it. Then he got out, looked around, and started running down the drive. I took the Ghost Shirt back to Coy's room. He was sound asleep, and I decided not to wake him up. After all, the Jeep was back."

The judge interrupted David's narrative with a question. "What did you notice about the man who was driving Coy's Jeep?"

"Not much, your honor. He was paunchy, and tall, and walked with a slight limp. But he took off down the drive, and I couldn't see him any more. But then a few minutes later, I saw the lights from another car. It must have been there for a while, because I didn't see it drive up. And I came across the pasture; I didn't follow the road, so I didn't see it sitting there. It must have been waiting for the driver, though, because all of a sudden it started up and took off."

"Did you happen to notice what time this was?"

"Yes, sir. When I rode up to the junction the guys were griping because they had to wait so long. They made a point of telling me it was just past two o'clock. They were getting afraid that Seneca had bucked me off, and that I was lying in the snow somewhere with a broken back. And when I went inside to put Coy's Ghost Shirt back I glanced at the kitchen clock. It was two thirty-five." He looked around at the crowd. "It only took me about twenty minutes to get from the junction back to the ranch. I thought that was pretty good time."

Again there was general laughter. Judge Kincaid banged his gavel.

Sheriff Carter stood up and said, with a rough edge to his voice, "The boy's lying to protect that Indian!"

I started to say something, but David shot out of his chair and said, "I am not! Everything I said was true! I wouldn't lie for anybody, not even Coy, because lying's a sin."

I gaped at my little brother.

John Ransom nudged me, and I turned to him. He smiled and said, "The kid's got guts."

Tears were stinging the back of my eyes and I was struggling to keep them from falling. I turned away from John. But he was already making his way over to his brother's side.

John put a hand on Coy's shoulder and said above the general hub-bub, "It corroborates Coy's testimony."

The sheriff stood to his feet. "I still say the kid's lying," he bellowed.

John gave Coy a gentle pat then walked over to the sheriff and asked, "Why are you so...unflinchingly...convinced that Coy murdered a man? Surely Coy is innocent until you prove him guilty, and now there's no chance of that."

Carter sputtered. "There's evidence..."

"And it's all circumstantial. Do you have any real proof? Like did you find Coy at the scene? Or even his fingerprints?"

"Harley Bishop said..."

John smiled. "You yourself said that Harley Bishop was roaring drunk. And Harley said he saw Coy's Jeep. He never said he saw Coy."

Harley was in court, and sober. All eyes turned automatically to the unshaven little man.

He shook his head. "I didn't see Coy. Just saw his Jeep."

The sheriff leaped toward David, venom in his voice. "You're lying, you little ba..."

He never got the word out. Coy struck the sheriff a blow to the jaw, and Carter crumpled slowly to the floor.

Everyone in the room gaped at the big Indian. He gave us all a rueful grin. "I may as well be hanged for a sheep as a lamb," was all he said.

But Coy wasn't going to be punished at all. There wasn't enough evidence to hold him, and my little brother's word, it seemed, carried a lot of weight.

Coy came into the diner the day after the hearing to talk to me. We went to a back booth, and no one bothered us.

"You have a very special brother," he told me.

"Thank you, Coy."

"I want you to tell him that I'm very proud of him."

I smiled at him. "For speaking out at the hearing, or for riding Seneca?"

"For both. But I also want to apologize."

I stared at him. "For what?"

"For losing my temper. For hitting the sheriff."

"Why on earth apologize for that?" I asked.

He looked at me, a serious expression in his dark eyes. "Because it wasn't a good witness."

I was thoroughly perplexed. "A good witness? I'm afraid I don't understand."

"It wasn't a good witness for the Lord," he explained patiently.

"Oh," I said a little feebly. "You're supposed to turn the other cheek. But Coy, you didn't strike the sheriff for your own satisfaction. You struck him for David."

Coy looked down at his hands. "Did I?" He shook his head. "I'm not really sure. In any event, I'm going to apologize to Carter, too." Then he grinned. "But maybe Carter ought to be grateful that I got to him before Johnny did."

"What do you mean?"

"Johnny was ripe for murder. And Johnny is the one with a temper—and a wicked left."

"That's what I've heard—heard, but not seen. If there is one thing I would be surprised at, it would be to see John Ransom lose his temper. I think you are all imagining it."

Coy laughed outright at that. "I hope you never do see him lose it. He really fights to keep it under control. But when it goes, watch out! If he would have got to Carter, our good sheriff would have a broken jaw right now, and not just a bruised one."

I watched my friend leave. He was on his way to apologize to a man who would like to have seen him get the chair, or whatever Nebraska uses to execute its capital offenders.

Turning the other cheek? What a lot of nonsense!

As I wiped off the table my thoughts turned to John Ransom. What was I going to do about him. He hadn't come into the diner for a while, and just when I thought my life was going to go smoothly, Coy gets himself accused of murder, and David winds up smack in the middle of the investigation. What insidious plan was God working on now? What was He thinking of, bringing John Ransom back into my life just when I had shoved him out of it?

"A penny for them."

I gasped. He had slid into the booth while I was scrubbing the paint off the table. I had no idea how long he had been sitting there, watching me.

I recovered my thoughts, and said lightly, "Oh, come. Surely they're worth more than that."

He shook his head. "Not even with inflation." His eyes were smiling, but he was watching me closely. For some reaction, maybe?

"You can have them for free. I was thinking about what Coy said to me just now." It was partly true.

"And what was that?"

"Ask him."

"I will. Later. Now it's my turn to say something to you. Just between us, Coy knew David was in the barn that night."

My knees were suddenly weak. I sank down across from John Ransom. "How could Coy have known?"

"When he gave Seneca the oats, he saw David's footprints, in the snow just outside the barn, and where he had tracked snow into the barn. Next morning he saw where Seneca had been taken out and brought back. Coy's a pretty good tracker, but he said this was so easy even I would have seen it."

"Then why didn't he say anything when he was arrested?"

"Because he wanted David to come forward voluntarily."

"Then why didn't *you* say something?"

"I wouldn't have, anyway, but Coy only just now told me. I didn't know until today."

I put my elbow on the table, and my head in my hand. "I don't understand you two," I said.

"I know," he replied ruefully. "But Coy was right, you know. David had to do it on his own. It's part of growing up, of being a man. He told what he knew, even though it might have angered his friends. Or Coy might have been angry. And it wasn't going to please a lot of other people either, including the sheriff. We've always liked David. Now we have a great respect for him, too. I just wanted you to know that."

He was gone as quickly as he had come. I watched as he said something to Pete, slapped him on the back, and left.

I made up my mind. I would sell out—to him, if necessary. I would sell out and move far away, before things got more out of hand than they already were.

244

Many are the plans in a man's heart
but it is the Lord's purpose that prevails
—Proverbs 19:21

Chapter 18

Coy was free, but so was the murderer. Sheriff Carter sulked for a few days after the hearing, but Jeb Truman, his young deputy, went out looking for clues.

David and I went to Scooter's funeral. It was a sorry affair. Everyone who went did so for the sake of Scooter's sweet little wife, Annie. There wasn't much Rev. Hurst could say that was in any way kind about the deceased. He had been a shiftless, alcoholic spendthrift with a nasty tongue and even nastier habits. He had never supported his wife or five children, and if it hadn't been for his son, Mark, the family would have starved.

I hardly took in Rev. Hurst's words. I was thinking about another recent funeral, about another man whose passing went unlamented. I kept going over in my mind those final few days in Chicago. There was my father, who had never done an unselfish or kind deed in his life. No one, not one single person, mourned the passing of my immoral, temperamental father. And today only a few tears were being shed for this man whose very existence had been a cross for his lovely family to bear.

The service was over and I, along with everyone else, paraded past the casket and took one look at the man whose death was almost responsible for the incarceration of one of the finest men I had ever known. And I thought again of my father, who was responsible for the death of a man who had devoted his life to the healing of others. Patrick Thornton, Carl Mathieson. Alike in life, alike in death. I wondered if they were getting acquainted now, and if so, where?

But life goes on, and even though some would argue that Carl Mathieson's life was worthless, it was still a life, and it had been taken. After word got out that David had testified at the hearing, three other boys went to the judge and told him that they had seen Coy's Jeep go past them at a little before two o'clock on that Sunday morning, and that they didn't recognize the driver. All they knew was that it wasn't Coy Youngblood.

Now that Coy's freedom was no longer in jeopardy, and Scooter Mathieson was laid in the little cemetery on the hill below the park, I turned my thoughts more seriously towards packing up and moving. If David could make friends so easily here, he could make them just as easily someplace else. Then he was doing so well physically, that he could surely get along with another doctor. I wondered with some bitterness if I should consult with Dr. Ableman again. I felt like telling him, "Thanks a lot for sending us here to Dr. Ransom's hometown." But I knew he had done what he thought was best for David. Then the fact that I had moved next door to the Ransoms was nobody's fault but my own.

I feared more than just John and Coy finding out, although they were my main concern. I had not forgotten that Rick would be coming home one of these days, and if he recognized me, my masquerade would be shown up for the sorry deception it was.

Morrowitz Plastics had been a large company, and a well-known one. Frederic Morrowitz had not only been a highly respected businessman, he had also been a well-loved philanthropist. His demise had not gone unnoticed by politicians, corporate heads, and certain members of the clergy. And when Patrick Thornton took over the company and ran it into the ground amid whispers of questionable ethics and disloyalty to the American cause during the War, that had not gone unnoticed either. Sooner or later I was afraid the past would catch up with David and me wherever we were, but especially if we stayed here. John Ransom's father and mine were irrevocably linked in death. My life, and David's, were enmeshed with the Ransoms, and I could see no way of avoiding the inevitable discovery. We needed to go someplace where, even if Frederic Morrowitz and Patrick Thornton were remembered, Samuel Ransom was unknown.

I would offer the place to John Ransom, and ask no more than what I had paid for it. I could be out by the end of the week. David and I could, by Saturday, be on our way to points west, or south, or even north into Canada. I hated quitting Pete without notice, but then I hated leaving all the friends we had made. I packed steadily as I waited for David to come home. My heart was empty, drained of emotion or feeling or hope. I would not be here when the cottonwoods turned green. The miracle of new life was not to be mine.

David was out riding. He had gone to the ranch, I suppose to apologize one more time for going into the barn without permission and borrowing Seneca, not to mention the valuable Ghost Shirt.

When he came home I would have to tell him. I dreaded that, and almost willed him to stay away. It was well past seven o'clock, and no moon shone on the white snow. The hills were dark and forbidding, the wind was kicking up, and now snow began to fall from the starless sky.

The clock chimed eight. I began to pace. Maybe David was helping the men with something, or maybe the three of them had started talking and forgot to note the time.

I put on my heavy coat, boots, and gloves, and went out to check the livestock. David always got a kick out of calling our thirty-odd chickens, one cow, and young horse by that rather grandiose term. The porch light did little to alleviate the gloom of a moonless night. I proceeded cautiously across the snow. But then I suddenly stopped, and listened. There it was again—the whinny of a horse. David had finally come home.

Goliath met me at the door of the barn. Goliath...without David!

I called, and the wind picked up my voice and twirled it around, then carried it off into the darkness. I called again. There was no answer. David wasn't there. Goliath had come home without him.

Urgency, now, was gripping me, pulling at me, making me frantic. Suddenly I was frightened. I jumped on Goliath. With little regard for the snow and none at all for the bitter cold, I turned the horse towards the big ranch house.

We galloped into the yard and before Goliath had come to a full stop I was off his back and running up the steps. I beat my fist on the door. John answered my desperate knock instantly.

"Is David here?" I shouted above the roar of the wind.

He shook his head as he pulled me into the warmth of his large living room. "He left," he looked at his watch, "nearly an hour ago."

"Goliath came home without him," I said with a sob.

Coy was in the room. Simultaneously both men went for their outer clothing.

"You call Jeb," John told Coy. "I'll get Lu some cof...er...tea." To me he said, "Come, my dear, into the kitchen. Here's the tea, and there's the kettle. Don't get yourself all worked up. We'll find him."

"I don't want any tea. I want to go, too."

"You don't know the terrain like we do. You'd best stay here, near the phone. We'll go to your barn and backtrack Goliath from there." He put his arm around me in a protective embrace, and squeezed my shoulder ever so gently. "We'll find him, Lu. I promise."

I said, on another sob, "Will you find him...in time?"

"I pray that we will," he said, and then he was gone.

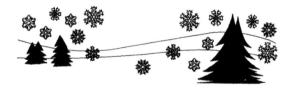

It seemed like hours, but actually barely thirty minutes had passed before the yard began to fill with headlights. Jeb Truman was there with half the men from the two churches—and Marty Maguire.

The men would split up and look in all directions. I recognized the dark little man who was approaching me as Freddy D'Angelo's father. I had contrived never to really meet him, but now he came up to me and hugged my shoulders though he had to reach up to do it. "Mama an' me, we unnerstan' how it is. But it's gonna be okay."

Jeb went to look at the place where David had mounted Goliath and turned him towards home, but snow had been falling heavily for over an hour and the tracks were nearly obliterated.

Only once before in my life had I been gripped by such ominous dread—when David was fighting for his life inside that horrible iron lung. I had been helpless then, too, just as I was now.

Marty sat there, watching me pace back and forth the length of the Ransoms' living room, and she talked to me, a gentle flow of words that fell around me unheeded. But though I didn't comprehend what all she said to me on that terrible night, I appreciated the soothing voice, and the fact that she was there kept me from falling apart. I know she said a few prayers, and answered all the calls that came on one long, one short ring.

"Anne Truman is praying," she'd say after she hung up, or "The Peabody women are having prayers." Once she called to me and said, "The teens at church who aren't with the searching party are meeting to pray."

Later she handed me the telephone. "It's Aggie. She wants to talk to you."

I wish I could remember all that Aggie said to me that night. A flow of comforting words said in a tranquil voice was all I could remember.

Father O'Brien was among the searchers, and several members of his parish called. Some of them were Pete's customers at the diner, and some were parents of David's friends. But it was obvious that nearly everyone in the little town and the surrounding country was in some way involved in the search for my brother. Only Sheriff Carter was conspicuously absent.

The night dragged on. Marty tried to get me to eat something, but I couldn't face any food. "You might help me get something ready, though," she said. "When the men come in they are going to need something hot."

So I worked in John Ransom's large and modern kitchen, making soup and sandwiches for the men who would—who had to—find David. Marty kept up her easy flow of conversation, and I was grateful to be doing something.

Then John Ransom came in, tired, worn, his blue eyes shadowed by acute distress. "We've found him," he said to me.

The strain was there, in his voice. "He's still alive. You better come. Coy and Jeb have taken him to Doc's."

Something was desperately wrong. I had felt it all night, and now it was there in John Ransom's weary eyes and taut voice.

Marty helped me into my coat, then John Ransom led me to his truck. Marty stayed behind to serve the food and hot coffee to the men who were beginning to straggle in.

That ride to town, seated beside John, who was grim and shaken and consequently silent, was the longest ride of my life. I was afraid to speak, to ask questions because I was terrified of the answers.

As we reached the crest of the hill that overlooked Lee's Corner, John finally spoke. His voice was utterly drained of inflection. "He's very sick," he said, his eyes never leaving the road. "The cold...he couldn't have lasted much longer. Lu, you must brace yourself for this. He's a sickly child, battling polio like he has."

"He can't die," I said through clenched teeth. "He can't. I won't let him."

He covered my hand, which was lying listlessly on my lap, with his. "We'll do what we can, Lu. We all love David."

Doc was already working on my brother when we reached the little clinic. Coy was in the back room with him. Jeb met us in the waiting room.

"He's coming around," Jeb whispered. "Doc thinks we may have got to him in time. The next few hours will tell. But David keeps babbling something about the sheriff. We don't understand what he's trying to tell us. I'm going out to look for Carter now. He probably doesn't know what happened or he would have been out helping."

I went to the treatment room and tapped on the door. It was opened by Coy.

"He's asking for you," Coy said softly. "And for Johnny."

John followed me into the little room. David was on a bed and covered with blankets. I bent over him on one side and John stood across from me, and gave my brother an encouraging smile.

David, his dark eyes glazed with pain and fever, said to John in short gasps, "I...didn't fall...off Goliath." His voice drifted away, and he dropped into a fitful sleep.

I would not cry, I told myself. David needs me to be strong. He doesn't need a weeping willow standing at his bedside shedding tears all over him. I looked up at John, who was watching me closely.

Suddenly he came around the bed and drew me away. "He's a tough kid," he whispered. "Anyone who can face Judge Kincaid and Sheriff Carter and an unruly mob of Indian-haters can face anything."

Doc put a cot in David's small room at the clinic and I spent what was left of the night in there. But I couldn't sleep. John Ransom never left the chair that faced me, and Coy made coffee and hot tea and kept those who inquired after David's health informed.

I must have finally dozed, but it couldn't have been for more than a few minutes, because John woke me shortly after six o'clock. I knew by his expression that something was wrong.

Doc and Coy were hovering over David, erecting a plastic tent. David's breathing was shallow and erratic, and even from where I sat I could hear a gurgling sound that was emanating from his thin chest.

"It's gone into pneumonia, Lu," John told me as I rubbed my eyes adjusting to the lights.

"Oh, no!" I cried. "It can't, it can't. He was doing fine. Doc said…"

He shook me gently, "You mustn't let David see you like this. Come on, he's asking for us."

Doc, looking bone-weary, was turning on the oxygen, and it filled the tent around David's head and upper body. My brother lay there looking young and defenseless; his face was flushed and his chest rattled pathetically.

"It turned on me suddenly," Doc said. "A high fever, and this cough. I'm going to pump him with penicillin."

I bent over the tent. David's eyes fluttered open. "I'll do anything in the world for you," I promised him. "Just tell me, and I'll do it."

His dry lips formed the word, "Pray."

I stood up and looked at him helplessly. Then I glanced at John, who was watching me closely. I turned and went to the window. The early pewter sky was dumping even more snow over the landscape. I could see the tall spire of the Catholic church, and just above it the steeple of Grace Community church. There was the town park, and the railroad tracks where Napoleon had pulled little Suzanne from the path of an oncoming train. And there was the cemetery, a stone's throw from Doc's clinic, where Marty's husband Mike was buried. John Ransom's mother was there, too, and Aggie's husband, and so many others who had lived and died in this little part of the West. Children who hadn't survived the influenza epidemic of 1918 were there, lying in pathetically small graves under small crosses or tiny monuments of guardian angels. The cemetery was the final resting place of a judge, a senator, and veterans from every war since 1860 in which the United States participated. Would there be a new grave even fresher than Carl Mathieson's?

I stood there hugging myself tightly to keep from crying, and wondered incongruously if the United States would ever go to war again, or if we had already learned enough about killing. And about dying.

There was David. Dying. He had asked only one thing of me. But how could I pray to a God at whom I was so angry, a God who had disappointed me so many times in the past? I didn't want anything more to do with this God of David's, or His Son, in whom David had so much confidence but in whom I had none. This Father, Son, and Holy Ghost combination that let sweet children like David suffer with a crippling disease, then when he seems to get better try to take his life by some other means.

John Ransom came up behind me.

"You pray," I told him. "I can't."

"You can! Do it for David."

I shook my head. "I'm too old to start believing that God is concerned with the heartbreaking events of human life. He hasn't seemed to notice David before. Why should He be so all-fired concerned about him now?"

"No one's ever too old to start believing the truth."

"He doesn't answer prayer," I shot at him. "When David got so sick before, I prayed. I prayed so hard my insides hurt. I begged for the polio to go away. But God didn't answer my prayer."

"Oh, but He did," John said softly. "His answer was 'no.'"

I rounded on John. "So you're admitting that God has allowed this."

"Of course I am. Lu, God does nothing without a purpose. Suppose His purpose in this is to bring you to your knees? Suppose all along He has wanted you to serve Him, and you've denied Him at every turn? Suppose He finally had to do something this drastic to wake you up? If this is His plan, and you turn Him away again…Lu, God will bring you to your knees, even if it takes David's death to do it. How long are you going to deny God? Don't you see, Lu, that if David dies it won't be God's fault, but it could be yours?"

I glared at him, but the caustic denial I was about to make died in my throat. I took a step back from him. I felt suddenly weak. My life had been spiraling downward for years. Every problem I faced I seemed to resolve, but then the next problem was a little worse. Every crisis was a little more serious, until now, *this*. Could John be right?

"You have nothing to lose, but everything to gain," John said softly.

"If David dies, I'll die," I said dully.

Doc came over and patted my arm. "I've done everything I can. Now he's in God's hands."

My eyes suddenly filled with tears. It had been a long time since I allowed myself to cry in front of anyone—years, in fact. Not since the day I was told David had polio. What was he? ten years old when that happened?

I tore past John Ransom and fell to my knees beside David's bed. I wept, and prayed, and begged, and made promises to a God I still wasn't sure I believed in. But everything that had been kept deep inside me for so long came out in desperate sobs. I don't know if I actually spoke the words, or if the prayers went unspoken and only my weeping could be heard. I don't know how long I knelt there, clutching at David's hand, my face in the soft folds of his blanket. I know John was beside me, and then he was gone while somebody else came and put an arm around me. I was only vaguely aware of other people coming in and going out of the room. People were talking. I heard soft questions, quiet answers. Then suddenly, the room faded and the voices seemed to be stilled.

I was alone with God, face to face it seemed, though I didn't want to face Him.

I fell asleep, there on my knees beside David's bed in the little back room of Doc's clinic. I sensed John Ransom's presence much later as he came into the room, picked me up, and carried me out.

I awoke on a cot in another room. John was there, sitting beside me. He looked tired, and grim.

I sat up. "How's David?"

"About the same. Doc thinks he'll reach his crisis sometime this afternoon."

I got up and went to the window. The morning was a dull gray, like tarnished silver. Snow was still falling, though not as hard, and all that could be seen of the sun's rays was an occasional glimpse of dim light through drifting clouds. "What time is it?" I asked.

"Nearly ten thirty. You've been asleep the better part of three hours."

I turned around, and took notice of John's appearance. It shocked me a little. I had always seen John Ransom at his best— immaculate clothes worn with a lazy grace, combed hair, a clean-shaven face, and an expression which suggested he was at peace with the world. Today his clothes were rumpled, his hair needed a brush to it, his face was shadowed with a new growth of black stubble, and he looked worried, and even a little fearful.

We went in to see David together. He was awake but barely lucid. "The sheriff," he said through parched lips. I could barely hear him.

"He keeps saying that," Doc told us. "Jeb's still out looking for Carter. Has been for hours. Apparently David wants him for something."

I picked up David's limp hand. "How is he, Doc? How is he really?"

Doc went to get the thermometer. He shook it down then stuck it under David's arm.

"Hold his arm down," he told me.

David moved his arm a little but I held it fast. Heat was radiating from his body.

"We've got to get him through the night," Doc said in reply to my question. "Then we'll take it one day at a time." He looked at me and tried to smile reassuringly. "Your little brother may not have a strong constitution, but he has a strong will. The two churches are having a combined prayer service. On top of that," he grinned, "he has a good doctor. I'd say his chances are better than nothing." Then he gave me a sober look. "But I can't deny that he's very sick, Lu. Very sick."

John Ransom's presence seemed to reassure David. Although David drifted in and out of consciousness John kept a constant flow of conversation, his pleasant voice telling the old stories of the Bible. David's favorite seemed to be the stories about the young shepherd boy who was chosen by God to be Israel's greatest king.

Whether David responded to the stories or just to the voice I didn't know. All I know is that my brother rested easier with John Ransom in the room, and I could only be grateful.

There was Jesse's youngest son, the shepherd boy who was chosen to be the next king. And there was the teenager who had to face down the dreaded giant Goliath. There was the boy as he grew, moving to the court of King Saul. There was the jealousy of the king against his young protegee, and the bond between the shepherd and the king's son Jonathan. It seems Jonathan loved David so much that he was willing to give up his natural place on the throne to his best friend. There was Jonathan's death, and David's inconsolable grief. And then there was Bathsheba, and David's great sin against God, followed by bitter sorrow, forgiveness, and redemption.

And I listened, while the quiet voice went on, and the shadows in the room lengthened, and David lay quiet and still, too quiet, too still.

The crisis came that night. His fever was high, and Doc and John and Coy took turns rubbing him down with alcohol.

His breathing was labored, and I knew I was losing him. In desperation I dropped to my knees for the second time. "Jesus," I cried, "if you're real, please don't let David die. I'll do anything. Anything!"

I don't know if I actually said the words aloud. I don't know how long I knelt at the bed and sobbed. But I'll never forget

John's gentle hands as he reached down for me and pulled me up. I couldn't have stood had he not been holding me. He let me cry into his shoulder, as he quietly whispered, "It's all over, Lu. It's all over."

I turned to look at my brother. He was smiling at me. It was weak, but it was there.

"His temperature is almost back to normal," Doc told me. "He's going to be fine. It's going to take a few weeks, but he's going to make it."

I collapsed in weariness.

~~~~~~~~~

I woke up between soft clean sheets in a room I recognized.

"Oh, good. You're awake. Or at least conscious," came the familiar perky voice of Marty Maguire. "Here. I brought you some hot tea and something to eat."

I tried to sit up, but my back and arms were sore, and my head hurt. "How's David?" I asked.

"When Johnny called a few minutes ago he said David was shouting for his dinner."

I sat straight up at that. "Dinner? How long have I been here?"

"Oh, Johnny brought you here about nine hours ago. You were passed out cold. He said you probably just needed some rest. Doc sent a prescription: a good meal, hot tea, and as much sleep as you want."

One thing stood out above the rest. "David's all right." I said to reassure myself.

She nodded. "Praise God! The whole town is enjoying a sweet sleep today after praying for two nights straight."

Praise God? I remembered sharing in those prayers. I remembered making some promises. "Yes, praise God." Was it possible? Had God actually said, "yes" this time? Gratitude flooded my soul, as tears again flooded my eyes.

"Oh, Marty, thank you. How can I thank everyone enough? We were strangers and you took us in." I wondered where I had heard that phrase. It had suddenly come to my memory from someplace deep inside.

"Don't you know we'll all be repaid when we see David out on that basketball court again, and think how nearly we ended up attending his funeral instead?" I had seldom seen such a serious look on Marty's face.

"Nine hours ago." I calculated. "That must have been about three in the morning. Yet you just said, 'Bring her on in,' I suppose. Marty, you are one of the most selfless people I've ever met. Thanks are so inadequate!"

Marty shrugged off the thanks. "I was up anyway. We were holding prayer at the church. Then Johnny came in with the news that David had passed his crisis and was doing much better. You've never seen a happier bunch of people." She cast me a sidelong glance and bit her lower lip. "It was a miracle, you know."

"I have to agree with you," I said calmly.

Marty threw me a questioning look, and I nodded my head. "A miracle. Who would have thought it?"

I picked up the teacup and relaxed back against the head of the bed. Life was sweet after all.

Marty smiled at me, a smile that lit up her face, "Almost everybody at the church seemed so surprised. There we were, praying for a miracle for hours, and then when Johnny runs in and tells us the news, we're shocked." She shook her head, "Oh we of little faith," she paraphrased. "Johnny took Aggie out to your house to pick up some clean clothes. When you feel up to it, come on down and get cleaned up. Then I'll take you to see David."

She left me. I heard her singing as she went down the stairs. I felt like singing myself. I jumped out of bed and ran to the window. The sun was shining from a cloudless sky. The snow glistened in its rays as if carpeted with a million tiny perfect diamonds.

I went to the mirror on the chest and took a good look at myself. I was a mess. My face was pale, my hair was tangled, and my clothes were badly wrinkled.

I fairly skipped downstairs. Marty had thoughtfully put my clean clothes in the bathroom. They were the skirt and blouse I was wearing the first time John Ransom had ever seen me, and I wondered then whether Aggie had really been the one who had picked them out.

I washed and dressed, and brushed my long hair back behind my ears. When I went out to the kitchen Marty was waiting for me with a worried, anxious look on her face.

I stopped short. "What is it? David? Is he worse?"

"No, he's fine. It's...you better sit down first."

I obeyed, literally falling into the nearest chair. My sudden buoyancy had disappeared and left me like a limp balloon.

Marty bit her lip. "It seems as though David has something he wants to tell—but he wants the judge, and Jeb, and you, and Johnny, and Coy all there when he does. But not the sheriff. He doesn't even want Carter to know he's better, but of course everybody in town knows and I don't see how we can keep it from the big, fat...Excuse me; that wasn't kind."

"Often the truth isn't. Maybe that's why people often don't tell it."

She was too distracted to even pretend to smile. "Come on. I'd better get you over there."

Wondering what revelations my brother had for us now, I followed Marty out into the cold sunlight and climbed into the Packard.

Beware the fury of a patient man.
—Dryden

Chapter 19

David was looking much better. Color—not the sickly flush of yesterday, but a healthy glow—was back in his face. He was still weak from the fever, but he had eaten a little and was now ready to tell us just exactly what had happened. As his story unfolded, we were all puzzled. None of us understood it, least of all David. His obvious perplexity somehow made the story believable.

He was riding home from apologizing for the umpteenth time to Coy, who assured him, also for the umpteenth time, that one apology had been quite enough. Instead of riding across the fields like he usually did when he came from the big ranch house, he decided to come home by the road because the snow had been packed down better. He worried that riding through the huge snowdrifts would be hard on Goliath.

A car went past him, and suddenly he recognized the driver. It was the same man who had taken Coy's Jeep and drove off in it the night Scooter Mathieson was murdered. Then, not two minutes later, Sheriff Carter came by. David waved him down, and the sheriff stopped and rolled down his window. He was still infuriated with David, and his whole tone was offensive, but David told him that he had just seen the man who had taken Coy's Jeep. The sheriff asked David which direction the man had taken, and when David pointed west, Carter grabbed his arm and yanked him off Goliath.

David was totally taken off guard, but when he hit the ground he tried to run from the sheriff. David, however, can't run, and

Carter managed to catch him without much effort. That was the last thing David remembered.

"And we found him five miles from his house, in shock, with a bump on his head," Coy said. "I don't understand this."

Judge Kincaid looked searchingly at my brother. "You didn't imagine this? You're not trying to get the sheriff into trouble because he was so obnoxious in the courtroom the other day?"

"Of course not," David said. "I would never do that. Would I, Sis?"

I shook my head. "I might," I told the judge, "but David never would."

"Well, this is incredible, but Jeb, you better issue a warrant for his arrest. Which way did you say he was headed?"

David answered, "He was going west. And I think I know where he was going. We...some of the other guys and me...we meet over at the old Lipscomb place for our...Well, anyway, once we saw the sheriff's car there, parked in the old barn. There isn't much to the barn anymore, just some leaning walls. The car looked like it had been hidden, and we barely saw it, but we went closer and checked, and sure enough it was the sheriff's. We were just getting ready to leave, when another car came, and a man we didn't know got out and went inside the old house. We didn't know what was going on, and we decided not to stay and find out. But then, a third man came. It was Scooter Mathieson. And he went inside the house, too."

"I don't understand any of this," the judge grumbled. "But Carter hasn't been seen since David was found, and I don't trust the man. So Jeb, let's you and me go to the courthouse and do this thing right."

"What reason shall I put on the warrant, Judge?"

"Just say I don't like him. No, no, that's not a valid reason. Well, it is, but not in the eyes of the law. Suspicion of attempted murder. Coy, you better come, too, and we'll deputize you."

John got up, too, but the judge snapped his eyebrows together and said, "No, Johnny, you stay here, you and that temper of yours. I want to bring him in alive."

The three men left, leaving John Ransom behind. He gave me a rueful grin.

260

But David was frowning. Something was bothering him. John searched his face, then said, "Was there something else, David?"

David had still been in somewhat of a fog. Now he seemed, gradually to be coming out of it. "You know," he said slowly, "I was in a car. I remember it now. My head hurt, and I felt a lump. I think Carter must have hit me. And then there was another voice, and Carter said, between curses, 'No, not the Lipscomb place. Those kids know about that. I think they've seen us there. The Barton place. Go there and wait. I've gotta dump this kid. He'll be dead in an hour.'"

The fierce anger that gripped me made me speechless. I looked over at John Ransom. Suddenly my blood seemed to freeze. It wasn't his expression—no, it was his total lack of expression, the cold mask that had come down and made his handsome face look like it had been carved out of ice.

David continued his chilling story. "I…guess I was only half-awake. I know I tried to say something, but nothing came out. I couldn't make my mouth move. Something was said about the 'split', and now it was only going to have to be two ways, and then I heard Cheyenne mentioned, and a guard who got in the way, and now this kid would end up like him. And the other man said something, and Carter said, 'I won't have to shoot him. They'll think the little cripple got thrown from his horse. Don't worry about him.'"

John Ransom's face, raging red as David's story unfolded, had now turned deathly white. Before I could stop him, before anyone could stop him, he was out of the room, and out of the clinic.

I wasn't going to wait for Coy or Jeb to come back. Marty grabbed my arm and tried to stop me. I said just three words to her—"The Barton place," and took off after John.

Of course that was where he was headed. But I knew something I feared John didn't: while the sheriff carried a .45 in the holster at his side in plain view of everyone, he also had a small-caliber pistol hidden inside his jacket. I hadn't thought much about it before now, but it suddenly dawned on me that I had noticed it one day when he came into the diner. His jacket was unbuttoned, and he bent over to pick up a piece of paper he had dropped, and I caught a glimpse of the black metal. I knew now what it was, although it hadn't registered then. John Ransom would be wary of a sheriff with a .45 in plain view, but he would be caught off-guard when he managed, as I knew he would, to get the .45 off the sheriff.

I jumped in Marty's old Packard and fumbled for the keys. The car was being as recalcitrant as a spoiled child. I pumped on the gas, pushed hard on the button, and begged it to start. I had caught Doc and Marty by surprise, but now they had recovered their wits and were running down the porch steps.

The motor finally kicked over, and took off, but it seemed to have a mind of its own as though it were reluctant to negotiate the hills in the deep snow.

And I wasn't the driver John Ransom was, either. He was used to speed, and snow, and the roads that tumbled over and through the hills. There was nothing reckless about that speed, or his driving. A calm, icy rage was making him drive with perfect composure.

I couldn't afford to be reckless, either. I went as fast as I could, as fast as I dared. But it wasn't long before I lost sight of John's pickup, and had to be content following in the path his tires had made on the snow.

Then I began to think. Some time had passed since David had been found. Maybe the sheriff and his confederate, whoever it was, had already gone. Surely they wouldn't have stayed and risked...but no, they had no way of knowing David was alive. Carter wouldn't know he was in danger, and he could show up with some plausible excuse for why he had disappeared for nearly forty-eight hours, and be ready to offer condolences for the poor little crippled boy who apparently wasn't able to hold a strong young horse.

And what was all this about Cheyenne, and a split. And then it came to me, in waves of cold, icy water. The bank robbery, in Cheyenne. The same day my parents had died, the same day they had killed Dr. Samuel Ransom. I remembered how angry I felt, that the robbery had been relegated to the second page while my parents' perfidy made the headlines.

So, my thoughts ran as I made my way through the hills driving in the tracks made by the pickup that was getting farther and farther ahead of me. Sheriff Carter was somehow involved in that robbery.

Then I remembered Scooter Mathieson's boast the day he came into the diner and accosted Coy. Something about him and the sheriff. Had Scooter been involved, too? I'm sure he was, though how I couldn't imagine. But if he was shooting off his mouth every time he got drunk, well, that made a motive for murder. And that led me right back to the sheriff, and also made it much more clear why he was wanting to pin the murder onto Coy.

Yes, it all made sense now, as I reached the crest of a hill and then slid down its other side. The Packard swerved, but I held on, and eventually it righted itself and kept on going, down into the gully, over a creek, and up another hill. Scooter had picked a fight with Coy. That must have given Carter the idea to try and frame him for the murder. Because Scooter had to be got rid of, and quickly, before he told everything he knew. And so, it was staged brilliantly—only David got in the way. And they had tried to get rid of David, too.

It didn't matter which one had killed Scooter—the sheriff or his confederate. They were both in on it, and it was the sheriff who had tried to murder David.

Then another thought send a chill down my spine. Was John going to be confronting one adversary...or two?

But I didn't dare drive any faster. Wouldn't it be better to get there late than not get there at all?

Finally I went through the broken gate that marked the beginning of the deserted Barton place, and off in the distance I saw the pickup parked. It was hidden from the house behind a small hill. I parked Marty's big, solid Packard behind John's red truck, and jumped out.

The pickup was empty. I clambered up the hill that overlooked the house. From up there I could see the Sheriff's car, hidden in a clump of evergreens that had gone wild. And I could see John, making his way around those same trees. He was trying to get to the back of the house.

The sheriff, unaware of what was happening, was coming out the front door. He was dragging something—a man! There was a sort of hump at the base of the hill, probably a storm cellar. Carter pulled open the door and dumped the body into the cavity. Then he closed the door on it and went back towards the house.

I scampered down the hill as fast as I could and made my way cautiously, as had John, around the trees. John had been as stealthy as a cat when he entered the house, and now I mimicked his movements. I ducked around the back door, which hung on its hinges, obviously standing open to the weather since the house had been abandoned years ago. John's jacket lay there on the porch where he had shed it.

I reached the kitchen door just as John made a lunge for Carter. I knew he wanted to get to the sheriff before he had a chance to draw his gun.

But the sheriff was quick, and whipped out his gun as he backed off a step. I plunged on into the kitchen in total desperation.

My crashing entrance was a second surprise for Carter, and his aim was thrown off. I heard the sickening smack of the bullet as it hit flesh, and simultaneously another crack where it hit the boards of a broken cupboard beyond, but John kept going, so I was hopeful that no vital spot had been hit.

I saw the gun, the .45, that horrible death-speaking weapon, go flying out of Carter's hand as John hit him. It landed under a small table, then slid into a big crack in the rotting floor, and dropped out of sight.

Blood was flowing from John's right arm, but he was on the attack now. He hit the sheriff with all of his weight, and they both went over with a solid thud. I dove under the table after the gun.

It was lodged just beyond my reach. I could feel it with the tip of my finger, but the opening was too narrow for me to get hold of it. I started pulling frantically at the rotten wood, all the while watching the two men flinging themselves at one another.

John had his youth and athletic skills in his favor, but Carter was a heavier man, and I knew now that he was a murderer and would hesitate at nothing. John was bleeding heavily, and it made me sick with fear. I was afraid if he couldn't overpower the sheriff in that first burst, he didn't stand a chance.

Then I noticed that Carter was in his shirtsleeves, and the little gun nowhere in sight. His jacket was hanging on a peg at the far side of the room, and I was sure that the gun was there, and that

Carter would try to get to it. I weighed my chances of getting past that furious combat and reaching it. I knew if I got within Carter's grasp he would use me to stop John.

I tried to yell about the second gun, the pistol under the sheriff's jacket, but my throat was dry, and I couldn't make myself heard over the noise of thrashing bodies overturning furniture, breaking glass, banging into walls, and knocking down plaster.

My eyes scanned the room for some other weapon, but nothing offered. So all I could do was still pull, pull at the rotting wood and try to get to the .45. My hands were bloody. I had opened the old wounds.

I started praying for the third time in just two days. Praying for John, for his strength not to give out, and for myself, that I could reach the gun in time. I hadn't thought beyond that.

John was on top, pounding at the sheriff. Then Carter, with a sudden vengeance, threw him off, and he was on top, and John was on the defensive, his hands gripping Carter's wrists to keep those strong, deadly fingers from his throat.

I kept pulling at the wood, and praying for a miracle. My hands were full of splinters, but piece by little piece I was pulling apart the rotted floor. I could get my whole hand through, now, but the opening wasn't large enough for me to get my hand and the gun out.

John's arms were straining. He was holding the sheriff at bay, and with what could only have been a super-human effort, he threw Carter off and jumped to his feet. But Carter rolled, and with lightning speed grabbed John's foot and twisted it. John was back on the floor.

Carter was up, and made a leap toward the jacket, but before he could reach it John had pulled him back down. Carter was taking the fight closer and closer to the peg. I wondered, suddenly, where Coy was. He could be my miracle, if only he would show up.

John threw the sheriff off, and both men jumped up, panting at each other. John's wound still flowed, and it was evident to all three of us that his strength was ebbing. The sheriff made a lunge at him, but John caught him with his famous left, and Carter staggered back. John, though, was in no condition to press his advantage. And the sheriff, instead of going for John, grabbed his coat from the peg, which was now within his reach because of the force of John's blow. He pulled out his little pistol just as I got a firm grip on the .45.

I ripped it from the floor, tearing skin from both sides of my hand, and instantly I had it pointed straight at him before he could level the one he was holding. My left hand came up to steady the other. "Drop it!" I shouted. "Drop it or so help me I'll shoot."

Both jerked their faces towards me. Now I knew they had forgotten about me if they had really even realized I was there in the first place.

Carter jeered at me. "You could never shoot me, little lady. Not even for David."

His gun hand was edging up ever so slightly as he spoke to me, trying to make me concentrate on what he was saying and not see what he was doing. But while I have done some stupid things, I have never been that stupid.

Carter laughed. It was an eerie laugh. "I know people," he said. "And you're just not the kind to point a gun at a person and fire it. Think of the blood, of the bullet ripping up flesh, shattering bone." I saw the gun still edging upwards.

At the edge of my vision I could see John Ransom just watching, a look on his face of neither fear nor anger, but intense curiosity.

Carter laughed again, and I said something to him. I don't know what, but something to let him know his danger was real. I was squeezing. If the gun had had a hair trigger, it would have exploded already. I never dreamed how much strength it required to pull a trigger. I was wondering if it would ever go off, or if I would still be squeezing with all my might when Carter gunned John down. Everything seemed to move in slow motion.

Then both guns went off in one roar. I only remember Carter's look of genuine surprise, before blackness engulfed me. I tried desperately to fight it, but couldn't. The gun slid from my hand, and I slumped sideways. I don't even remember hitting the floor.

Voices came to me from a great distance. Someone was asking me questions. I tried to answer but my voice didn't work. I felt suspended. I knew something terrible had happened. I shut my eyes tighter. I didn't want to wake up. I fought the voices, and the recent memories that were beginning to flood my mind.

But in spite of my best efforts the blackness started to recede.

"You're all right, Lu. You're all right," I heard a soft voice say.

I opened my eyes and looked straight into Coy's. That meant everything really was all right. I laughed weakly, almost more like sobs. He was holding me as though I were a baby. Turning my head I saw Doc, kneeling on the floor and tending John's wound. Marty was standing over him, acting as nurse. Jeb was there, too, and he was inexpertly handling the sheriff's bleeding right hand.

"I'm...hurt...worse'n...he...is," Carter complained, his voice barely a whisper and coming in gasps. "I...want Doc."

Doc grunted and said something I couldn't hear. John gave him a wan grin.

Finally Doc stood to his feet. "You'll be all right in a few weeks, Johnny my boy. No, no, there's no need to get up yet. Just stay there while I see what I can do for this miserable polecat."

"'Bout time," the sheriff grumbled as Doc let Marty take his place so she could make John more comfortable.

Carter had managed to pull himself over to the wall and was half-sitting up, leaning against it. I found out later that he had made one desperate attempt to get away but was overpowered immediately by Coy and Jeb. Now he was subdued, all the fight having gone out of him. Doc walked over to him, bent down, and looked at the injured hand.

Then Doc looked at me. "Mighty fancy shooting, Lu."

I gave another shaky laugh. "It would have been, if that's what I were aiming at."

The laugh dispelled all Coy's doubts, and he gently released me. "You shoot where you look," he told me. "I bet you were concentrating all your attention on that little gun."

I was still a little unsteady, but I insisted I was fine. The only difficulty I was having was meeting John's eyes. I knew they were on me—had been on me almost the entire time.

Marty stood up after putting Coy's jacket under John's head to make him a little more comfortable. I glanced quickly at John. His face was gray, and he winced a little when Marty moved his head, but he managed a smile. Besides the bullet hole in his arm, he had been mauled by the sheriff's hard punches to most of his upper body.

I met Marty's smiling eyes. "How's David?" I managed.

"Fine. Just fine. We left him in Aggie's care—and Mikey's," Marty answered.

"Mikey's guarding him like a dog with a bone," Doc said as he worked on Carter's wrist. "It *is* bad, Carter. The bullet completely shattered two of the carpals in your wrist. A big bullet, that .45—your own gun, I think. I'm going to send you to the hospital in Scottsbluff. Under guard, of course."

Carter was hauled unceremoniously out of the shack and placed in the back of the sheriff's car—only it wasn't his now. Jeb was driving. Doc had bandaged the wrist so that the handcuffs wouldn't tear into it. They were about to leave when suddenly I remembered the body in the cellar. Jeb and Coy went to investigate and found what was left of Carter's other accomplice. They put the body in the back of the pickup, and we watched without sympathy as Jeb drove Carter off the premises.

Doc wiped his hands. "Well, that's that," he said, his gruff voice full of satisfaction. "Coy, help John to your truck. Marty, you can drive Lu back in your rather extraordinary vehicle." He pointed a finger at her, and added, "And stay behind us, mind. Here, Coy. I'll help you."

Between them they managed to get John up and out into the pickup. I learned from Marty on the drive back to town that Coy and Jeb had returned moments after I left the clinic and taken off together in Jeb's car. Aggie, fortunately, had just arrived at the clinic with Mikey, who had pestered her to go see David. So Doc and Marty took off in Doc's car, and followed the two men to the deserted farmhouse.

The fight between Carter and John, which at the time had seemed interminable, actually had lasted only a few short minutes. I hadn't been that far behind John, Coy and Jeb hadn't been that far behind me, and Doc and Marty hadn't been far behind them. It probably looked like a strung-out parade, in fast motion, with all of us speeding over the snow-covered hills to a place that hadn't seen that much activity for a quarter of a century.

Marty took me straight to the clinic. David was sitting up listening to Mikey's version of David and Goliath. Aggie was in the rocker knitting and smiling fondly at them both.

It didn't take Marty long to regale them with the recent events and my part in them. When David was satisfied that I would survive, he inquired after John, who was at the moment in Doc's treatment room.

Soon Doc came in to check on David, and on me. He took one look at my face, went out, and came back with a glass filled with a nasty-looking liquid. "Drink this," he ordered.

I drank it. It tasted as awful as it looked, but Doc had had a trying day and I didn't think it advisable to argue. Before long I was feeling a little lightheaded, and Marty helped me to the bed in the room next to David's. I don't even remember putting my head on the pillow.

When I finally woke up I found Mikey my sole companion.

Before I could say "Hi", Mikey vanished. "Hers wake!" I heard him yell to someone, and in seconds Marty was in my room.

"About time," she said, grinning her gamin grin.

"What time is it?" I asked.

"Nearly ten o'clock."

"Oh, I've slept all evening."

"It's ten *in the morning*. You've been asleep for almost eighteen hours!"

I sat straight up. "Eighteen hours! Pete must be furious." I threw the cover off and started to jump out of bed. I discovered my hands were bandaged.

Marty gently pushed me back. "Carol went in early. Pete's managing just fine. Said he'd probably do land-office business today, with everybody gathering down at the courthouse."

"Oh?" I managed, a little feebly. "The courthouse?"

Marty nodded, "Jeb's being sworn in as sheriff."

I smiled. For some reason I felt that was the most comforting news I could hear at the moment. "And Carter?"

"He's been charged with so many crimes he'll be wishing you had hit what you were aiming at."

269

I shuddered. "That was the first time I ever even had a gun in my hands."

"No one would know it. John gave his statement already. He said you told Carter to put down his gun, and Carter said something to the effect that you wouldn't be able to shoot him, and then you said something to Carter and then you pulled the trigger and the bullet hit Carter's wrist and the pistol went flying out of his hand."

I searched my memory. I knew Carter had taunted me a little, but I couldn't remember saying anything to him just before I pulled the trigger. But then John's face swam in front of my eyes. His face, just before I pulled the trigger. Yes, Carter had given me a puzzled frown, but John had given me a swift, gentle smile. What had I said?

"Doc had to give Johnny a transfusion, he had lost so much blood. He wants to see you."

"Doc wants to see me?"

"No. Johnny. As soon as you feel able."

"That will probably be next August." I said weakly.

Marty bit her lip. That she wanted to say something slightly cutting, I knew, but I also knew that she felt I had been through an ordeal, and I watched in some amusement as her compassion gave in to her natural tendency to say what was on her mind. "He's in with David. Doc set up another bed in there."

Doc's small clinic only had two rooms for patients. I knocked at the door of the other room and two voices simultaneously told me to come in.

David was looking so much better that I could have burst into song. John, on the other hand, was pale. His arm was in a sling, and there was a bruise on his left cheek from the only hard punch Carter had managed to give to his face. It wasn't much of a bruise, either, because John had nimbly stepped aside and Carter's fist had only grazed him. John was sore, though, from other blows to his body, and he winced as he sat up.

I was still dressed in the clothes I had worn last night. There were blood stains on them, probably mostly mine. My hands were a mess—again. I had opened some of the old wounds. Some of the newly healed skin had been scraped off, and Doc had gone after the splinters. Marty had done her best to brush my tangled hair but it tumbled over my shoulders and down my back and wouldn't stay where she tried to place it. I stood there looking, I'm sure, like I had been on an all-night binge.

John smiled at me. I wished he would quit doing that. It always did something to the pit of my stomach.

"How are you feeling today?" he asked.

"All right. And you?" Very proper, very formal.

"Fine. Thanks to you." His eyes had clouded now to a smoky gray. "Why did you do it, Lu? Why did you come tearing after me like that?"

I stood there gazing at him for a moment before I answered. "Because I knew he had a gun—a second one he wore inside his jacket—and I was fairly sure you didn't know it."

"You're right. I didn't know it."

The conversation was apparently wearing him out. He laid his head back down and closed his eyes, the smile still lingering on his lips.

I went to my brother's side. "Feeling more the thing?" I asked gently.

"You should talk to Johnny like that," my little brother said petulantly.

"He's right, you know," came the voice from the other bed.

I turned to John Ransom. "Feeling more the thing?"

John opened his eyes and looked at me. "I am now."

That look nearly did me in. I quickly turned back to my brother. "I'm getting out of here tonight. You'll be able to come home soon."

Jeb Truman came over in the afternoon. He had heard the rest of David's story including the references to Cheyenne and a guard. He wanted to get any more information I might have. I let him tell me about the bank robbery, and agreed that I was sure the three had been involved. It was pretty obvious that Carter had killed "Joe," I remembered the name from Scooter's boasts at the diner. Jeb had fingerprinted the corpse, and sent the prints to the FBI for identification. I shuddered. I was glad he was sheriff and not me. From David's testimony we could be certain that Joe had killed Scooter. Which one had shot the bank guard didn't matter much now. Carter would have to bear the blame alone just as he expected to enjoy the loot alone.

271

Now Jeb broke into a wide grin, and I thought how good-looking he really is. Too bad he's so serious all the time. He told me he and Coy had gone back to the Barton place, partly to pick up his car, but they had made a search too. The money—all of it—had been concealed in the same root cellar, hidden under some filthy trash. And now he thrust a wanted poster at me. It said, "REWARD $10,000."

"I'm figuring half the reward money should go to David," Jeb was saying. My ears suddenly perked up. "He certainly supplied the information that led to solving these crimes, and with what he's been through he more than deserves it."

"Jeb, that is splendid of you! You made the arrest and you found the money, so I'm sure you're entitled to the full reward—but if David could get some college money out of this, it would be such a blessing." I was calculating—$5000 would go a long way at the University of Nebraska *if* I would settle down, so we could establish residency.

Jeb grinned. "Coy and I made the arrest together. Remember the judge had just deputized him. When I asked Coy if he figured he should receive part of the reward, he said it should go to the person who disabled the criminal and discovered the body of the third accomplice."

I didn't quite follow all that, except that it would have been totally uncharacteristic of Coy to accept any reward.

"So," Jeb continued. "I put your name down for the other half."

I just looked at him. Could it be? Had our luck really turned around that much? My conscience suddenly jabbed me hard. When things went wrong, I had blamed God. Now when something went right, I credited "luck?" "Forgive me," I murmured.

"What did you say?" Jeb wondered.

"I said—Praise the Lord."

"Amen," Jeb agreed.

I left the clinic at suppertime. Doc protested my going, but I had to leave, to get by myself, to sort things out.

I didn't go to work the next day. Pete was unusually sympathetic. I used my hands as my excuse, but the real reason was that my nerves were too on edge. The possibility of having extra money complicated everything even more. It meant I could afford to leave—but that I couldn't leave until the reward was paid, and who knew how long that would take? But the biggest complication was that now the thought of leaving seemed as impossible as the thought of staying. If we left, Where would we go?. I had come to realize that there was no place we could go where God wouldn't track us down, and probably Johnny Ransom too. I decided to pay a visit to Father O'Brien.

Several times during our conversation I almost told him about Chicago, and about Dr. Ransom. Almost. But for some reason I couldn't put my thoughts into words. The guilt was still there, something as tangible as a steel wall that stood between me and John Ransom. Father O'Brien wanted to help, but I couldn't verbalize the problem, so he was left feeling as helpless as I did. He promised to continue praying for David and me. The visit was a failure except that it made me realize if I told anyone about my part in that horrible and tragic night in Chicago, I would have to tell John Ransom first.

When I went to visit David, Johnny had already left.

"Coy came to get him around noon," David told me. "And Doc says I can leave tomorrow. Says he'll be glad to be rid of me." And David grinned.

I went home, and sat at my desk in the living room. I took paper and a pen from the top drawer, swallowed my pride, and poured my heart out to Missouri.

There it was, in writing. The guilt I had been living with ever since the night of the accident, the stratagems I had used to avoid John Ransom, stratagems that hadn't worked. And my feelings for him now, feelings I had no right to have reciprocated until he knew the truth.

"So I'm on my way to tell him about the Thorntons, and about my part in the tragedy. He has a right to know. I also intend to tell him that I love him. He has a right to know that, too. He may decide to throw David and me out of his life, but I'm praying he'll forgive me—my deceit, and my part in the tragedy. When it's over, I'll finish this letter. I'll let you know whether we're staying, or coming back to Chicago."

There. I had admitted it. Finally. The next step was to see Johnny Ransom. Then when I knew the outcome of that, I'd have to tell David.

Judge not the Lord by feeble sense,
But trust Him for His grace;
Behind a frowning providence
He hides a smiling face.
—William Cowper

Chapter 20

The old Chevy skidded down the lane. I felt I was going to my execution.

I knocked and Johnny himself answered. Now that I was there I didn't know what to say.

Although he was obviously pleased to see me, there was some reserve in his voice as he invited me inside.

I felt the ice thin under my feet, and it was trepidation that made my tone a little formal. "No, don't try to help me off with my coat. You must keep your arm in the sling."

"Nonsense," he said as he dragged the coat from my shoulders.

"I distinctly heard Doc tell you..."

"Never mind Doc." He suddenly grinned boyishly. "Rick's home!"

"Your brother?" My voice went shrill with shock. Well, maybe this was how it was meant to be. If he knew me, my little charade would have come to an end today anyway. But I wanted to reveal it myself, not be caught in my lies.

Johnny stood there looking at me, his blue eyes glittering, his expression unreadable. Finally voices from the living room brought him out of whatever thoughts he had been mulling over, and he gingerly took my bandaged hand, "Come on in. It's time you two met."

I pulled back, "But there's something I need to tell you first..." My eyes and face pleaded with him. He had always wanted to talk, to listen, and I was the one who had refused. What if he refused me now?

He nodded sympathetically, and gestured at a chair in the entry. I started to sit down...then I froze. Two people had just stepped from the living room into the entry—a young boy who looked as Johnny Ransom must have eighteen years ago—and Sylvia Bannister.

At first she looked as shocked as I'm sure I did. But as my shock turned to helpless despondency, hers turned to gloating triumph.

She stood, never taking her eyes from my face. Spite was in her venomous smile, and it spilled over into her voice. "Well, well. If it isn't the little princess." Then she turned to Johnny Ransom, who had gone over to a small table and was opening a drawer. "I've been hearing all about 'Lu Morrow' from Rick all the way from Chicago, and from Coy all the way from that horrible little airport." She nodded her head towards me and said to Johnny, who had apparently found what he was looking for and was coming toward us, "Do you know who she really is?"

I turned to Johnny. His eyes were on my face. "Of course I know who she is," he answered lightly. "She's Lucasta Morrow, at least to those of us who know and love her." Then he turned to his brother, and said gently, "Rick, come and meet the person who saved your life." He looked at me again, then added, "And mine."

I couldn't move. Neither could Sylvia. But whereas I had lost my voice, she still had hers. "But her father was responsible..."

"For many reprehensible things," Johnny finished. "All of which his children have rectified. Not that they needed to." He walked towards me, and took my hand. Into it he placed—the Contessa Elena Fire Opal!

I stared at it wordlessly, then dropped it as though the flame had actually burned me.

Coy was just coming in the door, but I brushed past him and, coatless, ran out of the house.

I jumped into the Chevy and willed it to start promptly for a change. The motor was still warm, and I tore out of there. So God was still playing games with me, I thought. When I was at last ready to be repentant and sincere, He laughs in my face.

It all came back now, Sylvia's boasts about her rich cowboy. The glitter of that diamond suspended above my piano at Nick's seemed to flash blindingly in my eyes. I was smoldering at Johnny, then got angry at myself for thinking of him now as "Johnny". When had that happened?

At the end of the drive I barely made the turn. I looked back, almost expecting to see the red pickup bearing down on me. But no, that was folly. I had behaved rudely—as usual. Johnny was still not well, and besides he had *company*. He would not follow me. I wondered briefly if God was getting even with me. I was sure I appeared to Johnny as the schemer, the deceiver I finally acknowledged myself to be.

He knew! All along he had known. He watched me fumble my way through, trying so desperately to pawn myself off as something I'm not. And he knew all along who I am, who my father was. And he never said anything. He just allowed me to make a fool of myself, and today I would have completed the job: Confess to everything he already knew, and beg his forgiveness. What a picture! But tell him I loved him—could I really have gone through with that? I could hear Sylvia's mocking laughter. Perhaps I would hear it the rest of my life.

One thing remained to be done. I had to tell David. I had to tell him before someone else told him. Johnny was in a revelatory mood. Why had he produced grandmother's brooch today? It had been so long since I had seen the opal, it seemed more like a ghost than a real object. I realized I wanted it very much. Maybe Missouri had been wrong about needing the money more. I needed something to hang on to that I didn't have to be ashamed of. I would trade the ranch for the brooch. That was fair. It was exactly what I had paid for it.

The tires skidded as I rounded a curve. I glanced off a snow bank. No harm done. Looking at the speedometer, I saw I was driving too fast. I was letting my emotions get hold of me. Where was I going? To Doc's office to see David of course, but after that?

All at once I saw myself clearly: I was Brittany Thornton. I was fleeing from my crimes just as my father and mother had been doing that night. "Pick up David and leave the country." And I was their daughter doing just as they had done. All these years I had felt myself so superior to my parents, so honest and morally upright. I wouldn't stoop to lying, to selfishness and self-pity. I had formed a life-long habit of blaming them for everything that went wrong, and now they were dead, whom could I blame?

The only question remaining was would I succeed in dragging David down with me?

I stopped the car beside the park and crossed the road to Doc's office. It was still early, but the day was so gloomy, his desk lamp was burning. I went in without knocking.

"That you, Lu?" he called from inside his office.

"No," I replied. "It's Brittany—Brittany Thornton. But then you've known that all along, haven't you?"

Doc rose from his chair and came into the dusk of the waiting room. I sank into the couch.

"Yes, Hiram told me your name before I ever met you. But I never put much importance on names." He sat down facing me. "Better tell me what's troubling you."

"Me. I'm what's troubling me." I dropped my face into my bandaged hands. "Tonight I was going to face up and confess who I am, and now I don't even know myself."

Doc did not respond at once. He went to the back room and returned with a cup of hot tea. I had to laugh.

"See," I pointed to the steaming cup. "Everybody knows me better than I know myself. Thanks, Doc, but this time I need more than just hot tea."

"I seem to remember promising to have a good talk with you. I guess I've put it off too long."

I shuddered. I remembered how I had rejected that promise in my mind when he first made it. I thought I had everything worked out. I didn't need anyone's advice. David and I were making a fresh, new start and everything was going to be beautiful.

Some things *were* beautiful. The Sand Hills were beautiful; I thought of David's marvelous paintings. In just a couple of months we had found acceptance and love in a community of kind, wonderful people. The only two men who hadn't welcomed us were now either dead or imprisoned. What would our welcome turn to when they knew we were the children of murderers? What would they say when they knew the connection we had to the death of one of their favorite citizens? Doc had said it wouldn't matter. He was right in one way. It didn't matter. Whatever it cost, I had to stop living a lie.

"All right, Doc. I'm defeated. Tell me what to do."

"Well, that sounds like a good place to start. Did you never hear that man's importunities are God's opportunities?"

"Then He certainly has me where He wants me."

"I'm glad to hear it. Does this have something to do with Johnny Ransom?"

I looked up startled. Was I that transparent? A denial was already forming itself on my lips, but I stopped it. I had had enough of falsehood. "Yes," I conceded, bowing my head again. "I just learned that he has known all along who I am. Probably Coy knew too. Anyway their kid brother just came home, and Johnny introduced me to him as the person who saved his life."

Doc took me by the chin and lifted my face to look into his, "You mean he didn't say, 'This is the person whose father killed our father.'"

The words went into me like a sword. I didn't know Doc could be that cruel. "No," I cried in anguish, "he left that for Sylvia to say!"

Now it was Doc's turn to be startled. "Sylvia! Who's Sylvia?"

"Ohh! Never mind! She doesn't matter!"

"You're probably right about that, but it seems to matter a great deal to you."

"She's...someone we both knew in Chicago. I guess she came with Rick."

"'We both' means you and Johnny I take it."

I nodded miserably. Even if I never saw Johnny Ransom again, he deserved better than Sylvia Bannister. Marty had said Coy was worried. He had a right to be. I had said it was none of his business, but that wasn't true. He loved Johnny. Did I? or was I just thinking of myself? When Johnny's life was in danger from Sheriff Carter I had fought with everything that was in me. Now he was in a different kind of danger, and what had I done? I had run away.

Johnny was right. I had been running all this time. From the past, from truth, and yes, from God. Now I was poised to run again. Grab David and run.

"My dear," Doc apparently didn't know which name he should use. "If Johnny—and possibly Coy—have known the worst all this time, can't you see that they haven't held it against you? They already forgave you before you asked. I don't claim personal knowledge of this Jesus they worship, but I believe forgiveness was one of the strongest points in His teaching. If He were any relation to Jehovah God, it would have to have been, because my God is a God of forgiveness. 'Bless the Lord, O my soul, and forget not all his benefits. Who forgiveth all thy iniquities.'"

"Psalm 103," a soft voice interrupted.

Both of us jumped. We had not heard David come in.

"David, you shouldn't be out of bed!" I gasped, taking in his bare feet and thin pajamas.

He rushed to me and threw his arms around me.

"And you shouldn't be eavesdropping, young man!" Doc said gruffly as he flung a blanket around David's shoulders.

"I couldn't help it. I heard you say, 'Is that you, Lu?' and I thought she would come right in to see me. When she didn't, I got up and was coming out, but then I heard her say she needed more than hot tea, and I started listening."

I pulled David onto the couch beside me as if he were still a small child. "And...did you understand what you heard?"

"Not at first, but it began to fit together. I had thought before what a coincidence it was that Johnny and Coy's Dad had died the same day our parents did. I guess I was so intent on keeping the truth from them, that I kept it from myself."

"It was my fault, David. I made you lie. Please forgive me."

"Like Doc said, I already have; but, Sis, don't you see? Just like going to Johnny and confessing—even though he already knew it all—that's how we come to Jesus. There's not a single thing He doesn't know about, but He wants us to confess just the same. And He's already forgiven us, because He paid for our sins way back when He died on the Cross.

280

"Sis, do it! Just like I did! Confess to Jesus and ask His forgiveness. Then receive Him into your heart."

I felt a struggle inside. Could David be right? I had been wrong about everything else. "David, you're too young to understand what you're saying. You..."

"Missouri is older than both of us put together, and she says the same thing. Or ask Doc!"

The good doctor was on the spot. I knew he was Jewish, but David didn't understand the difference. He looked at David's expectant face and then at me. "I should..." his voice came out as a squeak, so he cleared his throat and began again. "I shouldn't be surprised if the boy understands more than you give him credit for. Isaiah said 'a little child shall lead them.'" He rose and went to his office, closing the door and leaving us alone.

I had had enough. "All right, kiddo. We'll try it your way."

"Not my way, Sis—God's way."

It was late when I pulled into my own drive. My heart was singing. I had never experienced any joy like this in my life. I had sung "The Lord's Prayer" over and over all the way home, and I really didn't understand why it should make me cry, or why I was so happy crying. The burden of guilt was gone. Where? David said Jesus had taken it.

Just like David when he had come home that Sunday, I was filled with love for all of Creation. I could forgive Scooter Mathiesen and Sheriff Carter. I even loved Sylvia Bannister. If Johnny really loved her and decided to marry her, maybe he could change her as he had helped to change me. Yes, next to God, it had been mostly Johnny who had done this. Missouri had been working on it for years, and not without effect. David had certainly played a major role, and Coy and Marty and all of them had helped show me what was missing in my life. But mostly it had been Johnny and the way he had kept turning the other cheek no matter how rude and offensive I was. I would love him forever, and if I couldn't be his wife, I'd be his friend as Marty was. This was a new kind of love—I even loved David more than before. I had wanted to bring him home with me, but Doc said he was worn out and needed to rest—David, that is. I think it had been a pretty stressful evening for Doc too.

The red pickup was next to my front porch. My heart jumped into my throat. Even before I could start planning what to say, I saw the porch light go on, and Johnny stepped out the door to meet me. He was carrying my coat. I had left it at his house this afternoon—a hundred years ago at least.

He wrapped it around me as I climbed out of the Chevy. "Where have you been?" he sounded agitated. "I've been worrying the whole evening!"

"Didn't you think I'd be with David?" He held my arm as we climbed the three steps and crossed the porch.

"I've been worrying about him too! Why is no one at the clinic?"

I stopped in surprise. "We've been there all evening, Doc and David and I."

"Why didn't Doc answer the phone?"

It suddenly occurred to me what a quiet evening we had enjoyed. No interruptions. "The phone never rang. It must be out of order."

"Why didn't I think of that?" Johnny flung himself into my rocker.

I had never seen him distressed like this. When David was lost he had been a strong oak, and I had leaned on him. Even when we feared David was dying...yes, then I had seen a little of this same anxiety. "Johnny, what's wrong? Has something terrible happened?"

"No, everything's all right...now."

In that case it was time for my confession. I hesitated wondering how to word it. "Johnny, I...I have been living a lie ever since I came to Lee's Corner. That's no news to you. You've known it from the first, though I still don't know how. I was coming today to...to tell you the truth...about me, about everything. I waited too long. I didn't know of course that Rick had returned, and..." I bowed my head, "that you would be the one making the revelations—at least to Rick and Sylvia."

"Bother Sylvia!" he almost shouted, jumping from the rocker. "Do you honestly believe I could kiss you one day and fly into Sylvia's waiting arms the next? Is that what you've been thinking of me?"

I shrugged.

"Now let me tell you what I've been thinking." He ran his hand through his dark hair and loomed over me in a way that was almost frightening. "I thought you were gone! I thought you had run away again, taken David and vanished.

"I tried to explain a little to Rick, and then I rushed over here. But you didn't come home. I looked in your room and saw you had been packing, so I knew you were planning to leave. I thought I had upset you so much you had just taken off without bothering to get your things.

"I tore home again and called the clinic. I was going to tell Doc not to let you go. But he wasn't there, or at least I thought he wasn't. All afternoon I wore a path between the telephone and the front porch watching with the binoculars for you to come back. I called Jeb and Marty and the Highway Patrol."

He was pacing now, as if to demonstrate.

"When it was too dark to see the road I came back over here. I imagined you—with no coat—and David—still half-sick—driving along some road with no clear destination in mind, and finally getting lost or...running out of gas and freezing to death."

"I'm sorry," I shrugged helplessly. "How could I have known?"

"I kept telling myself you wouldn't do that; that you had better judgment. But then I remembered your face, and Sylvia's accusation. I wanted to kill her. But at last I realized it was I who had run you off, overwhelming you with unexpected confrontations; that if anything happened to you, *I* would be the one to blame.

"And why hadn't I stopped you? If I had thought that you were running out of my life...do you see how I've been going insane the last six hours?"

"I'm sorry," I repeated. At that he hadn't been far from the truth. I wouldn't have done anything to endanger David of course, but if I hadn't had him to think of, I would probably have done just what Johnny was envisioning.

"You should be!" he snapped.

Then suddenly he relaxed, and there was that smile. If I fled to the ends of the earth that smile would haunt me forever.

"And you should be especially sorry for what you were still hiding from me. I would never have known."

"Not known? Not known what? You know everything, have known everything from the beginning."

He smiled again. "Not quite everything."

I was at a loss, a terrible disadvantage. He knew what I was talking about, but I didn't have a clue as to what he meant.

He came towards me. I stayed rooted to the spot. Finally he was within an arm's length of me. "You would have left here, and I would have been unhappy for the rest of my life. I should be very angry with you, but I'm not."

I was still in the dark, and pointed out again, "You said you knew..." My voice faltered under his intense gaze.

"I said I didn't know everything. Until now."

He pulled something out of his pocket. I felt the blood drain from my face. My unfinished letter to Missouri Smith, the letter that I had left lying, open, on my desk in the parlor, was now folded in his hand. He opened it, saying, "When I came back the second time, I found this."

I didn't say anything, only stood there mutely as he slowly unfolded the letter, and continued, "I normally don't read other people's mail...but I made an exception in this case, my name having caught my attention." The letter was open now. "Shall I read to you from this particular page?"

"I know what it says," I was near tears now and trying to hide it.

"I'll read it anyway, in case you've forgotten the pertinent details. 'Dear Missouri' —I'll skip on down past the news and David's health. Here we are: 'So I'm on my way to tell him about the Thorntons, and about my part in the tragedy. He has a right to know. I also intend to tell him that I love him. He has a right to know that, too. He may decide to throw David and me out of his life, but I'm praying he'll forgive me, my deceit, and my part in the tragedy. When it's over, I'll finish this letter. I'll let you know whether we're staying, or coming back to Chicago.'

"You need," he said slowly, "to finish the letter."

I turned and went to the window in the dark dining room. I stared out at the snow that was falling, the flakes piling up on top of the snow that was already there. He came and stood behind me.

Finally I said, "I don't know how."

He pulled me to him; I could see our reflection in the window. "Tell her to pack her glad rags and catch the next train to Ogallala because she's got a wedding to attend. Tell her you're going to marry Johnny Ransom and live happily ever after. Tell her Johnny Ransom has been growing daily more in love with you ever since he heard you sing "Danny Boy" at Little Italy. Tell her," and he turned me around and held me fast in his uninjured arm, "that I finally got what I came after during those horrible days in Chicago."

"How did you know?" I whispered, my throat dry.

He kissed me, then answered, "To begin at the beginning, Sylvia took me to Little Italy one night. I asked her casually if she knew who the beautiful pianist was. She said she didn't, in such a manner that I was sure she did. I came back several succeeding nights to hear you play. Didn't you ever wonder who requested 'Danny Boy' so often?"

"You?"

He smiled, and nodded. "I found out your name, of course, and fully intended to meet you and ask you out. I felt confident I could get past Nick Costelli. But then—well—the accident.

"Someone had pulled Rick from the car, someone who had to be on the spot. No one came forward. Most people would have wanted the credit, you know. I went to the Tribune office and went over all the photographs from the scene. One of their press photographers was on his way home from covering a party when he came upon the accident moments after it happened, and he started taking pictures immediately. You were in several, in the background with other spectators. I recognized you, and knew you were involved in the accident. And in each picture the bloodstains on the coat pockets were a little larger. I knew you had pulled Rick from the car, and I could also surmise why you didn't want anyone to know you were there, though why anyone should blame you for your father's actions is beyond me. The main reason I came by to see you was to thank you for saving Rick. But you wouldn't even see me."

"I thought I had good reasons."

"Well, the reasons aren't important, now. But the first time I came, I wasn't completely sure it was you who had saved my brother. It was only when I saw your coat that I was absolutely positive. It was hanging by the door, and covered with blood, and it was green. Rick insisted that a beautiful lady in a green coat had pulled him from the wreck." He lifted my bandaged hands and kissed each finger in turn. His voice was husky when he said, "You...paid a price after all, didn't you."

"That's not important now, either."

He looked at me, his eyes smoldering with emotion, but he continued evenly enough, "I wanted to help you in some way. I knew about David. It was easy to dig up information about the Thorntons."

"That I can believe," I turned my face away.

"So I went to Missouri's apartment, and bought the brooch. She promised me she wouldn't tell you where the money came from. And obviously she kept her word to both of us. She wouldn't tell me where you had gone. She only told me that you had left for good. Dr. Ableman had been sworn to secrecy too, though the way he kept smiling should have tipped me off. I struck out completely with Nick. He was sure I wanted to sue you for damages. I was stymied. I *had* to find you. But with no clue where to start looking, I decided to come home with Coy. I was considering my options, including hiring a detective as a last resort.

"Believe me, I was just as surprised to see you standing at the door that day before Thanksgiving as you were to see me on your doorstep. Oh, yes, you were surprised. And very, very upset. Don't try to deny it."

"I won't."

"While I, on the other hand, showed no emotion whatsoever. I felt it, though. Inside me the 'Hallelujah Chorus' was playing and fireworks were going off. I was dancing with joy and praising God for His mercy and goodness.

"But Missouri had told me how humiliating your parents' affairs had been to you over the years, and I was wondering how on earth I was ever going to get you to give me a chance here when you refused to see me so often in Chicago. I could tell by your face that you had recognized me, but you couldn't possibly have known that I knew who you were. I've had to play the hypocrite too, for fear of scaring you into running away again. You were in quite a dilemma yourself, but you have given me a few bad months."

I pulled away from him. "I've given *you* a few bad months? Do you think I've been enjoying this? But..." I faltered, and he reached for me again. "No, let me talk. There's something else you don't know."

The worry came back to his face.

"All of this...I mean everything—my problems with my parents, David's illnesses, the accident—everything I've gone through, has just been leading me to this day. Today, at the clinic with David...I stopped running. As David puts it, I gave my heart to Jesus."

I was swept into a powerful embrace that nearly squeezed the life out of me. Johnny's eyes were tightly shut and tears were seeping from under his eyelids.

"And I'm asking your forgiveness too." I whispered when I could get my breath.

He laughed, "Just be grateful that the good Lord is gracious enough to have forgiven all the half-truths you've told, especially the ones you told to me. And I fully expect you to marry me, the sooner the better."

"Sylvia?"

"Is flying out tonight. Coy is taking her, gladly, to that 'horrible little airport'. Chicago can have her back."

"She told me..."

"I can imagine what she told you. The Bannisters were friends of my step mother. Sylvia showed me around the Windy City; that's all. At least, it was all for me. When Coy arranged for Rick to come back home as a surprise for me, he had no idea Sylvia would insist on bringing him. Rick doesn't especially like her, and she didn't make a good impression on Coy, either. And I

287

knew what she was the first time I met her. I don't care for spitting cats. Never did."

"But you gave her…"

"A little bracelet. It was in appreciation for a nice time; I was especially grateful to her for taking me to Little Italy. It was *not* a commitment." He pulled something out of his pocket. "*This* is a commitment." He slipped the ring on my little finger, the only one it would fit right now.

So—we were staying. I thought about the cottonwoods along the creek. At the first sign of spring I would go down to see them budding, and this year my long winter would come to an end at last. I could feel myself like those trees beginning to live, beginning to grow. Today was my first day of joy.

And I thought about Missouri's prayer that day, how she asked that some fine young man would come into my life. And then Johnny Ransom had knocked on my door.

I thought, too, about what God's plan had been for my life, and about everything He did to pull me back into His will whenever and wherever I tried to run. God really does "work in myster'ous ways."

Kingdom Press

"Helping Christians grow"
1869 Top Road
Mountain Grove, MO 65711
Phone (417) 926-6420
e-mail: *navajean@fidnet.com*

☐ Send me _____ gift sets of books 1, 2, and 3 $_____
   Regular $37.85, only $29.95 each
      Missouri residents add $1.42 per set sales tax.   _____

☐ I would like to order _____ copies of $_____
   Learning—Life in the Castle @ $11.95 each
      Missouri residents add 56¢ per book sales tax.   _____

☐ I would like to order _____ copies of $_____
   Laboring—Life in the Outpost @ $12.95 each
      Missouri residents add 61¢ per book sales tax.   _____

☐ I would like to order _____ copies of $_____
   Leading—Life at the Battlefront @ $12.95 each
      Missouri residents add 61¢ per book sales tax.   _____

☐ I would like to order _____ copies of $_____
   the Study Guide to Book One. @ $9.95 each
      Missouri residents add 47¢ per book sales tax.   _____

☐ I would like to order _____ copies of $_____
   the audio cassettes of Book One @ $15.95 each
      Missouri residents add 75¢ per set sales tax.   _____

☐ Send me additional copies of
   A Tree in Winter by Sherry Newcomb
      _____ copies @ $11.95 each $_____
      Missouri residents add 56¢ per book sales tax.   _____

                              Total amount enclosed $_____

Name_____

Address_____

City, State, Zip_____

Phone _____ e-mail _____
   Please make checks payable to **Kingdom Press**. *Thank you.*

Or order from amazon.com